WHEREABOUTS LOST

Alan Dunbarker

VANTAGE PRESS
New York

This is a work of fiction. Any similarity between the names and characters in this book and any real persons, living or dead, is purely coincidental.

FIRST EDITION

All rights reserved, including the right of reproduction in whole or in part in any form.

Copyright © 2008 by Alan Dunbarker

Published by Vantage Press, Inc.
419 Park Ave. South, New York, NY 10016

Manufactured in the United States of America
ISBN: 978-0-533-16009-9

Library of Congress Catalog Card No.: 2008901797

0 9 8 7 6 5 4 3 2 1

To my Mother, Mattie, who has always believed in me and my dreams.

One

It was in the fall of 2002 when I decided to follow a dream, or at least part of it. All my life I dreamed of living in the wilderness. But with a wife and children and a good job providing for the needs of everyone, that dream was just that, a dream, but it was my dream. Four years ago I retired at forty-eight and now I am fifty-two, no longer married and the children are grown and on their own. Now was the time to plan a trip, a chance of a lifetime. I figured I had all winter and spring to put it together. It would be a four or five week stay in a remote area of Alaska, dropped off by a float plane. It would be a great chance to experience the wilderness and all its animals while drawing on all my years experience of being in the woods and hunting. Needless to say, my family thought I was nuts when I told them of my plans. However, they all knew of my love of the great outdoors. All of those who have been around me or with me on an outing or hunting trip say that no one comes more prepared than I do.

My first goal was to start contacting bush pilots in Anchorage. I had stayed in this area in 1969 overnight on my way to Kodiak Island for a week and a half. I had a great time fishing, hiking, mountain climbing and more. I didn't have any time to explore the interior of Alaska but I vowed I would return. This coming year a promise I made thirty-four years ago will come true. I started compiling names of pilots and businesses from the Internet and letters to the Chamber of Commerce of Anchorage and also the airports. I figured it would take three to four weeks to compile the list. This would give me plenty of time to make up a letter of what I wanted and what I was looking for in this area. I also wanted to learn about the pilots so I contacted the ones with e-mail addresses first. This would give me a head start on the selection process.

It's the morning of September 15th. I got up at 6:00 a.m., made a pot of coffee and set down to my computer. I told myself that this is it, the start of an adventure, and pushed the on switch. As my computer took off, the coffee was done and I grabbed a cup and sat down. I was anxious to see what would come up on the screen so I typed in bush pilots, Anchorage, Alaska. Wow, thirty-three pages of names, so I printed them out. Next I typed in bush plane charter, Anchorage, Alaska, and I found even more! Then I typed in bush plane guide hunting and fishing, Anchorage, Alaska. Damn, I hit the mother lode; there were all kinds of names, I printed out six pages. Now I had eleven pages of names to work with. What a start! I got my marker and started crossing out repeats. The total so far was eighty-seven. Forty-two were from outside the Anchorage area. I wondered how many others there were. There were some with e-mail addresses. It's a nice group to start with. I went for another cup of coffee and started my letter. There were a lot of questions I needed answered so that I could make my choice. I also wanted the pilots to know a little bit about me and what I was looking for. I asked the following questions: How many years have you had as a pilot and how many as a bush pilot? What kind of planes have you flown and what were their conditions? How old are you and how much experience do you have? I then went on to explain what I was looking for and the area where I could spend thirty days or so in the bush with no contact with other people, good fishing and wildlife where I could watch moose, bear, sheep and goats. If possible, I wanted to do a little panning for gold too. Thirty days of just me and the wilderness would be a great time. I was figuring around the first of June 2003. I also needed to know the weight limit for gear and the cost.

    About myself, I am fifty-two and in good health; retired at forty-eight, but still work, I am a successful hunter and experienced woodsman. I have been all my life. I enjoyed camping in remote areas for a week or two at a time. I have hunted bear and lived and camped in bear country so I am not a stranger to the woods. It's always been a dream to live in the wilderness but a trip like this would be the experience of a lifetime. This would put it at number one of my list of been there done that. I was in Alaska once before in 1969. I loved it and spent a week and a half on Kodiak Island but I never got the chance to experience the interior of Alaska. I looked at the mountains around Anchorage and made a promise to myself that I would be back.

It was lunch time already and I needed to stretch my legs. This afternoon I will put in the program for bulk e-mail mailing and put in all the addresses I have collected; but before I do anything I will save my letter. Time for a break. As I ate my lunch my mind was going a hundred different directions. I was so excited, to say the least, and eager to get to the task at hand. I received the program that I downloaded and I was ready to go. As I was typing in the e-mail addresses I had to admit, there were a lot of colorful ones out there; Lone Wolf, Bighorn, Moose Head, Arctic Fox, Bear's Den, Beaver Tail, Flying Duck and many more. It took me longer than I thought to get the addresses completed but I still had to go back through them to make sure they were correct. This is going to be neat, 129 e-mails at one time. Everything looks good, send. My eyes and mind were tired after ten hours. Time sure does fly by when you are having fun. I think I'll spend the rest of the evening on my deck and watch the deer come in to feed. I began to do a little bit of daydreaming too.

The next day I had plans to help my daughter and son-in-law with their addition of their home. We had finished getting it closed in a few days ago. Today I will do all the wiring of lights, switches, receptacles and most, if not all, of the insulation. Drywall won't take long, all easy run, no craziness. All day I was wondering if any of my e-mails were being answered. I was guessing maybe five to ten. As soon as I got home, I fired up my computer to check my in box. I had twenty-eight; four from family and friends, and twenty-four were replies from my e-mail. I felt like a kid on Christmas morning. I got myself a beer and sat down to do some reading. The first ten or so didn't sound the greatest and I was thinking this might not be as easy as I thought it might be. So far bush pilot experience was one to ten years. Well after twenty e-mails I still did not get any warm fuzzy feelings, but I had four more left to read. I was getting tired. It has been a long day.

Number twenty-one, Flying Beaver.com. As I started to read his reply, I knew that I needed to look no further. I don't quite know where my tired went to, but I was wide awake like after a ten hour sleep. Jim Swenson was his name, fifty-four years old and flying since he was sixteen. He's been a bush pilot for thirty-four years. His father was also a bush pilot. He had two planes, one a single engine Cessna and his DeHavilland Beaver. Oh my gosh, I've always wanted to fly in a Beaver ever since I was a child and I saw them on TV. He went on to say he keeps it in prime working condition and has it certified every year. He said he has just seen the area I was looking for which is a hundred miles from anywhere. He's been going to this spot at least once a year for the last ten years and has never seen evidence of anyone ever being there. There is a small lake with one stream and excellent fishing. The valley is surrounded by mountains with moose and bear and smaller animals. Getting on the lake is easy but the weather and wind have to be right to get off. He went on to say that he has often thought about sharing this spot with someone. He wanted to talk with me more and gave me his phone number too. I was hooked after reading that. Tomorrow I will make a few calls to the Better Business Bureau and local small airports and see what they say about Swenson's air services. I wanted to make sure about him before any more plans or exchanges. So I shut things down and took a shower and went to bed. It still took a while to fall asleep.

Waking up today I felt whipped. I'm not sure whether I was overexcited or tired, but my mind didn't stop going last night. I must get some coffee going. I'm definitely not running on eight cylinders yet. I got a cup of coffee and sat out on my deck. It was a beautiful fall morning. It was sixty-one degrees and calm. It was the beginning of a spectacular sunrise. I've always enjoyed sunrises and the start of another wonderful day. The sunsets are great too. It's two shows that God gives us to watch for free. You just have to be there for the opening and closing acts. Well, that first cup tasted like more. I can't make any phone calls until this afternoon because of the time difference. I'll go over to my daughter's house and hang some dry wall and tell her what I have found out so far. She supports me on my plans but I can tell she is not totally for it. I guess it's the love between a father and daughter and not wanting anything to happen to her Daddy. She knows that I have always come back from trips and outings and have great stories to tell, but this one was different because I would be in the wilderness alone this time and it bothered her.

When I walked in the door, my daughter asked what I was doing there? "I came to hang drywall and tell you some news and get the coffee going, girl." She is not a morning person, bless her heart, but she's doing her best. We sat down at the table and I filled her in on the events of the night before. I told her about Jim Swenson, his plane and the area he would take me to. "What if this guy is talking bullshit, Dad?"

"That's why I'm going to make a few phone calls this afternoon to the Better Business Bureau and a small airport or two and find out about Jim Swenson and Swenson's air service. If everything checks out fine I will e-mail him and seal the deal."

"I wish you would take someone with you, Dad."

"I know, dear, but this is what it's all about; no people, just me and the wilderness for thirty days or so. You know I will be prepared. I don't do things half ass, it's all ass or no ass. I know that you are worried but as it gets closer to the day, you will see that I left nothing to chance."

"I understand, Dad, and I am behind you 100 percent but, make that a little but."

"I'll be fine."

It's 1:00 p.m. I got a lot of drywall up this morning and began to make some phone calls. I called information and they gave me the numbers I needed. The Better Business Bureau said that in regards to Swenson Air Service there have been no complaints. Swenson's Air Service was one of the best. I then called two small airports and each had nothing but good things to say about Jim and his dad and his air service. I also asked about his DeHavilland Beaver. I was told that it was in great shape. All I needed to do now was send an e-mail and it would be the start of an adventure and my dream. I finished the e-mail to Jim and thought a minute, took a deep breath, and pressed send. I checked my mailbox and responses were still coming in. After one week I contacted everyone who responded to my e-mail and thanked them for their time and told them that I found an air service.

I got an e-mail from Jim a couple of days later. He apologized about the delay in getting back with me. He was gone on a three day outing. He gave me the best time to reach him for the upcoming week. He was looking forward to the call and so was I. Thursday at 10:00 or 11:00 p.m. would be the best because of the Friday through Sunday Weekend Warriors, as he called them. I could relate to that because I have seen that many times in the woods or on the water. Thursday evening came and I planned to go to sleep early because of the time difference. I set my clock for 1:30 a.m. That would give me a half hour to wake up and get my wits about me before I called.

I punched in his numbers. I got two rings and a "Hello, Swenson's Air Service. Jim speaking."

"It's Alan Dunbarker. At last we speak."

We hit it off right away and before I knew it an hour had passed. I felt we were like old friends and hadn't seen each other in years when I hung up the phone. We talked about everything and agreed to keep in touch through the winter and spring. During our phone conversation, we set the date of June 15th, 2003 with a 7–10 day window for weather. I told Jim that I had planned to be there by the eighth or the tenth of June and I would drive because I hadn't driven the Trans Canadian Highway yet. I would sightsee on the way home. I had asked him if $1,000 would seal the deal. He said that $1000.00 would be plenty and if that date didn't work out we could do it another time or he would give me my money back. He would be putting this all in writing along with a receipt. I couldn't ask for better than that. I joked, "Visa or Mastercard." We laughed. "Either one," he said. So I gave him my numbers and everything was set.

It was getting towards the end of September and June was a long way off, but I had a lot to do to get ready. I knew that I didn't want things all over the house as I was gathering things to get ready for the trip. I rearranged the back bedroom so that I could use half for a gathering spot. I had already started a list but I knew it would be growing. There were things that I needed to order and what I couldn't buy locally I would buy from a catalog. I wanted to be prepared for anything. Where I am going, what you bring in is what you have.

Jim and I kept in touch through the winter and he was keeping me updated on the progress of the Beaver. While the engine was completely rebuilt, he was going through every inch of the plane, every nut, bolt, screw, rivet, and structure. Nose to tail, wingtip to wingtip. He said that he does this every winter on the plane and it's been five years for the engine. If I had a plane like that and it was my bread and butter I would not think twice about keeping it up either.

It's hard to believe it's the first of April already. I'll be leaving in sixty days. Time is getting short. I still have to check over my Ford Explorer yet. I want to replace all hoses, new serpentine belt, change oil, transmission fuel and filters, transfer case oil, check rear-end brakes, tires. The exhaust is good.

I've got to see my doctor for one more time check-up and I will be getting a few things from him that I want to take with me. When I saw him a few months ago I told him of my plans. He said I had a bigger set than he did but agreed that it sounded like a great adventure. I asked him for help since I would be one hundred miles from anywhere. I wanted penicillin or ampicillin, pain killers and few suture packs to go in my med kit that had everything else. He assured me that it was no problem and said that it was a good idea to have on hand. In the following weeks the preparation was getting complete. My Explorer was ready and I got what I needed from my doctor and then some. I also got some antiseptic cream, alcohol packs, hydrocortisone cream, and eye treatment solution. My med kit was ready.

The time was winding down quick. It was now May 25th. Today I will mail my Colt 357 so it will get there before I do. It should only take four days, five at the most to arrive. I will check with Jim before I leave to see if he received it. I have to stop at the hardware store and get the last few things that I need. I will start packing this afternoon. It is hard to describe the feeling that I have every day. I'm full of excitement, anticipation, and the wondering if I have covered all of the bases of what I need and what I should have. I will miss the times away from my family. They are happy for me and concerned at the same time. We won't be in contact for a month or more.

Well, got my gun mailed and the last things from the hardware store. A little lunch and I'll get started packing. Looking at my list and the pile of stuff that I've accumulated, one would think that I was planning a three or four month trip, instead of a four or five week trip. First I will begin with my tools and equipment which include one pair of eight inch pliers, one pair of six inch vise grips, one flat screwdriver, one single bit axe utility hatchet with a hammer head and pailer, one handsaw rip-cut file, sharpening stone, a fold-up trim saw, shovel, hunting knife, belt and holster, box of shells, two fish poles, one fold-up replacement line, hooks, lures, shots, boots, rain gear, a jacket, bibs, one roll of electrical tape, one roll of duct tape, one tarp 12' × 20', one tarp 20' × 20', four cords of nylon rope 5/66, nails, sixteen penny one box, one box of sheeting nails, one roll of 30-pound fish line. Eight two-inch bells, one box of eye screws, one fluorescent light and extra batteries and bulbs, two Led solar lights, one pack of light steel wool, a can of WD40, a can of bear pepper spray with holder, a roll of plastic, bug repellent, four rolls of wire 50 feet each, 24 gage. Oh yes, my gold pan and snuffer bottle; got plenty of time there. I might find some color.

Now for the clothes: insulated boots, extra liners, six pairs of socks heavy cotton, one Thinsolate pair and one wool pair, four pairs of long johns and one silk pair, four flannel shirts, four jeans, four bandana handkerchiefs, one flannel-lined jean jacket, one down vest, one down jacket, two stocking hats, two pairs of gloves, pair of insulated hiking boots, sleeping bag with outer liner, pillow, two blankets, two space blankets, four tee shirts and underwear and a bug netting hat. After putting everything in vacuum travel bags, if there is room, I'll put my hunting jacket and coverall in too.

Now for the food: two ten-pound bags of potatoes, ten pounds sugar, ten pounds salt, one large can of coffee, two boxes of Bisquick, one gallon jug of flour, bay leaves in both, four boxes of noodles, ten boxes of stew, dehydrated dried fruit and vegetables, beef jerky, beans, pears and bag of apples. The bacon, eggs, and whatever else I want I'll get in Anchorage. One cast iron pan, one gallon of oil, spatula, tongs, fold up cooling rack, large spoon, one fork, two cooking pots, food holding cooling racks, eating utensils, four plates, four cups, one thermos, one cooking

May 31st, this time tomorrow, I'll be on the road, yes! The get together is today at 6:00 with family and friends and I know it is going to be hard or nearly impossible to sleep tonight. No matter how much sleep I get, I'll be on the road 6:00 a.m. if not before. I will load my Explorer this afternoon, so in the morning, make coffee, fill thermos, travel mug and leave. Sounds like a plan to me. The get together was great. We cooked outside, some people stayed, others stopped by and wished me the best and some wanted to know all the details. It was over around 9:00 p.m. I told my daughter I would call her when I got to Anchorage and e-mail her the location of my camp area and also put it in a letter. A copy of my location will be in the glove box of my Explorer with the dates and times. I would call when I get back from the brush in July. As we said our good-byes and I love you's, we were both crying and she still begged, please be careful. I will, I said, I am a survivor and I will be home again and don't you ever doubt it. Driving home I was happy and sad. I arrived home at 10:00, took a shower and hit the sack.

It's 5:00 a.m., the alarm just went off. I got some sleep, woke up several times. At 3:00 good sleep finally came. I got the coffee going, sat my bag of road munchies on the table along with the travel bag. The coffee pot is belching it's last now. I took the two bags to my Explorer, went back, filled my thermos and travel mug. One last check that everything was shut off, lights and doors locked. I turned the key and fastened my seat belt. It's 5:30 as I pulled away. I said good-bye-house. I guess I've always done that.

As I got onto US 31 south, there was not much traffic. I set the cruise on 73 and my adventure has started. Other than the slow down through Grand Haven and Holland, I should be able to keep a steady pace. The skies were getting light and it was nice to be on the road again. I've traveled most of the U.S. and parts of Canada. I will just have to pace myself a little so road lag doesn't set in. It sure was a beautiful day for traveling. Getting around Chicago wasn't too bad and I was glad when I started into the countryside on 80 West. I've always enjoyed seeing how the land changes as the miles go by. I will stop in Semmine to get gas and stretch my legs and some fresh coffee.

pan, one cooler, two five-gallon buckets with lids, hand soap, dish soap, washing soap, four dish clothes, four wash clothes, four towels, toilet paper, two rolls of paper towels, coffee pot, small folding table and chair, camera, thirty rolls of film, binoculars, notepad, writing paper, pens, pencils, boxes of one quart and gallon zip lock bags, one combo heater and stove with propane, four extra small tanks, and eight by eight all weather tarps. Everything will be put in water tight containers and packages and bags. It took the whole afternoon but after the squeezing, stuffing, and labeling I was finished. I got to admit I am the master of packing.

The day before I leave some of the family and friends are having a going away party for me. I am looking forward to it and I know there will be a lot of questions. I will make time for them all. Tonight I think I will fire up the grill. T-bone steaks sound good, boil up a few red skin potatoes, green beans and spend a few hours on the computer. I know I have e-mails to answer.

Tomorrow I will get the travelers checks and put $5000.00 on my travelers card. I will carry my Visa card which is good for $10,000 as well as $100.00 cash. If there is a problem, I will be covered.

Well the banking is done. I got the travelers checks and cash. I've got to get with my daughter before I leave and give her the house keys and my checkbook so she can pay any bills that come in and check on the house.

I've got to weigh my food and equipment. I wanted to keep it to 500 pounds or less. Jim needs to know so he can make his calculation for the flight. The weigh in is final, gear 487 pounds; and with bacon and some meat that I'll buy when I get there, it should be 500 pounds, or less. I've packed enough food for two months without fish or anything else.

If the weather is bad it might be a week or two after the pick up date of July 15th. Far better to have plenty than not enough. The same with the clothes; you can't put on what you don't have and being that far north, the weather can be nice or nasty. I'll be ready for any condition. I'll be on the road in six days. Now to get the next few days behind me. I am ready, want to leave now but I can't.

I plan to spend the night in S. Dakota, somewhere between Michel and Rapid City or Wall. I would like to see the Bad Lands again. I was glad to put Iowa behind me, now it's 23 North to Sioux Falls where I'll get on 20 West and get a place to spend the night. Gassed up again in Sioux Falls and headed west. I wasn't feeling tired yet so I'll put more miles behind me. As I passed by Mitchel, I was thinking about the Corn Palaces and the Doll Museum. I had seen these years earlier, two good things to see.

I had decided to spend the night in Wall as I pulled into the motel. I had been driving 14½ hours. I am a driving nut! I got my room and walked across the street to get something to eat. A good meal, pork chops, mashed potatoes and gravy and salad. I was starting to wind down by then and headed back to my motel. The bed was comfortable and I would get the weather report and watch TV for a while. Clear skies for tomorrow, no storms, temp in the seventies. Perfect I thought. I will be able to see the Rockies long before I get into them. It's 11:00 p.m. and the sand man is beating me up. I set my travel clock for 6:00 a.m. and turned off the light. Sleep came quick as my thoughts of today's events and tomorrow's anticipation.

The alarm was buzzing. I sat up, shut it off, 6:00 a.m. I never woke up at all last night. I am not sure if I even moved. I quickly took a shower and shaved, gathered my things and headed for my Explorer. A quick check under the hood, everything's fine. One thing about the winds on the prairie, they are constant. One stop for coffee and hit the road.

The Bad Lands are always a wonderful sight, the thousands of different shapes and colors. The last time I saw them was eleven years ago. I would be in Rapid City before long, then on to Billings, MO. One thing about Wyoming, you start seeing Prong Horn sheep and the smell of sagebrush in the air, that's when you know the plains are behind you and the west begins. I planned to spend the night in the mountains around Helena, not sure where. Whatever looks good. A little slower pace today and tomorrow and take in the scenery. I couldn't wait to see the Rocky Mountains rising in the west. I will gas up in Rapid City and it won't be long I'll be in Wyoming. I saw a lot of Prong

Horn; they were dotting the landscape everywhere. I stopped in Billings for gas and a bit to eat. I figured to be in Helena by evening. It will give me plenty of time to find a place out of town. I didn't come this far to stay in a city. I found a nice place west of town, a few miles off the highway, nice cabins and a nice stream with fast water. You could hear it everywhere. I thought about getting out a fish pole but they were packed away so I was content to set by it awhile. The sun hadn't set yet but we were in the shadow of the mountains. The soft light and the sound of the water was very relaxing. The cool fresh air and I was ready for some sleep.

I got up feeling great. I had set the alarm for 7:30. I wanted nice daylight for the rest of the trip through the mountains then on into Washington. As I headed back to the interstate, the sunlight was lighting up the trees and rocks with such clarity, you could call it a Kodiak moment. I stopped to get coffee. The restaurant across the street was having a breakfast special: egg, toast, bacon and hash browns $3.50. It sounded good to me. I must have been hungry or the food was good. Everything I tasted was so good and everything was cooked just right—eggs over easy, bacon not overcooked and loose hash browns not patties. All the coffee you wanted, no waiting! The waitress should teach others; pleasant, friendly and made sure you had what you needed, coffee refilled, everything. I've had some waitresses, couldn't find them and others were in your face. I tipped her a five; it was worth it to me.

There were just a few hours of mountains ahead of me, left the rest of mountains and Idaho. I'll take my time and enjoy them. Not a lot to see in eastern Washington but it's been years so it's almost like seeing it for the first time. The mountains are ending and soon the foothills. I had several hours of driving till I got off of 90 onto 5 North. I'll spend the rest of day and night this side of the border and cross over in the morning. I've always wanted to drive the Alaskan Canada Highway but it's called Trans Can Highway by now; they call it what they want. I am still going to drive it.

I got my motel and looked over the Explorer, checked everything, all looks good. I needed to pick up a gas can just to be safe. A lot of miles ahead and not a lot of towns and people. I already had everything one would need: air compressor, tire repair, plugs, sealers, hose repair, clamps, tools you name it. There was a gas station down the street. I'll go to it in the morning. I can get coffee too. After I got my gas can, I saw a sign, all you can eat seafood $15.95, oh yes. Crab legs and shrimp, here I come. Damn, I got to stop going to places like that. I couldn't eat another bite. Got back to my motel room, watched TV, the weather channel and crashed for the night.

I got up at 5:00 a.m., showered, shaved and ready to go. I stopped for gas and coffee and to the border. Showed my passport and drivers license, normal questions, where I'm going, how long in the country, got any guns, weapons, drugs? Have a nice trip. Now the last stage of the trip, four days to Anchorage, five if I feel like goofing off. This is my fourth day. North to Alaska, this is new to me. The Cascade Range is always so interesting to see, being more arid on the west side. I was glad when I reached Seattle and headed north. Lyndon was twenty-five miles from the border and I was excited for tomorrow morning. I could see the coastal mountains to my left as I headed north on highway. Every curve and over every hill was something new to see and it will only get better. Who knows how many stops.

The first town I came to was Chiliwack; it was still expressway and would be till I got to Liadlow up by Harrison Lake. Then it will be two lanes the rest of way. That is what I was looking forward to where I could stop or pull over whenever I wanted. The day was real nice with clear skies; it was like you could see forever. Rosedale was the next town I went by and Laidlaw was next. I made a pit stop in Laidlaw, topped off the tank, fresh coffee and a nature call. I turned back on the highway, headed north toward Hope. I can't believe how much the land changes. I am just taking my time so I can see everything. I know I barely got started but with all my travels, seeing the area for the first time is special. I just passed Hope and unto Yale. So far they have the town spaced out pretty good. When I got past Yale, I was coming to the first tunnel on my way to Chapman. I had to stop for a few pictures. I went through Chapman. I had another tunnel to go through and a few more pictures. The next town was Boston Bar. I put Boston Bar behind me. I had 108 miles to go till I reached Lytton. There I will take a short break, get something to eat and gas up.

I got into town and got my gas first and got directions for a place to eat. I like the mom and pop restaurants. It's a lot better than the drive up, can I take your order? The restaurant wasn't far. The food and services was good. The people are always curious about where you're from and where you're going. I was anxious to get back on the road. I headed out of town. The sign said, thirty-seven miles to Spencer Bridge. I am not sure how far I'll drive today but one thing for sure, this trip will be driven in daylight. Hell, if I was pushing to get from point A to point B, I would be driving sixteen to eighteen hours at a time. This land is too pretty to miss.

Still heading north after Spencer's Bridge, I had forty-seven miles to go till I reach Ashcraft. There were quite a few RV's heading north, everyone with a dream of seeing the great north and I imagine, like me, it's the first time. Still following Highway 1, I passed through Ashcraft then Catch Creek then on to Clinton. I am glad I have a bag of film. I just finished my second roll since this morning. I had 164 miles to go till I get to Williams Lake, where I plan to spend the night. That should put me in town around 6:00 p.m. Counting picture stops and everything else. The time looks good. I'll be there in around 2 hours. Being the first part of June, all the green is out on the trees, valleys and fields with background of rocks, mountains and sky of blue. You couldn't ask for better than that.

I arrived at Williams Lake a little after 6:00. I got the tank filled up and checked all the fluids under the hood. Now to find a place to sleep and eat. I found a nice cabin for $50.00 for the night, off the main drag. It was owned by a couple around my age and they were real nice to talk with. They told me where I could eat supper and breakfast and that I wouldn't be disappointed about food. They were right. There were so many things that looked good on the menu. It was hard to choose. I had the half chicken with mashed potatoes, salad and homemade rolls. It was like a home cooked meal. My belly was full when I left and if their breakfast is as good as supper, I'll have something to look forward to in the morning. I got back to the cabin and sat outside for awhile trying to anticipate what the next day will be like and what I will see. It was almost 9:00 and I was ready for a good nights sleep. I set my alarm for 6:00 a.m. so I would have plenty of time to shower and shave and eat breakfast. The light will be good by 8:00; that's when I plan to be on the road.

I arrived at the restaurant around 7:00 and had the Woodman's special; two pork chops, fried potatoes, two eggs and toast with coffee. I had them fill my thermos too so I was good to go. I pulled out on Highway 1, it was 124 miles to the next town of Hershey. There wasn't much traffic yet and most other people weren't in a hurry either so that was nice. That reminds me, I got to put a fresh roll of film in the camera when I got through Hershey. The next town was Guestnal. I want to get to Prince George by around noon. I left Guestnal with 55 miles to Nixon. After Nixon I stopped at the river to take a few pictures then drive on to Red Rock. I had fifty-nine miles to go to Prince George. I still couldn't get over the scenery, it keeps getting better and better. When I got to Prince George, I needed to find a place to change the oil. I've got over 3000 miles on this oil. I found a fast oil and lube and I was back on the road in no time. Highway 1 and 97 run together and will for quite some time. The next town I came to was Salmon Valley then on to Summit Lake, stopping for pictures all the time. I had plenty of time to get to Anchorage so I am enjoying. When I got to Bear Lake, I had 136 miles to Mt. Le Morey and 384 miles to Dawson Creek. Each mile offered something new to see and something to get a picture of. At this pace I will be getting to Dawson Creek after 7:00. When I got to Mt. Le Morey I had 148 miles to go to get to Chetoyand. I still had 100 miles to go before I reached Dawson Creek. By the time I rolled into Dawson Creek it was 7:30.

I filled up the tank and got a room for the night. There was a restaurant across the street from my motel room. The food was good and as soon as I was done I headed back to my room. I want to start earlier tomorrow. The restaurant opened at 6:00 so I set my alarm for 5:30. I'll really be into the mountains tomorrow. I am going to try to get somewhere close to Watson's Lake on the border of British Columbia and the Yukon Territory.

I was at the restaurant when they opened the doors at 6:00. I ordered bacon and eggs, toast and coffee with a thermos fill too. By 6:45, I was walking to my Explorer. I pointed it north back on Highway 1 toward Wonowan. It was another nice day and I could see the mountains with the sunlight on the tips of the peaks. Ninety-five miles past Wonowan, the park mountains were on my left. After I get to Sekanna Chief and Trutch Mt. Summit, I had to take pictures. The elevation was 126 feet. It was 200 miles to Fort Nelson. I can only imagine what the army workers thought, when they cut this road out in 1942. There are still areas you can see where the original road was cut and how they improved it years later. So many lakes, streams and rivers. I could see Clark Lake to my right along with the Nelson River. I gazed up at Fort Nelson and got back on Highway 1, crossed Prophet River heading toward Summit Lake 112 miles away. The way I am going, my camera's going to need a vacation. If I had a camcorder I would have needed a suitcase of tapes. With Summit Lake behind me, Muncho Lake was the next landmark. I stopped at the Todd River for a picture or two then on to Muncho Lake. Mt. Prudence was off to my right. Of all travels throughout the lower 48 and parts of Canada, nothing compares to what I've seen already and I've got a lot more ahead of me. Muncho Lake was a pass through and Lisard was the next town. One thing I've noticed so far was that you can tell where there are moose crossing by all the skid marks on the road. Right after passing through Lisard I stopped at the Lisard Bine River for a few more pictures and down the road I stopped again at Smith Bine River. By the time I got to Coal River it was too late to continue on. The next stop was Contact Creek 277 miles ahead. I was ready for some sleep. I've got to get some miles behind me tomorrow; it's going to take many hours before I get to the Yukon.

  The restaurant opened at 5:00 and I planned to be on the road by 6:00. After having a breakfast of ham, eggs, toast and coffee and my thermos filled, I was on the road by 6:00 as I planned. The morning was cool, the skies and weather would be great for traveling. I got more good pictures on my way to Contact Creek, where I stopped for gas and a nature call. I pulled back out on Highway 1 and the next stop was Watson Lake, the Yukon. I finally reached Blue River and a short picture stop there, then on to Watson Lake. I topped off the tank at Watson Lake and picked up some road munchies and more coffee. When

I left Watson Lake, I had 135 miles to go get to Rancheria. For a long ways the Rancheria River was on my left. The next town was Swift River, trying to keep some of the picture taking contained along the way but it was hard. The hours and the miles were going by as the day progressed. I passed through Teslin then another one mile to Johnson's Crossing, where I gassed up again. I had another 129 miles to Whitehorse. Jake's Corner was the next town and you could see Marsh Lake on the left, more pictures. I had eighty-two miles to go to Whitehorse. The scenery is so vast and wild and you never know what you will see next. I would have stopped more for sightseeing along the way, but I'll do that on my next trip back home which will be weeks of traveling. I got into Whitehorse, saw a little town and headed back on the road. It was getting late in the day by now but I wanted to drive till dark. The town of Champagne was next then Boutillier Summit, elevation 1000 feet, then on to Haines Junction. I planned to stop in the town of Klulana for the night. When I left Haines Junction I had 107 miles left to go before I reached Klulana. I could see the large mountain range to my left and the sun was slowly setting behind it.

When I pulled into the town of Klulana, I got my gas first and found a place to spend the night. There was a cute little restaurant down the road; it looked like a good place to eat. Log walls and big glass windows in front. As I walked in the door, you could smell the aroma coming from the kitchen. I sat down and the waitress handed me the menu. The special was a rib eye steak with boiled potatoes, sourdough bread and salad. It sounded like a winner to me. She took my order and I sat sipping my coffee. They had pictures on the walls of the area, some from back in the '40s. My food was here and I was for some serious throwing down. The steak was tender and juicy with some moo left in it, the way I like. I was full by the time I finished but I still had room for apple pie with ice cream. I was stuffed. I drove back to my room and it didn't take long to fall asleep.

I got up at 5:00, showered and shaved. The restaurant was open when I got there at 5:45. I had eggs, bacon, sausage and fried potatoes and filled my thermos. I was on the road. Kluhana Lake went on for miles and miles and I even got a picture of a moose too. It was 263 miles to White Bine. I planned to be in

Anchorage by afternoon sometime. I would fill the gas tank at White Bine and drive on to Beaver Creek. I was still having fun seeing all the sights. It wouldn't be long until I reached the border.

I passed through Beaver Creek, thirty-two miles to go and I'll be in Alaska. After a short stop at the border and a moment of who, where and when, I was on my way. Toh was the next town forty-two miles away. The mountains were great, so much to look at and take pictures of. I topped off the tank in Toh and stayed on Highway 1 to the west. On my way back, I would go east to Sawson City and beyond. When I got to Highway 4 to the left was Valdez, Alaska. I had 328 miles to go to get to Palmer so I topped off the tank again. As I crossed each valley and ridge, my trip was getting shorter. Making my way through the mountains, I had to stop a number of times to take more shots with my camera coming out of the mountains. I could see Palmer ahead and after gassing up, and a nature call, it was on to Anchorage and find Jim's place.

It was nice to see Anchorage again in the distance. I've had a number of moose stops already. I sure wouldn't want to hit one first thing. What I've got to do is call my daughter and let her know I made it alright. I had my phone travel card so whatever calls I make it's put on my home phone bill. Ah, I see phones at a convenience store. As I got out I couldn't help noticing how nice the weather was. It had to be in the 60s.

I punched in the numbers, anxious to get through. One ring, two rings, hello, I am here. "Oh daddy I am so glad you called. I've been wondering about you ever since you left." It was nice to hear her voice again. I told her I just got into Anchorage and had a good trip and a great time so far. I told her I had to get to Jim's first. I also told her that I would send her an e-mail and a letter before I left for my location. I would get that from Jim. Oh yes, I will have a copy in the glove box of my Explorer too. We talked awhile more then said our I love you's and good-byes and I would give her a call the day I leave.

I pulled into Jim's place. His plane was there and he was loading up. As I walked up I asked if he knew of a pilot that could take me on a dream adventure. "You must be that dream-crazed guy I know from Michigan." We shook hands and had a good laugh. It was great to finally meet him in person. I gave him a hand getting the rest of the stuff in the plane. The plane was beautiful inside and out. I complimented him on his plane. "Thanks, it's my baby." Then Jim surprised me. "You want to ride along? I've got to drop these things off to a woman about sixty miles from here. She had just bought a cabin a month or two ago."

I couldn't wait to say yes. We untied and climbed in. I was excited to say the least. My first ride in a Beaver. When the motor started and I watched Jim check his gauges, controls, flaps and tail, he was all business. We motored out. I couldn't believe the power and lift that plane had when we took off. I thought to myself this thing is so sweet. In no time we were coming in for a landing on this lake. I couldn't help but be amazed. Jim and his plane were as one. He was the plane and the plane was him. We unloaded the supplies, gas, materials and headed out. As we talked, my nose was on the glass. I wanted to see everything. The trip might have been short but it was sweet.

We tied up to the deck and walked to Jim's house. His house was nice and cozy. Two bedrooms but one was his office, nice kitchen, living room and of course a woodstove. He showed me a picture of him, his dad, places where he has been and things he's done. As I looked at the pictures and heard him talk, I thought what a life this man has had. I had done a lot in my life and but not like this.

I asked Jim if he wanted to go out to eat? I'll buy. He asked, where I was staying? I didn't have a place yet. "I will tell you what you do. Down this road here, is some nice cabins about a mile. I know the owners and you'll get a good price. I'll give them a call and tell them you're coming. Do you like moose?" "Yes, why?" "Go get your cabin, get settled in and come back in about two hours. I'll cook for you."

The cabin was nice with all the comforts of home. I couldn't believe it. The price $25.00 a day. The owners were real nice. We talked awhile and they wanted to make sure I had everything I needed. They had moved here forty years ago. Jim and his dad were some of the first people they met. I put the things I wanted in the cabin. It was time to enjoy some home cooking.

As I pulled in the yard Jim was busy cooking. "I like wood, it's better than gas. Don't you think?" "You got my vote, damn that smells good." "Go in the house and get us a couple of beers. Food will be ready in about twenty minutes."

When I got back I told him this sure beats any restaurant. The moose steaks were fabulous, baked potatoes, veggies. It doesn't get any better than this. We couldn't stop talking and I couldn't help but look every time a plane came in on the lake. It was 11:00 p.m. It was going to take awhile to get used to this daylight, Land of the Midnight Sun. Jim was saying, this lake will be wing to wing planes at night and by 5:00 a.m. only a few will be left. He had a fly out tomorrow morning and would be back in the evening. We'll get together then.

Driving back to the cabin, my mind was on the events of the day. I was still too excited to be sleepy yet. As I sat in a chair outside the cabin I thought, this is wild, reading a newspaper at midnight. Well, must get some sleep. It's been a long day. The bed felt good and it wasn't long before sleep had come.

I awoke to the sound of motors roaring. It was after 4:00 a.m. The lake and the skies were alive, one after the other. A whole new meaning to fly the friendly skies. By 5:00, only a few planes were left. I must get to bed earlier tonight. Ya, if that will happen. It must be the air. I'm hungry. I am about ready to leave when I saw Mr. Miller sweeping out the front. "Where's a good place to eat?" "Go back to the main road, turn left, three miles on the right, you'll like it." "Thanks and I am on my way."

As I pulled in, I liked it already. Log building, mom and pop look to it. As I walked in the aroma of the food almost made my mouth water. So many things on the menu, the lumberjack special caught my eye, four pancakes, ten strips of bacon, three eggs, a slice of ham, fried potatoes and toast. I sipped my coffee as I waited for my order. There were pictures of Anchorage in earlier days on the walls everywhere and some from the earthquake of 1964. Wow, everything came on this big platter. Well, appetite don't fail me now. I dug in. By the time I finished the last bite, I knew I wouldn't need to eat the rest of the day. Sweet misery, I thought, as I walked out the door.

Think I will check out a bit of Anchorage. The day was early and I had time to kill. I hadn't driven only a mile or so when a moose suddenly appeared out of nowhere. Damn and a few other words, I stopped about 5 feet from this cow and she just stood there. I think she had a death wish or something. She finally walked off the road. I like moose meat but this one was too fresh for my grill. I want to keep my Explorer intact. I think they should change the name to Mooseville.

I spent the next few hours driving around and also found the store to get the last of my supplies the day before I leave. It was mid-afternoon when I got back to the cabin. The skies were clouding up like it's going to rain before long. I had driven by Jim's but he wasn't back yet. I think a little power nap is in order. I woke up at 6:30. I must have been tired. Guess I still had a bit of road lag. I drove over to Jim's. He wasn't back yet and the rain was starting to come down. I put a note on his door to call me. When I got back to the cabin, I planned to watch the weather and get a letter started for my daughter. Rain for the next four days and clouds clearing out by the fourth. I was glad to hear that. Today's the 9th and clear skies by the 13th. I had a real good start on my letter when the phone rang; it was Jim. He had just got in and his clients just left. I'll be over in a few.

Two

As I came through the door, I said "I am buying supper tonight but you're going to pick the place. How does crab legs sound?" On the way to the restaurant, I told Jim about moose today. "Got your heart going didn't it?" "You bet." The crab legs were real good and I ate too much. I've got to stop doing that. Back at Jim's, we sat at the table, enjoyed a beer and some conversation. "Let me have a look at your .357 mag." "I'll get it out of my gun safe." I opened the package, still taped and sealed as the day I shipped it. I pulled it out and handed it to him. "Nice feel. I like the full style grip you got on it, it makes it feel like part of your hand. What kind of shells do you have?" "Hand-loaded, ¾-jacketed, hollow points, a lot of bite for the bark. They are better than factory loads."

"Let's check the computer and see how the weather's doing and get an idea for the 14th." After taking in the information and a bit of calculating, "We might be able to leave the 14th if you like, I'll know for sure by the 13th." "If the door is open, let's do it," I said. Then Jim got out his maps and showed me the area and location where I'll be staying. "Damn, you weren't kidding when you said remote and nothing for hundreds of miles." I told him I needed to make a couple of copies of that area of the map. One to send to my daughter and one for the glove box of my Explorer. "I trust you, Jim, but if for some reason you can't make it back to pick me up, I want directions ready when the troops are called out." He agreed it was a good plan. Plus, I kidded him his spot was safe with me. After we made copies, I was talking with him about the terrain and the mountains. What we will be traveling over and through. "You won't see any rougher," he assured me, and with that we had a bourbon, a toast to the trip, to the adventure. We called it a night. I headed back to the cabin. As I settled in for the night, I drifted off to sleep with thoughts of the days ahead.

It rained the next three days and the morning of the 13th, clouds were clearing out. You could see the mountain peaks again in the distance. The weather report looked great for the next seven days.

Mr. Miller, the owner of the cabin, asked me to go fishing with him today for Northern Pike. All I had to do is bring myself. He had a boat, poles and everything. We unloaded the boat and started out. The waters were almost calm. I asked if we were going to troll or cast? He said troll till we get to his favorite part of the lake. Big lures, big fish, he said. I set out two poles. He already set up big lures. These buggers were at least 8" long. I don't think we had gone 100 yards yet when bam fish on. I grabbed the pole as Mr. Miller brought in the other pole. I tell you the fight was on. You could feel the power of that fish through the pole. After the first run was over, I was bringing him in but I've had experience with big pike before. There was a lot more fight left in this fish which I was about to find out.

He took off again, the pole was bent like a U and the reel screamed as the line went out. He stopped. My eyes must have given me away. Bob was laughing. "You've got a while before he's ready for the net" and laughed again. "What's the biggest Northern you've caught?" he asked as I worked to get some line back." "Forty-four inches," I said. "I'll be this one is well over four feet." I think he's right, hopefully. I'll get a look at him soon. He's still stripping line on his run but less now. Here he comes. Damn, is he big!

Almost to the boat, another run, got him to the boat and Bob was ready with the net. We got 'em! He pulled the fish over the side of the boat and there was more green than I've ever seen in that net. We pinned him down so he wouldn't beat us or the boat up. We got the lure out and I asked, "What's the policy? Keep or toss?" "Keep it." It's the biggest he's ever seen come out of this lake so we thumped and stuck him, got out the tape, 58½ inches. I told him, he must mount it and put it in his office. "But it's your fish." "It's our fish. It took both of us to get it. Just put both our names on the plaque. Pictures are fine for me," I said.

We caught more fish that day but nothing as big as that one. We got back around 4:00, took pictures and some of Bob's family came by to see the fish. I wanted to lay down awhile before meeting with Jim this evening. Bob said he would have some fresh cooked fish for me when I got up. Sounds like a plan.

I awoke to knocking on my door. It was Jim. "What's the matter? This northern life wearing you out?" "No. just saving myself for the better stuff." "Fish is ready, let's eat." We had a good time with Bob and his wife, Helen. The food was great. The stories funny and the time went by so fast. We said good night and left for Jim's house. Jim checked the maps and charts and radar and the 15th was a go. "So tomorrow afternoon, I'll check over the Beaver and we'll get everything loaded. Bring your cooler of food in the morning when we leave." I stayed awhile longer. Jim had paperwork to catch up on and I went back to the cabin.

I sat down and made my list for tomorrow; send e-mail and letter, get rest of food, put maps and directions in glove box and load up. It was 9:00 p.m. and I would see what is on the TV, maybe a good movie. I checked the TV guide. *The Edge*, with Anthony Hopkins. That will be a good one to watch before I go into the bush. I thought, I seen it before but it's worth seeing again. By the time it was over the sand man was ready to put a whoopen to me so I turned off the light and soon drifted off to sleep.

The next morning I was up and running, had breakfast and plenty of coffee. Then I went into town to get the rest of the food: five packages of bacon, three packages of Johnsonville brats, three dozen eggs, four pork chops, ten-pound bag of onions and a twenty-pound bag of potatoes. As I left the store, I decided to stop at this big sporting goods store, just to look around. As I wandered around the store, I kept telling myself I really don't need that. I don't need this either but then I saw a solar water shower, portable and light weight. I'll take one please. I was almost to the checkout and then it had my attention like it reached out and grabbed me, a wooden handle roasting fork. Must grab and run before another thing appears. Will that be all, sir? Yes, I paid for my items and headed out of town.

When I got back to the cabin, I finished my daughter's letter, packed away the fork, roaster, solar shower and put the meat in the frig. I'll send the e-mail when I get to Jim's. My ice is made in plastic containers half gallon jugs. Went to the office to talk to Bob and get some more newspaper for the cooler and the trip. We talked for awhile and thanked him and his wife for everything and told them I would be leaving in the morning. I had to call my daughter yet and mail her letter. Bob said just leave it on the counter. He'll put it with his mail. Great, thanks a lot. I left the letter with him. I went outside to make my call. UPS truck pulled up. He walked in with several packages. I could see that he set them down where my letter was. He left so now I could use the phone so I could hear. I let it ring ten times, no answer. I hung up and realized no answering machine either. That was strange. I'll keep trying the rest of the day. I glanced into the windows again and the counter was clear. Bob must have picked up my letter. I then put the envelope of the map and info in the glove box. I went back into the cabin to catch the Weather Channel. They had thunderstorms through Wisconsin and Michigan, high winds and thunderstorms, maybe that is why I can't get through.

    I went over to Jim's to bother him (not really). As I pulled in I could see him sitting in a chair by his phone. "You really look busy sitting there." "I was busy. I am busy and I am still busy. It's your turn to get busy." "Is it still a go?" "Yup, unless you are getting cold feet." "Not me." I backed my Explorer to the dock. I unloaded, Jim packed, keeping the load even. The only thing left was the cooler for tomorrow morning. I asked if I could use his computer to send an e-mail to my daughter. "No problem. I'll set it up for you." When I finished I checked everything over, info was right, location was right. I'll call when I get back. I love you, and hit send."

    "Well, Alan, tomorrow is your big day. You think you are ready?" "Well, Jim, put it this way, if I was anymore ready, you would have to have a bigger plane." I liked the humor we shared and looked forward to many years of friendship.

    We checked the weather reports, maps, and charts. "Everything looks right," Jim announced. "What time do we leave?" "5:00 a.m., I figure if there are no clouds on the mountains. Alan, how about you get a fire going, I've got a couple of T-bone steaks that's been screaming at me, eat me, eat me and now would be a good time to shut them up." I agreed we could do that. It wasn't long before the fire was ready and those steaks looked good waiting to be put on the grill. "How do you like your steak, Jim?" "I like 'em with a bit of moo left in them." I started to laugh. He said, "You never heard that before?" "No, that's what I always say." We both had a good chuckle over that one. There is nothing like the smell of meat cooking over wood fire. As we ate we talked about many things and the time went by so fast, several hours worth.

As I drove back to the cabin, I thought I'm going to miss this guy, the next thirty days. Last night in this place, I looked at the cooler on the floor. You're getting stuffed in the morning. I set my alarm for 3:30 and crawled into bed. I wasn't sure how much sleep I would get. It was not only the excitement and anticipation but a mental checklist as well. I finally had to tell myself "enough." You have done everything, get some sleep.

What time it was when I finally drifted off, I don't know. But when the alarm went off, I was up and running. Bob had brought over a coffee pot and sugar the day before. I fired that puppy up and took a shower. After getting dressed, I poured myself a cup and started loading the cooler. I first lined the bottom and sides with newspaper, then the meat and jugs of ice and put newspaper over the top of everything. This will be good for at least ten days. I filled my thermos and mug. 4:15 a.m., I took everything out to the Explorer. One last check around the cabin and I am out of here.

When I pulled into Jim's place he was up and waiting. "I'm glad I didn't have to come down there and drag your butt out of bed." "No chance of that, Jim." We put the cooler in the lane. I locked up the Explorer and put the keys in the office. Jim said pee now or forever hold it. As we walked to the plane, Jim commented, "You look like a tourist with that camera around your neck."

"Call me what you want. I plan to take a lot of pictures." We climbed in and the engines roared to life. Jim went through his checklist. "Are you ready?" "You bet!" It was ten minutes to 5:00. We taxied out on the lake and we were off. As we lifted over the trees, gaining speed and altitude, it was exciting, seeing the mountains in the distance, getting bigger the closer we got.

No matter what way into the bush, you have to cross mountains when leaving Anchorage. The view was spectacular and breathtaking and this was only the first part.

When we crossed into the mountains, I couldn't believe how rough and rugged the land was. I've seen pictures and on TV but it's totally different in person. As we weaved our way through passes and around peaks, it was definitely the last frontier. Jim pointed out sheep on a few mountains. As we traveled on, I told Jim this is no area to walk out of. "You're right about that. If a person tried he couldn't carry enough food or water to make it out." "I don't want to sound like a kid, but are we there yet?" Jim just smiled and shook his head.

I continued to take pictures and take in the sights. When Jim announced that our last pass was up ahead, he pointed out a crash sight from two years earlier. No one survived. When he went down the pilot was 150 miles off course from a storm. Our pass was coming up and we were through. I could see the whole valley, trees and the lake. We dropped down into the valley. Jim gave me a fly over look. I saw several moose and he pointed out a trapper cabin. It was caved in and not much left of walls. We banked to the left and dropped onto the lake. This place was all I expected and more. We motored to the north side of the lake where it will be my home for the next thirty days.

We got on our boots. I tied the plane to a tree and we started to unload. It didn't take long. Then Jim showed me where his campsite was "but you pick out what's comfortable to you." We walked back to the plane. While Jim was putting in the extra gas we carried, I was getting out my .357 holster belt and knife and loaded it. I was getting the last of my stuff to higher ground. Jim was ready to leave. We said our good-byes. I tossed him the rope and helped push him out. He motored across the lake—that wasn't far—and he did a half circle, powered up to pick up more speed. I waved as he passed then lifted. He cleared the trees at the end of the lake by only a few feet as he circled once more to gain speed and altitude and disappeared through the pass. That's when the reality sets in.

Did you ever have a time or place where you ask yourself, what did I get myself into? Well for a moment this was one. But not long. I had a lot to do before I called it a day. First get out of these boots and get my shoes on. I picked out a spot for the tent next to small clearing Jim showed me, high ground good run off. I smoothed the ground and put up the tent with a tree at the back and another out front of the tent. Next to put up tarps first, put a rope between the two trees two feet above the top of the tent, then the tarp next. After tying it down and anchoring the bottom edges, it made a good shelter. Next to do, the food shack. I had picked out some spruce trees about forty feet away with good limbs to work with, around twelve to fourteen feet up. I will have to make a ladder.

It took a while to find the poles I wanted. I laid them out and started notching for the rungs. I cut and notched the rungs and fitted each one with a few nails and some wire. A nice sturdy ladder. First I trimmed off all the branches on the four trees to the level where I wanted the bottom of the catches, put two cross logs and several across them. It was good enough for today. I hauled my food supplies up and secured them. I will build the rest of it tomorrow.

The fire pit cooking area was next, plenty of stones around and my cooking rack fits fine. Gather firewood and I'll be ready to do a little fishing. I was getting hungry. I got out my 6½-foot pole and tied on a gold and black spinner with a tail. All I wanted was a couple of fish. I'll try first down from the campsite, second cast a trout, a little over twelve inches. A few more cast, number two, about the same size. I cleaned and rinsed them right there and headed back to camp. It wasn't long and the fire was burning good and I'll have a bed of coals before long. That fresh trout hit the spot. I tossed the skin and bones in the fire. I don't need a lot of smells around camp. Now to set up the bells and fish line, had to do a bit of brush clearing. I wanted a thirty to forty-foot area around camp. I got out the pack of eye screws and six of the eight bells. One bell per side, got up the eye screws and line. When I fastened the bells, I left the line loose enough that if something runs into it, several bells would ring. The last two bells, I'll put up on my food catches.

I was getting tired and I was happy with what I've accomplished today and it was time to set awhile. The fire was out. I didn't plan to start it up. As I sat on my chair, I wanted to take in the smell of the woods; the wind was calm and any sounds would carry a long way. It would take a week or so to get your senses tuned in, then you can identify sounds and smells and everything. Wow, that was neat, a wolf a long way off several miles. There he is again. What a way to end the day. I still haven't got used to the way to end the day. I still haven't got used to the skies being light. I looked at my watch—it's after 12:00, time for some sleep. I climbed into my sleeping bag. It felt good but I definitely got to soften the area underneath.

It was my body that woke me up. No noise, just plenty of screaming. As I stepped out of the tent, I could smell the spruce along with the cleanness of the air. The sky was clear and blue and the sunlight was on the upper part of the mountains and soon down in the valley. A beautiful day, Lord, you do good work. Time for a little breakfast. Get the fire started, get out the fry pan, bacon, eggs and potatoes. The smell of that bacon cooking outside like this would make anyone hungry. The food, round potatoes done, and now the eggs. I like it, one pan cooking. Everything tasted so good. It can't get much better than this. Now for the clean up. Hey, I can use the solar shower bag for rinsing dishes. A little Dawn Foam and quick rinse works good.

Think I will take a walk to the stream and see what it's like. It's only a hundred yards or so. I stayed close to the shore line till I got there. I didn't see any sign of bear so I was glad of that. I carefully walked up where the mouth of the stream emptied into the lake. Just as I figured there were trout everywhere feeding on whatever they could coming out. The stream was about eight feet wide at the mouth but narrowed as I went up stream to five or six feet or so. There are a few good spots to do some sample panning, find a little color. I've got more work to do around camp. I can play later.

As I got close to camp I could detect the smell of bacon in the air, not strong but there. The grease I poured on the fire didn't all burn. I will get a fire going and stop the smell. I don't need to be sending an invite on the wind. I got the fire going and tossed some green boughs for smoke. That should do it. Might as well make a pot of coffee. Time to break in the twelve-cup perk and open the coffee up and the sugar. Today I will build the rest of my food shack a few more logs on the floor, then back of the wall and roof. The containers are tough and waterproof but I wanted more to detour critters big and small. I am ready for some coffee and get started.

It took seven more six-inch logs to finish the bottom row to build the sides. I could build each one on the ground and pull them up. My plan was to build them with the least amount of nails as I could. It would be more work. I started gathering limbs to work with. There were plenty on the ground and dead ones on the trees. The walls I wanted around three feet high and used the saw and hand ax to taper two sides on each end and two rails for the top and bottom. I used one nail on the corners and fitted each stick together between the rails till they fit tight and put in the last nail. It was sturdy and looked pretty good. Three more sides left, one with door. The two ends took longer to build and put in place. I liked the way it was looking and I will do the roof tomorrow. After supper I will make my sleeping area a lot softer.

I've got the fire going and put a potato on first, got out some dried veggies, put them in water and a steak out of the cooler. A good meal for a good day's work. It was nice to watch the fire and hear the wind whisper through the pines while I waited for the potato to get done. One more check, yes, time for the meat as the fire danced against the meat. The fat sizzled and the aroma filled the air. My mouth was watering for that first bite. I dumped the veggies on the plate, mashed down the potato, a couple hits of butter spray, flopped down the steak, a little salt and the feed was on. What a meal. I took my time and enjoyed every bite. As I sat there listening to the fire, I looked around and was proud of all I had accomplished since yesterday. I'll just rinse the dishes. I'll wash them with the breakfast ones.

I gathered moss grass and leaves and made a nice padded area under the tent bottom and fastened the tent and went inside. A little arranging, spread out my sleeping bag and took a feel, much better. I've done enough for today. I'll set by the fire awhile. The wild and grandeur of this country and solitude one can experience, is the opportunity of a lifetime for a few who will dare. This truly is a dream come true. The fire was almost out and I was ready for some sleep. I think I'll check the bells and line around the camp. Everything looked good, time for bed.

I awoke to a raven calling; by the sound he was close. I don't know if he was greeting me or cussing me out. As I came out of the tent, I could hear his wings as he left. I hope he doesn't make a habit of it. The morning was cool and it would be awhile before sunlight will warm things up. Time for some fire and get the coffee going and make breakfast. Bacon, eggs, and coffee, a good combo to get the body jump-started. I made sure the smell was gone before the fire went out this time. After dishes were done, I started on the roof of the food shack. I like that name. I had most of the wood cut out for it from yesterday. It took about two hours to fasten the wood down. I covered the roof with plastic then a layer of moss to keep it cooler inside. A few hold-down sticks tied down, and the food shack was done.

The next thing is my alarm system around the four trees of the food shack. I put the eye screws in around eight feet off the ground, strung the fish line and fastened on the last two bells. A little tug, works fine.

I think I will play this afternoon and check out the stream. I grabbed my gold pan and shovel and headed out. If I could find a little color I'd be happy. That water was cold. I had to do a hand warm-up after each test pan. No color, yet some black sand, that was a good sign. I will go upstream further and try it there. No luck. Maybe there isn't any gold to find. I thought for sure I would find a flake or two. I was getting tired and my hands and fingers were yelling obscenities at me. Time to head back to camp. The sun was about to go beyond the mountains so it definitely was time to go. I got the fire going and took off my boots, at least the feet warmed up a bit on the walk back. The fire made the chill go away and life is being restored in the hands and fingers. Now to make supper, potato, veggies, Johnsonville brats and fried onions. That does it for me. Wow, another great meal. I don't want to move, my belly's full.

The fire is warm. I'll just set awhile and enjoy. I'll see what the skies look like in the morning. I was thinking about finding that old cabin and look around maybe find a souvenir to take home. The dishes are rinsed and the fire is almost out. Time to get some sleep.

Morning came quick. I must have fallen asleep when my head hit the pillow. I admit it was a little stiff and sore but once

I get moving around I'll be good to go. I am going to have to build an outhouse or something with a roof so when it rains, I'll have a bit of protection. I got plenty of time for that. Finish the first package of bacon at breakfast. I'll wash dishes when I get back.

My guess was that the cabin was two to three miles away. From what I've seen of wood and underbrush, it would take me a while to find it. I checked my compass to landmarks, rock formations, and mountain peaks and I knew the general direction to go. I loaded my backpack with water, jerky, a couple of apples, hand ax and got out my can of pepper spray. I put it on my belt with my hunting knife and .357 Magnum, time to go. I'll have to walk around the lake but I plan to take my time and keep my ears and eyes open. The skies were clear as I started out; it will be a good day to explore. I was looking forward to it.

About 1/8 mile from camp, I saw my first moose tracks, about a day old and a good size, according to the size of the tracks. As I rounded the end of the lake, I checked my compass to where I was and where I wanted to go. The mountains helped a lot for landmarks. The underbrush was a lot thicker than I thought. I had to really keep my wits about me because visibility was short and I didn't want to stumble upon a bear. I still had a ways to go before I would be into the tall trees, so senses don't fail me now. I had traveled about 100 yards or so when I saw an old log torn apart. It didn't look fresh; definitely a sign of bear.

I was glad when I reached the tall spruce. I checked my compass, still going in the right direction. I walked on. I could see a glimpse of the mountainside. I was getting close but not sure where it was. Trying to remember what I had seen from the plane. My guess it's to the left of here. There it was. I found it! There wasn't much left. The roof was gone. Only some of two walls, brush and a small tree was growing on the inside. I was surprised to find a cast iron box stove with the lid missing. The stove pipe was gone. There is a window, two of the panes were still intact, about six by eight-inch glass. I was digging around some more and found what looked like a part of a gold pan; most of it was rotted away. A few rusted pieces of tin cans. It didn't look like any souvenirs. I wanted to look at the old stove some more. The door was still there and the legs were still attached.

Whoever was here had to have pack horses. This bugger was at least sixty pounds.

As I stepped back, my foot dropped about six inches in a hole. That was strange. I got down on my knees and examined it closer. It was caved in. I found a miner's stash. I took out my knife and started to dig and removed the dirt and wood. There was a tin rusted and broken. It looked like a lid to a large can, maybe two-gallon size. I removed the top. There was dirt and rotted cloth. As I removed the cloth I couldn't believe my eyes—gold. It was a miner's stash. I got my backpack and started loading the nuggets, one handful after another. My fingers bumped something hard. It was a tin filled with dust, lid still on it. There had to be forty pounds total. Well, I got my souvenirs alright.

I checked my compass with the landmarks and thought about doing a straight line from here. No, I'll go back the way I came. Clouds were starting to come in. I wanted to make use of the good light and headed out. In no time, I reached the fallen down trees, where I turned coming in. One quick check of the compass and I was on my way. I was making good time with the help of different trees and rocks I had passed earlier. My eyes caught sight of something different about 150 feet away. It was a bear. His head was down. I stepped behind a tree, still watching. The wind was in my favor. I was glad of that. Now to find out what direction he's headed and hopefully it's not a sow with cubs. It raised its head and sniffed the air. It was a male. I was saying to myself, please don't come this way. Needless to say my heart was doing overtime. Even though it was a minute or so it seemed like forever before he moved. I breathed a sigh of relief when he continued sideways to me. I waited a half hour and I hoped he would keep walking before I started out. I carefully walked with my hand on my gun. As I reached the thick underbrush area, the clouds had moved in and you could no longer see the mountaintops. I checked my compass again, still on course. I was glad when I reached the lake. It was starting to rain. I could see the trees by my campsight and I was glad that I would be home soon. I was dripping wet. I didn't pack my raingear. I didn't think I would need them. At least it was dry under the tarp.

I needed to get out of these wet clothes and into warm dry ones. I was glad I brought my heater. I set it up and before long it was comfy in the tent and getting the chill out of my body. I was getting hungry so changed over to burner and set it up on the table outside the tent. I needed to slip into my raingear to get the food and the fry pan. The food shack was dry inside. I had done a good job on it. I'll finish the pack of brats and have some veggies. It would take a little longer to cook this way but time I had plenty of.

As things were cooking, I sat and listened to the rain hitting the tarp overhead. I remembered I hadn't built an outhouse shelter yet and wasn't looking forward to the moment when it would be to go. A few more minutes and supper will be ready. I guess I was hungrier than I thought. I was glad the only thing growling was my stomach. Well, that hit the spot. A quick cleanse and the dishes are done. I still had some coffee in the pot from this morning. I heated it up and had a cup.

I cleared off the table. I wanted to look at today's find. I removed my things from my backpack and took out the tin and dumped out the gold. I proceeded to remove the dirt and debris. There were nuggets of every size and shape from pickers to one the size of a quarter. What a pile! I'll need to find something to put it in. I picked up the tin and tapped the lid all the way around with my knife. I then pried it open; sure enough, gold dust, and it was full almost to the top. I put the lid back on and sealed it with duct tape. I had a carry on bag. I emptied it. I put the gold in that and put it away in the tent.

The rain had slowed down and I decided to get something out so I could get under to take a dump. A few sticks, a bit of rope, plastic and I've got a dry spot and not too soon, nature was calling. I put the tools away, grabbed the paper and made a run for it.

The sky was a solid gray and no sign of the rain stopping. I sat on my chair for a while more and decided to get some sleep. It was warm and dry inside my sleeping bag. Along with the sound of the rain, in no time I fell asleep.

I awoke next morning and the rain was still coming down. I got dressed and stepped outside. The clouds showed no signs of letting up. I thought about making a pot of coffee. I'll wait. I want to save the propane. I slipped on my raincoat and took a pee. It's a good day to sleep and I'll lay back down. I was just dozing off when the bells rang out on the back side of the camp and brush breaking. I jumped up, strapped on my .357 and shoes and I opened the tent. As I stepped out I was looking behind the tent and the sound of the rain is all I heard. I slipped on my jacket and stepped out, checking the area the noise came from, still nothing. I knew something tripped the bells and broke branches. As I walked closer I could see a couple of branches that were broken. With each step, I checked for movement; there was none. I could see that the fish line wasn't broken, sagging a bit though. Then I saw it was moose tracks. Boy, was I relieved!

Three

Well, I am awake now. I went back to my tent and sat down and dried my gun off. I'll go down to the lake and get a couple buckets of water, one for wash, one for rinse and let the rain do the final rinse. It's only a few days of clothes and it won't take long. I already had a drying line up. I had one pair of jeans to go and the rain was letting up some. Maybe we'll get a break from the rain for awhile. The clouds were getting a little brighter in the distance. After I dumped the water, I sat down for a while. I thought about how surprised that moose must have been where he had run into the line. There was a bell right there. I bet that was a Kodak moment.

The rain is letting up. I can start a fire and make some coffee. I got out some dry wood and kindling I had stashed under the tarp area. Soon the smoke and flames climbed higher and higher. I added more wood. The light rain wasn't going to stop me now. The coffee's on and it won't be long before that percolator will be belching out its brew. My body was in need of caffeine. The pot was starting to rumble and soon the sound of success. Ten minutes later and coffee is served. I filled my mug and my thermos, now I am good for the rest of the day. As I sipped my coffee, my thought went back to the cabin. What was the story that's been laying there for so many years? Was there one miner or two? How long were they there? What circumstances led up to their demise—starvation, bear, greed? The cabin was on the edge of an avalanche area. I could tell that by the broken trees. Other trees laying on the ground pointing downhill and even the backs of the trees. They sure wouldn't leave their gold behind. If I had a map, I could guess how they got here. One thing for sure, it wasn't the way we flew in. There is nothing for hundreds of miles. We'll never know.

Got to feed the fire again. I want to build up a good set of coals so it will last a while. I think I'll have fish tonight for supper. The rain almost stopped. I think I will try by the stream. I grabbed my pole and tackle and headed out. I could hear the stream before I got there. The water was moving with anger, many times the normal flow, ready to sweep away and destroy anything in its path. I started fishing about thirty feet down from where it entered the lake. It looked like a good area. First cast, one fish, this is almost too easy. Second cast, a trout, no two. Well, Jim said the fishing was real good; that was an understatement. I think I will fry these this time, a little flour and salt, a splash of oil in the pan. I'll be eating good in the neighborhood. By the time I finished supper, the skies was clearing and only scattered clouds remained. After a quick cleanup, I poured another coffee and moved my chair by the fire.

The evening was calm and damp and the smells of the woods laid heavy on the air. The sound of a red squirrel broke the silence of the moment. He chattered for about ten minutes then quiet. The sound of the fire and the wood snapping and popping was the only sound against the calm of the evening. I felt happy and content; making this trip a reality was worth it. In life if you take time to do things and follow your dreams, you won't be saying what I've heard many say, "I wish I did." Tomorrow a big day, going to build the outhouse. The bed is going to feel good tonight.

Wow, I slept like a baby. A few more stretches and it's time to drag these bones out of bed. I put another X on the calendar, 19th of June, 6th day already. Time sure flies by when you are having fun. As I stepped out of the tent, I could see it was going to be a nice day. First get a fire going then coffee on. I'll eat a little later on. Coffee will do me fine for now. The lake was calm with its reflections mirroring the trees, mountains and sky. I must get a picture of this. One more on panoramic, yes, this one will be great. Coffee should be ready by now. Time to get to work.

It took a while to get the wood I needed. I want it to be tall enough to stand up inside three walls with lean-to roof. I had to use larger wood because of the length. The four corner logs were longer to put in the ground to keep it solid. After a couple of hours it was taking shape. It was getting to be lunch time. I thought I would have beef stew I brought. Just add water and cook, there is enough in this thing for two meals. It will seem good to sit down. I've been going all morning. The roof and seat area to build yet and dig the hole. The stew looks like it's done and smells good. A little taste, it's a keeper, not bad at all. I had two bowls of it and plenty left for supper. Now back to my sawdust therapy. After I got the roof sticks in place I put down plastic then moss and tied down a couple of holding sticks. I then cut the seat braces and smoothed 2–4-inch logs to set on. I dug the hole and fastened the seat logs in place. Now for a butt check. Feels good. I've got a dry place to do my business. One more thing, make a hole with a screwdriver and hammer and made a peg, pounded in it. My john is complete with paper holder; damn, I'm good. Now for a bit of cleanup. I can take some pictures of my campsite now that it's done. Four regular shots and one panoramic that shows everything: my tent with tarp, fire pit, cooking area, outhouse and food shack.

    I think it's time to play. A couple of hours of catch and release. I got out my tackle box and bent the barb over on a couple of lures, grabbed my pole and walked down to the lake. Let the games begin. I never in my life caught fish like this, one after another. The only time that comes close to this is when I was fishing salmon on the American River on Kodiak Island in 1969. I was worn out after a full day of fighting fish. After an hour I thought I would try something different. I didn't bring ant flies but I had some floating peppers and gave a toss. It didn't take long and the water erupted, fish on. I fished a while more. I was having a blast. I was getting tired and the fish needed a break, maybe not but I did.

    By the time I got to camp, the adrenalin was wearing off. The body was telling me it had enough for one day. I couldn't agree more. I got the fire going and I was glad supper was a heat up. The stew tasted good as I finish the last spoon. It felt good to sit down and the warmth of the day. I thought what a picture it would be if I had all the trout on the rope with a heading of trout in two hours. You should have seen the one that got away. I couldn't help but laugh with that thought. It was time to call it a day. I was in a silly mood. I'll plan tomorrow in the morning.

I must have been tired, the sunlight was bright. I looked at my watch, 10:45. I've wasted the whole morning but as I climbed out of bed, my body was telling me I didn't miss anything this morning. I could hear the wind in the trees so I got dressed, unzipped the tent and stepped outside. A breezy day alright. I was still moving slow when I reached the outhouse. I think I will lay around camp today. Made a small fire enough to make coffee and cook breakfast. Got to get dishes done, yesterday's and this morning's. After a couple of hours the stiffness was going away and I was moving like normal.

I needed to cut more firewood and build up the supply under the tarp area. I'll just take my time the rest of the afternoon. Think I will have steak tonight, boiled potato and veggies. I was glad there was a good supply of dead wood close by as the afternoon went on. The pile of wood had got a lot bigger. A little more wood and I should have enough for the rest of my time here. As evening came, the wind was died down. I could have a good fire to set by. I put the potato on to boil and the veggies too. The potato will take the longest, moved the veggies off to the side. They were ready. Checked the potato, almost done, time for the meat. Boy, it was smelling good. I got to leave some moo in the meat, a slice to check, it's ready and so was I. Think everything tasted better when cooked and enjoyed outside. That was a good supper I told myself as I set back in my chair. After the dishes, I've got to wash up some, plus the pits need a little attention especially after the wood cutting today.

Tomorrow I will go exploring some more. Right now I've got to get warmed up after the wash up. I sat by the fire and planned what I will do tomorrow and where I am going, to the other end of the lake and beyond and the end of the valley. It will be quite a hike. So I had better get to bed and start early.

I woke up feeling good, got dressed and marked another day on the calendar, June 22. I stepped outside, the skies looked good. I made breakfast, loaded my backpack, water, food and my raingear this time. I was ready to head out. The sun was just clearing the tops of the mountains. I haven't explored that way yet so it will be new to me.

Following the lake about 150 feet was a small stream, clear cold water. I followed it back to its source. It was only twelve to fourteen inches wide. It was a natural spring 200 feet or so from camp. I will make a trail later on. I continued to the end of the lake. There was a lot more water and low ground and marsh further on so I stayed on high ground. The area past the spring to farther past the end of the lake was an avalanche area, trees down, trees broken and debris. I had several miles to go to reach the end of the valley. There had to be an outlet for this water because the lake rose and went back down when we had the last rain. It was rough going; the underbrush, rocks, trees and terrain. The terrain was changing into more rocks now. I climbed up this ridge for a better look. I could see the wet land and water and there it was, the outlet maybe fifty feet below, sheer wall rocks zigzagging past the rocks and boulders. It was well hid and I wasn't going to look any closer. I sat down for a while to rest. I could see several moose off in the distance feeding. I looked at my watch; it was after 2:00, time to get back to camp. I got at least five hours of walking ahead of me. I was making good time, always watching for bear, only stopping to rest for a few minutes at a time. I must have been around half way when I came face to face with a moose, a young bull in velvet. I stood still and he didn't know what I was. He turned and trotted off. I was probably the first human he'd seen. I would bet on it. I was happy to see the lake only a short distance to go and it will be home sweet home.

As I walked into camp, my watch said 6:40. I slipped off my backpack and sat down. The fire can wait. If I venture out again it will be back to the miner's cabin. No more long ones like today. I got up to start a fire and much stiffness was setting in. I won't be up long after supper tonight. I got two pork chops, sliced up some potato and onion, and slid the pan over the fire. After the chops started cooking and the potato got its head start, I tossed in the onions. Things were smelling good. When I finished eating I was ready for some sleep. I'll do dishes tomorrow. When I took off my shoes, my socks were wet. I hung them up and stuffed newspaper in the shoes. They will be nice and dry in the morning.

I woke up and it was darker than usual. I checked my watch, 9:20. I crawled out of bed, unzipped the tent and looked out:

foggy, very foggy, that explains it. I was surprised. I didn't feel too bad as I got dressed. The legs felt the worst and the back was stiff but considering what I went through yesterday, not bad. The fog was thick—fifty feet maybe was the farthest you could see. With the lack of visibility and the moisture dripping from the trees it gave me a bit of an eerie feeling.

I started the fire and checked the alarm system. The fish line and bells were good. I wanted to be ready if there was going to be a close encounter of the worst kind. I will have pork chops and eggs for breakfast, then get the dishes done. The more I moved around the better I was feeling. The mobility was coming back. I added more wood on the fire. It felt good against the dampness. Must turn around and warm the backside. I do like a good fire! I was thinking about marking out a trail to the spring and do a little trim and clearing but I'll wait till this fog lifts or burns off. I got out my chair and sat down to watch the fire and daydream a little. There was nothing better to do right now. The smell of smoke hung in the air as the flames licked at the fog and I thought about the fishing a couple of days ago.

Why don't I make some smoked fish, I've done it at home many times. All I've got to do is build a smoker. The more I thought about it, the better it sounded, fresh smoked trout. Sounds like a plan to me. The spot would be between the food shack and the tent area. Will have to gather enough rocks to make the fire box and figure out a way to control the flames and smoke. Next to get the wood, the four corner posts and the rest for the sides and top. The things I do for fun. Got the four corner posts in the ground and nailed a few sticks across the top to hold them in place! Then started building the fire box, chipping and fitting each rock for a good fit, kneeing it all within the corner post till the fire box was a foot deep. I had found a couple flat rocks to use on top to control the fire. Then I put sand around the outside of the rocks that will stop the air. I stepped back to take a look. I like it. The sides will be made like the food shack but instead of up and down, they will run sideways, each side will be three feet wide. I had a lot of pieces to cut and tape. Fitting each one with as little gap as possible was going to be more time-consuming. The more you can control the heat and smoke the better.

It was time to take a break and get myself another coffee. Two sides are done. As I sat by the fire and sipped my coffee, I still had to figure out a door for it yet. I think I'll make it like the food shack, hinged from the top. Break time is over, back to work. Boy it doesn't look like this fog is going to clear today. The last side went up well. I am getting pretty good at this. It's time to call it a day. I should be able to finish it tomorrow.

I think I'll have brats, potato and veggies for supper. While supper was cooking, I couldn't help looking at today's work. It looked good already and I couldn't wait to see it done. After supper I rinsed the dishes clean and dried my tools and put them away. I then set by the fire awhile. Let's see, tomorrow is my 10th day, twenty days left. Hell, if they had me on *Survivor* they wouldn't know what to do with me. The fire is getting down so it's time to turn in for the night.

I awoke and was anxious to get started. I dreamed about smoked fish last night. As I stepped out of tent, the fog was a lot less and looked like it will clear off today. I started the fire and put on the pot; got to have my fiens, nectar of the gods. The pot started perkin'. It won't be long now. I got my mug and thermos ready, sugar added, time to pour. I will eat later. I want to get started.

The roof will have a good slant to it so the rain will have a better chance to run off. I made it so it hung over four sides and enough gap to let smoke out. Now to build the door. After the door was built, I had to trim it to fit, put on three wires for hinges and pulled it open. That will do it. I got back to take a look. I liked it a lot. I will make a rack or two out of green willow and make some hooks too. I cleaned up the area around the smoke house, tossed the scraps on the fire. Now to cut some willow. It didn't take long to cut an armful. I sat down in my chair and started stripping the bark off, then used a couple of sticks to get the measurement I needed. I used some wire and fish line to put the first one together with ¾-inch space between each one. I hung it with wire. I'll see how this works before I do anymore. I added more dirt around the outside. It looked like it was time for a test fire. I slid the flat stones back, put in the kindling wood and small sticks and started the fire. I let it burn till I was getting some coals built up and closed the door and the smoke got thicker. The heat coming out at the top was good. I let the fire burn itself out and put the willow sticks away.

I cleaned up the areas and put my tools away. I've got to touch up my knife. It will only take a few swipes with the stone. I think I will mark out the trail to the spring now and tomorrow I can make a path. I was done in a half hour. A few squares of toilet paper on twigs and bushes. It's ready for tomorrow. I think trout is on the menu for supper. I grabbed my pole and headed to the lake. A few minutes later there are two fish for supper. I love it! I had to put more wood on the fire and I'm ready to get this show on the road. Pan fried trout and potato. From the water to the pan in minutes. Who says fast food isn't good for ya. After I finished the dishes, I am going to set by the fire and enjoy the rest of the evening. Now I am ready to watch the fire dance but I'll set this one out. As I looked at my campsite, the only thing missing was a cabin. No, I am not going to build one. I've got everything I need. Tomorrow I will clear the path to the spring, then take my pan and shovel and check it out farther upstream. The water is back down and I want to find some gold in my pan. The eyelids are getting heavy and I will turn in for the night.

Wake up, wake up, wake up, rise and shine, got another busy day ahead of you, I kept telling myself. I had a comfortable spot and really didn't want to leave it. But there was adventure in the plans so I got up. Morning tradition, fire and coffee. I think I'll make pancakes and eggs, that sounds good for a change. If it was later on this year, I could add some blueberries with the batter, but it was good anyway.

Time to trim the path. It should work. I had it almost done. I need to go back to camp for the saw. I've got a couple of fallen trees to move at least part of them. Another job well done. One good drink from the spring and it's back to camp. I'll rest a while then put on my boots and try to find some gold. The stream was down like I figured so I started following it upstream. I started test panning beyond where I was the other day and still nothing so I kept going. Up ahead, I could see an area of rocks from the height of twelve feet or more. I made my way around the rapids and above that was a pool fifteen to twenty feet wide, close to forty feet long with the water falling about three feet into it.

Sheer rock walls all the way around and it was deep, ten maybe fifteen feet, I was thinking. If there was any gold around, this is where it would be at. I got up alongside of the pool. I wasn't sure I could see bottom. I worked my way to above the falls and found a few nice pockets, shallow enough to work a shovel. I dug out a pan of material and there was a nugget right on top, the size of a pea. I took my pan to an area a few feet away to pan it out. After finding that nugget, I was getting excited. The water swirled and splashed as I worked the pan, stopping time to time to pick out chunks of broken rocks less and less and it was time to look, two more nuggets and pickers. I gathered them up and panned some more, going slower, working the ripples on the side of the pan; one more look and there was a good teaspoon of flakes. I got out my snuffer bottle and sucked up all the flakes. My gosh, this is only one pan from one spot. There is a lot more here and heaven knows what is at the bottom of the pool. I would say many millions. I found what I wanted. I am heading back to camp. On the way back I told myself that I will come back next year and put a gold claim on this area, maybe the whole valley. Jim is going to be surprised when I show him this and what I found the other day.

    I arrived back at camp. Everything looked normal. No visitors of the wrong kind. I took off my boots and put on my shoes, grabbed my pole and tackle box and headed for the lake. I wanted about ten fish for the smoker. It didn't take long to get the fish I wanted, four big ones, sixteen to eighteen inches and 6-6 to twelve or fourteen inches. I cleaned them and headed back to camp.

    My cooking pot wasn't big enough so I used a dish pan to put them in. I split all of them in half, leaving the skin in one piece. I took the bones out of four, the other six, I left the bones in; that way I could see what way works the best in the smoker. I put the fish in the pan, added water then some salt. I'll let it set overnight. I better set this in the food shack. I set the ladder in place and opened the door and propped it open with a stick. I will have to drain most of the water into a pan then take it up; I'll add the water back to it. Then I snapped the plastic lid back on and closed the door. I laid the ladder back down and cleaned up the area to get rid of most of the fish smell. I tossed what I could into the fire, and added some green boughs to the fire to smoke up the area some.

I think I'll make a pot of stew, two meals one cook time. While supper was cooking, I got out the gold I got today. I put the nuggets and pickers in a plastic bag and the flower gold in a vial. Impressive I thought for one pan! The stew is ready and I'm hungry. As my taste buds were getting smothered from the flavor, I was thinking about tomorrow's smoking process. I think I will try doing a couple of the fish as dried after the heat and smoking is done. I will see how it tastes and how long it will last. Well my belly's full and I am content. A little cleanup, put the stew away, then it will be my time by the fire for the rest of the evening.

I am glad the weather's been good so far but that can change fast when a front goes through. So far it looks like tomorrow will be nice. In a little while the fire will be down and it will be nice. In a little while the fire will be done and it will be the end of another day. In the distance, I heard a wolf again then others. My how their howls carry through the still air of the evening a few miles away beyond the lake. They went on for at least twenty minutes then stopped. I got serenaded before I go to bed. How cool is that? I smiled and headed to bed. As I fell asleep, I thought about the smoked fish I would have tomorrow.

I slept good last night. I jumped up, got dressed. I was eager to get this day started. Stepped out, blue skies, yes! First things first, fire and coffee. I'll have the rest of the stew for breakfast. I've got plans for the last of that package of bacon, bean soup! The coffee is done, the stew is hot, breakfast is served. I think the stew tastes better today than yesterday.

Time to get started, get the fish out of the food shack and open the smoke house. I put the fish on a rack to drain while I got the fire going. After I got a bed of coals I put the fish on the rack skin down. I had sliced most of the two fish I wanted to dry in one-inch slices. I added a few sticks, slid the rocks closed and shut the door. I knew it would take a while to figure out the right amount of wood but this was a start. I got a pan of water and put in the beans to soak then. I dumped the fish water in the lake and rinsed the pans. I checked the heat coming out of the smoke house, a little more wood next time around in about twenty minutes. Time for a coffee break. Time for more wood. I slid back the rocks and it was down further than I expected. I got the wood in place and blew on the remaining coals till I got flames. I tossed a few more pieces of wood in till it was burning good. I closed the rocks and shut the door. We got smoke and heat now. I could see that I would have to stay on top of this the rest of the time till it's done. So I grabbed my chair and got comfy. After three hours of chasing fire and eating smoke, the fish were starting to look good. Another two hours and I'll start tasting. Too long of smoking and you will get a bitter taste. At that you have passed the point of no return. Five hours into the project, time to test smoke flavor is good, need bake time now. I took a shovel full of coals from the pit and put them in the fire box. I'll get the heat I need to bake a while. I drained the beans, sliced up the bacon and precooked it, dumped the bacon and grease and added fresh water and put it on the rocks to start cooking. I checked the smoker for heat, it felt good. I would say about an hour and I can starting enjoying. I stirred the beans and moved the pot back some away from the fire. I didn't want to burn it. Time to set a while, it was almost 4:00 p.m. and it won't be long now.

A faint noise caught my attention. I sat up and cocked my head; it's a plane. I jumped up and ran toward the lake for a better look. A float plane, who in the hell is this? As the plane turned out of the sun, I could see it good now. Well I'll be damned, it's Jim! He planted that bird on the water with ease and motored to the shore in front of me. He killed the engines, climbed out and tossed me the rope. "Are you missing me?" I said. "Hello, I just wanted to see if you were bear food yet?" We laughed and greeted each other. "Help me unload a few things and you can show me your camp." "Just head up the path, I am right behind you," I told him. I couldn't wait. What the hell, as the bells rang out. Alarm system Jim, well I'll be. It must work, it got me.

I was still laughing as we walked into camp. Seeing the look on Jim's face was priceless. "What's that?" "A smoke house! The trout will soon be ready. You didn't bring a cold beer did you?" "Yes I did." "Check out the food shack." "Nice job, looks good inside and out. Where does this path go?" "To a spring." "Really,

I didn't know there was a spring back here. You got an outhouse too? When are you going to start the cabin?" "Maybe next year I was thinking. You ready for some smoked fish?" "Bring it on."

I told Jim to hold the plate as I opened the door. He was looking it over good when I was taking the fish out. "That's quite the smoker you got there." I added more coals to finish drying the last two fish and shut the door. We sat down to smoked fish and cold beer. "I am impressed with what you have done out here. What else has your alarm system worked on?" "A moose, it scared the pee out of him too. Well does my first batch of fish pass the test?" "It sure does."

"What brings you around this way?" "I had to drop supplies off to a village a couple hundred miles from here so I thought I'd drop by." I told him about everything I'd been doing except about the gold. He laughed when I told him about the two-hour fishing frenzy. "Did ya find anything panning yet?" "Yup, I'll show ya." His eyes got big when I handed him the zip lock bag. "How long did it take to get this?" "Well, a lie would take longer than the truth." "What a day or two? What? One pan? You're kidding." "One pan and there is a lot more." I told him where on the stream and would show him tomorrow. Jim was still amazed.

"Now I've something real good to show you." I brought the bag out of the tent and set it on Jim's lap. "Damn that's heavy! What's in here?" "Open it and find out." Jim didn't speak, move or anything. "You get this out of the same place?" "No, I found it." "What do you mean you found it?" "I found it at the miner's cabin." "I was over there about eight years ago. The only thing I seen was the stove." "You wouldn't have seen it either, it was buried in a large tin. I was looking at the stove when I stepped away my foot sunk in about six inches. I dug it out. I found the top, opened it and the rest is history." "What do you have here in pounds?" "About 40 at today's price, it's over $125,000.00." "What's in the tin?" "Gold dust. The way I figure, it pays for my trip this year and next. But I need a partner, you interested, Jim?" "Yes." "Since you have the plane or know-how with plane or helicopter. We can get the equipment in here to go after the stream. I know I can find where the miners were digging. You're the plane man. I am the equipment man and I can do about a four-month's work to start with next year. We should take out of here at least 500 pounds and a good chance even more. We will have to file a claim and both our names will be on it." I could tell Jim was thinking as I talked. It's a deal and we shook hands on it.

"What time are you leaving tomorrow?" "Sometime in the afternoon. Rain's coming the day after tomorrow." "I've got bean soup with bacon ready." "I am kind of full from the smoked fish."

"How about we do a little fishing now? We can eat when we get back." "It sounds good to me." We played catch and release for a couple of hours. It was nice to have Jim here to share the fun with. We had a great time, laughing, joking and kidded each other. Jim lost a huge one. That fish made his pole beg for mercy right till the end and got off. Jim just dropped his head. "That's ok," I told him, "that one was needed in the lake to make more babies." "Yes, you're right, I guess." "Let's head back to camp. These fish need a break."

I heated up the soup and we dug in. It tasted pretty good, damn good. We each had our fill and settled back to enjoy the fire. Our conversation soon went back about the gold and plans for next year. All the equipment we need. "I will get like a three-foot dredge and air pump, a high banker with two-inch dredge hose and contractor to get the fine gold and pickers. We can gather our concentrates into containers and process them on days when the weather is bad because after the rain, it will take a few days before we can get back at the stream. We will head to the stream tomorrow morning and grab a handful of gold. Our operation won't be big but it won't be small either. I don't want to kill ourselves with a lot of bulk and weight." "Hell, after we take what we want, we could sell the claim." "No, we'll keep it." "Why is that, Alan?" "If a company came in here, they would ruin this place." "You're right. We will be rich enough, we could buy it and retire here, if not year around at least for the summers." We tossed around idea after idea. We laughed and joked and planned. We knew we would be friends for the rest of our lives. Jim reached into his bag and pulled out a bottle of bourbon. "A toast to our friendship, our partnership and our future." "Well, tomorrow comes early. Let me rearrange the tent and we'll hit the sack. Jim, you're cheating, you have an air mattress." "I know, I like roughing it but not too rough." We talked awhile longer and Jim was out like a light. It wasn't long I was too.

I was up first getting the fire going when Jim crawled out of the tent. "Coffee will be ready in about ten minutes." "Good, I'll be ready for a cup. Don't get anything out for breakfast. I have that in my cooler." "What's that?" I asked. "Steak, eggs and bread for toast." I said, "Deal." Everything smelt and tasted so good. Afterwards, Jim did the dishes and I checked my dried fish. I bagged them and took them along. We got on our boots, grabbed my pan, shovel and bucket and headed out to the stream.

When we got to the pool area, Jim agreed, there wasn't anything coming out of there that was being washed downstream. We got above the waterfalls. I showed Jim the spot I dug the pan out. I dug deeper this time, scraping the bedrock. The pan filled. "Look at that," was all Jim could say as several nuggets fell into the pan, nickel and quarter size. There was a lot more this time because I was getting material next to bedrock. I panned it down far enough to get the big stuff and the rest in the bucket. We did a few more areas especially behind rocks and came up with good gold every time. When we had a bucket of concentrates, we called it quits. We each had a pocket of nuggets and headed back to camp. We both took turns carrying the bucket and when we could we both carried it. It was heavy. It felt good to set down when we finally got back. We looked at each other and laughed like a couple of school kids. I told Jim, I wanted him to take all the gold back with him, cash it in and pay for an assay and claim. I didn't know if they charged by the size of the claim. I imagine, the bigger the claim, the more it cost. If not the whole valley, just the north and south sides. "Take ten or twenty thousand out for yourself and put the rest in the bank for me. I will give you my personal info to take with you to do the paperwork." "Are you sure about the ten or twenty thousand?" "Yes, cover your cost, time, travel and new seat covers if you feel like it. Plus, when you get back here in two weeks, I will have more gold to take back. I will know where the miners were digging too." Jim gave me the rest of the ice and I gave him the rest of the smoked fish to take with him. We loaded his plane with his things and the bag of gold and said our goodbyes. I kidded him a bit, "Don't forget to come and get me on two weeks." "I won't, partner." I tossed him the rope, pushing him out and he was on his way. A half circle on the lake and he was on his way. A half circle on the lake and he was off the water and cleared the trees, gaining altitude till he disappeared through the pass.

I was sad to see him go but I'll see him again in a couple of weeks. Now to get back to camp routine. I guess I will start panning out these concentrates, it will keep me busy for a while. I got my water and pan, set up my chair and gold rush was on. It was fun seeing this much color in every pan, a lot of pickers and flower gold. By the time I finished that bucket my arms were tired. There had to be over fifteen pounds or more. I put it away in the tent. It was late and I was tired. I had some smoked fish and a couple slices of bread. All I wanted to do now is get some sleep.

I woke up to the sound of rain. Jim was right, he said it was going to rain today. Well it's a good day to rest. I turned over and went back to sleep. When I woke up two hours later it was still raining. I had to get up, nature calls so I got dressed, slipped on my rain jacket and dashed to the outhouse. The way this rain is coming down, it's going to be at least two days before I could get back on the stream. So today I'll be lazy, the air was damp with a bit of a chill. I'll crawl back in the bed, it's warm dry there plus a little rest would do me good. Tomorrow or the next, I'll make a trip to the miner's cabin. They had to be working east of the cabin from what I could see the other day. There might be a wash over in that direction. As I laid on my back, my thoughts were of next year. I will have it all planned out for everything. The rain is not letting up and I think I'll take a nap.

I woke up around noon and it was still raining. I guess I will have to cook by the tent. I've done it once before. I opened my last package of brats, took out two, grabbed two potatoes and closed the food shack and climbed down. I then set up the camp stove on the table and started cooking. I hung up my raingear and kept stirring the potatoes and turning the brats. I was almost finished when the tank went empty. I got out another and I was back in business. After I finished lunch, I cleaned the dishes and fry pan and put the stove away.

I wanted to do some figuring on next year and started my list. It felt good inside the tent away from the dampness. I looked at my calendar; today was June 29th, my 15th day. About an hour has passed since I got into the tent. The bells sounded off in front, then all of them rang out. Something hit it hard. The second line either broke to shake all the bells or was pulled a lot. I drew my .357 and zipped the tent down a ways and grabbed my can of bear pepper spray. Oh shit, it's a grizzly! He's by the fire pit, looking and sniffing. I thought about lunch time and I knew he was going to come in my direction. My heart was pounding so hard. I was sure he could hear it. His head turned toward the tent where I cooked earlier and he sniffed the air under the tarp and a few steps and he would be under the tarp and a few feet away from me. The element of surprise was on my side. I could hear him breathe and smell his wet musty fur. I had the pepper spray ready at the opening and my .357 too! He sniffed around the table and growled. He picked up his head two feet from me. I hit him with the pepper spray at point blank. That son of a bitch got a face full. He busted out backwards knocking over the table, that's when I touched off two rounds of my .357 not hitting the bear but let him feel and hear the muzzle blast at close range. It worked! He was on the run. I jumped out to keep track of where he went. I could hear brush and sticks snapping as he ran away. I've got to calm down and try to get my heart and breathing back to normal. I reloaded my gun.

I got my raingear on. I didn't even notice the rain. Talk about close encounters. I took out the bottle of bourbon and took a drink. That helped settle me down. I've got to fix my alarm system. Yup, like I figured. He broke the thirty-pound test fish line. I got it tied back up and checked it all the way around. Everything is good again. No more cooking under the tarp. The adrenaline was still high when I sat down under the tarp. Looking at the size of the tracks and remembering how he filled the space where I was at, that bugger was big! Hopefully, this was enough to keep him away. I've been too relaxed lately and from now on I'll pay attention to my senses and feelings. I was lucky this time. I must have sat there for several hours watching, listening, smelling the air, still playing out today's events over and over.

The rain has almost stopped so now I'll get a fire going. Everything is damp or wet. I will have to use some steel wool with the kindling, a spark from the lighter and a good breath of air and let there be fire. It wasn't long before I had a nice fire going to chase away the chill. I think a beef stew will do fine for tonight, maybe some bread to soak in the juice. The skies are clearing and the rain is over now. I'll be able to enjoy the rest of the evening by the fire. The stew warmed the insides and I had enough for a meal tomorrow. I cleaned the dishes and put the stew in the food shack. Tomorrow I will go to the miner's cabin and look around. If I start early I will have plenty of time to spend exploring. I watched the fire till the flames were gone and only the glow of the embers were left. I was tired but not tired and today's experiences were still on my mind. I must get some sleep but I'll keep my ears open. It took a while to fall asleep.

When morning came, I was ready to get the day started. I got the fire started and put on the coffee, got out the stew and slid it on the rack to start heating. I packed my backpack with what I needed for the day. A soft breeze was beginning to stir as I filled my thermos and poured a cup. The stew was ready and I was anxious to get going. I did a rinse on the dishes, put on my backpack, grabbed my shovel and headed out. It was going to be a nice day, a few puffy clouds in the sky.

I was rounding the end of the lake when I watched an eagle snatch a trout out of the water; what a move! As I made my way into the underbrush, I kept my eyes and nose working, keeping track of any danger. I was making good time and before long I was in the tall trees. When I got to the fallen down tree, exit stage left. I'll get to the cabin in ten. When I reached the cabin, I took a short break and then headed east. There was a spring about fifty feet from the cabin. That's why they built it back here. There was a lot of soft stones on the side of the stream from the spring. It looked like tailings left over from panning. I walked on toward the area that looked like a wash and sure enough it was. This is where they were digging alright. There were piles of rocks that wasn't normal. I traveled up the wash a ways and dug down to a spot that looked good. I filled my pan with material keeping out the big stones and headed to the spring. I knelt down and filled the pan with water and began working the material after a few minutes. I was getting close to the bottom, time for a look. I saw color pickers. I worked it some against the ribs of the pan till most of the black was gone. I tilted the pan back and smiled, a lot of color. I picked out what I could and swirled the remaining black sand away. A few more taps on the pan and I sucked up the rest with the snuffer bottle. I test panned a few more areas of the wash and got color every time. Next year is going to be fun!

It was already mid afternoon and it was time to be heading back to camp. I found what I wanted over here. I won't need to come back again. I slipped on my backpack and headed out. I was used to the trees, rocks and other landmarks now so walking was a lot easier; all I had to do was keep track of anything out of the normal. I saw fresh moose tracks as I got closer to the lake and saw bushes they were feeding on. When I reached the lake, I could see where my camp was and before long I'd be home. As I walked up the path from the lake, the fish lines and bells were still up.

When I walked into camp everything was as I left it. I was glad of that. I'll get the fire going and rest a while. I should get my notebook and write down what I found and where, so there will be a record of it other than in my head. I think I will have some noodles with butter with the last of the butter. I should get a pot of beans soaking too. Supper was good, noodles were a nice change. When I got the dishes washed, I filled in my notebook and put the pot of beans to soak. Tomorrow I will need to empty the fire pit, it's getting full with ashes. But tonight I'll just sit by the fire and relax. I must be tired, I woke up and the fire was down to a few glowing embers. Time to go to bed.

Boy, did I sleep good. I laid there for a while planning my day. Come on, drag your butt out of bed, I told myself. So I got dressed and stepped outside. Today will be camp day and for a little fishing too. I grabbed my shovel and got the fire pit cleaned out. First I built a fire and started a pot of coffee. Pancakes and bacon for breakfast. I can get the bacon cooked, some for the beans too. When I finished breakfast, I drained the beans, put in the bacon and some grease too and set it on the side of the rack to slow cook. I've got to clean clothes and take a shower. I'll heat the water for the bag instead of the sun. I should make a little wind protection. The water felt good but the open air was a different story. The fire helped get the body another back. I finished cleaning the camp area and went to the spring for more water. The beans were done so I took them away from the fire. I will go fishing a little later. I need two for supper and eight or ten for the smoker. The bigger ones turned out better the last time. The fire is getting down so I can leave. I've got to put the beans away. I'm not leaving anything out in the open again.

I spent about an hour but I got the size fish I wanted. I cleaned them and headed back to camp. All I had to do was cut them in half and let them soak overnight. As I climbed down the ladder, I thought the smell of musty fur, like I smelled that day. I couldn't see anything and I did smell it again. I stayed on the ladder for ten to fifteen minutes, looking, listening and sniffing, still nothing. I climbed down but I was still going to keep a bear alert going. I heated up the beans and bacon and fried the fish and sat down to eat. After dishes were done it was time to relax by the fire but still mindful of my surrounding. I really don't want to be that close to a bear again. I need to check the alarm system before I go to sleep. After walking the line, everything looks good, time to go to bed.

I didn't sleep at all last night. I kept waking up all the time. Well, get your butt out of bed, got things to do. I marked the calendar—my 18th day. The skies looked good when I stepped out of the tent. Did my nature call and started the fire and put on the coffee. Wow, those beans have caught up with me. The air is still and if I am going to keep this up, I am going to be forced to keep moving. I am not really hungry yet. I'll fix something later. After I got a cup of coffee down, I got the fish out of the food shack and set it out to drain while I got the fire going in the smoke house. I loaded the rack, added more wood, closed the rocks, shut the door and let the smoke and the good times roll. I dumped the fish water in the lake and rinsed the pan. I set down by the fire and kept an eye on the smoker. The water should be down good by tomorrow and I will go back to the stream. I will pocket the big stuff and bring the concentrates back to camp. I figure two or three buckets a day, maybe more, then spend a day or two at camp working at the concentrates. I'll keep doing that with weather permitting and I'll have a big pile by the time Jim picks me up.

Sitting here by the fire, it's easy to reflect back on all I've seen in the past weeks and each day offers something new. All the mountains and this pristine valley, the wildlife and birds. The small ones have no fear of me here. I would like to feed them but I don't want them to get out of their natural habits. I got to tend to smoker again, very little smoke coming out. The fish are starting to look good but they have a ways to go yet. Well, that batch of wood should last awhile. Sitting back down, I was thinking about the rest of the journey when I get back to Anchorage. I'll spend a day or two then drive to Fairbanks, see the sights then head north and take the Dalton highway to Pouts Bay. I'll do a little fishing along the way. I want to catch a Galling and Arctic Char and see herds of Caribou and the Arctic Tundra. I will be right in the bug season too. At least I'll be leaving here before they get too bad. Then I am going travel about the Yukon and British Columbia, the Rockies before coming back to Michigan. This will be a year I'll never forget.

I've got to get my binoculars. I can see sheep on the side of that mountain. Boy, they stand out good against the rocks. There is ten to twelve, yup, twelve, they sure move when they want. This is more things I can add to my list of things I've seen. Boy, I am so glad that I took time to make this dream come true. It has turned out better than I ever imagined.

Smoker needs my attention again. That smoked fish is going to taste good tonight. Smoke is rolling good, shut the door, I think I'll have a couple pieces of Jerky. I'll save my appetite for the dish. It feels nice to laze around today. It gives me time to reflect and make plans. An hour or two of smoke, then heat to finish it off and it will be my time to enjoy the rewards. Jim said this place was way off the travel routes for planes. I believe him. I haven't seen or heard any planes except Jim's. As nice as this place is, I wouldn't have told anyone where it is either. I've got to slow down on the daydreaming and pay attention to the smoker. I don't want to oversmoke the fish, time for a taste, that's good stuff, just right, time for just heat. I couldn't help myself to grab a few pieces by the tail area. They are thinner and were done.

    I put in the coals and shut the door and sat down to munch. Damn, it doesn't get any better than this. At least I will be well fed and rested up for tomorrow. I am going to need it. Time for the finish, check, the fish is done to perfection. I ate my fill and then it was hard to leave it alone. I was full but still you wanted to grab another bite. I had to put it away or I may not stop. As soon as the fire goes down, I'll get to bed. It's been a good day.

Four

I slept a lot better last night than I did the night before. The skies were clear when I stepped out of the tent. I was eager to get started. First things first, fire and coffee and a quick trip to the outhouse. Things were moving this morning. Coffee's ready and some fish for breakfast and I'm ready to head out.

The stream was down to normal and I made my way above the waterfall. I started to dig out a new spot, trying to get the bedrock where the gold was laying. I got a pan full of material and started to work it down to put the rest of the concentrates in the bucket. The bigger nuggets were put in my pockets, the rest in the bucket. I kept trying different spots and was coming up with color every time. The bucket was three-quarters full already and I would take it back to camp and return; when I grabbed the handle and lifted it I knew the trudge was on. By the time I made it back to camp my arms must have stretched an inch. I dumped the bucket and headed back. I started right back at it trying more spots while going upstream. I was finding more nuggets and bigger ones too! I only filled the bucket a little over half this time but it was heavy too. There was a lot of gold in there. Round two wasn't much easier than the first. But a short break and headed out. I got back to where I left off and started digging and working material down. To think this is only the placer gold, the mother lode is still ahead yet. I moved upstream about twenty feet to a pocket I found a little deep about three feet and started digging out material. I had a feeling that this would be a good spot. I was seeing nuggets on the first shovelful. Let me tell you that's exciting. I kept digging till I hit something solid and I moved it with my shovel; it wasn't a rock. I finally got under it getting wet in the process. It was a chunk of gold almost the size of my fist. What a lunker! I could hardly hang on to it. I got out of the water and sat down. I couldn't believe what I just found.

I better get heading for camp. I was tired, cold, wet and my fingers were numb. The bucket may be half full but my pockets were full and I had this lunker too. I had to put my hands in my armpits to get some feeling going. They were too cold to hang onto anything. Wow, you'd think I just stuck ice in my pits. After the initial shock wore off the feeling was coming back after about fifteen minutes. I was ready to go. It was a lot slower walk back to camp. By the time I walked into camp, it felt like someone wiped my wookey. I quickly got the fire going and got out of the wet clothes. I was warm from the walk but parts of me were still chilled. I sat by the fire till all spots felt normal. As I went to get up there were many parts of my body expressing their displeasure of how they were treated today. This prospecting is hard work. I think a shot of bourbon will do me good right now, plus I have to celebrate. I looked at the piles of nuggets on the table from today. There was more gold than what Jim took back with him. I had over two five-gallon buckets of material to pan out yet. I will have some fish. I am too tired to cook. So I sat by the fire and sipped my drink thinking about today. I will fill in my notebook tomorrow. It's time for bed.

I was asleep before my head hit the pillow. I think I was laying in the same spot when I woke up. I went to move and my body said, don't want to. Everything hurt, my hands wouldn't close either. I am done with prospecting for this year. I kept moving till I felt I could get out of bed. It took a while to get dressed; moving slowly, I stepped outside. The day looked better than I felt. Got to start the fire and coffee going. The heat felt good and helped loosen things up and by the time I poured my second coffee I was feeling a lot better. I will make some pancakes for breakfast, a good stack of them should hold me till supper. I'm just going to take it easy the rest of the day. The fire felt good on the hands. They took most of the beating yesterday. I'll start panning out the material tomorrow. Oh, a good idea I had! I will warm up the water I will be using. Damn, I am smart. I think a power nap would do me good right now. I entered the tent and my notebook reminded me to get the info and location of yesterday's finds entered in. I like writing the word lunker and closed the book. It felt good to lay down, it was another good idea.

I was just dozing off when the bells went off, son of a bitch. I don't need this crap now, I told myself. I got my shoes on and strapped on my gun. I slowly stepped out of the tent. I didn't see or hear anything. Slowly I stepped out further till I was by the fire pit; it sounded like the bells between the camp and lake. I stood still for ten minutes with my .357 cocked and ready, still nothing. I was hoping it wasn't a bear waiting to pounce at the right moment. I walked down the path toward the lake ready to fight off an attack. I could see tracks and breathed a sigh of relief, wolf. After looking closer at his tracks I could see he was favoring his left front leg; three paw prints, one print was light. He was probably looking for a easy meal. I wish I had the chance to see him. He won't be back. He might have been curious about the camp and the smells. I am not tired now but I will still lay down to rest. After a while I did drift off to sleep. I woke up and it was late afternoon. I'll make a stew for supper and have the rest tomorrow. From the ashes I coaxed the fire back to life, then put the stew on to cook. I think I'll set a snare or two, see if I can get a rabbit. I've seen tracks down by the spring several times. I'll do it after supper, maybe I'll be lucky. After I finished eating, I put the rest of the stew away and did the dishes. I grabbed the wire and pliers and some rope and headed for the spring. I set up two snares, twenty feet apart, two trails. I'll see what I get in the morning. On the way back I took a walk around the alarm system; everything looked fine. Sitting by the fire, I was thinking I've been visited by all the animals that I know of this place—moose, bear, wolf. I doubt if there are any mountain lions, plus we're too far north. No deer or elk, sheep will stay high. The only thing left might be wolverine, and caribou but they wouldn't show up till winter. I am not going to stick around to find out. I've got twelve days left and I am just going to kick back and enjoy my last days here. I sure am going to have a good story to tell my family when I get home. I think I will keep a camcorder for the rest of the trip. I thought about getting one for this part of the adventure but pictures are fine. I've still got a lot of film left. One of the things I am going to miss is the Northern Lights. It's not dark this time of year. The fire's down and it's time to call it a day.

Morning came too soon but I felt pretty good. Got dressed and headed out to greet the day. It looks like it's going to be a nice one. Fire and coffee morning tradition, can't do without either one. The coffee is cooking and I put a pan on to heat water. I was anxious to get started panning. As soon as the coffee's ready, I'll head down to the spring for more water and check the snares. No rabbit yet. I'll check it again tonight. The water's hot so I got out a dish pan, filled it with cold and hot water. The temp felt good, a lot better than the water in the stream. I grabbed my pan and a bucket of material and started in, only doing a few handfuls at a time should work out good. I was glad I had worked the material down as far as I did at the stream. There were still a lot of small nuggets and pickers, those were easy to get. The flower gold, however, takes time and time I had plenty of. I imagine some people would just grab the easy stuff and toss out the rest. That would be like working all week to buy a nice steak at a restaurant and eat half and leave the rest. Hell, after all that work, sit down and enjoy it all.

I've been at this for a little over an hour. Time for a short break. I don't want a bad case of prune hands or a stiff back. A little smoked fish, that sounds good right now. Break time over, back to work, you dog. I shouldn't talk to myself like that but it's fun. Humor must have humor. Pan and pick, pan and pick. I panned all day till it made me sick; maybe I should write a song with that line. I couldn't help but laugh at myself. I was having fun. Gee, if Peter Piper picked a peck of pickers, how many pecks can Peter Piper pick? A bunch! Time for a break. I am getting silly and my fingers have a bad case of prune syndrome. I'll just rest awhile and enjoy the fire.

After about an hour, the fingers were looking normal. I'll get back to the panning later. I am going to do some fishing, catch and release. It's been a while since I did that. I'll bring one back for supper to go with the rest of the stew. It sounds like a plan. I grabbed my pole and tackle box and headed down to the lake. I got to my spot and it didn't take long, the fight was on. After about three hours, I won most of the battles and only lost a few. I grabbed my fish and headed back to camp. It's been a good day. Who says you can have too much fun? Not me. A short rest and I'll start supper. I am glad I don't catch and release every day. It would get old too quick. Well get your butt off the chair and get started. No one is going to do it for you.

    I got the fire going and got the stew out and started frying the trout. It didn't take long before the aroma was tickling my taste buds. A few more minutes and supper is ready. Between the trout and the stew, I was stuffed. I am eating good in the neighborhood. I cleaned the dishes, looked at my gold pan, no, tomorrow is another day. I need to do a quick check on the snares then I can enjoy the fire. Well nothing yet and took a cold drink of water. I looked over to the side of me and there were a few blueberries. I knew it was getting about time for them. If I can find enough, I will make blueberry pancakes in the morning. That sounds good. There wasn't a lot around here but I managed to get a couple handfuls, that will do it. Maybe tomorrow I will check out other areas.

    I got back to camp, put the berries in a bowl. I was tempted to munch a few but I'll save them for morning. A few more pieces of wood on the fire, it's sit time, my time to reflect and relax. I am going to miss this place when I leave but at least I'll take home great memories of this adventure. I couldn't help but smile as I looked out across the valley and the mountains shadowed from the evening light. Well, tomorrow is another day, time for bed.

    No problem waking up this morning, that raven's back. He's got to be in the tree above me. Okay, bird, I am up. I stepped out from under the tarp and sure enough there he was right overhead. I pointed my finger like a gun and said bang. He looked at me, sounded off again and flew off. Hell, the sun wasn't even peeking over the mountains yet. Damn noisy neighbors, there are some of us who work, you know. Might as well get a fire going and get fresh water and check the snares.

    I'll be damned, I got one fresh rabbit tonight. A young one about three-quarters grown. He'll make for some good eats. I got the water and headed back. I put the water down, picked up my shovel and got away from camp to skin and gut the rabbit and bury the rest. A quick rinse in the lake and I was done. I didn't want the smell of blood and guts by my campsite. I put it in a pan of water to soak the rest of the day.

Now to make up those blueberry pancakes. I wound up making more than I could eat but that's fine. I can munch them later. They sure were good. The sun is up now. It takes a while to get past the mountaintops. I think I will get me some more of them blueberries. I can pan this afternoon, the picking is not the best yet, a lot of green ones. I spent three hours to get a quart and half. I was glad I didn't see any bears, you can bet I was looking.

I got back to camp. I need to put fresh water on the rabbit and have some smoked fish for lunch. I put a pan of water on the fire and sat down while it heated. I'll only pan for three to four hours I told myself. I don't want to overdo it. Water's hot, time to get started. My, how I like yellow gold. There is gold in them there hills and gold in the pan and some in the hand. Jim should have the claim filed and paperwork done by the time I get back. Man, if the word got out about this place, there would be so many people and crap hauled in that this valley would be destroyed. I don't even want to see that. Well it looks like I'll get the first bucket done today. Time for a little break then I'll finish it up. I was looking at what I collected so far, what a pile! Tom and Jim Massic from the Prospecting American and the gold fever shows, Eat Your Heart Out. By the time I finished that last pan, I was ready to quit for the day. I'll take a short rest then start supper. I've got ten days to get the rest panned out. I'll do a baked potato with the rabbit. I put the rabbit in the roasting rack and slid a nail into the potato to speed up the baking. I've got a lot of coals built up that will work fine for both. It took around an hour to get the rabbit done and it was worth the wait. Having fresh meat for a change was nice. All I need was salt. I had some left over. I'll enjoy that tomorrow. I was ready to sit down after things were cleaned up. Now it's my time to relax and enjoy. After sitting there a couple hours, I was starting to nod off. Time to hit the hay.

I woke up early, had a nature call. The sky was red. We got a storm coming. Red sky in the morning, sailors take warning. I want to lay down a while longer. I woke up to the sound of a mouse under the tent in the bed area. I climbed out of bed and moved my sleeping bag with me then waited for it to make a noise. It didn't take long, he's right there and I stomped down with my foot. I will have to check to see if I got it. I had to loosen the tent to check. I got the bugger. I refastened the tent down and started the fire and got the coffee started. Things were starting to cloud up more. I'll make up more blueberry pancakes and make extra for later for when the rain comes. By the time I finished breakfast and put stuff away, it was getting darker out. It looked like I was in for a good one. I could see the storm coming over the mountains and lightning with it. This does not look good. The rain is starting and now the wind; as the lightning crashed, the thunder echoed through the valley. Pouring rain and high winds, lightning strikes one after another. The wind and rain was slamming to the camp and everywhere else. It's been years since I have seen anything like this. It seemed like it was slowing up after twenty minutes. Now I am getting wave after wave of rain, skies a solid gray. I don't get the chance to play outside today. That was one hell of a storm. I am glad the worst is over. I dedicate this day lazy day. I don't have to cook or clean. I can live with that. Listening makes you sleepy. I'll have something to eat when I wake up. It was around 2:00 when I woke up; still raining. I grabbed my thermos and poured a cup. I am listening to the rain come down, sipping my coffee, when a feeling came over me, that something was wrong, not here but somewhere else, family, friend or something wrong or something bad. I've had this experience before with my mom and my daughter. When things happen to them and this was no exception. Something has happened to someone. I decided to put on my raingear and get something to eat out of the food shack. I'll eat the rest of the rabbit and have an apple. The pancakes and smoked fish I'll have tonight. It doesn't look like it's going to stop raining anytime soon. I sat under the tarp to eat. Damn it, I can't shake this feeling. Now I wish Jim was picking me up tomorrow instead of eight days from now. I laid back down and thought about my time out here and the gold and next year. But the feeling wouldn't go away. I finally dozed off listening to the rain; when I awoke I felt better but something was not right. The rain was still coming down. I bet that stream looks like a raging river right now. I've got to stay up now so I can sleep tonight. There is nothing I can do right now so I'll daydream awhile and plan for next year when I come back. I laid there dreaming for hours, then it stopped. The rain stopped. Like someone shut off the valve.

I stepped outside and the last of the clouds were going away. I looked at my watch, 8:45, I can have a fire now. I'll have to dig down in the woodpile to find drier wood but I've got enough of the small stuff under the tarp to get it going. I was glad the rain stopped, now I can enjoy a fire for a few hours otherwise it would have made for a long night. It didn't take long before the flames were blazing against the dampness. I was totally enjoying the warmth, turning every so often to get my backside too. I got out the last of the pancakes and some more smoked fish. A good way to end the day, good fire, good food! It was almost midnight before I started to feel sleepy. It was time to turn in for the night.

It felt good when I woke up. I was ready to get the day started. When I stepped out of the tent, the sun was just peeking over the mountaintops and the sky was clear. It's going to be a beautiful day. I am ready for a cup of this as I sat the pot on the fire. I've got a half a fish left. I'll eat that this morning. I'll go fishing for more later today. I've got to get some more water heated up. I am standing here like a dummy staring at the coffee pot. I've a lot of panning to do. The water's on the fire and the coffee's almost done. Finally, it's coffee time, caffeine do your thing, my senses have been awakened. I finished the fish and the water was ready. It's time to get started. I've got to get some beans soaking so I can use the last of the bacon.

Now I am ready to start panning. I was surprised to see how good it was going, a good amount of rest works wonders. A few hours had passed and my wrinkled fingers were telling me to take a break. As I stood up to stretch, the rest of me was saying the same thing. I dried my hands and sat by the fire, taking in the beauty of the day. I still had that thought in the back of my mind from yesterday. There is nothing I can do about it now where I am at, so forget about it. There are too many things to enjoy and I've got eight days to do it. After an hour of rest, the hands are looking good, let's get back to it. Gee, this could be a whole new meaning to the word panhandling. I think I'm coming down with a fever, it sure feels like it's gold fever. I'm sure I can keep it under control. I hear there is no cure for it. It's something you have to live with and I am living with it quite well. The rest I can finish tomorrow. The arms are tired. I'll rest for a while I have some coffee and go fishing.

The lake was up from all the rain but that didn't affect the fishing any. I had the ten I wanted plus one for supper. After the cleaning was done, I headed back to camp. I prepared the fish and put them in water for tomorrow's smoking, then I got the beans and bacon ready and started cooking it. I felt good! I am doing the things I like to do. I've got time yet before I cook the fish. I need to get more water. I had put the snares up the other day when I got the rabbit. I'll set them back up. I might get another before I leave. When I got back, it was time to check the beans; they're not ready yet. Might as well sit a while and feed the fire. It looks like it will be calm tonight. The breeze is letting up. One more check on the beans, they are done; slid them off to the side and started the fish. I am trying rack cooking tonight, something different. I think I'll have a bowl of beans while I wait for fish to get done. I must have been hungry, that bowl didn't last long. Now for the fish, a little salt and enjoy. I think one more bowl of beans and bacon and that should do it just fine. I did the dishes and put the beans away for tomorrow. I was just about ready to sit down. A few blueberries for dessert sounds good, so I grabbed the container and took my spot by the fire. Boy, these are tasty! I am definitely going to pick some more. Between the fire and the food, I was getting very relaxed. I should sleep good tonight. I thought about sitting here longer but my bed was calling me, come here, come here. I gave in and went to sleep.

I am going to kill that bird; out of this whole valley, he's got to set above my camp. Well I'd better get up because he is not shutting up. Maybe if I surprise him, he'll stay away. I came out of that tent with a vengeance, yelling and making noise and he was heading out to someplace different, hopefully that will do it. I had a feeling that raven would be back. Well I am getting an early start today I told myself. The sun is not even close to showing itself yet. I'll get the fire going and put the coffee on, it should be ready after I check the snares. Well, I had a rabbit, the snare still there completely out of place and fur and pieces of hide all over the ground. Wolf tracks, it might be the one from the other day. He's got to eat too. He probably needs it more than me since he's favoring that one leg. I moved the snare to a different spot and tried again.

The coffee was ready when I got back and I was ready for a cup. I got the fish out of the food shack and set it out to drain while I got the smoker started. I put the fish on the rack and shut the door. The water was hot so let the panning begin. I should be finished by noon. I got more breaks since I had to keep adding wood to the smoker, that was fine with me. It was a goldfish day anyhow. I was glad when I put the last of the concentrates in the pan, with the last slurp of the snuffer bottle I was done. I looked at my watch; it wasn't even noon yet. The rest of the day will be tend to the smoker. After eating those beans last night, there has been quite the air about me this morning, good enough to clear a crowd. Can you imagine what it was like at a mining camp years ago when they were eating beans every day? I bet the comment was made, did something crawl up you and die? I couldn't help but laugh at that thought. A few more hours of smoking fish then heat dry. Time to kick back and enjoy the fire.

There are several ravens raising a fuss across the lake. I can't see them but you sure can hear them. Boy, I almost feel like a nap but I can't, it's getting close to taste time on the fish. I opened the smoker and checked. It's heat time now, they had enough smoke. I put in some coals and shut the door. An hour or so will do it. While I waited, I got all the gold out to figure how much I had. It turned out to be a lot more than I realized. It was too much for my table so I spread out my rain jacket and piled it on it. I know it's well over 100 pounds. It's more than twice what Jim took with him. One thing about that lunker, it's worth a lot more to a collector than face value. What a pile! I put it back into the tent, it was time to take out the fish.

I started to heat up the beans and bacon while the fish cooked a bit. Tomorrow I will get myself some more blueberries. After supper I cleaned the dishes and put the fish away. I've got to remember to check the snares before I go to bed. I'll just sit for a while. A new visitor to camp. I was wondering when mosquitoes would arrive. My first one, slap, he won't get the chance to tell the rest I am here. It must have been all that rain that got 'em going. At least I'll be out of here in two days. I'll check my snares and get inside my tent. I don't want to start a feeding frenzy. The snares are clear. Now it's to the tent. By the end of the month through the next I know it will be intense around here, I've got repellent, I may have to use some before I leave. Tomorrow when I get back from berry picking I'll start packing. It's been a great twenty-eight days. I am ready to do the rest of my adventure on the road. So with those thoughts I fell asleep.

When I woke up I realized I slept in. I got dressed and stepped outside. It's a clear day and the sun is over the peaks already. I got the fire started and coffee going. I need to get more water and check snares, nothing yet. I got the water and headed back. As I drank my coffee I was figuring to get two quarts of blueberries today, enough to munch and for pancakes in the morning. I got out a couple zip lock bags and headed out. The picking was slow and I had to keep a watch out for the bears too. I cut through some trees heading to another area that should be real good. I stopped just inside the trees to check the opening and there on the other side, a bear was feeding and two more, mama and cubs. I already knew I was downwind. I came in that way; she didn't see me so I quietly slid out of there and kept going. I found other patches but there was still a lot of green ones on. It was noon by the time I got the two quarts I wanted. I covered a lot of area to get these. I was glad to see my camp when I walked up.

Time for a rest and a cup of coffee. I was surprised there weren't more mosquitoes than there were, when I was out there. I'll get some smoked fish out for lunch then start packing this afternoon. It felt good to sit. I put a pretty good walk in. I'm getting good at doing smoked fish. This bunch even tasted better than the first or second batch. It didn't take long to get things ready for tomorrow. When Jim gets here, I'll take down the tarp and tent. I might as well grab my pole and play with the fish awhile. I can't wait to call my daughter tomorrow. I know she's been worrying about me. She will be excited and relieved when she picks the phone up and it's me. I miss her too! Tomorrow I am going to have my camera ready so when Jim comes in for a landing, that will make quite a shot with the Beaver in the air, the water, woods and mountains in the background. I know right where I want to stand to take the shot. The fish aren't getting tired but I am. It's time to call it quits. It's time for some fire and rest. I've done plenty today. I spent the next few hours reflecting back on the last twenty-nine days. Tonight will be my last night here. I have no regrets. This experience is one for the books and it's not over yet. I've got all that traveling to do before I get back to the lower forty-eight. As the fire burned my thoughts were changing toward my family, to trips, to experience, to leaving and to camp. I like the camp I created. Well the sooner I get to sleep the sooner morning will be here. I must have laid there for an hour before sleep finally came.

    I didn't sleep well last night. I guess I was anxious for today. The noisy neighbor—that bugger—brought a friend. They are either eager to see me leave or they enjoy being annoying. I might as well get up because they won't leave till I show up. I unzipped the tent and jumped out from under the tarp with a sharp yell and they took off. That's the last time they will wake me up. I'll get the fire going and take down my snares. I won't be needing them anymore. I'll start the coffee when I get back. No rabbits and in no time I was back. Now to get the coffee started and start making pancakes. I'll make a good bunch, that should hold me over till I get back to Anchorage. Jim and I can eat smoked fish on the plane ride back. After breakfast, I'll get the dishes cleaned and put away. I filled my thermos and mug. Another job well done.

    Now it's wait time. I've got the camera ready so as soon as I hear the plane I can take pictures. Time sure does fly by when you are having fun but waiting is a whole different thing. I got up and added more wood to the fire. It's 11:00. I sat back down with my ears tuned to the sky. I enjoyed some blueberries while I waited. 2:00, Jim should be showing up anytime. I walked over to the clearing and gazed at the pass where he would be coming from. After a while I went back and sat down. 4:00, maybe he'll get here late and spend the night and we'll leave in the morning. I bet that's what he's got planned. I built up the fire and had some smoked fish, still waiting for the sound of the plane. By

8:00, I told myself, Jim will come tomorrow. I made my bed and cooked up some noodles for supper with a little butter spray. The weather was good today too. I got out my calendar, yes today is the day. I was feeling down. I was expecting to leave today. I'll go to bed. Tomorrow Jim will come.

I woke up feeling good. I stepped outside; clear skies that's a good sign. I need to get out the coffee pot and cooking tinsels and go to the spring for water. When I got back I got the fire started and the coffee going. I looked to the skies and listened, nothing yet. I poured myself a cup and sat down. I laughed as I told myself at least I don't have to pay to stay an extra day. I think I will grab me a trout for breakfast and cook it over the fire. I will leave the fry pan packed. I was back in five minutes. I like fast food! I took my time cooking it and when it was ready to eat, I made it disappear and no one saw me do it or how I did it. I am good! I sipped my coffee and waited. It was noon when I checked my watch. Come on, Jim, this waiting is killing me. The afternoon into evening and still nothing. I guess I'll make a pot of stew, that will give me two meals. After I ate, I put away the rest of the stew and went to bed.

When I got up I told myself today is the day. Jim wouldn't leave me waiting. If he couldn't make it he would send someone. I'll do the fire and coffee morning routine. There were a few clouds in the sky but the rest is clear. By the time it was noon, the feeling of something wrong was entering my mind. But all I can do is wait. When evening came, I was getting bummed out. Three days of waiting. I ate my stew and went to bed.

The next two days was the same. No plane, no Jim. I know by now, my daughter has been making phone calls trying to find out about me. By now the camp was almost the way it was six days ago before I packed up. The smoked fish was gone. I still had food I brought so I am doing good in that department. I will put the snares back out and try to get fresh meat, at least it will give me something to do. I've got to cut some more firewood, the last is on the fire now. It was 5:00 when I finished with the wood. I took a short break, then went fishing, some for supper and the rest for the smoker. I know I could be picked up tomorrow but I may not be either. I'll have smoked fish if not. When I got back I fried two trout and put the rest in water to soak overnight. I sat by the fire, trying to figure out why this is happening to me. Tomorrow my 6th day of waiting. Jim knows where I am. My daughter knows where I am. I sent her an e-mail and a letter of my location and a map plus I have the info in the glove box of my Explorer where I am. There is no plane, no reason, no nothing. If something happened to Jim, my daughter would have contacted the authorities by now. The more I thought about it, the madder I was getting. If no one shows up by the 10th day, then no one is coming.

It's the morning of the 6th day, a little cloudy. As I started the fire and the coffee, I told myself I think I am screwed. While I am smoking the fish I will clear out an area for a signal fire and tie out my big blue tarp, twenty feet by twenty feet. It should stand out nicely against the green. The fish are smoking now. I cleared an area about fifteen feet by fifteen feet. I put down dried brush with a pile of kindling and covered it with plastic and stacked pine boughs and brush limbs up to shed water. There was plenty of green for smoke the way I piled it, it will take off good. I got out my can of WD-40 and set it on some rocks close by. If I see a plane, rain or shine, with the WD-40 and my lighter I will have big smoke in seconds. I then unpacked the blue tarp, stretched it out and tied it down.

I got two sources of visual now. The rest of the day I tended the smoker till the fish was done. I ate fish while sitting by the fire that evening. I was thinking about what I'll have to do. Stay put or try to walk out the way we flew in. I could try following the streams out of this valley but to what river or rivers. I've got a compass but no maps plus the amount of food, clothes and a bit of shelter would be more than I would want to carry and if I got hurt, no one would know where I am at. I will stay put. I left behind where I am and this is where I'll stay.

I'll sit on my ass. Three more days after that, it's survival mode then. I've got three days to make a plan then do it. I am not going to sit around for a month or two then say gee I'd better do something, it will snow soon. If I do get rescued between now and a few weeks from now at least I was making good with my time. I went to sleep, knowing I would have to rely on every resource and knowledge. I had to make it through this, if no one shows up.

I woke up tired, so many things going through my mind last night. I won't make coffee, I will try to save what I got. The fire is going good. I need to get water and check the snares. I filled my water container then checked the snares. Nothing in the first, just my luck. I got to the second and jackpot! I got a rabbit, yes! Fresh meat tonight. I cleaned the rabbit and buried the rest and put it in water. The sky was mostly clear, visibility would be good. I still kept an ear out for the sound of a plane. With each day the chances would be less that a plane would show up but I still didn't know why.

I need to take a check of trees for a log cabin. I've got enough tools to carve one out but only a little over two months before bad weather will start or colder weather. Might as well get started. It took me about an hour but I found enough trees the size I could handle. That's going to be a job. I've got to have heat, can't make a fireplace, got no clay. Wood stove! Miner's cabin! It's a start but no stove pipe. Well that's an idea screwed. Son of a bitch, unless I come up with a way to vent that stove, I may have to try to walk out and I really don't want to do that. I kept racking my brain for an answer but no solutions. Where are my rescuers? A plane, a plane, my wish is for a plane. Wait a minute, there is a plane crash fifteen to seventy-nine miles from here. I could get metal for a stove pipe and roof cap for the pipe. That will work! I've got two days to work it out.

Well today has been like the rest, nothing, nobody, ZIP. It's like I stepped off the face of the earth. I can't be that hard to find. The only plane I've seen is a jet liner at 35,000 feet and they sure as hell are not looking. Maybe if I went down with a plane, they would look but eight days and not a thing and weather perfect. I just don't get it.

I'll cook my rabbit, maybe it will help take my mind off this situation. The skies are cloudy up, looks like it's going to rain tonight. The rabbit's done and I'm hungry. Well that was good timing. It just started to sprinkle. I moved under the tarp and none too soon. It's coming down now. I ate my fill and I've got some left for tomorrow. I set in my chair for a while listening to the rain and thinking. Well I wanted an adventure. I am in for a big one.

The rain was still coming down when morning came. I laid there listening to it come down. I got dressed and went outside. The clouds were low and gray with no sign of the rain letting up soon. There won't be any planes flying in this. I went back into the tent and laid down. I was thinking if it rains all day I will have to wait till tomorrow to start building a litter to drag that stove back here. It will be easier than dragging deer but I've never dragged a deer that far. I will start out early and should be back around mid afternoon. I better rest when I can now; once I get started the long hours will start. With that thought I drifted off to sleep.

It was noon when I woke up. I need some coffee. I'll just make a half a pot, got out the propane stove and I was ready to cook up some caffeine. That first cup hit the spot. My motor's running now. I'll make a quick drawing of the litter I need to build. Two green poles about seven feet and four cross pieces all will be notched. The longest next to the end so I can push against it while my arms can balance the poles. I will be able to save my arms and shoulders. The two center cross pieces will support the stove and the last to stabilize the end. Keep it wide enough to move inside and tapered to around one foot at the bottom.

Time to finish the rabbit. I'm hungry. I hope the rain stops. I want to get busy building. The afternoon dragged on with the rain coming down non stop. Getting the stove here should be quite easy compared to the walk to the crash site. That will be a two day trip. I'll cook up some noodles to go with the fish for supper. I am sure glad I like fish, if I didn't I'd be in trouble.

Damn, it's been raining for twenty-four hours. I might as well get on my raingear and check the snares. It felt good to walk after setting all day. The snares are empty. I didn't think I would be that lucky. When I got near the camp, I really didn't want to sit down so I decided to walk over to the stream for a look. I could hear the water long before I got to it. The stream was a raging torrent of fast water, sweeping away anything in its path. Definitely not a place you want to be. Now I know what this place is like when the rain comes down.

When I got back to camp I shed my raingear and got inside the tent. I'll stay up a little while longer then I'll go to bed. I had quit trying to reason why I am not being picked up. I've already made up my mind—if I am not going to be saved, I will have to save myself or die trying.

It's the 10th day, I told myself when I opened my eyes. I was glad not to hear the rain anymore. It had stopped sometime during the night. I got on my clothes and rushed outside, clear skies. I'll get a fire started and get myself a couple trout for breakfast. I am anxious to get this day going. I am glad the fish are still cooperating and they keep biting the way they do because later on I will need to catch a lot and dry them for winter. I pan fried the fish and by the time I finished eating the second I was full.

Now to start building the litter. I cut the poles and the cross pieces and started notching and fitting with everything in place. It looked good. I used wire to fasten it all together. I stepped in and picked it up. It felt good and I had good control of it. I think I will put a tower around the cross piece. I'll be pushing on, I'll have more comfort. I tied a rock on it for a test run. This works nice. Tomorrow I'll put it to the real test.

I grabbed my shovel and went over to the spot I picked out for the cabin, farther back into the trees, about twenty feet beyond the food shack. I spent the rest of the afternoon clearing and leveling the ground and getting the rocks out of the way. I liked the spot, plenty of room to work. From what I could see this was not an avalanche area. To the east it was but not here. Time to call it a day and enjoy the fire. A little smoked fish and a apple for supper. I've got a handful of blueberries left. I'll save them for morning pancakes. The fire's getting down so I need to get to bed. I got a big day tomorrow.

Wow, I slept like a rock last night. I couldn't wait to get started. I did a quick check on the snares, nothing in them. In no time I had pancakes cooking. I wasted no time getting them down. I loaded my water, food and rope in my back, grabbed the litter and headed for the miner's camp. As I rounded the end of the lake I forgot to put a note out so I went back to camp. I wrote a note, put it in a plastic bag and tied it to a tree. So if by some chance someone came, they would know where I am and how to get there and when I'll be back. Well this puts me a little behind.

I got back to where I left the litter and started out again. It was a little rough getting through the underbrush but the tall trees were just ahead. As I walked along, I could keep track of the landmarks quite well. Then I saw something that stopped me in my tracks. A territorial marking tree with fresh claw marks reaching ten feet and the smell of urine. I didn't even go close to it. I kept moving on looking everywhere, including in back of me. When I reached the fallen trees, I didn't have far to go, turn left and I'll be there in ten.

When I got to the cabin, I removed my backpack and started removing the stove. The bugger was heavy. I probed around awhile, trying to find the lid but no luck. I got out my rope and tied it secure to the litter, put on my backpack and headed back. My creation was working good and it was easy on me. I didn't care for the noise I was making, dragging this thing along, but I had no choice. I was a bit uneasy as I passed the marker tree, hoping that bear was somewhere else, only stopping a few minutes at a time as I went along. By the time I was getting out of the underbrush, breaks were a little more often.

It was a welcome sight when I could see where my camp was. I just got to get around this part of the lake. As I set the litter down in camp, I could tell my legs had a good workout, my hands and arms felt good. I'll catch a couple of fish for supper and rest by the fire. I could tell the body had a workout by the time I finished supper. It was talking to me. Tomorrow I'll rest.

I slept in this morning and it felt good too. As I got dressed I was hoping the weather would be good the next few days. The body was a little stiff but once I got to moving around it was gone. I headed to the spring for water and check the snares. My lucky day I got one in the other this time. More food for the trip. I got the fire going and cleaned the rabbit and put it in water. A little coffee this morning will hit the spot. I untied the stove and looked it over more. For the age and all the years out here it's in good shape. I can use a rock or a piece of metal over the plate area.

I've got to gather the things I need for the trip to the crashed plane. My hatchet, screwdriver, pliers, vice grip, rope, first aid kit, warm clothes, space blanket, extra socks, 2½ gallon of water and food enough for four days. The hardest part is getting up over and down the pass and I do not know how rough the terrain is on the other side or how far the plane is. The pass is seven to eight thousand feet. I figure on leaving camp around 4:00 a.m., at least the skies are still light yet. While I am sitting here, I will write the note: "I have gone to the plane crash sight, west-northwest of here beyond the pass fifteen to twenty miles away. It's July 27, I should be back in three to four days. Alan Dunbarker." I slid it in the bag and tied it back to the tree. I was thinking this is the craziest thing yet out here. I have climbed mountains before so I do know what I am getting myself into. This will be harder because I have to find my own way.

I think I will take a power nap, the added rest will not hurt. That is a way to use up three hours and a nice rest. Time to play fisherman. I need fish for supper and to take with me tomorrow. Fast food, four in fifteen minutes—that included travel time and cleaning. Time for some fire. I have a lot of cooking to do tonight, one rabbit, four fish and pancakes so this will take me awhile. So far, the mosquitoes have not been too bad. That reminds me, headgear and repellant. I'll put that in my pack right now. It took two hours to get everything cooked. I ate some rabbit and fish and bagged the rest. I added sugar to the pancakes, a little extra boost. My backpack is full and ready. Time to get to bed.

I woke up around 3:30 got dressed and stepped out of the tent. Made my trip to the outhouse and I am ready to get started. A couple adjustments on the pack. I am ready to go.

I made my way to the end of the lake; now it's the underbrush and trees till I get to the base of the mountain, about two miles or so. From what I could see I had an idea which way to start. There are some areas higher up of loose rocks. I'll need to avoid those areas if at all possible. So far I've had good hard rock. I will try to stop every half hour for a few minutes break. The rocks are getting more difficult. I need to make stone markers for the return trip. Damn it, I can't make it this way. I'll have to find another. The going is a lot slower now, one wrong move and I am screwed. I've got to keep picking away. I want to get to the top sometime today. I looked at my watch, 10:00. Shit, I am only three-quarters the way up. I've got a steep area above me about 30 feet. I will have to climb it and pull up my backpack. When I made the distance up, I could see a lot easier area ahead. I should be at the top around 2:00. As the hours went by, I made it to the top at 2:45.

I could see the saw tooth peak where the planes were near the bottom. Damn, I've got a ways to go. I look back to the area where my camp was, it looked a lot farther away from up here. I've got to get moving. I've got to find a way down. There is a lot of loose rock on this side. I found a hard rock area to the north that looked good. One thing nice about going down, you can see where you're going a lot easier. One thing for sure I'm not walking out. This is about all I want of dealing with mountains and rocks.

This valley is not as deep as the one I am at. It's a few miles wide but it's long. Damn, there is a lot of loose rock, almost every step you dig for something solid. My butt is going to be sore before I am done. Finally getting more solid rock, you still have to watch your step. This is going to be a bitch on the return trip. When I get to the bottom, I am not sure if I will keep to the rocks or the brush. I want to make the best time I can. Wow, I made it to the bottom, 7:00 now. I've got miles to go. I started through the brush but there's a tundra soft bottom. That's all I need is to step into a hole or mud pocket. The rocks are the way to go. I am keeping to the north side of the valley because that's the side where the crash sight is. I'll keep moving till I get there. I can see the saw tooth peak and hour by hour it's getting closer. I had to stop to rest for a few minutes. I am getting exhausted. 10:30 and I am not there yet. Must keep going. I can rest when I get there after climbing over this rock ridge. I finally see it, about two hundred yards ahead. I made it, 11:50, what a walk—almost twenty hours. I'll look the wreckage over in the morning. I am making a place to sleep. I had a few bites of food, put on my netting over my head and went to sleep.

I awoke a few hours later and the air was a constant buzz of mosquitoes. I made sure I was covered and rearranged the moss and went back to sleep. It was 8:00 when I woke up. I thought to myself, these mosquitoes are intense here. There was one part of me that didn't hurt.

As I got up, damn, someone wiped my wookey. The air was literally gray with bugs. I am going to have to figure out a way to pee so I won't get bit. I finally ran for fifty feet or so, I made it quick. Running didn't feel good either.

I looked over the plane and picked out the areas I'll go after. A lot of rivets to deal with. Great! Plus there is one side window that's not broken. I'll take that too, along with the wiring. I got out my screwdriver and hatchet and started cutting rivets. The sheet metal may be soft but the rivets are a lot harder. This is going to take a while. By the time I started chopping and cutting, I think every mosquito in this valley knows I am here. It was hard trying to damage the metal. I was at it an hour and progress was slow. I took time to look around the site for something to help speed up the task. There was a door toward the tail of the plane. I had to pry it open. There wasn't much light to see inside. It looked empty then I spotted a box jammed between the framework and the cockpit. I got my hatchet and chopped it loose. I could hear things inside, possibly tools. I pried open the lid, sure enough, pliers, screwdriver, pop rivets, pop rivets gun, a small crank hand brace, four drill bits, a couple bolts and yes! a chisel. Thank you Lord! What a difference, in no time I had my first chunk of sheet metal. Now I need two more panels. It was afternoon already when I finished the panels. I got to get the wiring yet and get the window out. I pulled the rubber seats from the doors and started to get things packed up. The sheet metal I rolled up and tied with rope. The window wouldn't fit into the backpack so I tied it on. The rest I stuffed in my pack. I had three-quarters of a jug of water left. I needed to get the hell out of here. I am not spending any more time in this valley than I have to. I strapped on my backpack and grabbed the sheet metal and headed out.

The gray cloud of mosquitoes followed me as I walked. I carried the sheet metal when I could and dragged it the rest of the time. The pace was slower than when I came. I knew I would spend another night out here but I wanted to do it on higher ground. It's around 4:00 p.m. and I had miles to go before I could start heading up. We were starting to get more clouds showing up and it didn't look good. I've got to push myself to get some distance between me. It was 7:39 when I reached the base of the mountains. There was a lot more clouds now. I got out my first aid kit and took some pain reliever. I will keep going till I can't go anymore. It's not a good plan, being tired and having to climb larger areas of loose rock. It is going to take everything I got. The farther I get up, the less bugs. Plus I want to get past the loose rocks before the rain starts. I've been into the climb now about twenty minutes and the pain reliever is helping. I am having to stop for a minute or two more often to rest. I have reached the first loose rock area and no more mosquito land. I was glad of that! I could put away the netting. I knew it was going to be hard climbing but being tired wasn't helping. For every two steps, you make one. There was a constant clatter of rocks sliding down behind me. It was slow, hard work, take a few steps and stop. Take a few steps and stop. I still had a way to go before I would get to hard rock and it's starting to rain. I found a spot where I could get my rain jacket on. The rocks would tear the pants up. My knees and shins have already been taking a beating. The climbing was treacherous; now the rocks were wet. It's muddy and with each step my feet were sliding. My energy was about spent. There were about fifty feet to go and I'll be on hard rock. That last step onto hard ground was a welcome one. I need to find a place to stop.

It took about twenty minutes or so to find a place. A rock hangover that would give me shelter. It was high enough to be somewhat comfortable. I got out my warm clothes and put them on and also my rain pants. My knees and shins have really took a beating. I don't even want to look at them now. My hands and knuckles were beat up too. I was tired, cold and sore. I took some pain reliever. I had less than a quart of water left. I unfolded the space blanket and tucked it in around me. I looked at my watch—it was after 1:00 a.m. Between the raingear and the blanket I was retaining body heat and by morning what was wet will be dry.

I don't remember falling asleep but the rain had stopped. I tried to get up and couldn't. I kept moving my legs and feet and the rest of my body. I was stiff and sore beyond description. I finally got to my feet, hanging onto the rocks to keep my balance.

Slowly I regained the use of my muscles. Once I could walk, I started moving around till I was feeling stable. I took more pain reliever and had a good meal. I've still had to make it to the pass yet and down the other side, at least the worst loose rock area was behind me. I removed my heavy clothes and raingear and put them away.

I strapped on my backpack. I had no problem following my markers and was enjoying the hard rock climbing. I had two hours of rock areas yet, but they will be easier and not as steep. I should be at the pass by noon. I'll take a short rest there. The body was still letting me know there had been too much use and abuse. With every step, I was getting closer to home. I was sure glad to see the pass. It was all downhill from here. I sat so I could see my camp area. I couldn't see the camp but knew where it was. There was no plane on the lake so no one came. I rested about twenty minutes. I didn't want to sit any longer, must keep the endorphins going. Boy, going down is sure a lot easier. I was doing good making my way down the side of the mountain. A few butt slides but not bad. When I got to the area, I had to lower everything with a rope. I was around halfway. I'll tell you, it felt better climbing than it did going down. Making the wrong steps means sudden stop. I breathed a sigh of relief when my foot touched bottom. Still following markers, I made my way down and the valley was getting closer. When I got to the bottom I took a break, ate the last of the food and took a sip of water. I've got a mouthful left and I will be drinking a lot when I get back to camp. I can feel that I am dehydrated.

I started across the valley heading for the lake and the worst was behind me. I was almost to the lake when I drank my last swallow of water. Knowing I would be in camp soon gave me more energy for my steps. Here's the lake and I'll be at camp soon. Walking up the path was a welcome sight. I am home!

As I took off my pack, I looked around—everything was the way I left it. I was glad of that, no unwelcome visitors. I headed to the spring for fresh water. It felt nice to move without the load on my back. As I knelt down for a drink my knees let me know they were in dire need of attention big time. I got my water and headed back. I had to set awhile. I dropped my pants and was shocked. I knew they were bad but I didn't think it was that bad. I grabbed the first aid kit. There were more scrapes, gouges and bruises than I want to count. I washed the dried blood away and cleaned with alcohol, applied cream and bandages and took ampicillin to fight the infection. I got a fire going to heat water so I could get cleaned up. I started a pot of stew. I could feel it now as things slowed down. I didn't want to sit for any length of time. The stiffness was setting in. After supper was done, I put away the stew and set by the fire. It was 8:30. I got up and got out the bottle of bourbon and had a drink. It wasn't long the day had caught up with me. Bed was calling me. I slid in bed and covered up and I was out.

It was noon when I woke up. I felt good as long as I didn't move. I started with my fingers. I had to push on them to get them closed then worked on my hands, arms and shoulders, next my feet, legs and back. When I stood up I was wobbling like a new calf. Today is a nothing day. I am sitting back and just lick my wounds. I wobbled outside and sat down. I might not do anything tomorrow too, the way I feel. Must get up, get a fire going and make some coffee. That will help get me going and Lord I need the help. Man, it's been days since I had coffee. I almost forgot how good it is. The more I moved around the better I felt. I untied the window from the pack and got out the wire and tools and hung out the clothes. The pop rivets will come in handy and let see the drill bits, ⅛, ¼, ⅚, ⅜; that ⅜ will come in handy for drilling peg holes. This was a nice find. I got a nice amount of wire too. I am going to need it all to build the cabin and I've got to get started on it soon. It's July 30th. Well, it's been fifteen days and no one came, not even a plane in the sky. It's like no one knows I am out here. Piss on it, I am not going to think about it anymore. You can wish in one hand and crap in the other and see which fills up first.

I should sit around and rest but I want to start doing things. I could start whittling out pegs but that would be a good rainy day project. I could start trimming tree limbs and marking out logs. There is a lot of down trees to work from to the east. I won't go crazy at it, just take my time. I'll cut out marking pole so all the logs will be the right size and length. Front and back logs fourteen feet, side eighteen feet, keeping the size no more than eight inches. I got weeks of cutting and dragging logs so whatever I do now is less I'll have to do later. I got out my ax and saw and headed out for a little cut and trim. It only took a few minutes to change my mind. My body was not ready for this, maybe tomorrow. I guess the mind said yes, the body said no way in hell.

When I got back to camp, I put the tools away and sat down. Yep, rest is good. I can handle that. Well since I can't handle an ax, I'll start whittling pegs. I got out the hand brace and 3/8 drill bit and drilled a hole in a piece of wood. Then I cut a few willow sticks, debarking and shaping to size and checking to the 3/8 hole, keeping them on the tight. I am going to need a lot of these for the roof poles. I don't think I would have had enough wire and nails to hold them all. So as the afternoon went on, the pile of pegs grew.

By the time evening came, I was ready to call it quits for the day; not bad, I had thirty-two done. I got out the stew and heated it up. I needed to catch some fish for tomorrow. Must not let the smoker set too long. I'll do that after supper and dishes. In no time I had my tenth fish and was back at camp. I prepared them and put them in water. I needed to do a food inventory too. I still had a good amount and some I hadn't touched yet. Time to set by the fire. Tomorrow, no day after is the 1st day of August already. Tomorrow will be my last rest day, then the push is on. I intended to get the cabin done and get settled in before the weather got bad. The fire was getting down and I couldn't wait to get into bed. The eyelids were getting heavy.

I was surprised how good I felt when I woke up. A little stiff, a little sore, far better than yesterday. I got dressed and stepped outside, another nice day. I started the fire then headed to the lake to catch breakfast. Two in the hand means two in the pan and it won't be long till breakfast is ready. The fish was good. Now it's time to get busy.

I cut four logs about four inches size and made two log horses by the cabin site. I was lucky, no big rocks when I dug the four holes. I notched the logs and tied them together and packed the dirt tight. The V was just the right height for working. It was time to check on the smoker again and add some wood. Then I started gouging pine trees. I needed a head start so I could gather pitch to seal the cabin. It was just after 12:00. I've got a nice bit of work done this morning. I will tend the smoker and whittle pegs this afternoon. I know I've got a hell of a lot of work ahead of me but I am really looking forward to it. By the time it was 3:00, the peg pile was getting bigger and it was heat time for the fish. I think I'll rest the hands awhile. As I sat, I was thinking about my plan of attack on building the cabin and attack starts tomorrow. It was getting time to check the fish, they are ready. I took out a big one and started eating. I hope I don't ever get tired of smoked fish. As long as it's food I won't complain. I am definitely full now. I'll put away the rest and whittle more pegs till it's time for bed. I don't know why the mosquitoes aren't bad here. A little repellent works good. I hope it stays that way. The peg count for today is forty-six. I am happy with that. I only have a few hundred to go. Time to hit the sack, big day tomorrow.

I feel good today. I slept good last night and I am ready to turn and burn. As I stepped out of the tent I saw it was going to be a nice day. I couldn't wait to get this show on the road. I had some smoked fish, grabbed my tools and got started.

There were four trees close by. I had picked out four base logs close to the cabin sight; they would be the biggest I have to work with, ten inches. These trees were already dead so they wouldn't be too heavy to work with. After trimming the limbs I marked out the two end logs fourteen feet, the two side logs at eighteen feet. I rolled them to the site then started to mark and cut and chip out the cross lap. I tried to make each joint as tight as possible. It took several hours to set the logs right and square. I had to dig down the two ends so the side logs would touch the ground, once everything was where I wanted. I took pitch and grass to make a seal and packed dirt all the way around nice and solid. I stood in the center and imagined what the rest will look like. It's been a good day's work. It's time to rest and have a bit to eat. Tomorrow, logs will be smaller but I will have to drag them. If I can get eight to ten a day that won't be too bad and trade off every other day to set logs. There is going to be a lot of fitting and trimming to have a little to no gap between logs. I figure setting three to four logs a day or more. I'll find out when I get to that point. As I laid down, my thoughts were on tomorrow.

I couldn't believe it was morning already. I will make pancakes for breakfast. That should hold me over till lunch. I was eager to get started. By now I had trimmed and cut fifteen logs—now to start dragging. After the first two were at the site I had to try something different. The holding and pulling at the same time was wearing me out quick. As I was resting I was thinking about my problem, then it hit me—I could use the backpack with rope so I only need to lift the log a foot and drag with my shoulders and arm. I think that should work fine. I took the pack off the framework and tied up a snatch rope with loop. I put the framework on for a tryout. I got on my knee, put the rope around the log and stood up. Holding the rope I could steady it and started walking. A lot better, one-quarter the effect than before. The first trip like this took twenty minutes. I rested a while that afternoon. I got four more logs hauled. I had enough. I definitely put the P in pooped today. I had some smoked fish and went to bed. I was too tired for a fire.

As the daylight greeted my eyes. I knew the night was over. Ouch, I found a few muscles I forgot I had. I'll fix myself something to eat and I'll be ready for more use and abuse. I'll get the other eight logs hauled today. It was slow going. That first log felt like a tree but as the muscles warmed up and the adrenalin kicked in, it wasn't long I was hauling the mail. By 4:00, I had the 8th one at the site. I am not ready to quit for the day so I started to trim and cut. I needed to cut one more fourteen foot then sixteen to eighteen foot. I have an even amount to work with. I cut five logs and drug the 14th back. I had enough. When I got back to camp I was pleased with the progress so far, still a long way to go. I grabbed my pole, I needed fish for supper. By the time the fish were done cooking it was after 8:00 p.m. I sat by the fire afterwards till the fire died down. I was ready to get some sleep.

Wake up, it's August 5th. Time's a wastin.' So let's get your motor stirring. I'm glad I have humor. I can laugh at myself and with myself at the same time. I've got to admit I am getting these muscles toned up. Hell, by the time I finished I looked like the incredible hunk. I'm going to have to move the snares to a different area. I need some fresh meat, a little break from fish. I could get some beans soaking, yes, I'll do that for supper. I had a fast food breakfast, fish. I moved the snares to a different area, then grabbed my ax and saw and headed out. I've got thirteen more eighteen-footers to trim and cut then I've got to haul all sixteen back to the sight. I spent the morning and half the afternoon trimming and cutting the eighteen-footers. I took my tools back to camp and rested a few minutes. Now to start hauling. I needed to pace myself so I don't burn myself out. It took over an hour to get the first one back, taking breaks between pulls. I went for the second a little over an hour. I still felt good. I think I found my rhythm. Number 3 took a little longer, the strain was catching up to me. I'll do one more. I was glad to get the 50 feet over with.

Time for some R & R. I got the fire going and started cooking the beans. That chair felt good and I've got twelve more to get for this bunch then I'll start setting what I've got hauled up. With what I've cut I will have enough to get the walls up around 4½ feet. I plan to get them up to 6 or 6½ feet on the sides. A quick look, beans are done, time to eat. It's just not the same without bacon. After supper was over, I went to check the snares, nothing. It was getting late and I was tired. Time to get to bed and hit it hard in the morning.

The skies were cloudy when I got up. We might get some pass over rain showers today. I ate breakfast, checked the snares, nothing yet and started working.

The forenoon went well—I got four logs hauled, only a brief rain shower. The afternoon I got five hauled, only three more to go. It's 6:00 now, I am going to go for it; if I stop for a rest I won't get it done. I kept a steady pace of determined go and when I set the last one down it was 10:00 p.m. I did it, I told myself as I sat down. Tomorrow is fit and trim, setting logs. While the beans were heating up I got out the bourbon and had a drink. I was proud of what I had accomplished so far. I finished the bean soup and climbed into bed.

Morning came too soon. I felt like going back to sleep but I can't slow down now. The skies were mostly clear; that was a good sign. I caught two fish and cooked them up. Went out to check the snares. I got one, yes, fresh meat. I cleaned it and let soak in water.

Now to start setting logs. First I've got to set the two end logs, a lot of cutting and trimming when I got the first one where I wanted and almost no gap. I drilled and pinned each end. It took just as long to get the other end in place. You can only go so fast with a saw and a hatchet. Now that I've got both ends in place and pinned, I can start on the side logs. I had three logs done and a start on the fourth when I called it a day. It was almost 8:00. I had rabbit to cook yet. I put away the tools and got the fire going and added some rabbit to the fire. It will take a while before it's done. At this rate it's going to be around the 20th when the sides are up. I am going to have to find a way to make up time or not be so picky. Extra time I don't have. That means work rain or shine. The rabbit's done, it smells good. I ate half and I'll eat the rest in the morning. I've got to get four or better in place tomorrow. Time to hit the hay.

Five

I woke up early, got dressed and ate breakfast and went right to work. I started trying different ways of doing things and made up some time, the fourth log was in place and pinned. I started on the two ends again and by noon they were in place. I got one side done. It was fighting me and then I went for the fourth, by 7:30 I was driving the last pin. So I started on an end one. I got most of it carved out when I called it quits for the day. Gee, guess what's for supper. I'll bet it's fish. I know I won't go crazy. I have therapy every day, sawdust therapy. Must go to catch supper, eat and go to bed.

Rise and shine, daylight in the swamp, cock a doodle do. I'm awake. I need to treat myself to something good for a change, coffee, it's been days since I've had some. Must check the snares too. I'll fill my mug and take a walk, nothing yet. Time to make sawdust and wood chips. I finished setting the log I started, pinned it and continued on, one after another. By noon I almost had three in place and by evening I had five and I started on the sixth one. If I keep this up I will have gained several days. If I had a wood chisel and a draw shave, I'd be farther yet. At least I'm on the 13th log, three more and I'll have half of what I cut up. I'll cook up stew for tonight and have half of it. As I waited for the stew to cook I was thinking when I got the other half of the thirty-two logs set. I will be around 4 1/2 feet on the walls. Three more rows I'll be at six feet. I'll need twelve logs for that. The stew is ready and I am hungry and I am going to bed as soon as I can. I've got a lot to do and a short time to get it done. I should sleep. Good night, I told myself as I pulled the covers over me and that was the last thing I remember.

I woke up to the sound of rain. Oh well, I've got pegs to make. I got dressed and slipped on my raingear and cut an armload of willows and set it under the tarp area. Then took a walk to check the snares; no luck, so I went back to camp, removed my raingear and started making pegs. If the rain lets up, I'll start back on the logs. I really need all these pegs, so this time is not wasted. By noon the pile was getting bigger and the rain was still coming down. I ate the rest of the stew and went back to whittling pegs. Around 4:00, the skies were getting brighter. The rain should be ending soon. It was 5:30 when the rain stopped. I was glad of that. I was getting tired of pegmaking. Now I can go after the big sticks, logs. I finished setting the log I started and started on the next ones. Things were going together real good and before I knew it, I had three more done. I wasn't tired so I kept working. When I quit I had another row done, twenty logs so far. It was almost midnight when I sat down. Wow, what a day. I got a lot done. I'm glad I have daylight yet next month. It will be getting dark at night.

When I woke up I had high expectations for the day. First things first, catch some fish for breakfast. I need to get another batch in the smoker. Maybe I'll do that tomorrow. With breakfast done, I checked the snares, nothing. I can't be lucky all the time. The skies were clear and I should get a long way today so let the chips fly.

I think I found my niche on doing these logs. I had four of them set by noon. With every log, the look changes and I was liking the way things looked. I kept up the pace and by 7:00 p.m., I had five more done. I should stop but I've got to keep pushing forward. I got one more set, it was 9:00. I guess I was too tired to think. It seemed the harder I tried the more it fought me. But considering it was the 10th log of the day, I had a reason to be tired, mind and body.

I got the fire going and then went to catch fish for supper and the smoker. The trout I was catching were around the same size as before but my arms felt like they were five pounds heavier, each one. I walked back to camp with twelve trout. I put ten in water and cooked two for supper. My bed was a welcome sight as I closed the tent and climbed in with my belly full. Sleep will come soon.

I woke up laying in the same spot. I didn't move at all. Well let's get back at it. Drag your butt out of bed. The skies looked good for working. I started the fire in the smoke house and added the fish then did a snare check. No luck in that area. I'll use the luck on the cabin. I put more wood on the fire. The smoker will be good for awhile. I've got six logs left then I will have to cut more. It was after 3:00 when I pegged the last one. I checked the smoker one last time. Heat is the only thing needed now. I had a good amount of coals in there so I let it set.

I grabbed my saw and ax to trim and cut more logs, six for the sides and six for the ends after getting the twelve cut. I started cutting the ones I needed to complete the gable ends to the peaks, starting at fourteen feet and shorter as I go up. It was 9:00 by the time I got through cutting out what I wanted. The fire was out in the smoker but the fish was done. I ate two of them and put the rest away. I was glad I would be getting to sleep earlier tonight. A little extra sleep would be good.

When I woke up I felt pretty good and was eager to get started. Today will definitely be a drag. I'll do the long ones first the 18th then the 14th foot. By 2:00 I had the 18th foot one done and started on the rest. So far I felt good. I am in better shape now than when I started days ago. It was 6:30 when the last of the 14-foot ones were at the cabin. The end logs were the only ones left, by 9:45 I was done. I didn't realize how tired I was till after I sat down awhile. I finished my fish and headed for the tent. I had a date with my sleeping bag.

When I woke up there were a few muscles letting me know they were not happy with me and what I had put them through. But after I got moving around it wasn't so bad. I checked the snares and ate breakfast and started back on the cabin. I am going to have to make another ladder shorter than the food shack one, around eight feet will do. The logs are getting high enough, working from the ground is almost impossible. When I get this row done, I'll need to make two saw cuts part way through the log where the windows will be so I can cut it out later. At least I can still get the logs where I want them. Set one end on the wall, pick up the other and slide it up. When I finished the second row it was 8:30. I had enough for the day; a lot of extra lifting and wrestling logs today. I started a small fire and set down to eat. Things are getting high enough now. I'll need to make some stop sticks to help logs from rolling and to keep them in place. The fire felt good as I made my plans for tomorrow. It wasn't long before the eyelids were starting to close and it was bedtime.

Why are the days so long and the nights so short? I asked myself, rubbing the sleep from my eyes. As I got dressed I looked at the calendar. I've been here for two months and it's the 14th day of log cutting and cabin building. A little coffee for breakfast sounds good. Oh waitress, someone fired her. I guess I will have to get my own coffee. I think I caught all the rabbits around here.

The last row, I told myself as I started. I made some stop sticks and nailed them in place. When I got the first log up, the sticks held it so I could control the log. It was 1:00 when I finished the fourth log. I made two saw cuts where the door will be. I changed my holding sticks and started on the front end of the cabin, a fourteen-foot log first. After I set it in place, I set up to do the same to the back end, when I got that one set in place. I needed to cut out the cross log for the center of the cabin which is fourteen feet also. After I got it setting on the two sides it was easy to work with. I got it set at eight feet center and pegged it. It was 5:00, I needed to trim and cut some long logs now. I had picked out some trees that were the size and length I needed, twenty-six feet. I cut one out first to see how I could handle it. It was long and slender like a Hemlock. I picked up one end and pulled. It's going to be a struggle but I think I can handle it. I might even use a short log or two to roll it on. I cut and trimmed the other four and quit for the day. If I can't handle it, I'll do a half lap after I cut it in two.

I got a fire going and cooked up some noodles to go with the fish. When I finished eating I couldn't wait to lay down.

It's morning, it can't be. I just laid down or it seemed like it. I stepped outside and it was partly cloudy. No rain clouds in sight. I ate the last of the smoked fish and started out.

I made it to the cabin with the first log in an hour and a half. The short logs helped. I'll make a couple more as I can pull longer. The second log took an hour. By 1:30, the last one was on site. I've got to get the two sides on first. I've got three areas to notch out. Once I got one end up on the wall, I walked up the ladder. It was easier when I left a one-third of the log hanging over the end then slid it to where I wanted. I will have an 8-foot overhang on the front of the cabin to close in on, two sides to store wood. By noon, I had both side logs in place. Now to start to finish the ends to the peak.

The next log will be just over twelve feet, I could carry that. I marked it out so it would fit against the two side logs and took it down to cut to fit. The third try it slipped in place. I took it down and laid it on the ground. I fitted four more logs against it and nailed two tag sticks to keep everything in place. I then marked the roof angle for cutting. I removed the tag sticks and cut the angle on each one. I was glad I made the log horses. This is the fun part. One by one the logs went up. I nailed and pegged each one. The front of the cabin looked great. I got things set up on the back end of the horse and repeated the same process and before long I was nailing and pegging those logs in place. I stepped back to take a look. What a change from this morning. It was after 7:00. I didn't want to handle anymore big logs today so I set a log up on the horses to start cutting the door casing and threshold plate, after marking out three pieces, 1½ inches thick, six feet long. It's a long cut to make, just follow the lines and let the saw do the work, don't force it. My arm was tired when the fourth cut was made. Then I made the last cut at six feet. The thickest log on that wall is eight inches so I'll cut the side and top at eight inches and the threshold plate at ten inches. It was 9:45 and the door casing board was ready. I didn't bother with a fire. I just wanted to eat and go to bed.

When I got up I felt pretty good. The power of motivation was slow. I definitely need some coffee today. I've potatoes left. I'll fix some and a trout. I'll take a walk to my fast food place, the lake! The potato tasted good. It's been a while since I had a good meal and coffee. I was feeling normal. I moved the snares to a different area. I'll see how that works out.

I'll need to cut the door for today's work. I used fish line and a rock to make a plum bob and marked where the cuts would be. Cutting out one log at a time, I drilled and pegged one log to another to hold them in place. When I got to the bottom I cut and chopped a flat area for the threshold plate, making sure it was a tight fit. I put down pine pitch and grass on the logs and tapped the boards into place and nailed them. Now for my first step into the cabin. I liked it a lot! Looking at the walls, I could see I had a lot of mud chinking to do. Now for the hard part, getting the peak log and the two roof logs in place. I measured and knocked the peak log for the ends and anchored two poles to the side of the cabin and nailed the stop boards in place. I put one end up on the wall so it hung over like the other and put a stop board up to keep it from rolling off. I walked it up unto the top edge of the wall then I tied it off. I still had to get it to the peak yet. I then tied a rope on the log at each end of the cabin around the stop board. I could push and hold it with the rope, changing from end to end. I was a foot and a half from the peak. I will change position and pull it the rest of the way. I got one end up and moved to the other end of the cabin. I pulled the other end up. All I need to do is nail two more stop boards on and slide the log in place and hope my notches fit. Boy, was that a nice sound when it fell in place, a couple of hits and a good fit. I pegged and nailed in place. After a short break, I started on the next roof support log. I measured and notched the log and slid it on the wall like the others. Once I got it up, I could push it up to where I wanted it. I tied it off so I could nail the stop boards on. Then slid the log down and let it drop in place, a little trim and it was looking good. I pegged it and one to go. I set up on the other side of the cabin and got the last roof support log in place. When I finished pegging it, it was 6:30. I used three of the logs from the doorway for braces between the cross support log in the center to the peak log and the two roof support logs. After trimming and cutting each one fit real good. After the pegging was done everything was solid. I was happy the hardest part was done.

It was almost 9:00 when I sat down. I started a fire and enjoyed my supper. After eating, I felt like a drink to celebrate and relax. Things sure are going good so far but there is still a lot to do. My bed was calling so I'd better go join it.

In the morning I knew I was still alive when I went to turn over. There were a few parts of my body doing a mild scream, letting me know that they were not happy. Despite their protest, I got up and stepped outside. The weather looked good and I had another big day ahead of me. I need two fish for breakfast.

The fast food restaurant is open and I am hungry. After I eat I'll check the snares; the new area looked promising. Nothing yet, time to get started.

Today I'll get the log post in and the support on the overhang. I will do a flat lap on the joints for the cross log and the ends with a post. I dug a hole down a foot and a half with stone on the bottom. The post I left so I could move them when I needed but I finally got everything in place. I nailed and pegged and packed the post. I cut and fit the three supports in and I was done and it was only noon. Now to start cutting roof poles: upper end two inches thick and bottom will be three inches, most I will have to trim to size. It will be three inches wide and four per foot. I will need 104 per side 208 total, that's a lot of poles. So I better get started. Let's see, they will be no longer than eight feet, no less than 7½ feet, cut the small end first and measure back to cut to length. It was taking eight to ten minutes per pole, at that rate plus hauling time, six per hour, sixty in ten hours. Maybe seventy per day. It's going to take three days or less. Most of the poles were tops of trees, some limbs. All the trees I am cutting are from the avalanche east of the cabin. When I hauled the last bunch back for the day it was after 9:00 p.m., I got forty-three done. I went to bed right after I ate.

I got an earlier start this morning. Cooked a potato and fish for breakfast and caught a rabbit too. I took care of the meat and went to work.

I was trimming and cutting like a madman all day, hauling branches back to the cabin and back for more. I started the fire and while the rabbit cooked, I was whittling out more pegs. I don't even want to think how many of these things I'll need. It was almost midnight when I fell asleep.

I got up at 6:00 a.m., ate my traditional trout breakfast, checked the snares and started at the poles again. It's looking like we were going to get some rain. I have got seventy-three to go. It started raining at 2:30, another forty-eight done. I got on my raingear and started hauling. I was done by 3:30. The rest of the day will be making pegs. I got an armload of willows and started in. A few boxes of spikes would be nice. Plus I would need a ride to the hardware store anyway. I could even pay in gold, who needs paper or plastic? I'm not crazy to do this hour after hour, just determined. I stopped to eat at 8:00 and made pegs till 1:00. My hands weren't gripping anymore. I've still got several hundred to go; what a thought to fall asleep to.

I woke up to the sound of rain; that meant only one of two things, go back to sleep or make pegs. I can't afford to sleep so I make pegs. So after some stretches and finger exercise, I was ready.

Let the pegs fly. We got mass production going here. One peg at a time. I can see where this day is going. I'm pegging out. If I put up a fence, I could have a peg pen. Have you heard the story about the three little pegs? At least when I get done with these, I'll get a chance to beat every one of them with my hatchet. That makes me feel better. I was glad to hear the rain letting up and the clouds were clearing out. I took off to cut the last twenty-five roof poles. It's 5:00 when I walked in dragging the last bunch. I still had to cut out and fit the short logs between the peak log and to the side edge, four for each end. When I finished the last one it was 8:15. I had to put up a few roof poles. I nailed a bump board on the peek log and trim. I trimmed off any high spot that might poke through the tarp and plastic. I drilled the holes on an angle so the poles won't lift or pull loose. It felt good to drive those pegs with my hatchet. I got six poles in place and it was time to quit. I need to touch up the drill bit with my sharpening stone, it's not cutting like it should.

I got to get another batch of fish for the smoker so I better be off my butt and get going. I can sit more later. I had my twelve trout and walked back to camp. I got ten ready for tomorrow and started cooking the last two. I got out my sharpening stone and in a few minutes, I had the cutting edges razor sharp, drilling will be easier. As I sat eating, I was thinking about tomorrow's work. My hatchet could use a touch up with the stone too. I did that after I finished eating. I was so tired I headed to dream land department, my bed.

I was eager to get started when I woke up. When I was getting dressed I noticed that the belly fat I had was gone. I didn't have a lot to begin with. Damn, I'm one lean, mean working machine. I checked the snares first, then got the smoker started and put in the fish.

Now back to the roof poles. Almost everyone had to be trimmed somewhere. I didn't want the roller coaster look on the edge. I would drill and pin six holes at the bottom first, that took longer. The drill bit couldn't go deep enough into the side log after going through the pole so I had to move the pole and drill deeper before I could drive the peg. Then I would move to the peak, drill and peg. The end of the pole is two inches so I didn't need to drill deeper. For the center log, I grabbed every other one; so far it looks like it will work fine. So far it takes an hour to get six poles down, that equals 1½ feet and twelve feet in eight hours. For a fourteen-hour day, I should cover twenty-one feet. It's 8:00 now, I've got three feet done from last night and this morning. So the race is on now plus I get my chance for payback with every peg I beat in place.

The smoker needs more wood. I've got to keep a closer eye on that. I sure like it when I get a pole I don't have to trim, just pull and drag. The roof is coming along nice so with a break now and then to tend the smoker, time is coming out the way I planned. The fish is looking good. It's time for just heat. I kept the push on to get as many poles on as I could. By 10:00, I was at twenty-four feet total, two feet left and this side of the roof would be done. It was nice to stand inside the cabin and see half the roof done. I got a small fire going and sat down to eat, all the while looking at what I've accomplished in three weeks and there is nine days till September. I ate my fill of fish and put the rest away. It was time for some much needed rest.

I got up early so I could get as much done as I could. It's cooler this morning than normal, an indication of colder days ahead. I checked the snares and ate breakfast, then started on the roof. It's 7:00 now.

I completed the last two feet first then set up to start the other side. I am going to try something a little different. I will peg the top and bottom then go back and peg the center standing on top, that way I won't have to keep moving the ladder. This was working out good, instead of six per hour, I could get ten down, 2½ feet versus 1½ that equals eight hours for twenty feet. I should have this side on in twelve hours or less. Damn I'm good! At least one was in place. Now to drill and peg the center. Drilling from the top will be a lot easier and quicker. I was surprised when I finished at 10:30. What a day! I climbed down and walked inside; it made the cabin look smaller but I liked it a lot. I rested for a while while I was eating. Tomorrow I will cut out the window and make the casing. I was more than glad to climb in bed at that point.

    I overslept, it's 8:00. I was still tired and stiff. A good morning for some coffee. I got the fire going and set the pot on. When the coffee was done, I filled my mug and took a walk to check the snares. On the way there, I saw several moose feeding. I thought to myself when cold weather sets in, I'll be bagging one of you. Nothing in the snares today. When I got back to camp, I was feeling pretty good. I got out my file I brought and did a little sharpening on my saw. It was in need of some TLC.
    I could tell the difference with the first cut. The window I brought back from the plane was fourteen by eighteen inches, the opening in the wall seventeen by twenty-one inches. I drilled and pegged each log of the opening. Now to 1½ inches thick boards for the casing. I applied the pitch and grass and nailed the boards in place. I cut out the trim pieces for both sides. When I got the trim in for one side, I sealed the window with pitch and nailed the rest of the trim. The window was done. I walked inside for a look. It's just as I figured it would be. The railing around the edge of the roof is next to keep the moss in place. I cut boards for the ends of the roof and wired poles to them, one foot up with two rails. It was 5:00 when I finished that. I went up on the roof to round the ends more at the peek of the roof. By 7:00, I was done. The only thing left was to brace and cut where the stove pipe cap will be. The cap will be twenty-four inches by twenty-four inches. The hole will be around twenty by twenty inches. I cut the brace board at thirty-six inches and tied it in place with wire to each roof pole. The hole is two feet from the back wall alongside of the center roof log. It's 9:00 and time to call it quits for the day. I'm climbing into bed right after I eat.
    It felt good to get extra sleep and rest. It was a cool morning. Nothing in the snares so it's time to punch the clock.
    I marked and cut out the stove pipe cap. I then took down the blue tarp. The rescuers had plenty of time to see it. With the tarp being twenty by twenty, I had extra to fold over the

peak and use the tarp over the tent for the rest with overlap. I got the blue tarp in place and put the stove roof cap in place with half under and half out. I had also curved the sides to help channel the water. I used pitch to seal it up. I was ready for moss. I need a two by four piece of sheet metal for a sled. It worked out ok but not the way I wanted. I made a box frame and pressed the metal to it. That worked good. I made sides for it and I could haul twice as much. After making several trips, I didn't have a lot of it covered, packing it tight. The first layer is around six inches thick. I plan for a twelve-inch thick. By the time I quit at 9:00, I had around five feet done on one side. Tomorrow I'll get a lot more done. It will be cut, haul and stick moss.

    The next day I was up at it at 7:00. I'll get a lot done today. I know my legs are getting a workout, dragging the sled and all the trips up and down the ladder, an armful at a time. I had the one side done by noon and started the other side. I had a bigger patch of moss cleared than the size of the roof. This is taking me a lot more effort than I expected. By 8:00 the cabin part was covered. I had the overhang part to go. I'll save that for tomorrow. I stepped inside the cabin, it was dark and you could really see all the chinking I had to do yet. It seemed strange to see my tent without the tarp over it. I have to move everything into the cabin before I go to sleep. I started the fire. I wanted to spend some time to think and watch the flames. It feels like tonight is going to be the coldest night yet. The fire felt good. I will finish the roof first and start mudding the walls. As I watched the fire, I ate my smoked fish and thought about tomorrow. I may wind up putting the tent up inside. As I laid down I made my mind up, that's what I am going to do. I didn't like the tent being out in the open.

    I was stiff and a little sore when I woke up. It had to be in the low 40s. I ate a little fish and got started.

    I only had eight feet of roof to go. It was 11:00 when I packed the last of the moss in place. The skies were starting to cloud up so I emptied the tent and moved everything inside the cabin, tent and all. I hauled in rocks for the stove. I made up a bucket of mud and grass and started chinking around the stove area.

It didn't take long and the bucket was empty and only a small area filled in; it was enough for the stove. I got out my chisel and tools and started building the stove pipe. After getting it cut to size with a 5/8 extra for a right and left hand hook seam, bending the metal was easy with the vise grips and the hatchet. It took a while to make the joint so the pipes would slide together. I used the vise grips to bend the metal upward on the stove pipe cap till the pipe slid through. I put the stove in place and connected the pipes through the roof. I will need to make a vent cap to help keep sparks from getting out and make some kind of pipe damper. It's been raining for a half hour now and it's dry in here. I made another bucket of mud and grass and started packing the seams and gaps. I started a fire in the stove to see how it worked. I had a rock over the lid hole. I didn't put too much wood in at a time because I need a damper to control it better but otherwise it's working good plus it will help the mud to dry. It took five buckets to mud the north end of the cabin. It was 9:00. I got out the solar light and turned one on, not too bad. I set the tent up and made my bed; there was a lot of air going through the cabin; the east end west walls and the south wall are still open spaces yet. Someone left the door open. Oh, I didn't build it yet. It's going to take seven or eight buckets for each east and west wall and five for the south. Then I've got to do the outside. It's getting late and tomorrow's another day to turn and burn. The rain is still coming down and no leaks. I must be doing something right. It took a while to find a comfortable spot in bed but when I did I was out like a light.

Well, my first night in the cabin went well. I'll be able to take down the tent in a few days. It was still raining. I didn't mind, my work is inside for a while. I ate some fish and started playing in the mud. I had an idea last night. I'm going to try adding some ashes to the mud and grass to make it more pasty. It takes time to cut the grass up for mixing. I like the way this is going on. I'll keep it up. I wanted to get the west wall done next. I was right—four buckets done and half filled in; by 2:45 the west was won. I started a fire in the stove to get some heat going to help dry the mud. Then I went after the south wall; by the time I finished it, you could tell the difference. It was 7:00 when I started the east wall, still using ash in the mix. My hands had enough after two buckets. It's 9:30. Tomorrow I'll get the rest of the mudding done There is a lot of area to pitch and seal yet. I can get that later. I was thinking about what I needed to do the next while having something to eat. In the morning, I'll keep on this wall till it's done. I'll keep a fire going in the fire pit. I will need more ash. Well let's get some sleep, there are many more long days ahead.

    I got a little better sleep last night. It's not like my old bed but I'll manage. At least the rain has stopped. I got the fire going in the pit, checked the snares, no luck. I spent an hour getting grass to make mud. I'll need at least two days of fire to get the ash I need. I've got to cut more wood, after two hours I had a nice pile. I started a fire in the stove then made up my first bucket. With each gap I filled, it was getting warmer and the drying was coming along good. I was done with the inside mudding at 3:30. Now it's time to build the door. I set the log I picked out on the horse and laid it out for all the cuts. I was glad I sharpened the saw up because cutting with the grain is a lot harder than cutting across the grain. When I got the four boards cut I needed, the hardest part was done. I had to cut brace boards now for both sides for a Z pattern. I used my knife to smooth and fit the door boards together. It was longer and wider than I needed. I'll cut the size after it's assembled. I used rope and a stick to draw the boards together, using pitch on each joint. Then drilled and pegged the upper and lower brace boards and did the same to the two cross boards completing the Z look. All that's left is cuts to size. The opening was approximately thirty-three inches by six feet. After the cuts were made, I stood the door up in the opening, allowing enough gap for expanding to weather. It was going on 9:00; I'll make the hinges tomorrow. I ate supper and turned in.

    Man, morning came too soon around here. I tell ya, these hands are well callused but I've put them through hell. I got the pit fire going and went to the lake for fast food, two for breakfast and ten for the smoker. I'll start drying fish now to build up my supply for supper for winter. I've got to get back at the mudding process on the outside. The weather looks like it will be nice for awhile. After eating, I fillet the trout and put 'em in the smoker.

Well, it's time to play in the mud again. The outside is going faster because of the mud on the inside stops it and I can fill the gaps quick. I got to keep track of the smoker too. When I am busy, I forget about it. What a difference, it took five buckets to do a side instead of eight on the inside. I did the west side first, then started on the north. It was 7:00 and two sides of the cabin were done. I took a break and ate some smoked fish and started on the door hinges. I made three for the door, 1½ feet long, two inches thick with a hinge area three-inch thick. I cut and shaped them all the same. It was after 9:00, when I gave up for the day. I sat by the fire for a short while till it burnt down. I was by then ready for some serious sleep. I added coals to the smoker and let it go for the night. The inside of the cabin is drying good; by the time it gets fully dry, I will have to do touch ups.

Where have all the hours gone? I remember laying down and now it's morning already. I checked the fish, they're not ready yet. I grabbed a handful for breakfast and got the fire going. Must check the snares before I get started. Well, I'll be damned, it's my luck day. I got a rabbit. I'll be eating good in the neighborhood tonight. I put the rabbit in water.

I started mudding. Damn, it's 8:00 already. I need more grass too. I need about a week of good weather to get drying time I need. I was moving right along on the east side and the end of the wall was getting closer. One more bucket and I will be through and the south side is next. I'll be glad when I am done with this. Record time when I stepped off the ladder, it was 7:30. I'll eat later; if I sit down I'll be done for the night. I want to cut out the hinge blocks tonight and I can hang the door tomorrow; by 8:15 they were ready. I started the fire and proceeding to cook the rabbit. When I finished eating it was bedtime. Got a big day tomorrow, the door.

Good morning north woods. The new kid on the block is awake. The mind is willing and the body is a little slower. The fish were dry like wood and I put them away, checked the snares and started on the door. I mounted the hinges on the door with pegs and nails, pre-drilling was everything. Everything was put in on an angle, less chance of pulling loose. Then put a couple door stops in the casing. I had pre-drilled holes for the nails I will use as hinge pins. I set the door in place and put in wedges, bottom and side and started fastening the hinge blocks. The block was securely fastened. I inserted a spike into the hole and drove it in the rest of the way. I removed the wedge and opened the door, sweet. I opened and closed it several times. I couldn't help but smile, my door had a cabin go to with it. Now to make a handle and a latch. In no time I had the handle cut out. I shaped and smoothed it with my knife. I drilled the holes on an angle and drove a peg in after applying pitch to the holes, nice and solid, no wiggle. The slide bar lock took longer. The bar was twelve inches long, two inches by 1½ inches. I then made two holding collars for the bar to slide in. I drilled a 3/8 hole through the bar and through the door at each end of the stroke. Then I drilled a line of holes between the two on the door, and took my knife to trim out a slot for the pegs. After fastening it to the door, I cut out a board for the bar to slide into. After drilling and pegging it in place, I had a completed working door. The door seat, I'll do on a rainy day.

It was 2:00 p.m. I took time to eat the rest of the rabbit and started back on the moss for the roof. I still had another six inches worth to put on it. The extra will be on the cabin, not the overhang. At 8:00, I had half of one side done. I was tired and needed to catch some more fish too. I got the fire going and in no time I was back with my fast food. I fillet the ten and got them in the smoker, the other two were supper. I haven't run the smoker this late but I will load it with coals before I go to bed. It's after ten and I am ready to crash for the night. It sure was different to see that door in place and knowing it was more secure and quiet too.

I slept real good. A little longer than I planned. It was after 8:00 when I got dressed. I got a fire going in the stove to keep up the drying process. The morning was cool but the skies were clear. Keep the good weather coming, Lord. The smoker was broken into and the fish were gone. With the claw marks and paw prints, it was not what I wanted to see, a wolverine. The baddest pound for pound animal in North America. What I know of them, they have a large range of travel. I just hope he's passing through. I checked for tracks by the food shack and cabin, nothing. I just hope I don't have to deal with him later on. I'll take care of this mess later. I was on moss detail. I had the rest of the moss up on that half by 3:00. I kept up the pace; cutting, loading, hauling, carrying up and stacking. I quit at 9:00. I'll be done tomorrow.

I went to the lake and picked up my order, two fish to go. When the fish were done cooking, I took them inside to eat, thinking about tomorrow, finishing the roof. Let's see today is September 1st. Winter is not far away. If the weather holds out and I keep up the pace, I'll be ready. Good night cabin, I said and fell asleep.

The cabin felt colder this morning. I stepped outside and there was frost on everything. I started right back on the moss detail and by noon, I was packing the last chunk. I got out my roll of plastic and rolled and stretched it out over the roof, using poles to hold it down. I went out to cut nine poles; after a few hours I had enough. I used wire to fasten one end to the side rails with everything held down and all edges tucked in, the roof was done. I'll look at it again in a few weeks.

Now to repair the smoker. Several sticks and some wire and it was good to go. I will start more fish tomorrow. I just won't leave any out at night again. I left and got two for supper, then cooked them up. I ate them by the fire and listened to the woods. It's been a while since I took time for that. It was getting dark for a while at night now. Days are getting shorter and the nights are getting longer. My eyelids are getting heavy so it's time to go to bed.

Morning was waiting when I opened my eyes. Today I will do the easy stuff and give this body a break. First off catch fish for the smoker and breakfast. The fish were ready and I fired up the smoker and cooked breakfast. Today I will pack and seal every seam, joint, crack and crevice there is on the outside of the cabin. The inside is a rainy day project. With a screwdriver I began stuffing, using grass moss pitch. The area of the roof poles took the longest. So between packing and tending the smoker, I kept busy. I was done with the outside by 3:00. I was going to wait on finishing around the door but I'll do that now. I cut out the wood that I'll use for the seal. The rubber seal I got from the plane will work. I will have to trim off part to make it work. I put a dead stop in the upper and lower corners and used the rubber and boards on the rest. It's pretty much tight. I'll keep running heat on the smoker till bedtime and I'll bring 'em in for the night. One last thing to do on the door is making a handle for the inside. It didn't take long. I made one before. I drilled and pegged it and I was done. I've got to keep an eye out for bears a lot more now. They're putting on their last feed before hibernation in October or early November. I was setting by the fire eating my fast food. Thinking that could be dangerous. I need to get the two sides up on the overhang for the wood. It's going to be a long winter too. There are going to be times of extreme cold, ten to twenty below or more; with temps like that, the cold will go right through that wood. I think I figured a way to keep the cabin warmer. Moss on the sides, put poles in the ground up to the sides of the roof around four feet apart and wire poles sideways. I will stuff moss between the framework and the cabin about a foot thick. That should cut the wood consumption in half. It means more work but it will be worth it. I took the fish out of the smoker and brought it in the cabin and went to sleep.

    I woke up thinking about my idea. I'll need twenty poles to do three sides, then cross poles for the sides. This is where all the wire from the plane will come in handy. I put the fish back in the smoker to finish drying and got started. I will do the west side. I got the eight poles in place then started attacking the side poles around six to eight inches apart. I started stuffing moss at two foot when that was full. I put more rails and more moss and packed it right under the eve to the roof poles. It all looks a little strange. I wasn't out here for pretty. I put the fish away and I'll start another batch tomorrow. The air has a chill to it tonight, it definitely feels different. I'll catch a couple fish for supper and go inside to eat. I can take the tent down. I got time to do it. I started a fire in the stove and in no time it was toasty in here. I got my bed inside. I'll make a bed off the ground later on. It didn't take long and the heat was making me sleepy.

The sound of the wood snapping was the only thing I remembered.

I got up and looked out the window, some clouds but windy. There must be a front going through. It's colder out now. It took longer to catch the trout I wanted. The wind made the lake rough. By the time I got the fish ready for the smoker my fingers were getting numb. By the time I got the fire going in the smoker I was enjoying the heat on my hands. I'll cook my fish on the stove. I've got to break it in for cooking on anyway. The warmth of the cabin felt good as I ate. I'll need to make a table top later on. My work awaits me, I announced as I walked out the door. I think I'll get all the poles up first on the east and north side, then start with rails and moss. When I got to the window, I used sticks around it for an opening.

It was time to add more wood to the smoker and I am going to take a break out of the wind. The cabin was getting more soundproof; by the time I get the rest of the moss up it really will be quiet. I don't think I'll do the south end, that will be somewhat protected by the walls and the overhang. Break time is over. I want to get the east side done today. The rest of the afternoon, the temperature was dropping. When I finished the clouds were getting thicker and I could smell snow in the air.

I took some fish out of the smoker for supper and added more wood. It felt warm in the cabin compared to the outside. I started a fire and sat down to eat. If we do get snow, I don't think it will last. After this cold front gets past, it will warm up. I was glad I kept this marathon push up to get the cabin done. It would have been a cold night in the tent if I was outside. It was time to bring the fish in. I'll be in bed by 9:00 tonight. There were snowflakes in the air when I went outside. I was glad to be back in the cabin. The warmth was like a welcome home.

When I got up there was four inches of snow and the wind was a lot less than yesterday. It was still cloudy. No moss packing today. I'll work on the two walls of the overhang. I got the fire going and put in the fish. When these get dried, I'll have around twenty pounds dried. I've got just the logs I need left from the trees I got logs from. These only need to be around eight feet, four to six inches thick. I'll need around forty. I grabbed my ax and saw and headed out. I was dragging two to three at a time. All I need was closer by. By noon I had thirty hauled up. I added more wood to the smoker and went for the rest. After I got the other ten back, I hauled up more firewood for a few hours. At least the snow melted some today.

In the morning I should be able to pick out better spots for the storm. I'll be able to pick out a traveled area better. I cut and split two armloads of wood and took 'em inside, then I got a fire started. The fast food restaurant was open so I stopped by to get supper. Maybe I'll put out a few more snares, more meat for a change won't hurt. After supper I'll need to take the fish out of the smoker and put them away. The skies are clearing and tomorrow should be a sunny day. There is a lot more snow higher up than here. With supper done and the smoker emptied, I sat down and made four more snares. It was time for bed, another big tomorrow.

When I woke up I could see the sunlight coming through the window, good. I thought it would be warmer. I got dressed and went to set up snares. I moved the two I had out and set up the other four. I should have a lot better luck now. It was 9:00 when I got back to the cabin. Today I'll get the two walls up. I first dug a trench to set the ends in, chopped a notch on the upper to fit the support legs, shaping the side for a tight fit. To keep the wall going straight some logs I turned around. It was noon when I finished the west wall. the south took longer because I had to fit them to the peak drilling and pegging each one. By 6:00 I was done. I've got nice area for wood now. It was warm enough today that all the snow was gone. So I'll be back on the moss tomorrow and get the north side of the cabin done. I was thinking about getting into some of the food I've been saving that I brought, but no I'll need it later. I'll eat fish, so with that thought I went and got two. Fresh fish tonight, yum yum. While the fish were cooking, I was figuring how to make a bed, table and shelves. At least I'll have plenty of time to be creative. I've got enough room for more than four cords of wood under the overhang with plenty of room to come and go. I should start cutting wood after I eat. I can do that tomorrow. So far I am ahead of the game on getting things done. I think I'll just set and enjoy. Before I knew it was after 9:00. Early to bed and early to rise makes a man healthy, wealthy and wise. I am. I got all three, right now the first and last count. I woke up feeling good, I had a nice sleep and felt well rested. I got dressed and went outside. It's going to be another nice good day. I wanted to get out and check the snares, it is a good day! I caught two, one in the second and one in the 6th. I'll not be eating fish today or tomorrow. I'll be splitting hares, bad joke but still good. I cleaned them and let 'em set in water.

Now to get the north wall done. I had a couple feet to go to the peak when I took time out to cook and eat. It was my guess it was in the mid-50s outside. I was cooking outside today. There still was snow on the mountains that might stay till next year. I tell ya that rabbit tasted good. It was a welcome change. I ate half and saved the rest for tonight. Now to get that wall done; within an hour the last handful was stuffed.

I could see clouds off in the west. I'll spend the rest of the day cutting firewood. I changed my mind; if I get a day or two of rain, I'll need material to work with for inside. I went out and brought back a couple of logs to make boards. I marked out for one inch thick boards all at seven feet long. The log was almost eleven feet as I made each cut to about ten feet then moved the log to cut the rest. I just need to cut out the legs for the bed. I'll make them two inches by four inches by twenty-four inches. I can cut to size as I build. I took the boards inside and gathered more grass and pitch. It is definitely going to rain, maybe snow too. I cut and split a few armloads of wood and I was done for a day. I got some noodles to go with the rabbit and a handful of veggies. I wanted a celebration meal. It was starting to rain by the end of my meal, so it looks like tomorrow I'll be building my bed. I went to sleep with a full belly and happy mind.

I slept like a baby. I looked outside, still rain so I went back to sleep for a while. When I woke up it was almost 9:30. I got dressed and put on my raingear to check the snares. I couldn't believe the temperature change between inside and outside. It was a cold rain; it's got to be in the 30s. By the time I got back, I was ready for the warmth of the cabin. I brought in the rabbit so I could cook it at lunch time. I started to mark out the boards for the bed. I was out of nails so everything is drilled and pegged. I planned a box bed so I could stuff it with grass; it should make a good cushion for the sleeping bag. It was time to cook the rabbit. I had all of the boards cut out. After I eat, I will use my knife to shave everything smooth. I was enjoying the rabbit because after tonight, it's fish again. I liked the way the bed was going together. The pegs were put in on an angle, fitting nice and tight. The sides were six inches high and from the floor to the top was twenty inches. All the edges were rounded and smooth, same for sides and corners. I filled the box with moss I was sleeping on and the rest with grass. I covered it with my sleeping bag and gave it a test try. I am in heaven! I've got to do something about the area alongside the bed.

After the weather clears, I will cut a bunch of boards and stack them inside for projects this winter. I don't feel like eating yet so I'll start sealing seams, gaps and what have you, so this place will be airtight as possible. The corners filled in quick, the areas by the roof poles took a lot longer. It's after 8:30 and time to quit. My arms are tired of reaching up. I was looking forward to sleeping on my new bed. It felt good and I was off the ground.

Morning was here too fast. It was nice to set on the bed and let my feet hang over the side. When I got dressed, I stepped outside. Still cold and wet, I stepped back inside. I'll get on my raingear and check the snares when I get back. I'll catch a couple trout for breakfast. While checking the snares, I found a log that was torn apart recently from a bear, not a good sign. It's the first bear sign I've seen in quite a while. They're on the move looking for food and it's only a matter of time before one shows up. I may not be as lucky as I was the first time. No rabbit today as I walked back to the cabin, I was looking out for anything out of the ordinary. When I got back to the lake, it's fast food time. I was almost to the cabin, I stopped in my tracks. There in the dirt where I walked in earlier were bear tracks. I had my hand on my gun in a blink of an eye. That son of a bitch followed me back here. I was looking around to see if I could hear or spot him. He's been over by the food shack but not the cabin. It sure gave me an uneasy feeling. I went inside to cook my fish. I was eating and thinking of different ways to protect myself. There was too much rock to dig, a dead fall and I wasn't up to building a fort either. Maybe some kind of fence to detour or slow him down.

Today I'll work inside, get the rest of the sealing done and catch up on a few other things too. It was noon when I finished up, I need my WD40 to get the pitch off my hands. I have to get more water. I am in need of some clean clothes and a much needed body wash. I got my two five-gallon buckets and headed for the spring, the second trip for one more bucket. Both times I felt uneasy like I was being watched and my gut feeling was working overtime. I got back with the water. I've got to move my bells, they are too far from the cabin to hear when I am inside. I've got a bad feeling that bear is going to come back and it won't be a walk in through this time. I hung two bells across the opening of the overhang. The others I'll put elsewhere tomorrow. I am going to make the door more safe too. I made two slide bar locks for the inside three-quarter the way up on both sides of the door with a slide board so I could look out before I opened the door. I almost felt like a prisoner in my own cabin, maybe it's a little paranoia but I don't want to be caught with my pants down either. With that done I started heating water to start washing. I put up a line to hang the clothes on and afterwards, I got washed up. It was getting bad when I could smell myself. I got out my last clean clothes to wear, while the rest dried.

I got out a box of stew for supper. I had one box left. It seemed different moving around the cabin not wearing my gun and knife. The only time I take it off is to sleep. The stew tasted good, it's been a while since. I saved some for tomorrow. I will need to take some of the sheet metal and put in an air vent, a small one in back of the stove. The fire is causing a vacuum in the cabin. I could see and feel the difference when I opened the slide board on the door. I was ready to get some sleep. This is the earliest I've ever laid down, 7:30 and the skies are still light. I laid down and found a sweet spot right away. I hope this rain stops soon. I've got a lot of work to do yet.

I had just dozed off when the bells on the opening sounded out. I was on my feet and my pants were on in a heartbeat. With gun in hand, I was listening; I could hear the bear breathing on the other side. My heart was racing as I listened but he wasn't going away. Then he bounced on the door and I could hear his claws scraping the wood trying to get in. I knew he wasn't going to stop till he got the door open. I yelled as loud as I could. That pissed him off more and he growled and slammed the door more. One thing for sure that bear wanted a piece of my ass. So far the door and locks were holding. If I didn't make my move soon, he would be through the door. I had one chance to do it right and make it count. With my left hand on the slide board and my gun in my right, I waited till I heard his claws at the top of the door. I slid open the board, stuck the barrel of my .357 through and emptied the gun into its chest. All hell broke loose the other side of the door. Things were being knocked over and he slammed the door again. I was reloading when the door was slammed again as I got the barrel out of the opening. The bear bounced off the wall of the overhang and I shot two more times as he stumbled out the open side. I was ready if he came back but everything was quiet. I looked out the opening for at least an half hour, listening for anything, still quiet. It wasn't till after the shooting was done when the shakes started. My heart was still beating fast. I closed the slide board and turned on the light. That's when I spotted the blood spatters on me and the gun. I opened the slide board and there was blood in the opening too. I closed it and sat down. I know that son of a bitch is dead but I am waiting till morning before I go outside. I was wound up. I don't think I ever had adrenalin going like this. I got out the bourbon and took a drink. I sat there playing and replaying all the events in my mind and I knew it wasn't going to be easy to get sleep tonight. One thing for sure, bear is on the menu for a while. I laid there in bed for hours. It was 3:00 the last time I looked at my watch.

I woke up 7:30, got dressed, checked my gun, took a look and opened the door. There was blood everywhere, on the walls, on the door, on the ground and out the opening. I looked around the edge and there he laid face down, thirty feet away. I still walked up slowly, he was dead and he was big! One side of his head was opened up from a bullet. I had to use rope to turn him over on its back. Damn, I need to take pictures. I had hit him with all six rounds, four in the chest, one in the neck and one to the side of the head. They were all almost in a row. I was glad that it's cold out. It will give me time to process the meat.

Now I've got to gut him out. I can't move him so I'll have to do it right here. After I got the guts out and dragged off to the side, I started skinning him out. On his left side there were two more holes behind his leg in his rib cage. When I emptied the rib cage, there was nothing left solid inside. Those hollow points did the job. I removed each hindquarter and hung them in a tree, then I cut out the front shoulders and hung them in a tree. Then I cut out the backstraps and gut loin. Seeing all this meat had made me hungry. I started a fire and cooked the loins. I've had black bear before. This was my first grizzly. Not bad and a welcome change from fish. All the meat is hanging. Now to clean up the mess. My poor door looked like it went through a war. There were scratches, gouges, chunks of wood ripped off. At least the hinges were good. Two pieces of wood were cracked on the latch. The wood pieces I can replace. The rest held up. I was glad I still had the soap water from the night before. I washed the blood off everything, even my shovel scooped up the sand and blood until all the ground was clean, right up to the carcass. I cleaned the hide and hung it up. The hide weighed more than me. I put the backbone and ribs in the fire and added more wood. I dug a hole for the head and blood and guts. After I burned the bones, I will bury them too.

I had to make two more racks for the smoker so I could make jerky and dry the meat to eat later. The temp is around forty degrees so it's perfect to get this done. I filled all three racks and it didn't make a dent in the pile of meat. I'm eating bear steaks tonight. This first batch in the smoker is jerky. I'll keep after this till late tonight. When I sat down for a break it was 6:30. The only thing to bone out yet was the two hindquarters. All the meat I put in the food shack is going to freeze tonight and I'll start at it tomorrow. I removed the bones from the fire and buried them and got two steaks ready to cook. The jerky was looking good. I added coals for heat then started cooking my steaks. The bear was a bit tough but I was tougher. I am going to let the hide hang out. Let it be a warning to others. It was almost 10:00 when I added the last coals to the smoker for the night. Tomorrow I will do dried meat then jerky after that.

I'll be done in four or five days. I was whipped by the time I walked inside. I got the stove going and in no time it was nice and warm. As I laid down, I knew sleep wasn't far behind. What a chain of events these last twenty-four days have been. I wanted adventure and excitement. I am getting it.

When I got up and looked outside, it was frosty out. It had frozen hard during the night. Stepped outside and the frost glistened in the sunlight. I'll go pull up the snares. I don't need them right now. Everything crunched beneath each step I took, disturbing the stillness. I was glad I hadn't caught anything. I didn't need to kill any more at this point.

As soon as I got back to camp, I got a fire going and emptied the smoker. The jerky was good. It needed salt but I was saving what salt I had left. I was getting meat out of the food shack for the smoker and breakfast when I spotted a wolf watching me. I didn't see any others. I wonder if it's the wolf that has been here before. It was neat; he was looking at me and I was looking at him. I think he was more curious than anything, maybe hungry. I turned to cut him a chunk of meat, when I looked he was gone. I didn't feel he was a threat to me at all. I'll leave him this where he was, maybe he'll come back. I climbed down the ladder and put out the meat.

I then went back to my work, with the smoker filled and the fire going; it was my turn to eat. I sure do like the taste of meat cooked over a wood fire. Since I am on smoker detail the next four days, I can make good that time to cut boards and firewood. I spent the rest of the morning dragging logs and limbs up to the cabin plus feeding the fire in the smoker. The colder weather was nice for working. I got out my roasting stick, which I hadn't used yet, sliced some meat about one-quarter inch thick, stuck a couple pieces on the metal roasting stick and cooked it that way over the fire. In a couple minutes they were done. A small pinch of salt and the feast was on. I ate my fill. I'll have to do this more often. It was good! I walked over to where I had put the meat out earlier for the wolf—it was gone. If I see him again, I'll give him more. I knew I can't make him a friend or a pet but maybe an ally, where we could help each other. At least he's taking free food.

I started cutting and splitting wood. I put some poles down in the ground in the overhang to stack the wood on to keep it from freezing to the ground. They say you get three heats from wood: when you haul it; when you cut it; and when you burn it; and it's true. The meat has got enough smoke so it's heat time to finish drying. Before I get back to the wood cutting, I'll put the rest of the bells up around the food shack. So now I've got six on it and two for the cabin. I cut wood the rest of the afternoon. I had a good start on what I will need.

	The evening was calm. I would spend my time by the fire, adding coals to the smoker. The skies were clear and I think I will stay up later and look at the stars since it's dark at night now. I've always enjoyed looking at them since I was a boy. With clear skies and no lights, it should be good. I went inside to put on warmer clothes. It was freezing already. I roasted more meat for supper. I call it bear on a stick. It was calm and quiet. The sound of the fire was the only noise. As the skies got dark, the stars were coming out after all traces of sunlight was gone. The skies were dark; that's when the show begins. I haven't seen stars like these in many many years. The Milky Way was in full display like I've never seen before. It was almost midnight, then I saw them, the Northern Lights had started. I watched them for years but nothing like this—the colors, the brightness and the way they moved. I had chills running up and down my spine and it wasn't from the cold. It was mesmerizing to watch. You just couldn't look away. What a show. Before I knew it, it was 2:30 a.m. I tossed more coals in the smoker and went inside. I got a fire going in the stove and went to sleep.

	When I woke up, the day had started without me. It's after 9:00. Well it was worth it. I went outside, it was calm and frosty. I opened the smoker and the meat was done, hard and dry. I emptied the racks and put away the meat. I was looking to see the wolf again but no luck. I got more meat out and filled the racks again and got the fire going. Gee, I could have fish or bear for breakfast, bear!

	Today I'll start cutting boards. I need to do a little sharpening first. I had two nice logs I dragged up yesterday for boards stock. I intend to have a nice stack for this winter project. So I marked out the first one all one-inch stock and started cutting. It's time consuming, making cuts like this, but I've got plenty of time. It was after 3:00 when I finished the last cut.

My arms needed a short rest. I checked the smoker and its heat time. I was cooking some meat over the fire, thinking about what I had to get done yet. While I was enjoying my food, I was admiring the way the sun was shining on the snow in the higher elevations when I spotted a speck in the sky. It was a small plane many miles away beyond the mountain ridges. I ran and got my can of WD40 and lit off the pile of brush and boughs. In a matter of minutes I had enough smoke in the air that Smoky the Bear would have panicked. The tiny speck of a plane kept going and disappeared behind the mountains. I knew it was a long shot but I had to try. It was the first small plane I've seen. I was bummed out after getting my hopes up like that.

I put my boards in the cabin and kept track of the heat in the smoker. Setting by the fire I got to thinking about my family and what they were doing and how they were feeling not knowing anything about me. Damn it, this is not going to be a pity party. I don't have time or the luxury of those thoughts. Myself is all I need to worry about and do whatever it takes to survive. I'll cut and split wood for a while. I'll go after the boards tomorrow. It was 7:00 when I starting stacking what I cut when I laid down the last piece. The first pile was just over four feet high eight feet long and twelve inches wide. I think I'll have bear for supper. I do make some good choices. When I finished eating I was ready to go in for the night. I loaded the smoker with coals and shut the door. I was cold in the cabin. I hadn't had a fire in the stove all day. In minutes it was nice and warm and I went to sleep.

I woke up tired, even my mind was tired. But I've got work to do so I dragged my butt out of bed and got dressed. I've got two to three days of meat drying yet. Outside I started the fire; it was cold out again. I was glad of that. The meat in the smoker wasn't totally dry yet. I emptied the fire box and when I had enough coals for the fire, I shoveled some in. Two or three hours yet of heat needed. I put up the ladder to get some meat out for breakfast. I was getting ready to shut the door and guess who was watching me? The wolf! I grabbed a chunk of meat I had saved, if he showed up again. I tossed it at him around four feet or so. He took it and left. Well it's a start, I told myself as I climbed down.

After eating breakfast I decided to make some improvements to the food shack. I will use some of the tent material to cover the top and sides so the snow doesn't get in this winter and make some racks to set the meat on. I got out my tent and started my plan of attack. The top will have to be one piece. I'll use wire and pitch to hold it. I need to get the meat out of the smoker and reload it. I took all the meat and fish I dried so far and put it in the cabin. Then I took the rest of the meat out of the food shack and the boxes of dry goods and I put it in the cabin also. It wasn't long before I had the top done. When I got the sides covered, it was ready for winter. I had a few pieces of bear on a stick, then boned out the two hind legs and sliced them up. I saved the bones and the tough parts for the wolf. I'll give him some every time he comes back. So far it's been a good day. I got a visit, a good amount of work done and it's only the middle of the afternoon. It won't take long to make a couple racks and get them up. At 6:00, I was putting food back in the food shack. The meat is still drying. I'll keep the heat going the rest of the evening up till bedtime.

I'll have trout for supper. I don't want to get burnt out on the taste of meat. After supper I will set up the next log to be cut into boards so I can start on it tomorrow. Stayed by the fire till 9:00, then got the stove going and added coals to the smoker. When I came inside it was comfy in the cabin. I set my light back up after charging all day. I got out a few pieces of jerky and laid on my bed. It's been three months today since I came here and I'll be here for a long time too. When the cold weather sets in for good, I will try to get moose. The bears will be denned up hopefully. If I can get one somewhat close and the snow's not too deep, I won't have to drag it, just chop off what I want to eat. It can stay frozen. More work tomorrow. Time for some shuteye.

I can't believe it's morning already. It's the time of year the nights are supposed to be longer. I know what I need is coffee. It's my caffeine level, it's low. Hell, it's been nonexistent. I got the stove going and put in the pot. When that bugger started perking, the whole cabin smelt good. I couldn't wait for that first cup. I think my whole body woke up after that first sip. The weather is still cooperating. I got to get the smoker going, the meat's dry so in with the meat batch. Oh waitress, I'll have bear steak this morning to go with my coffee. You want it, you cook it, somehow I knew it was going to be that way. After I ate my steak, I began cutting boards.

    I am just taking my time today and sit down more. The body is telling me to slow the pace down. I'll be ready when winter comes. The cutting was going quite well. The sound the saw made with each stroke gave off a rhythmic sound in the morning air, great sawdust therapy. I was about to take a break when I noticed I had company, my new friend, the wolf was laying down watching me maybe forty or fifty feet away. He was probably curious but content to watch. I couldn't help but smile to myself. I talked to him in a soft voice: morning, wolf, how you doing today? He still laid there. His head cocked a little when I spoke. I climbed to the food shack and got a piece of meat and tossed it to him. He stayed and ate it and didn't move this time. I wasn't going to push trying to get closer. He was content where he was at and I was at. He watched me cut for a while then he left. I will have to come up with a name other than wolf. His coat was gray with some black and from a distance that I could see him from, he looked like he was still young yet. I wish I knew some Indian names, something fitting for such an animal. Well, since he was watching me, I'll call him Wantalook. Wantalook, I like it. My work had a different feeling, a little happier feel. I was making a friend out here. If Wantalook chooses to get closer it will be his choice. If not that's fine too.

    I finished that log and added coals to the smoker. I wasn't tired so I started cutting firewood. I will need to drag more wood up tomorrow. I had cut up everything I hauled a few days ago. I stacked it with the rest and took the boards inside. I checked the smoker; it wasn't quite hard as wood yet. I had one more batch to do yet so I'll start them in a day or two. So I sat by the fire, enjoyed bear on a stick till the meat was ready to take out. I got the last batch started and went inside. As I started the fire in the stove I thought I really need to get that vent in and make a pipe damper too. I sat on the bed looking at my pile of boards. I'll need more than this to keep me busy this winter. As I laid here waiting for sleep to come I was thinking of Wantalook and was looking forward to seeing him again.

I felt good when I woke up. The body didn't feel like it's been abused. I went outside to start my day. The weather was still cold and the first thing to do was get the fire going in the smoker. I should make smoked fish again, maybe tomorrow. I ordered up two fish from the fast food place for breakfast. The cook had the day off so I did it myself. Today I will haul wood till I have a big pile to work with. I kept looking for Wantalook but he wasn't around. So with saw and ax I headed out. Trimmed and cut till noon. I walked back to camp, took care of the smoker and sat down for a rest. I ate some meat from the smoker; it was cooked, but not dry yet. Break time is over.

Six

Time to make like a mule and get your ass moving. The things that come out of my mouth. I went after the heavy stuff first, the board logs. I had six of those puppies. I kept those at ten feet or so. In a few hours, I had them hauled up. I took a short break and went after the rest. By 7:00 the pile had grown a lot but at least I had everything hauled I cut. I got a fire going and cooked up the last of the fresh meat, enough for morning too. There had been a wind all day but it was calm now. I was enjoying the sit down time while I ate. The cool fall evening along with the fire was my entertainment. If the weather looks good in the morning, I'll catch a bunch of fish to smoke. I was getting relaxed watching the fire dance its last dance, till the embers only glowed. It was time to go in. I started a small fire to warm the cabin and crawled into bed.

    The night seemed short but it was 9:00 when I woke up. The extra sleep I guess I needed. I got a fire going and heated up the last of yesterday's coffee. I filled my mug and went outside. The skies had a few clouds but nothing that looked like rain. Today I will be smoking fish and cutting wood. I grabbed my pole and went fishing. It was fun to catch a bunch of fish again. It wasn't long before I had what I needed. I was on the path from the lake when I spotted Wantalook. I called out his name and held up the fish. When I got to the edge of the camp clearing, I left him a fish. I was hoping he would come more in the open to get it. I was putting the last trout in the smoker when he showed up. I got the fire going in the smoker and got ready to cook mine. He had went back into the brush; I'd see him now and then. I'd call his name every time. I think the fire pit was too close for him. After I ate, I got out a bone with meat on it and set it where I left the fish.

    I then started marking out the first log for boards, still glancing over to see if he showed up. I was about one foot into the first cut and guess who showed up. Matter of fact he laid down and was enjoying himself. I called his name. He stopped, raised his head, looked at me and went right back to eating. I kept on cutting, looking over now and then when I'd stop for a breather, I would talk to him more. He was giving that bone a good working over and when I spoke he had a ear turned in on me. There was thirty feet between us. I knew as long as I stayed where I was, he would stay put. I kept on cutting and at times it looked like he was napping. When I had to add more wood to the smoker he got uneasy and stared at me. When the task was done, I went back to cutting boards and he laid his head down. I was surprised that he stayed around as long as he did, almost two hours.

I kept pushing the saw the rest of the day. I had two logs cut into boards and sat by the fire eating smoked fish. I kept watching for Wantalook but he didn't show up. I took the boards inside and put away the fish. I was ready to head off to dreamland.

I got up early and I was glad I did. I saw a beautiful sunrise. Those clouds were lit up with color. I had warmed up some but still cool. Hell, it might get to fifty degrees today. We are having a heat wave, enjoy it while it lasts. I still had some cooked meat left so I ate that for breakfast and some fish.

I started back on cutting boards. I am having a zoopa party. That is the sound the saw makes—zoopa, zoopa, zoopa. I kept a look out for Wantalook but so far no show. Speaking of shows, I thought mine was a pretty good performance, maybe it was too boring for him. I could try a little song and dance with this next time he shows up. That's alright, our friendship is in the early stages anyway. So I kept up sawing the rest of the day and by the time it was evening I had one log left. I went to the fast food place and picked up two trout to go. Got a fire going in the pit and started cooking. When I finished eating, it was starting to get foggy. I carried in the boards and decided to say in the rest of the night. After the fire was started I laid on the bed; thoughts of my family rushed into my head and the devastation and feeling of loss they are going through. I've been mentally telling my daughter I am alive. I am fine. We've always been close and know each other's feelings. I believe in my heart she knows. I fell asleep.

I was ready to go when I woke up. I looked outside and it was pea soup fog. You could cut it with a knife. Get out the foghorns, thirty feet if you were lucky to see that far. Dead calm and the only sound was the moisture dripping from the trees. It sure gives you a strange uneasy feeling. I started a fire in the pit and the smoke hung in the air. I got out some smoked fish to eat. I could go back to bed but I wanted to work. I'll cut firewood for a while so I spent the morning cutting and splitting wood and the fog still hadn't lifted or thinned out. I had some jerky for lunch. I decided to make and put in the vent for the stove. It felt good to get out of the dampness for awhile. I used my chisel I needed for the vent. I bent and shaped it, punched holes on one end to put wires through to keep out mice. Then cut a slot on the other end so I could slide a piece of metal to control the air flow. I had to move some stones out of the way to get a hole through the wall and slide the vent through. I used a stick to make an opening through the moss and slid it in place. I sealed around it and went outside to repack the moss, then replace the stones. I then removed one section of stove pipe, set up a log on the horses so I could slide the upper end over and cut the slot for the damper plate to slide into. Then I cut out the damper plate, filed and fitted it to the slot and pipe. I'll be able to control how fast the fire burns now. I put the pipes back in place and I was ready for fire. It was a day and night difference with the stove now. I could bring the wood to a slow burn. Another job well done by yours truly.

After cleaning up and putting the tools away, I went back outside to cut and split wood. The fog had lifted some and visibility was around 200 feet. I worked on the wood till into the evening before calling it a day. I sat by the fire eating some fish. I've been looking for Wantalook off and on all day but he didn't show up, maybe he did this for noon. The fog was too thick to see. It's going on 9:00 and it's time to head in. I restarted the fire in the stove and sat on my bed for a while. I was pleased with what I had accomplished today. I liked the even heat coming out of the stove. I laid down, covering up and I was out like a light.

The next morning the cabin was warmer. The wood had burned a whole lot longer and I didn't load the stove heavy either. I got dressed and went outside, the fog was clearing and it should be burned off by noon. It will be a good day to work outside. I got a fire going in the pit then left to catch breakfast. When I returned the fire was ready for cooking. I left a fish out for Wantalook and when I was eating mine he showed up for his. I kept talking to him as I ate, he didn't seem to mind. I got up to get him the other leg bone and meat. He made no effort to move. I tossed it over to him. He got up, moved over to it and laid down to enjoy. He knew I meant him no harm. I sat by the fire a while longer, talking while he ate, turning an ear from time to time as I spoke. It was neat and today we sat twenty feet from each other. I let him know I was getting up to start working and he stayed put. I set up the 6th log and started sawing and Wantalook was content to watch. He stayed around all morning and I was glad for his company. After taking a break and eating lunch I had a couple more cuts to make and I would be through with this one. I needed to clean up around the cutting area. There is getting to be too much sawdust and bark plus I've got to keep the place looking good, I can't have complaints from the neighbors. After that mess was cleaned up and in the fire, I started gathering small stones from the lake for a path into the cabin so less dirt will be tracked in. I feel like I need to do something easier. I could put down a wood floor in the cabin or at least part of it. For now it will be a thought, the necessities come first. It only took eight buckets and the walkway was done. It looked good; hell, in the spring I could make flower beds and start a garden, ya right.

After a short break I started back at the cutting and splitting. I will finish with this pile by evening. When everything was stacked inside, I sat by the fire for fish and jerky. The air was getting a chill to it, like old man winter was announcing he was coming. Without a doubt he would be here in a few weeks and I have to keep cutting and hauling wood. I got another handful of jerky and started a fire in the stove so the cabin would be warm when I came in for the night. The fire was getting down by the time I was done eating the last piece of jerky. It was cold out and time to go in. I added more wood to the stove and laid down to sleep.

I can't believe morning is here already. I slept like a rock. I got the fire restarted and got dressed. When I stepped outside, you could really feel the chill in the air and the wind was starting up. I ordered four trout this morning from the fast food place; I was sure Wantalook would show up to join me for breakfast. I was cooking mine when he did and he's already waiting. He had his gone before I was done cooking. I tossed him a piece of cooked fish and he liked it. It was time to cut and drag wood. When I was trimming and cutting I was surprised to see Wantalook watching me work. He followed me out here. I kept talking to him from time to time and when I started dragging wood back to the cabin, he was walking off to the side. I took a break at the cabin and was tossing him smoked fish as I ate. He stuck around pretty much all afternoon. There were a few times I didn't see him but when I quit for the evening and sat by the fire, Wantalook was there with me. I got some jerky and dried meat. I sat down to eat, tossing pieces to Wantalook. He had laid down about ten feet away and we enjoyed the rest of the evening. It was time to go in and I told him good night. I was sure he would be back in the morning. The cabin was cold but I had the cure for that and in a matter of minutes it was toasty. I laid down thinking about the day and my new friend, Wantalook.

After I got dressed, I couldn't wait to go outside. I didn't see him around. I got the fire going and walked down the path to the lake. It was smoked fish day. I was getting ready for the first cast when Wantalook showed up. I asked him if he overslept and he just looked at me. He sure came to life when the first fish came out of the water. You could see his anticipation in his movements, he was ready to eat. When that fish hit the ground flapping he was on it. When I caught the second he was waiting as I tossed him that one too. After that he was content to wait but he ate two more before we left the lake. I brought back fifteen, two more for breakfast. I started the fire in the smoker and laid the thirteen trout in it. Now I could cook mine. While I was eating, Wantalook was content to watch. I offered him a piece of cooked and his tail started to move even while laying down. I tossed it to him. We still kept our distance. It never got closer than ten feet. I figured when he wants closer, he'll get closer. It was time to make one pile smaller and another pile bigger. The saw he didn't mind. The ax he was not crazy about. He just stayed farther away when I was using it but all in all he didn't mind watching me work. When it was time for a break and a bite to eat, he was ready to take one too. Just wait till I figure how to put him to work. The fish were coming along good and it will be heat time soon.

I was back cutting wood and it looked like Wantalook was taking a nap. I stopped for a break around 3:00. I don't think it got above freezing yet and the way the clouds looked coming in from the west, it was going to snow. I added coals to the smoker and decided to drag up some more wood. I made quite a few trips by 7:00. It was snowing heavier by then. I got the fish out of the smoker. I gave Wantalook a chunk and took the rest inside. The snow was coming down hard and the wind had picked up. It wasn't long before the stove had the cabin warmed up and it was time to eat. It's hard to say how long the storm will last. It might be over by morning or last a day or two. So far I had over half of the hangover filled, part of it to the roof. I started making a measuring stick for when I start work in here. My tackle box had a one to fourteen-inch scale. I used that to make a three-foot ruler. It was after ten when I finished it. I took a look outside and it was coming down hard and heavy. I put more wood in the stove for tonight and went to bed.

When I woke up the wind had stopped. I looked outside, the snow had too. After I got dressed, I took a measure, around ten inches. I need to change to boots for today. There was some snow to remove from the fire pit and got it started again. It sure looked different out with the snow on the ground and on the trees. All the sounds were deadened; it's like soundproofing. I was getting ready to catch some breakfast when Wantalook showed up. He knew where I was going and followed me to the lake. He had his spot picked out, ready for the first fish. He was almost dancing in the snow by the time I got the hook out. I think he forgot where he was in the excitement; when I tossed him the fish he was about five feet away. He backed up after he got it. He was standing back some on the second fish. I dropped it in the same spot and he ate it right there. I was winning his trust. He ate two more and I carried four back to camp. I think the snow perked him up. He was running and jumping having some fun with it. He sat and watched me cook and of course had to have some too. I put the last two fish up for later on. I cleaned off some of the snow and went back to cutting wood. I looked over and Wantalook was laying by the fire next to my chair; he's coming around.

When it was lunch time, I got out smoked fish for me and a raw fish for him. Wantalook got up before I got to my chair. I tried to see if he would take the fish from my hand, not yet. When it touched the ground, he had it. He was eyeballing my fish and I gave him a bite, then went back to work. Wantalook laid back down by the fire. I cut wood till evening, then stacked it inside. I sat by the fire a while and gave Wantalook his fish and I was ready to go in. I was tired. I know after some heat and some eat, the next thing was sleep and it didn't take long.

Wake up sleepy head, I told myself as I rubbed the sleep from my eyes. Drag your butt out of bed. I got dressed. It was time for breakfast. I just had to catch it first. Wantalook was waiting, when I stepped outside. He was happy to see me, tail wagging and all. He even beat me to the lake. You're not hungry this morning, are you? He was so excited waiting for me to get my line in the water. He was like a kid on the last day of school. When I brought the first one in, he was ready. I handed him the fish and he took it. I'll be damned and with each fish I gave him, he took those out of my hand too! I had the four I needed, he already ate his. I went back to camp. The fire felt good on my hands. They were numb, after fishing. The fish were cooking and my fingers were getting back to normal. When I sat down to make my plans for the day, Wantalook moved closer. My hand was on my knee and he sniffed and licked the back of my hand. This was turning out good. It was like he was thanking me. I slowly went to move my hand and he pulled away, not ready to be patted yet but close. I ate my fish and gave him his piece. He took it with a little coaxing. It wasn't as big as a whole fish but he still took it. The weather is good. I will haul wood today and tomorrow. I picked up my saw and ax and started out. I traded off from time to time to cut and trim to hauling. On one of my trips back to the cabin I watched Wantalook marking out his territory. I smiled. I am part of his territory now. Imagine that, I am owned by a wolf. I can live with that. It's better than having a watchdog tied outside.

It was time for lunch and rest some. Wantalook was waiting for his fish and I had mine smoked. I figured I would have all the wood I needed by tomorrow night. One thing nice with the trail made and the snow on the ground, it made dragging wood easier. So the afternoon was more of the same, cut and haul. I had enough for one day by 7:00. I got the fire going in the pit. I was ready for some sit down time. I got myself out some jerky to go with the fish and handed Wantalook his. We both were enjoying the fire so he listened and I talked. He wasn't eager to move anymore. When I got up to add more wood, he laid there and watched. When I sat back down he put his head down. It was time to go in so I told him good night and went inside. I should have came in and got a fire going earlier but it won't take long to warm it up in here. The bed was still cool when I laid down. It warmed up quick and the eyes went shut.

I know why the night goes by so fast, you sleep right through it and it's morning already. Get up. You have a date with a breakfast partner. I got a fire started and got dressed. From what I could see out the window, it looked like another nice day. It was cold and clear when I stepped out. If this keeps up, there will be ice on the lake. Wantalook was waiting and happy to see me as I headed to the lake. There was some area that had ice on it. Wantalook was ready when the first fish came out. I had him eating out of my hand for a second day. He got his four to eat and I carried the rest back to camp. I was getting the feeling back in my fingers, while the fish cooked. Hell, it was cold enough that the eyes on my pole were icing up. I was eating my fish when Wantalook smelt something in the air. He was off in a flash. I couldn't smell anything different but he did. It was either something he liked or didn't like. I got back to cutting and hauling. When it got to be noon I took a break and had some jerky.

The rest of the afternoon I kept watching for him with every trip I made, still no sight of him. I got the last of the wood up by 8:00. I started a fire in the stove and the fire pit. Wantalook wasn't back yet. I ate my smoked fish and sat by the fire till 10:00. I then went inside for the night. I think I'll make a pot of bear stew for tomorrow. I've got dried veggies and noodles. It will be more meat than anything else. I loaded the stove and crawled into bed. It was warm this time.

I barely remember covering up last night. I told myself in the morning. Rise and shine, another day awaits you. After I got dressed, I went outside to greet my friend but Wantalook wasn't around. He must have found a girlfriend or something. I went to get water and got the stew started. I had a piece of dried meat; once you get it moist it was good. The fire was going and I had the pot to the side for slow cook. I looked at the pile of wood from two days of hauling. I will have plenty for this winter. The overhang will be full except where I'll walk. The rest of the poles, I will lean around a tree, if I don't get it cut. I guess it's time for another zoopa party. I've got enough here to party for days. So let's get this party started. The stew was up to a boil. I added noodles and let it set. The wood cutting went on all afternoon. At 5:30 I put the party on hold till tomorrow. My arm needed a rest. I was heating up the stew when Wantalook showed up. I was glad to see him and he was glad to be back too. He licked my hand. He had been eating something. It looked like his belly was full. He laid down and was content to watch me. I added some flour to thicken up the broth; it was ready to eat. I had two bowls of it and there was plenty for tomorrow. It was after 8:00. Wantalook was falling asleep and so was I. I told him good night and went inside. The cabin was warm and I was more than ready to get in bed.

When I woke up my shoulders to my hand hurt, more my arm and shoulders. I knew better than to push myself that hard. I finally got dressed. I kept my hand in my pocket to help keep it from moving. I went outside and greeted Wantalook. I got out the two fish I saved for him. It took him a little longer to eat. They were frozen. I got the fire going and sat down. Wantalook could tell I wasn't myself. He was paying a lot of attention to me and licking my hand. He didn't pull away this time when I patted his head and petted him. What a moment, the bond was made between us. I wish I had a picture of that moment. We spent the rest of the day around the fire sharing food and petting now and then, that he liked more and more. That evening I gave him some of the stew and he cleaned up every bit. It was 9:00 when I came in for the night. It was nice to pet him when I told him good night. I took some more pain relievers and went to bed.

The arm and shoulder felt better when I woke up. I am just not going to handle the saw or anything hard for a few more days. Wantalook was waiting when I came out. After our morning greeting, we headed for the lake. There was light ice on the edge of the lake. I had to go by the stream where there was open water I could get to. Fighting the fish wasn't too hard and Wantalook was glad to get his share. I brought back one quarter to smoke and eat. After breakfast I decided to get more. It looks like there is a storm coming. It may be weeks before I can catch fish again. The ice is safe to get onto. I am guessing what weather and temps are going to be. We might even have a warm spell. I caught and brought back thirty more and by noon it was starting to snow. I felt like laying down a while. I'll see what it's like when I get up. I added more wood to the smoker and went inside. I got up at 2:30 and we had a couple inches of new snow. I checked the smoker, added wood and sat down a while under the overhang. Wantalook is out doing his thing. While watching the snow come down, I couldn't help but think about the winter coming up. The long days and nights and the hard cold; as long as I can get the food I need, I'll be fine. I must have sat there for an hour or more with my thoughts, till the reality of the cold brought me back to the here and now. I was eager to get back inside where I knew it would be warm. The heat felt good as I stood by the stove and before long the chill from the outside was gone. I kept looking at the stack of boards, wanting to start building things for the inside of the cabin. I kept telling myself later, that's for later.

It would soon be time to get the fish out of the smoker and I was ready to eat some too. I put on my coat and went outside. I opened the smoke house door for a look and taste—they were done. Well, look who showed up when the food is ready. Wantalook, where have you been—out chasing a girlfriend? After the greeting was done, I gave him a chunk. He has acquired a taste for smoked fish. I saved out two and put the rest away. I sat under the overhang. Wantalook didn't want to get by me but with a little coaxing and bites of fish he finally sat beside me. He's never been this close to the cabin before that I know of. He was liking the food and petting and it looked like he had gotten used to it. I got out a couple fish and he was glad to get them. I sat out there as long as I could, till the cold won. I had to go in so with the last pat, I told Wantalook good night and went inside. Maybe someday his curiosity to look inside will come but right now we are still taking small steps. I filled the stove for the night and went to bed.

When I got up the next morning I could see the snow was still coming down. I put on extra clothes and went outside. Wantalook was there to greet me. It looked like he spent the night under the overhang, according to the tracks. He was acting playful when I petted him. As I walked toward the food shack, he pushed me, almost knocking me down. You want to play huh? I tried to catch him but he was too fast. He kept challenging me to try. If I moved, he moved. When I stopped, he'd stop. As hard as I tried, he managed to stay out of reach. We had a good game of cat and mouse going. I had to stop and catch my breath. The second I took my eyes off him, he'd knock me down. We rolled and wrestled in the snow and he was winning. I had to quit. I was exhausted. When I stopped I was on my back and he was on top of me. Face to face, he still wanted to play. I told him to quit. I quit, you win! I dropped my arms. I have to admit it was little unnerving, looking at a wolf at point blank but then he started licking my face. I rubbed his ears and laughed. Get off me, you big wolf! You won this one, next time you won't be so lucky. He just looked at me like anytime.

I got him his fish and went to get mine. I grabbed my camera, to get some pictures of him. I got a couple good ones while he was eating. He wanted to check out what I had in my hand that made that noise. I set the timer so I could get some pictures of us together. I took five in all. I should have some good ones.

I put the camera away and sat for a while. Wantalook was laying at my feet. I was thinking about our playtime and the pictures I took.

The snow was letting up and the sun was peeking through now and then. Come on, Wantalook, let's go for a walk. We headed east. I haven't been out there since after I got here. I could see where moose have been feeding before this last snow. It was beautiful out with the snow on the trees and still coming down at times. We were out for two hours by the time we got back. I was ready for some time and a bite to eat. I got the fire going in the pit so I could spend the rest of the afternoon outside. I thought about cutting wood but I'll try tomorrow. Today is a nothing day so the rest of the afternoon and evening was spent eating and enjoying the fire. It was time to go in. I petted Wantalook one last time and went inside. I added more wood to the fire and sat on my bed. It's September 30th tomorrow. Time sure does fly by when you're having fun. I was looking forward to getting back to working tomorrow. I am not used to sitting around. I pulled the covers over me and went to sleep.

When I woke up, I felt pretty good. The arm and shoulder almost normal. As I got dressed I already knew what I wanted to do today. I'll make a pot of bear soup and set out some snares, then cut wood. Wantalook was waiting with wagging tail when I stepped outside. After our morning greeting, I got out the fish for breakfast. When we were finished, Wantalook wanted to play and wasn't taking no for an answer. So I wrestled with him a while till I got him to stop. I picked up the snares and I headed out with my shadow close by. The rabbits were out last night and it didn't take long to find traveled areas. Wantalook stayed back and watched as I set them up. Then we walked back to the cabin. I got a fire going and put a bunch of meat in the pot of water to let it slow cook. Now to test the arm and shoulder—not too bad, just keep it slow and easy.

I had made a lot of progress by noon and I was getting hungry. The meat was falling apart and I added some flour to it. When it was ready to eat, I dished up a bowl. I would have liked to add some salt but I didn't have much left. So I might as well get used to it. Wantalook was enjoying his fish while I ate.

I went back to cutting wood the rest of the afternoon. Wantalook was watching me. I quit around 5:00. I had done enough for today. I put more wood on the fire and sat down. The evening was getting colder and with the skies being clear it was going to be a cold one tonight. Wantalook was waiting for his fish and I gave him some of my meat too. Afterwards we stayed by the fire and enjoyed each other's company. It was time to go in for the night. I petted him on the head and said good night. It was nice inside the cabin. I sat on the bed a while and ate a piece of jerky and went to sleep.

It was cold and crisp when I stepped outside. Wantalook was waiting for his morning greeting and his share of food. After we ate it was time to check the snares. Wantalook was like a kid on Christmas morning when I held up the first rabbit. He wanted a piece of that. I had caught one more before heading back and Wantalook danced around me all the way back. He was eager to get the leftovers when I dressed them out. We got fresh meat for two days now.

The air was getting warmer as the day went on, by afternoon it was above freezing. I kept the wood cutting up all day and the warmer weather was a welcome change. Maybe we'll get an Indian Summer. When I quit that evening, it was still nice out and I was looking forward to setting by the fire after supper. I think Wantalook's mouth was watering while I was cooking the rabbit. He stared at it from start to finish. I had the back legs and he had the rest. Later on I got him a fish to eat while I had some smoked. It was dark out and I was watching the stars. Wantalook kept looking up but didn't understand what I was looking at. I was waiting to see the Northern Lights. It was 11:00 by now. It doesn't look like there will be a light show tonight and I was tired. I gave Wantalook his petting and went in for the night. That bed was calling me for a couple hours now. When I laid down closing my eyes was the last thing I remember.

That bed felt good when I woke up. I just wanted to lay there but things don't get done by themselves. I laid there for a few more minutes and dragged my butt out of bed. I was surprised how nice it was when I got outside. It's going to be another day above freezing. Wantalook was waiting for me like usual to get his petting and a bit of play too. I got him his fish and I had some jerky. When it was time to check the snares, he was ready and full of piss and vinegar. On the way out he was trying to get me to chase him, running, jumping, bumping me, just being a pain. This went on for several hundred yards and I caught him off guard. I snatched him off his feet and held on tight, my face buried in his fur at the back of his neck and my arms around his chest. He struggled some but soon gave up. "I won this one!" I said as I let him go. I petted his head and he licked my hands. It was a truce for now. There was nothing in the snares and we walked back to the cabin.

We were within a hundred feet of the cabin when Wantalook was all over camp with an attitude to kick ass. It didn't take long to see what had him pissed. There were fresh wolverine tracks by the base of the food shack and smoker. Then I saw tracks going to and from the cabin. He didn't get in but the little bastard pissed all over the cabin door and the wood under the overhang. Damn, did it stink. He just declared war on himself. By now Wantalook was nowhere around. I don't think the two would fight. I think he wants to make sure he's out of the area. I started the fire in the pit and washed down the door and any other piss spots I could see. If I get a chance to get that son of a bitch in my sights, he's history. I was cutting wood a couple hours when Wantalook showed up. He was busy remarking his territory around camp. When he was satisfied then he came to greet me. He looked OK. So I knew he wasn't hurt.

I went back to cutting wood and Wantalook was laying down watching. The snow's been melting all forenoon; it felt like it was about fifty degrees now. It was time for a break and some lunch. The sunshine felt good as we ate our fish. I just hope the warm spell will last a while. The overhang was getting full and tomorrow the wood cutting will be done. It was 6:00 and I had done enough for today. A lot of the lake was open. I might be able to do some fishing tomorrow. Now it's time to sit by the fire and enjoy the evening. The snow was off the trees and they stood out against the background of white on the mountains with the blue sky. The evening air was cooling and the sound of the fire is all I heard. My thoughts went back to this morning and the wolverine. I know it will be back, it's a matter of when. While we were eating our rabbit, I noticed Wantalook was restless like he had somewhere to go. I know he's got a hot date tonight. It was almost 8:00 and I planned to get to bed early tonight. I gave Wantalook his petting and went inside. I could still smell where that wolverine had pissed. It's going to take days till it goes away. I think I'll need a little more locking from the outside. The slide latch alone is not enough. I added more wood to the stove for the night. I was thinking if that wolverine gets into the food shack or the cabin, I'll be screwed for the winter. I am going to do whatever I can to not let that happen. I laid a while thinking about what I can do till I fell asleep.

    I woke up eager to get the day started and get things accomplished. I got dressed and headed outside for my morning greeting with Wantalook but he was nowhere around. I am going to have a long talk with that wolf about not coming home and staying out all night as if I thought that is going to work. The temperature was below freezing—only mid to upper 20s. I got the fire started in the pit and was warming my hands. I might as well go check the snares. I put two logs against the door of the cabin in case that wolverine comes back.
    When I got to the area where the snares were, every one was gone or destroyed. I could tell by the tracks and the smell who was responsible as I examined the tracks closer; there were two. Shit, this is not good. I immediately headed back to the cabin. Thankfully they didn't show up while I was gone. I know damn well they are not going to leave me alone. I got a pot of bear meat ready and put it on the fire to start cooking. I got my saw and some wood out to make a swing latch for the door with a locking peg. It took over an hour and it was in place and working fine. I was taking a break by the fire trying to figure what I will do about the food shack. I can't do anything on the ground because of Wantalook. By the way, where is that wolf? Well I can do one of two things or both—sharpen pegs in four trees and put snares on the tree. I think I'll do both. They started this war and I will finish it.
    So I started making pegs. I think I've done this before at least one or two. I spent the rest of the morning making pegs

and took time to eat lunch. Wantalook still wasn't back yet. It was starting to concern me some but he was a big boy and could take care of himself. I got out my shorter ladder and started drilling and pounding in pegs. I drilled the holes on an angle of about twenty-five degrees and offset each peg keeping 2½ inch space between each one. When I finished I had forty pegs in each tree eight feet off the ground. I have to admit it looked nasty. Next I cut one pole to extend the platform by four feet beyond each tree. That will be tomorrow's project. I added more wood to the fire and sat down to eat. Wantalook was still not back. I put the rest of the food away and sat by the fire for a few hours till it was time for bed. I banked the stove for the night and went to sleep.

    I laid there a while before getting up. I had found a sweet spot and didn't want to move. Thinking about the work I needed to get done, I got up. I had my battle plan in my head and I was ready to get started. Well look who decided to come home, I said when I opened the door. Wantalook was dancing on his toes waiting to greet me. I was happy to see him too. Our greeting was a lively one. He couldn't get close enough, almost knocking me down several times. I got out the rest of the fish for him and he didn't waste any time eating every bite. I got the fire started and put the pot on to heat. The lake was open so I'll get some fishing in today. I ate my breakfast and started back on the food shack. Each pole sticking out was sharpened to a point. I put three snares on each tree above the sharpened pegs and the poles. All I need is to catch a front or back leg and they will spend the rest of the time impaling themselves on the pegs. There were no other trees close so they can't jump onto the platform. With that job well done, it's time to go fishing. When Wantalook saw the pole he knew where we were going. He was bouncing on the shore waiting for the first fish. I had to keep turning away till I got the hook out. By the time he got the third one he had slowed down considerably. I got the ones I needed to smoke and the rest for us to eat. When I got back I loaded the smoker and got the fire going and shut the door. I put the rest of the fish in the food shack. I won't be finished with the smoking by tonight. I'll put them up here as well.

I might as well get the rest of the woodcutting done. It's a nice afternoon for it. Wantalook was taking a nap while I worked. I guess he's worn out from running around the countryside. The overhang was full and I leaned the rest of the logs on end against a tree so I could get at them later if I needed them. I need to feed the smoker some more wood then I'll cook me up some fish. Wantalook was making sure his property markings were fresh and joined me right after I sat down. He wanted a little loving and I was the right person to give it to him. He just sat there and took all the scratching and petting I could dish out. I got us two fish each. I started cooking mine and Wantalook ate one of his. Oh now your belly's full. He just looked at me like oh please. I sat down to eat mine and he did eat his last one; maybe he didn't want to eat alone. We sat by the fire till after dark. It was time to put away the fish and get to bed. I figured as long as Wantalook is around the wolverines won't come back. We'll take a walk in the morning and see if they would try for the food shack. I gave Wantalook his petting and went in for the night. I was tired and as soon as the stove was ready for the night so was I. I didn't take long to find a sweet spot and it was lights out.

Damn it's morning already. It seemed like I just laid down. I sat on the edge of the bed a while trying to get the cobwebs out. Well, time to get the show on the road. I got dressed and headed out the door. Wantalook was waiting and glad to see me. I got the fire going and heated up the last of the meat while Wantalook ate his fish. After I ate we headed out for a walk and to find new areas to put snares at. I was guessing that the wolverines would show up at camp. We were out for over an hour before we started back. I was within a hundred yards of camp when we heard the noise. Wantalook took off and I was right behind. I knew I had caught one. Wantalook was at a stand-off with one on the ground while the other was caught under the food shack. I tried to get a shot at the one on the ground. I didn't want Wantalook to tangle with it. The sucker zigged when I zagged and I missed. Wantalook went one way and the wolverine went another.

He had not heard my gun before and it surprised the hell out of him. The one caught in the tree was still screaming its growl. I drew a bead on its head and squeezed that trigger. That one is dead. It took a bit of reassurance he was fine. I let him smell the gun too. I got the ladder out and took the wolverine down, a female. I wished I hadn't missed the other now. We followed his tracks for a while. He was going away, no turns, no doubling back. We got back to camp and I wasn't sure what I was going to do with it. I put the fish back in the smoker. They needed a couple more hours to be done. I thought about skinning the wolverine and put the hide on the end of the overhang with the bear hide or hang it in a tree outside of camp for a warning to others. I know the other is going to come back and those two options could piss him off more. I think the best thing to do is destroy it. I'll burn it and bury what is left. I was glad the wind was blowing away from camp till the hair was gone. I had plenty of wood and a lot of flame. I repaired the snares on the tree so that would be ready for round two. It may take a day or two or even weeks but he'll be back and with an attitude.

Wantalook and I went to the lake for more fish. I let him eat his fill and brought four back. The smoked fish was ready to take out and I had some for lunch and put the rest away. I sure was enjoying the warmer temperature. This warming spell wasn't going to last too many more days. I did a little cleanup around camp and kept the fire burning hot. I dug a hole to bury what was left which wasn't much. The smell's been gone for over an hour. I figure a few bones is all that will be left. I sat by the fire till all that was left was coals and picked out the bones and buried them.

I built the fire back up and sat patting Wantalook and thinking it's been quite a day so far. I want to make use of the bear hide yet, since the weather's good. I might as well get started. I cut the hide into two halves so it would be easier to handle. I got on my boots and took them down to the lake. I submerged them in the water and held then down with rocks. The water will soften the hide up and make it easier to remove the hair. I hope to make snowshoes this winter and I'll have hide strips for tying things. I sat down and removed my boots and put them back in the cabin. I got Wantalook his fish and I ate mine smoked. I wish I could do more to protect the cabin and campsite but I can't for Wantalook's safety. I sat by the fire the rest of the evening taking in all there was to see and enjoying. It was time to head in. I gave Wantalook his petting and went inside. I got the fire going in the stove and laid there thinking till I fell asleep.

I slept in this morning. I woke up earlier but the bed was feeling too good to get up then. It was 8:30 when I got my clothes on. When I went outside, Wantalook was acting like he hadn't seen me for a week. After our morning ritual of petting and wrestling around was over, we went to the lake for fish. I still had two left at camp so I brought back four and Wantalook ate his. I cooked two for breakfast and the rest I'll hand out at lunch and supper.

When breakfast was over, I set up an area away from camp to work on the hides when they were ready. If I did it in camp there would be hair everywhere. I was enjoying the morning. It was going to be another day above freezing. The smoke from the fire was going straight up and drifted through the tree tops as I sat there. The peace and quiet of this place along with the scenery gives a person a chance to appreciate everything else there is. Thoughts of my family always comes up: the great conversations, the warmth of a hug and the loving touch that bonds people together. They got to know I am still alive. I know they won't give up. I sure don't have a clue why no one has come to get me. I may never know. Well I don't need to be going down that road.

I need to get up and do something. I guess I could cut some green wood for the snowshoes and peg them in the shape I want them to dry. I found four limbs to work with very little knots. I then cut and trimmed them to size and length of five feet. I got out a board, drilled and pegged to bend the wood around. I used hot water to make the wood more flexible. It took several hours to achieve what I wanted. Now to let them dry in the cabin. Tomorrow I'll start removing hair. The weather is still looking good. It was getting toward evening and I was getting hungry. I gave Wantalook his fish and sat down to eat mine. We sat by the fire an hour or so till it was time to go to bed. I could smell the green wood as I entered the cabin. It was a nice change. The stove is going good. It's time for some sleep.

When morning came I awoke with an ambition of taking on the world. I felt good and couldn't wait to get started. I could see that it was going to be another nice day when I stepped out the door. Wantalook was his happy to see ya self and the petting wasn't enough, he wanted to play. When I saw he wasn't taking no for an answer the game was on. We chased each other, pushed and challenged and never quite gave me the chance to grab him. He tried his best to knock me down and almost did several times. We must have kept this up for ten minutes or more. I tried calling a truce but he wanted to win. He managed to trip me and when I hit the ground, he had me pinned before I could find my feet. No matter what I tried he made sure I was staying put. I had to give up. I was out of breath when I let him know he won. I petted him and laughed. He licked my face and let me up. I told him, he's got two wins, I got one win. He was still full of piss and vinegar on our way to the lake. He finally started to settle down after the first fish. He was settled down fully by the fourth fish and was content to watch me catch the rest.

I made a fire as soon as we got back. I cooked up two trout for me. My plans for today is remove hair from the hide right after I eat. With my stomach full, I got on my boots to get the first hide out. Holy crap, that sucker is heavy. I had all I could do to drag it out of the water. I let it drain in for a while and it was still a fight to get it to where I was going to work on it. I got it draped over a trunk of a downed tree and took a short breather. Wantalook was having fun watching me struggle and at one point wanted to play tug of war. I never tried working a hide before so this will be new to me. I soon found out there was nothing easy about removing hair. The way it's going, I'll be lucky to get this one done by the end of the day. I wound up using a board to have a flatter surface to work on. I had to keep the edge sharp on my knife all the time. The things I get myself into.

It was noon and my fingers needed a break. I think the only part of me that doesn't have hair on is my hat. It felt good to set a while and after lunch I was right back at it. How in the hell did people do this years ago? I fought for every inch the rest of the afternoon into the evening before I was done. What a hell of a job.

I gave Wantalook his fish and restarted the fire and sat down. The heat felt good as I warmed my back and hands. At this point I was not looking forward to doing the same thing tomorrow but I've got to get it done while the weather is good and this warm spell is not going to last long. I ate my smoked fish and set back in my chair to enjoy the rest of the evening. When I did get up I was stiff, not a good sign for tomorrow morning. I gave Wantalook his petting and went inside. I put more wood in the stove and crawled into bed.

I couldn't even close my hands when I woke up. I laid there and kept rubbing and bending my fingers till I could move them. The rest of me wasn't doing much better. By the time I got outside, Wantalook was waiting. The first thing I said was, you win. I give up, no contest. I think he could tell I wasn't myself and just petting will do. The sky to the east was red from the sun. We got bad weather coming so I've got today to get the other half of the hide done. I got a fire going and the heat helped getting things back into working order. I was on a mission after I ate; I was started. This one wasn't any lighter or easier than the last and I was determined to get it done today.

Wantalook was out and about all day. He stopped by to check on me now and then. The sky was clouding up more and as the day went on you could feel the dampness in the air. Around 5:00, I had to stop to put on my raingear. It had gotten colder and I needed a couple hours to finish up.

It was after 7:00 when I stepped inside the cabin. Wantalook was gone somewhere and I couldn't set out. Now to get the fire going in the stove. I was tired, cold and wet. After getting cleaned up and clothes hung, I just stood by the stove a while absorbing the heat. I ate some fish and laid down. I was glad that I was done with that past. I was tired but the arms and hands just wouldn't give me any relief so I got up and took some pain relief medicine and laid back down. They were feeling better after a while and I drifted off to sleep.

I slept so soundly if there was an earthquake I missed it. I just laid there a while. I didn't want to move. The next thing I knew I was waking up again. I looked at my watch—it was after 9:00. I sat on the edge of the bed working my hands and fingers. I think coffee would be a nice change for today. I could see it was still raining out so I put the pot on the stove. I stepped outside to greet Wantalook and he was not around. I stepped to the edge of the overhang and looked around. I still didn't see him. Then I noticed the smoker was tore up and broken. I slipped on my rain jacket to investigate. I didn't take long to figure out who was the culprit. Between the teeth and claw marks and the smell, the wolverine was back. Well it has started. I checked the food shack, everything was good. The smoker will have to be totally rebuilt. What he couldn't rip and chew apart, he pissed on the rest.

I'll go in and have some coffee and think about all this. The first time he comes around when Wantalook and I was gone. Now he's come around when I was here; maybe he didn't know I was here. One thing for sure, he'll be back. I need to take time out to enjoy my coffee and I did. It's been weeks and I was enjoying every drop. I put the rest of the coffee in my thermos and went outside to take apart the smoker and burn it, saving what wire and nails I used to build it. I will build a better one next time. The first thing I've got to get this son of a bitch. The only way this son of a bitch will stop is when I am gone for good or he is dead. I know I will be able to outthink him. I will have to make him believe I am gone when I am not.

I emptied the ashes out of the fire box area and rinsed the stones. The air and rain will do the rest. It was lunch time when I finished. I put the pot on the stove with a pound or two of meat and ate smoked fish for lunch. There are only two places left that wolverine will go for, the food shack and this cabin. My guess is the cabin. I've got a spruce tree off the back of the cabin. I'll make a tree blind in it. I'll do a little at a time so it will look natural and I'll clear a path so I can double back when I leave the camp. I got on my raingear and went to check out the tree. There was a spot about ten feet up, that would work fine. I cut some poles to tie on to, two limbs for a platform. When I got them securely fastened, I climbed on it. I had a good view of the side and back of the cabin. All I need is some boughs for the side and a couple for the front and it would be done. I got down and looked at it from different angles. It looked normal. I then cut some spruce boughs and tied them in place. It still looked normal. I was happy with it. I then made a path from the tree around the cabin to the trail that heads out of camp.

I was putting things away when Wantalook showed up. After our greeting, he went to where the smokehouse was and smelt around. You could tell he didn't like it and his attitude had changed. His space had been invaded and he didn't like it. With Wantalook back the wolverine won't come around, at least I hope. He was enjoying his petting but his attention was on the woods, listening and smelling. He wanted a piece of that wolverine and so did I before he did. I wasn't going to do anymore today, rest was in order. I just remembered I need to get some fish so we went down the lake. I made sure Wantalook had his fill and brought back eight for a couple days' worth. The rain was changing into snow by now.

When we got back to camp, I put the fish away and I had bear meat for supper. I sat out with Wantalook for a while till after dark. I was getting cold so I gave him his petting and went inside. The warmth of the cabin felt good. I stood by the stove until my chill from the dampness was gone. With this new snow will give me the advantage to find out where the wolverine is coming from, if he's got an area where he is watching or any pattern of travel. When he makes a mistake, I'll be there to take him out.

It was still snowing when I got up and Wantalook was waiting. He had never left the overhang area all night. He was his happy to see ya, want to knock you down self this morning. We played for a while till he let me get him his food and we ate breakfast. So far the wind hasn't come up and it's a light steady snow. We took a walk. I wanted to see if I could find tracks. We were about one-third mile from camp when I found tracks an hour or two old. They were heading toward the cabin. I followed the tracks to a tree when he went up and came back down, then I proceeded toward the cabin. The little bastard's been watching. Wantalook beat me back. He had tried to get in. There were tracks by the food shack but nothing touched. The cabin was another thing. He not only chewed everything on the door latch and hinges but he dug the mud chinking from between the logs a couple feet up and he pissed all over everything. I won't track him. I'll let him think he got away with it. I spent the rest of the morning remudding the logs and cleaning up what I could. Wantalook was out on his own. I think he was trying to find him.

That wolverine will head out a few miles and double back. I hung a fish in the opening of the overhang. I got on warm clothes and headed out so I could sneak back to the tree blind. I sat there the rest of the afternoon. Just before dark here, he came sneaking in the same way he had come in earlier that day. That fish kept his attention. I knew I had one shot at twenty-five feet. I had a bead on his chest and squeezed the trigger. All hell broke loose for the next few seconds, flopping around, blood everywhere and took off the way he came. I knew he didn't go far. I got down and where he was standing when I shot, there was blood, meat, fur, hide and parts of lung on the ground. I blew a hole in him so bad, no way in hell he would live. I got my light out and started following the blood trail. He was laying about fifty feet from where I shot him. I held the gun on his head and poked him with a stick. He was dead. I turned him over and there was a 3-inch hole on his left side of his chest, broken ribs and shoulder, and from what I could see his lungs were totally destroyed. Now maybe life can get back to normal. First the bear and two wolverines. I just want to be left alone so I can survive the upcoming winter in peace.

I got back to camp and Wantalook showed up. He tore into that wolverine just for spite and to get his revenge for violating his space. I cleaned up what I could by the cabin and hung the wolverine in a tree till tomorrow. We sat under the overhang for a while, shared some smoked fish together and looked into the darkness. This time, Wantalook, we won! As I said it I patted his side. He looked at me as if to say, you are right. It's been quite the eventful day and I was looking forward to getting back to a normal routine again. I gave Wantalook his last petting for the night and went inside. I've got some mudding to do in here tomorrow and some latch repair. I loaded the stove and slid into bed. I laid there thinking about the events of today. I was glad it was over. I can leave camp now and not have to worry about things being torn up.

I was feeling good when I woke up and more relaxed than I have been. It was still snowing when I looked out the window. It wasn't windy, just a steady snow. When I stepped outside then I could tell how much snow had fallen, about a foot's worth. Wantalook was waiting for his morning greeting and playtime. I don't know if it's the fresh snow or what but that wolf is wound up like a clock this morning. He was running circles around me, diving in, trying to knock me down, and I am trying to grab him when he gets close enough. One time I almost had him. He twisted out of my grip, damn he's fast. He got his chance when I slipped. He knocked me in the snow so quick. I didn't even get a chance to do anything. I was pinned face down. I played opossum. He sniffed and licked my head. I still did not move, and then he nudged me with his nose and used his paw. I still did not move as I watched him out of the corner of my eye. I waited for my chance to grab him. When I got my chance, you would have thought someone lit a firecracker under him. He jumped and I grabbed and rolled; I was on top of him. I started laughing so hard I couldn't hardly hold him. He licked my face and I got up. I won that one! Wantalook, that's not fair, all you do is shake it off. I am in need of some serious snow removal. I had snow up my sleeves, down my neck, inside my jacket, even in my pants pockets. I had to go in and get dry clothes on.

After changing, I put on my raincoat and grabbed my pole; we needed fish. The lake was covered with snow and slush. I had to go down by the stream for open water. The fishing was a lot slower. I couldn't cast very far out. It took till noon to catch thirty fish to bring back. Wantalook was piggy this morning, he ate six. By the time I got back I needed to get my hands warmed up. The raincoat worked well keeping the snow off me. I had some smoked fish while I warmed up. I wanted to get started rebuilding the smoke house. I cleaned nineteen fish for smoking, the other twenty I put away. I spent the afternoon getting the poles I needed for the smoker. Then started putting up the sides and framework. It was getting dark so I quit for the day. The snow was still coming down and I got a couple fish out for Wantalook and I finished the last of the smoked fish. The wind had started, the tops of the trees were shedding their snow. I was tired and wanted to get out of the cold. I petted Wantalook one last time and stepped inside. Well it looks like winter has arrived. I loaded the stove and sat on the bed, enjoying the heat. If it stays cold now, I'll try to get a moose in a few weeks. The bears should be denned up by then. I've had enough animal confrontations to last me the rest of my life. I hung up my socks and liners to my boots and stuffed newspaper inside the boots. My bed was calling me, it was time for some sleep.

Good morning northwoods, I called out as I got out of bed. I could hear the wind in the trees and when I looked out the window, white is all I could see. Not a day to spend outside. I got dressed and stepped outside. Wow, there was snow flying everywhere. Wantalook was waiting for me. After our morning petting was done, I got his fish out of the food shack. The wind and snow as intense. I was glad to be back under the protection of the overhang. I sat with Wantalook till he finished eating, then I went inside. I think I'll make bear soup today. I got out the pot and dried meat and sat it on the stove to start cooking. The TV reception is bad today. The weather and outdoors channels are snowy and the rest are no better. I made up more mud and grass to fill in where the wolverine messed up the wall. It took me a couple hours to make the repairs. I was taking my time. I put on my hat and went outside to spend some time with Wantalook. With the coat he's got he is right at home when it's cold. I spent a good hour setting with him watching the snow swirl around the end of the cabin. I like it when he rests his head on my leg and takes all the petting and ear scratching I can hand out. He was truly a friend and there wouldn't be a thing I wouldn't do for him. I think he would do the same for me. I was getting chilled and I needed to go inside for awhile. I tried to coax him to come in but he only comes as far as the doorway.

I ate some soup and decided to make a coat rack. I definitely need one. I had a slab of quarter inch round that will work just fine. I cut it to fit between the door and the west wall. I removed the bark and smoothed it with my knife. The wood was almost eight inches wide. I cut 1½ inches off one side for a flat edge. I then cut a board the same length for a shelf. I used my knife to smooth the surfaces. I will be shaving the wood with the right edge on the knife, it will make it smoother than if you used sand paper. I made two support pegs for each end from the quarter inch round to the bottom of the shelf and pegged the shelf to the one-quarter round. I put five pegs in the quarter inch round to hang things and fastened it to the wall. It looked nice—my first piece of home improvement. It was nice being able to hang my coat and stuff and set things on the shelf and this is only a taste of what's to come for the rest of the inside.

It was time for supper. I put on my coat that was hanging on the peg, convenient. I liked it and went outside. I got Wantalook his fish and got myself a bowl of meat and soup and sat there with him. I shared my meat with him and you couldn't believe how gentle he would be taking food out of my hand. He was setting, leaning against my leg, happy to be next to me. I stayed outside although soon I was getting cold and went in for the rest of the night. It sure was nice to hang a coat up instead of flopping it down somewhere. I filled up the stove for the night and got into bed.

In the morning I could see the snow had stopped. I could work outside now. I got dressed and went out. Wantalook was out somewhere. It looked like he left right after the snow ended. First I've got to clear some snow out of the way. After clearing a path from the cabin to the food shack and fire pit, I cleared out around the smokehouse. I needed to make a push board or something. This point shovel doesn't quite get it. We had fifteen to eighteen inches of snow not counting the drifted areas. I cleaned the snow out of the fire pit and got a fire going. I was warmed up from all the shoveling but a fire always feels good. After a short rest, I started back on the smoke house.

It was noon and time to eat. I was coming right along on the walls and by tonight I shall have the roof and doors on. When I finished eating Wantalook was not back yet. He'll be hungry when he does show up. I started cutting quarter-inch logs in two length ways for the roof and door. That took most of the afternoon. I had to trim the sides of each for a tight fit on the roof; by the time I got the last one pegged in place, it was getting dark. The door will have to wait till tomorrow.

I put more wood on the fire and got out my chair and sat down. I liked the way the smokehouse is turning out. It's bigger and a lot stronger than the old one. I had some soup left and was heating it up. I turned around to set down and Wantalook had snuck in behind me. I sure wasn't expecting that. He about scared the crap out of me. My heart was pounding and I had to catch my breath. Wantalook, you little shit, was all I could say. You got me, next time make a noise or something. We got our greetings in and I got out his fish and we ate our meal. I still wasn't settled down, to see a big and furry behind me with only the light of the fire! The thought of dealing with the wolverine was still fresh on my mind for that split second. I tell ya, it got me going, bad wolf. We sat by the fire and Wantalook had his head on my leg and was enjoying his loving. It was getting late and time to go in. The fire had gone out in the stove so it took a while to get the cabin warm. I opened the covers on the bed so they would be warmer when I crawled in. I got to get more water in the morning. I am almost out. It's been a half hour now since I came in and the cabin is warm now. I packed the stove for the night and went to bed.

From what I could see out the window, it's going to be another nice day. I slipped on my coat and went outside. It was cold but the skies were clear and guess who was eager to knock me down, before I even made it away from the cabin? One of these days I am going to find a way to make use of the energy this wolf's got. After petting, pushing, chasing and rough playing was over Wantalook was ready to eat. I got out his fish. I then got the fire started to cook up some bear meat for myself in the frying pan with water. When we finished eating it was time to head to the spring. I need a lot of water for dishes and cleaning clothes. I made two trips and all the containers were filled now including the shower bag.

Now on to building the smokehouse door. I used one-inch lumber to hold the half logs together with a Z pattern on the outside. Then I finished cutting the door to size. I made two hinges and used pegs for pins. It worked quite well. I made a simple latch to keep it closed. I took the measurement I needed of the inside to make the racks. I cut a bunch of willow and put in the cabin. It will be a lot easier to build them inside than out here. It felt good to get out of the cold and get my fingers warmed up before getting started on the racks. Since I've made them before it won't take long to build them, stripping the bark will take longer. After I got the first one together, I took it to the smoke house to see how it fit. Everything looked good. So I went back inside and made two more. By 6:30 I was fastening the last one in place, my smoker was ready for business. I started a fire in it to cure the wood and cover over the smell of wood. I had to clean up the mess I had in the cabin and I took all the scraps to the fire pit. Wantalook was through being patient, he wanted some attention. We played for a while and I wanted to get a fire going. I had just started the fire when Wantalook grabbed my glove. He wasn't through playing yet. He stood there daring me to get the glove. The more I tried, the better he liked it. When I stopped, he'd stop, he'd move. He even went as far to drop the glove in front of me and wait for me to go for it. When I did, he would be gone with it and teased me some more. This went on over a half hour and I quit. He still stood there with the glove in his mouth. When I got the fish out things were different. I got my glove back.

I got out some fish to cook; they were frozen so it would take a while before they were ready to eat. I gave Wantalook a few more fish. Tomorrow I'll check the ice on the lake so I can do some fishing soon. My fish was finally ready and I sat down to eat. The fire felt good against the cold. The skies were clear and the stars were shining bright. I went inside and put more wood in the stove. It will be nice and warm when I come back in. I was only going to set by the fire a little while but the light show had started. The Northern Lights were running wild in the land of the midnight sun. The sun may be gone but the lights were doing real good. I can't help but get goose bumps every time I see them. I wound up watching them several hours. If I had some 1600 speed film I would be taking pictures. I finally had to quit watching. I was cold and tired; when I looked at my watch it was 11:55. I petted Wantalook good night and went inside. I knew I was cold but when I got inside that's when I found out how cold I was, even my legs felt cold to the touch. I stood by the stove till the chill was gone. I was getting into bed when I noticed that today was October 14th. I've been out here four months now and it looks like winter is here to stay too. Well get to bed, the party's over.

When I woke up the day had started without me. I put more wood in the stove and got dressed. I guess I was ready to get attacked by an attention loving wolf. Damn Wantalook let me get out the door. As far as he was concerned, it was playtime. Well game on, it's too bad, I couldn't get these times on tape. We played for a good half hour when I finally made it to the food shack and up the ladder. I got a break. I tossed down his fish then came down. I'll eat when I get back. It's been clear and cold and it's a good time to get some snares out. The traveled trails will be easy to see now. It didn't take long for Wantalook to figure out what we were doing. I was surprised to see him staying away from the areas I was setting up. We didn't go to the feeding area where I've seen the moose. I want to keep the area undisturbed till it's time to hunt one. I got six snares and we should have some good luck. The snow wasn't too bad. There were areas deeper than others but I'll want to make those snowshoes before it gets deeper.

It was a nice walk back to the cabin. I was looking forward to the warmth of the fire for a while. I sat for a while by the fire to get the hands warmed up before I check the ice on the lake. I am guessing three to four inches. I grabbed my ax and went down to the lake. A few spots next to shore were not solid yet but I found a spot that was. I kept checking the ice and it was safe to be on. I chopped a hole around forty feet out. Wantalook wanted nothing to do with being out on the ice.

I went back to camp, got warmed up a while. Now it was time to do some fishing. I got out my travel fisherman pole and tied on a jig lure. I grabbed my tackle box and headed for the lake. Wantalook was anxious about fishing but he wouldn't come out to where I was. He almost changed his mind when the fish were flopping on the ice. I caught fourteen and clipped them on the stringer. Wantalook was waiting to get one when I reached the shore. I gave him one so he would leave me alone. I think I have a spoiled wolf on my hands. When we got back to camp I cleaned the fish. Wantalook was more than happy to help. I put twelve in the smoker and one for me to eat. It was nice to have a smoker again and the chance for fresh fish too. The fire's going good in the fire pit and I slid the rocks over and shut the door. Now it was time to cook my fish. While my fish was cooking I was thinking I need to make a table so I can finish the hides. My camping table isn't strong enough. Well my fish is done now, I can eat. I should be able to cut everything out for the table this afternoon.

I got my saw out of the cabin and started cutting the legs first. I then stripped the bark and trimmed the knots. I then cut the boards to brace the legs and support the top. Then I cut the boards for the top of the table. I was planning the size to be thirty inches by forty-eight inches so I could get it in and out of the door if needed. I took a break and put more wood in the smoker. Now the job of shaving and smoothing the pieces. I got the leg braces smoothed and rounded and it was getting late and it was time to eat. The smoked fish was ready.

I put more wood on the fire and got out Wantalook's fish from the food shack. I was stuffed by the time I finished eating. I haven't ate that much in a long time. After putting the smoked fish away, we sat by the fire like normal, with Wantalook's head on my leg so he could get his loving before I went in. The skies were clear but I wasn't going to stay up for the light show. I will have many more nights for that. It was time to go in. I was starting to doze off. The fire in the stove was almost out but with some fresh wood and a little sweet talking, the fire was back to life. It felt good when I settled in the bed. The sandman won't need to come tonight. I'll be out before he gets here.

I opened my eyes. Wow it's morning already. I slept like a log. I don't see any sawdust so I must not have been sawing logs last night. I got up, added more wood to the stove and got dressed. I knew that crazy wolf was waiting for me to come out the door. Oh happy was glad to see me and was more than ready to start playing. We carried on with our morning ritual till Wantalook tired me out. I got out the last of the fish and let him eat his fill while I got the fire going. It was time to check the snares.

Wantalook was excited this morning, running around me as I walked. I almost had to threaten him with great bodily harm if he knocked me down, although I wouldn't but he didn't know that. When we got to the first snare we had a rabbit. I reset the snare and went on to the next. That one was clear; by the time we got to the sixth we had three rabbits. Wantalook couldn't wait to get back so he could get his share when I cleaned them. When I was cleaning the rabbits I told Wantalook in a few weeks we will be eating moose. We'll have one for lunch and the other rabbits tonight. The rabbits were cleaned and it was time to get after the table. I smoothed the table top supports next. Then I started to assemble the base, notching the logs and drill and peg the brace boards in place.

It was time for lunch. I put the rabbit in the cooking rack and set it over the fire. It took about an hour to slow cook it. Wantalook was waiting for his share and didn't waste any time eating either. You could say he wolfed it down. I wasn't finished with the first back leg yet. Now you will have to watch me eat and he did, waiting for me to hand him the bones. Well, Wantalook, I've got to get back to work on the table. I had to fasten the top supports on next and one with a half lap in the middle. I shaved and smoothed the table top boards next and pegged each one in place. All the holes on the table were drilled on an angle so they won't pull loose. When the last board was in place and pegged I did the finish shaving on them to make the surface even, then smoothed the ends of the boards and rounded all the edges. I liked it. It was solid and looked good. I couldn't wait to see how it looked in the cabin. When I got inside it looked great, a nice addition to the interior. I had to put away my tools and clean up the area where I was working.

It was evening by now and time to get supper going. I'll only cook one rabbit and have the other tomorrow and I'll have some smoked fish too. When I got out the rabbit I got out a chunk of bear meat for Wantalook. It held him over till the rabbit was ready. He was patient till the rabbit was done but after I removed it from the heat, it was a whole different story. I removed the back legs for myself and gave him the rest. I no more started eating and he was done. Damn Wantalook, did you even taste it? I gave him the bones as I finished each one. I waited a while before I got out the smoked fish. I added more wood to the fire and now it was our sit time and Wantalook could get his petting. I've got a spoiled wolf on my hands. I got up after an hour to get the fish and Wantalook was willing to share it with me. That sure was nice of him. We sat for a while longer till it was time to go in for the night. I brought in half the hide so it would be thawed out by tomorrow so I could finish scraping it. I banked the stove for the night and climbed into bed.

I was eager to get started when I woke up. I had places to go and things to do. When I put on my coat and headed out the door, I was ready to rumble. Today I am going to win. I looked around, Wantalook was gone. He's out doing his thing. I still win. It's a no show. I went out to check the snares. I caught one rabbit. I dressed it out when I got back to camp. I then headed to the lake for more fish so I'll have a supply on hand to feed Wantalook. The fishing went quite well. It didn't take long between chopping a hole and catching the fish. I was back at camp in over an hour. With fish put away, I went inside to work on the hide. I had all the inside to scrape yet. Having the table now will help a lot. My wandering wolf isn't back yet so I'll keep an ear open while I work. Being able to stretch the hide on a flat surface sure makes the job easier. I don't know how to treat the hide so I am hoping it will turn out. I think one process they use is limestone because of the acid in it. The only things around here with any acid to it is ash.

It was time for lunch and my hands need a break. I went outside to check if Wantalook was back yet, but he was nowhere in sight. So I went back inside and ate lunch. It took me the rest of the afternoon to scrape and clean and wash the hide. Then I stretched it out to start drying. After cleaning the table and the cabin I went outside to get the fire going so I could start cooking rabbit for supper. Wantalook wasn't back yet. He'll show up before too long. The fire was ready to start cooking. I had decided to cook both. I was hungry. While the rabbits were cooking I was enjoying the heat on my hands not to mention other parts of my body.

The evening was calm and I could feel the sharpness of the cold against my skin. I not only turned the meat but myself as well. Well, look who showed up for supper. Are you done running around the countryside? Wantalook was his happy self to see me after our greeting was over. I got him some fish to hold him over till the rabbit was done. When the food was ready, I tossed more wood on the fire so I'd be warmer while I was eating. Wantalook was ready for his share of the rabbit. I think the fish slowed him up some. He was taking his time eating now. It was nice having Wantalook back. I always wonder about him when he's gone.

It was a good evening. A nice fire and a friend by my side. I know we both look forward to this time. It makes our bond all the stronger. The fire was getting down and it was time to go in. It felt good to get inside where it was warm. I think tonight is our coldest yet. I filled the stove for tonight and climbed into my warm bed. I found a sweet spot right away and was off to sleep.

Seven

When I got up, I could see that it was overcast. When I went outside it was a lot warmer than it was last evening. Wantalook was waiting to greet me and was showing a lot more energy than I was. He was ready to play. We pushed and chased each other till I was exhausted but he surely wasn't. He finally let me get his fish, then I could get mine. We ate our breakfast and left to check the snares. Wantalook was his playful self as we walked, running circles around me, challenging me to catch him. He was finally slowing down by the time we reached the first one. He changed into serious mode now. He knew we were after food. We got one in the fourth snare. The rest were empty.

When we got back to camp, Wantalook just couldn't wait for me to clean the rabbit. He was excited as a kid on Christmas. When I was done, I put the rabbit away for tonight. I went inside to check the hide. It was just dry enough so I could cut it in shape. I put a board on the table to cut on and sharpened my knife. I hung the strips over the dross support log in the cabin. Each strip was about three-eighth inches thick. I was sure I had enough hide from the half the hide for the snowshoes. It took me longer than I figured but by 1:00, I was hanging the last strip. I cleaned my work area and it was time for a break and a bit to eat.

Wantalook was ready to eat too. He's always ready to eat. After our lunch, I decided I need to cut wood for the fire pit. Wantalook and I will be sitting out here whenever we can through the winter and when the snow gets deep. I don't want to be chasing wood for a fire. I spent the next four hours dragging wood to camp. I still needed more but tomorrow is another day. After a short break I started cutting the wood into two-foot chunks till around 6:30.

It was time to start cooking supper. Wantalook was right there overseeing the cooking. He was making sure that he didn't miss a thing. We ate our rabbit and fish and it was our time by the fire. The skies were still overcast and it's warmer than last evening. We sat together till after 9:00, with Wantalook taking all the petting I could hand out. I was getting tired and I could hear my bed calling me from out here. I told Wantalook good night and went inside. I filled the stove and got into bed right away just to shut it up.

After a good night's sleep, I was ready to get my day started. Wantalook was waiting for me as I came out the door. Happy to see me and eager to play. I am glad I am a morning person; taking on this guy every morning would be hell if I wasn't. I surprised him this morning. I took off after him first. I almost got him on the first grab, almost. He tried his best to knock me down but I was used to his moves by now. We pushed and wrestled till I got my chance to grab and pick him up. He tried to get loose but with his feet off the ground he couldn't do anything. I won this one. I let him down, petted is head as I turned away and he hit me from behind. When I hit the ground he was on top of me. When I moved he'd move. I finally managed to turn over; his face was in mine. I had to give up. He licked my face and let me up. I guess he doesn't like losing. I had to get some snow removed from myself before I could do anything.

I got Wantalook his fish and ate mine smoked. It was a nice day out, partly cloudy skies. A good day to work outside. I swear that wolf's getting tamer every day. He couldn't wait to check the snares. Walking out he was acting like he was gloating over his win this morning, rotten wolf. There wasn't anything in the snares so I moved them to a different area a lot further from camp. I followed the edge of the lake back and saw several moose tracks. I just hope they stay close for a few more weeks. A half mile or less would be good. We were gone from camp several hours and I was ready to set down.

I started a fire and got out my chair. After a short break, I'll start bringing more wood up. Wantalook was still playful but after he saw I was going to stay setting then he sat beside me. Break time was over and it was time to drag this job out, one bunch at a time. This isn't right. I am dragging this wood and Wantalook's running around like he got kicked in the butt by the energizer bunny. All that energy and no way to use it. I kept making my trips the next few hours. Oh, now you're tired and now you're just going to lay there and watch me work. You are a spoiled rotten wolf. It didn't matter what I said, he still laid there and watched. It was time for a break and lunch. Wantalook was hungry too. He had worked up an appetite running around. We ate fish and I started cutting wood. Wantalook was going to take a nap by the fire every time I saw him shut his eyes, I would toss a snowball in his direction. At first he didn't know who or what but he caught on to what I was doing. He looked at me like he's about to open a can of whoop-ass. So I left him alone and went back to cutting wood. Taking breaks every now and then throughout the afternoon.

I quit around 6:00. I wanted to cook up some bear meat for supper. After getting out the fish I'll need to catch more tomorrow for Wantalook and for smoking. I think I've got the best fed wolf in the neighborhood. Wantalook had his fish gone long before my meat was ready and when I started to eat, he watched my every bite, waiting for me to give him some. I finally did. We sat by the fire the same way we have for a long time now, his head on my leg enjoying all the petting I could give. It was getting late and the fire was a glow of embers. I petted Wantalook good night and headed to the cabin. The stove was hungry. It was starving for wood so I laid there listening to the wood pop and snap. It took me back to my younger years growing up at Mom and Dad's. When we would set around the wood stove at the end of the day after being outside all day. A nice meal and the heat from the stove would make you fall asleep.

I woke up still wanting more sleep, but I don't waste mornings either so I got up—a few stretches, a couple yawns, I was ready. But not ready for Wantalook. Maybe I can make it a short one today. I slipped on my coat and opened the door. I was greeted by the ball of fur and teeth. As we played, I was moving toward the food shack. Within five minutes I was on the ladder. I took out the last of the fish and fed my poor starving wolf. Alright, you would have to dig deep to feel a rib on him. We ate our breakfast and took off to check the snares. Wantalook wasn't so wild running around today. I think his full stomach slowed him down. Well, Wantalook, we came up empty-handed today.

We walked back to camp with mild play going on between us, or should I say it wasn't as hard and heavy as normal.

I sat a while before heading to the lake. When I picked up my pole Wantalook knew where I was going. I got him to come out on the ice. I have to admit he was not overjoyed but after the first fish came out he was fine with where he was. The first one he ate, the second he played with, tossing and chasing it around. I finally had all the fish I needed. When I got back to camp, I cleaned the ones for the smoker and put the rest away. I loaded the smoker and got the fire going. By the time all the wood is cut, the fish should be done too. I was glad Wantalook was content to watch while I worked. I would cut for an hour or so, take a break and check the smoker and start all over again.

By mid afternoon, I was on the heat process of smoking, and by 6:00 I was done and so was the fish. I wound up with a bigger pile of wood than I planned. That was time to sit down to a nice meal of fresh smoked fish. First I got to feed Wantalook so he will let me eat in peace for a few minutes before he'll want some of mine. We sat by the fire for the next few hours enjoying our time together till the flames were gone and it was time to call it a day and go in. I was ready for some sleep. The body was letting me know too. I loaded the stove and crawled between the halves of my sleeping bag and was out like a light.

Where did the night go? I felt like I just laid down but the skies were light. I sat on the edge of the bed trying to work the stiffness out. No way was I ready to take on Wantalook this morning. I added a few pieces of wood to the stove and got dressed. I know I'll walk outside, flop down on the ground and give up. But I know he won't. Well, I've got to get this over with. I put on my coat and slipped out the door, expecting to be attacked at any moment and nothing. Wantalook was gone. Wow, I get a break this morning. I looked around just in case to make sure he wasn't laying in waiting to surprise me. He was gone. I started a fire and had some fish for breakfast; afterwards I went to check the snares. I did have a rabbit in the second one but no more. The tracks told everything—a bear. You would think they were in hibernation by now. I didn't like the look of the way he followed my tracks to all the rest. That will mean a camp alert now. Damn it, I don't want to have to deal with another bear. I had pulled up all the snares and I'll put them back later on. I was glad to see that the bear proceeded on after the last and didn't follow my tracks back to camp. I was looking for any signs of bear all the way back to camp.

I put more wood on the fire and sat down for a while. I couldn't help but think about the bear tracks I seen earlier. I plan to start hunting for a moose in about a week and I don't need them still out there with the smell of blood in the air. The wind was changing directions and the wind was feeling different. I think we are going to get some snow. I was making plans to start working on the snowshoes but I am going to enjoy sitting by the fire as long as I can today. I was just finishing my lunch and the first flakes were coming down and it wasn't long things were turning white. I put my chair under the overhang and went inside. The wood for the snowshoes was dried and keeping the shape I bent them in. I marked out the wood for the nose pieces, then cut them out and used my knife to shape to fit. Then I drilled small holes through each strip, and fastened them with a wire. After both nose pieces were in place, I cut and fitted the tail end of the strips. Each were around eight inches wide and about twelve inches long. I took a look outside and it was snowing real good now. Wantalook wasn't back yet so I'll keep working. I marked out the foot support piece. Two for each and shaped each one to fit snug, with the ends wider than the rest for more support to the side.

It was after 6:00 and time to eat. I was eating my smoked fish when I heard Wantalook outside. The wandering wolf has come home. I put on my coat and went outside. Sure enough there he was, bouncing up and down, glad to see me. After our meeting and greeting, I went to the food shack to get his fish. He was ready to eat by the time I got back under the overhang. I had to brush the snow off me. It was really coming down. I had to go inside and put on more clothes so I could sit with Wantalook a while. With the fish being frozen it does slow him down but not much. I sat with Wantalook for over an hour, petting and talking to him. I was getting cold. It was time to go in anyway so I told Wantalook good night and went inside. I tried again to get him to come in, not yet. I filled the stove and got into bed, tomorrow is another day.

When I woke up, I looked out the window and it was still snowing. I thought to myself maybe this is what it will take to put the bears to bed for the winter. I got up, put wood in the stove and got dressed. I slipped on my coat and opened the door. Wantalook was waiting. We did our greeting with a bit of pushing too. He tried to knock me down on my way to the food shack. Maybe I could teach him what "no" means. I will have to work on it, maybe "stay" too. I sat in my chair while he ate. It looked like we got at least six to eight inches of new snow so far. I petted Wantalook for a while and I wanted to get back to the snowshoes so after about an hour I went inside to work.

I put a bunch of hide strips in water to soften them then worked on fastening the foot supports to the sides of the snowshoes. Now to figure out how to lace them. I changed the water to hot on the strips to soften them better. First I tied strips two inches apart from end to end. Then I tied strips on an angle from one side to the other and did the same the other way making a diamond pattern. The strips tied together where they crossed each other. It was solid and tight. I took a break with Wantalook for a half hour, then it was time to get the other one laced. One thing nice about doing something more than once, the second gets done faster. It was late when I finished lacing the second.

I went to the food shack to get out some bear fat I've been saving. I heated it up on the stove so I could saturate the strips so they won't get brittle. After they get a few days of drying, I will coat them again. Wantalook was waiting to eat. I was hungry too. It was already after 12:25. I loaded the stove and got ready for bed. My thoughts were on the snowshoes and what I needed to do before they were done as I fell asleep.

I woke the next morning to a sunny day. I could tell by the brightness coming through the window. I put more wood in the stove and got dressed. I knew I had snow to clear out as I put on my boots and coat and my morning wolf attack. I didn't even get out from under the overhang and it was game on. Wantalook wasn't wasting any time getting things started and by now I knew his moves as we pushed and wrestled around. I had all I could do to stay on my feet as he jumped on me trying to knock me down. I was just getting my balance from my spinning out of the way. Man over, when his body slammed me. I was down for the count and when the snow settled, I was face to face with my attacker. OK, Wantalook, you win. I give up, now you can let me up. He licked my face and got off me. While I was trying to get rid of the snow accumulated inside my clothes, Wantalook tried to knock me down again. I yelled no and he stopped and looked at me. I guess I surprised him. I had never raised my voice to him before. I petted and praised him for it. Well it's a start. I got him his fish and sat on my chair eating mine. Now I've got a chance to look at all the snow we got. With the snow hanging on the trees and the blanket of white on the ground with the sunlight, everything sparkled like diamonds. The shovel I have isn't going to work well with all this snow. I need to make a push board for clearing snow. After eating, I cleared out the fire pit and got a fire started.

I went out and cut a two-inch pole around five feet long for a handle. I then cut a board two feet long and ten inches wide. Next I cut two support pieces. I mounted the handle flat to the center of the board with a slight angle. I then notched the handle for the support boards. I pegged what I could and wrapped the supports to the handle with strips of hide. Afterwards I shaped the handle with my knife so it would fit better. The last thing to do was shave the surface smooth. It took me a few hours to complete it. In no time at all the yard was cleared. I cleared a path to the spring.

After lunch I got a pot of bear meat started for supper to make a thick soup. One thing that made it nice for the paths was the base snow that was already on the ground. All I had to do was the new stuff that fell. I was finished with the snow by late afternoon and from now on, it won't take so long. I put more wood on the fire and sat down for a while. It looked nice to see the camp cleared out. The day was still calm and it made it a lot more enjoyable setting by the fire. After Wantalook got his petting, he laid by my feet. Its sure been a nice day and if it stays clear it will be cold tonight.

I went inside to get strips of hide so I could make boot straps for the snowshoes. I braided strips together with plenty on each end to tie on the snowshoes. After each one was braided, I went inside to secure each one, giving enough room for my boot to move and make a wrap-around strip to go around the back of the boot. When they were both done, I coated everything with bear fat. Now I will let them dry for a few days till everything dries and sets up.

By now it was time for supper. I got Wantalook his fish and I had a bowl of soup, matter of fact I had two. It was the part of the evening where the daylight gives way to the darkness and the stars start appearing in the sky. Even though I've sat here many times each time is different but the reality is the same. I am just a small speck in this vast wilderness. Wantalook had his head on my leg taking all the petting I gave and we both enjoyed this time, our time. It was time to go in for the night. I gave him my last pet and said good night.

The fire was down in the stove so I had to give some attention to it before filling it for the night. As I sat on the bed I couldn't help but look at the snowshoes hanging on the wall, for homemade they looked pretty damn good. Well the yawns are getting bigger so I better get into bed and chase a dream or two.

I must have chased too many dreams last night. I woke up tired. The sky was already light from the morning sun so I better get my butt out of bed. I added some wood to the stove and just sat there a while. It felt like a coffee morning. I filled the pot and added the coffee before I got dressed and it wasn't long before the smell of coffee was all through the cabin. I really don't think I was too anxious standing there watching the pot and holding my coffee mug while counting down the last minutes of perking. Yum, yum, what a way to start the day. I put on my coat and stepped out the door with mug in hand. Wantalook did give me time to set it down before we started our morning rough and tumble session. How did this get started anyhow? I don't remember. We've been doing it so long. I was holding my own against him this morning; twice I managed to get him off the ground but what a handful and I lost my grip. When we went to the ground I managed to get my arms and legs around him and I had him pinned to where he couldn't move. He finally licked my face. I had won this one. I was brushing off the snow when he tried a sneak attack and I stopped him with a sharp no. I like it, he learns fast.

I got Wantalook's fish out of the food shack and heated up the soup. It was another nice day, cold but nice. I got myself another coffee and ate my soup. I need to do some fishing. I got only two fish left for Wantalook. When I finished my coffee I grabbed my ax and pole and headed to the lake. I got the hole cut in the ice and cleared. Wantalook was right there looking in the hole. When I pulled up the first fish, he was ready. I removed the hook and tossed him the fish; that will keep him busy for a minute or two. He was a pig this morning—he had four at camp and he just finished his third one. We were on the ice for several hours till I had enough to last a while. I plan to fry up two or three for supper. By the time we got back to camp and put away the fish and equipment, the morning was gone. I put more wood on the fire and got another coffee. The fire felt good and my fingers and hands were absorbing some much needed heat. After all the feelings were back, I had some smoked fish. Wantalook was laying down trying to take a nap. I guess he figured it was the best thing to do since he had a full belly. I let him sleep.

I had some preparation to do for the upcoming moose hunt. I got down my sled I used for moss. I checked it over and made sure the metal was smooth. I wished I had wax for it but you can wish in one hand and crap in the other and see which fills up first. The sled was ready. Next I went inside and got my backpack. I put my ropes inside and a large piece of my tent for the sled and some plastic. I got out a plastic jug for water. Next I touched up my knife so it was as sharp as it could be. A dull knife is a dangerous knife. A sharp knife you can control. Afterwards I put my sharpening stone in my backpack too. I checked over my .357 Mag and I was ready. I don't know how it will work out with Wantalook with me hunting. I may have to wait till he's gone on one of his outings. With this last snow the bears should be in their dens and I won't have a problem with them. I know I will still keep my guard up because I won't rule out anything. I went back outside by the fire and Wantalook was catching some serious Z's when I walked up. I added a few more pieces of wood to the fire and it wasn't long before I had some nice flames. I sat there a while petting Wantalook enjoying the afternoon. I was looking forward to doing the moose hunt and having fresh meat instead of dried. I'll go out in the morning and if Wantalook is here he'll go with me. That will be interesting. One thing for sure, I will need to get close to one for a well-placed shot.

It was nice to just set around but I felt like I had to get up and do something. I do have two logs I could cut into boards. I went inside to calculate if I had enough for my winter projects. It looks like it but I might as well be sure I have plenty. I did a little sharpening in the saw and set up the first log. After marking it out for one-inch boards it was time to get the zoom-pa party started. The saw was sharp and the cuts were straight and the sound of the saw made its sound with each stroke zoom-pa, zoom-pa, zoom-pa. I carried the boards inside and put them on the pile with the rest. Now it's time to fry some fish. I gave Wantalook his and my two were in the pan. The evening was clear out and it's going to be a cold one in the morning. Well, my fish were done and I was ready to eat. Wantalook got his few bites too. I sat with Wantalook for a while till it was 8:00. I needed to get to bed early. I planned to be heading out at first light. I gave Wantalook his last petting and went inside. I filled the stove and fell into bed.

Morning came early. I woke up several times before I got up at 6:00. I added some wood to the stove and got out the rest of my heavy clothes. I had packed and got dressed. I went out to feed Wantalook; I made it a short greeting. He wasn't used to seeing me before sun-up. I went back inside, filled my water jug and had the last of the bear soup. When I came back out with my backpack Wantalook knew I was up to something.

I grabbed the rope of the sled and started out making my way eastward toward the feeding area. I left the sled about one half mile from the camp. It was too noisy to take closer. I proceeded on walking slow, watching ahead for any moose feeding. Wantalook was still staying by me. How long he'll do that we will soon see. I was about a mile from camp when I saw a moose around 150 yards ahead in some thick brush. I started my stalk, one step and paused; when the moose moved I moved. I was slowly getting closer, paying attention where I was stepping around trees and limbs and brush; keeping quiet while still watching the moose. I stopped to see where Wantalook was and he was gone. I had no idea where he was. I told myself this is not good. I looked back in the direction where I had last seen it. After twenty-five minutes I spotted the moose about fifty yards and, still too thick to shoot. I had made it ten yards closer and I was sure I would get the shot before long. I had gone another five yards and the moose didn't know I was there. I had my sights on its chest waiting, then Wantalook ran up and the moose was gone. Well moose won, me nothing.

I continued walking to see where the moose went following his tracks. I found a traveled area where a number of moose have been traveling to and from this feeding area. Well since they don't go as far as the campsite, I will have to find a way to get to this area to cut them off. I found a good place to ambush with a few limbs and brush; I had a ground blind. The only way I could sneak in here was to come down the lake then come inland. The lake ice was thick enough so I wasn't worried about that. I'll just walk a trail out of here to the lake and back to the cabin. So I will have something to follow later on. I will just have to wait for Wantalook to be gone before I can come out again. As I made my way to the lake I cleared some brush out of the way so I can make a quiet walk back in here. Wantalook was still by me. He didn't know what my plans were out here. All he knew was we were going for a walk. When we got on the lake I made a beeline for the cabin, kicking up mounds of snow. I want to mark the trail better.

It was late in the day by the time I walked back into camp. I put my backpack away and removed some of the heavy clothes. I was ready to sit down as soon as I started the fire; I had put a good walk on today. As I sat there I was thinking about the moose I saw and the area I picked out to hunt at, that's over 1½ miles from here. When I do get one it's going to take me several days to get all the meat back here. I've been sitting about an hour. The sun was down past the mountains but the sky is still light. I got up to get out our supper, fish raw for Wantalook and smoked for me. Afterwards we sat there by each other, Wantalook getting his petting till it was time to go in. The fire was out in the stove so it took a while before the cabin was warm. I sat on the bed thinking over the events of the day. I just hope Wantalook doesn't wait for a snowstorm to leave on his outings.

The cabin was warm by now and I was ready to lay down. I remember shutting my eyes but that's it.

I got up before daylight and looked out the door. Wantalook was outside. Well, no hunting today so I went back to bed and got up after it was daylight. I would have loved to go back out hunting but I am saving my energy for when the hunting time is good. I got dressed and headed outside and greeted my crazy wolf and he was ready for fun and games more than I was. We pushed, wrestled and chased each other for a good half hour till I called it quits. I got down his fish and started a fire and sat down. I wasn't hungry and I would eat later on.

I might as well get started cutting up the last log into boards. I would rather be hunting, but oh well. I marked out where to make my cuts and got the zoom-pa party started. I would cut for a while and sit, cut for a while and sit, just making the job last. Wantalook just laid there and watched as I worked. I finished the cutting and took the boards inside with the rest, then cleaned up the area. I sat by the fire for a while till it was time for supper. I need to get the sled back here; it's way out of the way from where I'll be hunting. It's only a half mile away. I'll be back here before you know it. Wantalook came along, running around like he was half crazy. Maybe this little outing will give him the energy to go on his own. I reached the sled and headed back to camp. It was dark by now but there wasn't any problem following my tracks back home. We ate our fish and did our nightly ritual of setting by each other by the fire. It was getting time to put an end to the day and go inside. I've got to get up early. I might make it out hunting. I gave Wantalook his last petting and went in. I filled the stove for the night and went to sleep.

I woke up at 5:30 with a hopeful chance of going out this morning. After adding wood to the stove and getting dressed, I checked outside. Wantalook was gone. I was excited now. I put my battery powered lantern in my backpack, ate some fish and packed some food for the day. When I went outside, I checked the skies and there was a cloud cover with no stars in sight. I adjusted my backpack and picked up the rope to the sled and headed down to the lake. Even though it was dark the snow made it quite easy to see. Following my tracks across the lake to the east shore went by fast.

    I left the sled on shore and looked into the woods. The skies were just starting to show signs of light and I had a ways to go yet to get to my blind. I was glad I had tracks to follow. It was easier than not. I got to my spot and got settled in for the hunt. The woods were getting brighter when I could see pretty good. The wind was starting up coming out of the west northwest. It still was a light wind. It was perfect. My ground blind was on the east side of the funnel area of tracks. After setting there for several hours, I haven't seen a moose yet. It was just starting to snow small flakes at first and as time went on they were getting bigger and coming down heavier.

    By noon I was having my doubts if I was going to see moose today. I already knew I was going to shoot it to stop it so it couldn't run off. I was having a bite to eat when I saw some movement coming. It was a moose. He was walking right toward me. I had my .357 Mag ready as he kept walking closer and closer. He's going to be less than ten yards away the way he is walking. I had my sights on his backbone just above the front shoulders and squeezed the trigger. He went down and couldn't get up no matter how hard he tried. I got the chance to finish him off with a shot to the head. I only had a few seconds to stick him with my knife so he could bleed out before his nerves kicked in. I stuck the knife into the base of his neck into the chest area and drew the knife downward toward the bottom of the chest cavity to cut the arteries where they cross. This is almost like butchering a beef. Now the work begins. I removed some of my clothes because I was dressed for sitting, not working. I went to get the sled first and when I got back I started removing the hind legs, leaving the skin on to protect the meat. I removed the lower leg at the joint and dragged the first one over to a tree. I got a rope over a limb fifteen feet up or so. I tied the end of the rope through the gamble, pulled it up and tied it off. Then I went back and cut off the other hind leg and got them hung up. I removed the lower front legs and cut the front shoulders off and hung them up. After I got the back straps out, I rolled them in the hide, tied them and hung them up. Then I proceeded to bone out every piece of meat I could and filled up the pieces of tent material I brought. I tied it closed and hung them up as well. I continued to bone out the carcass, filling the plastic on the sled. I removed the heart, liver and the sled was full. I still had the neck to bone out yet and it was dark by now. I got out my light and finished boning out the neck, putting that into my backpack. The last meat to cut out was the gut loins.

    I caught glimpse of movement in the shadows and drew my gun; much to my relief it was Wantalook. He was happy to see me and happy to see what I had. I told him to eat what he wanted while I stripped down for the long haul. I tied my extra clothes on my backpack and put it on. With all the snow coming down the visibility was poor and my tracks coming in were covered. I stepped into the rope from the sled and put it on my hips and started walking. It was after 8:00 when I started out. I would go for a ways and stop. The trail out to the lake was not an easy one. I was glad of limb marking and trimming, at times I couldn't see that. I was carrying fifty pounds or more with my backpack and over 100 pounds on the sled. I lost track several times and being in a white out too sure wasn't helping. It seemed like I would never reach the lake and each time pulling the sled was getting shorter. There were times I had to check my compass to make sure I was still going in the right direction. I was glad when I reached the shore of the lake but being in the open was not a good place to be. When I got onto the ice, I couldn't see any of the snow mounds I had made a few days earlier. My compass was the only reference I had to go by to get back to camp. With each step my load felt heavier. I was only pulling maybe thirty feet at a time now. It was taking everything I had to keep moving through the snow. It seemed like I was walking much further than I needed. I moved closer to shore trying to find landmarks of some kind. When I spotted the leaning tree, it was a welcome sight.

    I was just down from camp. I don't want to stop for anything till I get all this put away. I saved out some meat for myself to eat when I get inside. Wantalook was cleaning up the scraps I left him as I went into the cabin. My clothes were wet from snow and sweat. I changed up after I got the fire going. I hung up all the clothes and my socks and boot liners. I put newspaper inside my boots to dry them out. I had the meat in the fry pan before

I sat down. I was whipped. While the meat was cooking, I got out the bottle of bourbon and took a pull and put it away. As I sat on the bed there wasn't a single part of me that wasn't tired. The meat was ready and I couldn't wait for that first bite. I sure have been looking forward to moose meat a long time. I happened to look at my watch and was shocked to see it was after 2:00 a.m. When I finished eating, I think I was out before my head hit the pillow.

When I woke up I didn't remember dreaming or anything. When I went to get out of bed I felt like a herd of moose put an ass whooping to me. Just getting to a sitting position was a job. I need some pain relievers like right now. That means I have to get up. I think all the good muscles went south for the winter and the ones left are letting me know they are still alive and very unhappy. I sat on the bed a while before starting to get my clothes on. The pain reliever was starting to work. I was moving a lot easier by the time I put my coat on. There is no way in hell I was going to wrestle with Wantalook this morning.

I opened the door and stepped outside. Wantalook was right there to get his greeting in. The first thing I did was a sit down in the chair so he had to settle on his petting that way. The snow was still coming down with the wind making it worse. Actually not much different than it was when I got here late last night. Let's see, it is what, 2:45 in the afternoon? Well the rest of the day will be resting and eating and some snow clearing. As I climbed the ladder to the food shack, my legs confirmed no trips today. It was too nasty to cook outside so I gave Wantalook his meat and fish and I went inside to cook mine. I need to drink a lot of water today and replace some of the calories I burned yesterday. If this weather breaks tomorrow, I'll be making trips. It will depend how things go whether I make one or two trips a day. After I get done eating I will try out my snowshoes. I had cooked up enough food for two meals but I'll eat this the rest of the afternoon and cook more tonight. I ate till I couldn't eat another bite.

I took down the snowshoes and went outside. I slipped my boots into the straps and tied on the heal straps. They worked quite well. Well my legs were not used to the different way of walking. My mind instantly thought three-plus miles walking like this per trip. I will be earning every piece of meat. I sat under the overhang with Wantalook for about an hour, giving him his petting before moving some snow clearing the yard out. The way I figured the more I do now the less I'll have to do later. I was just taking it easy and taking my time. I even managed to get the path cleared to the lake. I had done enough for today.

It was time to make supper. I cooked up a pan full of meat for tonight and to take with me tomorrow. I got down Wantalook's food and sat with him while I ate mine. Afterwards we sat looking out into the night with his head on my leg. The snow and wind were letting up, that's a good sign for tomorrow. I gave Wantalook his last pet and went to bed.

When I woke up the next morning I felt pretty good, a little stiff but not bad. I got dressed and filled my water jug and had some meat for breakfast and bagged the rest to take with me. Wantalook was waiting for me. I quickly sat down. I like this trick. I need to save my energy. So after a good bit of petting, I got up and got Wantalook his food. It had stopped snowing during the night and the skies were partly cloudy. It looks like it will be a nice day. By the time I got the snowshoes on, Wantalook was done eating. I grabbed the rope to the sled and started out. I've got to find my rhythm, walking with these snowshoes. At least when I get a path made it will be easier with each trip. I've just got to keep Wantalook off these snowshoes so I don't do a face dive in the snow. When I got to the end of the lake, I was getting pretty good on these things. The snow was deeper as we entered the woods. Wantalook was content to walk behind me with his long legs and big feet; the snow really didn't bother him much.

I was glad to see all the meat hanging when we got there. I let down the two front shoulders and got them on the sled. I figured it would be enough for the first trip. Wantalook was excited with the sight of meat before him. I hacked off a couple pieces for him and he sure didn't turn them down. I started heading back. The sled was pulling hard but not as bad as it was two days before. I would stop every so often for a breather and keep pushing on. When I reached the lake I could see the trees by the camp. I was on the home stretch now. When I got to the path, I removed my snowshoes and pulled the sled the rest of the way to camp. It sure felt different to walk normal again. I took a short break then put the shoulders in the food shack. I got out fish and meat for Wantalook and some for myself. I got a fire going in the pit and had moose on a stick. It was 12:30 when I finished eating and I wanted to make one more trip today. I grabbed the sled and went to the lake to put on the snowshoes. The path was packed down now and walking was no effort at all. I had made good time across the lake and started off into the woods. It sure was a lot easier now than when I came in the morning. When I reached the tree, I took down the back straps I had rolled in the hide. It will make a lighter load for this trip but it will still help pack the trail for the heaviest loads to come.

I started back and I could keep moving right along. I only stopped a few times on the way back. I felt good by the time I reached the shore by camp. I really wasn't tired after removing my snowshoes. I headed up the path into camp. After putting the meat away I decided to make one more trip—it was only 3:00. I tied on my showshoes and took off across the lake in no time. I was in the woods. By the time I reached the meat tree it was 4:00. I got down the bag of trim meat I had put in the tent material. This one will be the heaviest load yet. It took a while to get it on the sled. I gave Wantalook a few pieces and started back. The sled pulled hard but with the trail being packed down it was pretty good. I made frequent stops so I wouldn't burn myself out. By the time I reached the lake I could feel the fatigue. I stopped for about ten minutes before proceeding on. As I walked the last part of the trip, I was thinking of the two trips left for tomorrow.

I was glad when I reached the shore at camp. I removed the snowshoes and took a short breather and dragged the sled the rest of the way to camp. I got the fire started and pulled the sled up to the food shack. I put the bundle of meat at the base of the ladder and used a rope to pull it up the ladder into the food shack, not an easy task. It took everything I had to get it up there. I brought down some meat for supper for Wantalook and myself and a few fish too. I had to sit a while first before I did anything. Wantalook was chowing down and had his gone before I even started to cook. I had my chair close enough to the fire that with my roasting stick I didn't need to move, which was fine for me. After I was done eating, I needed to take a couple pain relievers. When I went to get up, stiffness had set in. I was stiff all over, maybe three trips was too much. When I went inside, I started the fire in the stove so it will be warm when I came in for the night. I went back out to set with Wantalook. I was feeling better after sitting there a while. I was still petting Wantalook and scratching his ears; he was quite the wolf and a good friend. The heat from the fire was making me sleepy so it was time to go in. The cabin was warm as I stepped through the door and as soon as I am through hanging up my sox and boot liners, I was going to bed.

Boy, I remember laying down last night but that's it. I was a little stiff and sore when I got up but it was nothing that moving around wouldn't take care of. I got to my feet and tried my legs, not too bad. I got dressed and went outside. Wantalook wanted to romp around but I didn't. I needed to save all my energy for the rest of the day. I had sat down in my chair when I first came out so Wantalook got his petting that way. I got our food down and had moose on a stick for myself. I was eager to get started and get these last two trips over. Wantalook was ready to leave also. I grabbed the sled and went to the lake to put on my snowshoes. Wantalook was running and jumping circles around me; definitely too much energy for one wolf.

I started out across the lake. The path was hard and it made walking a lot easier. The sun was out and only a few clouds in the sky. There was no need to stop till I reached the meat tree. I let down the hind leg and got it on the sled and started back. I had only stopped twice, getting to the lake where I stopped again at the shore for a minute or two. Then I proceeded across the lake to camp. After putting the meat in the food shack, I was ready for the last trip. I was putting on my snowshoes while thinking about the meat and insurance of making it through the winter. It felt like I had a new stride to each step as I crossed the lake and I was proud of myself of what I had achieved so far. Wantalook was a bit playful too, running around and jumping in the snow. We started out through the woods having a good time, kind of like playing tag with each other. As we got to the tree,

I could see fresh claw marks in the bark and the tracks around the base. I automatically had my hand on my gun. I couldn't see anything so I untied the rope and let the hind leg down, still watching for the bear.

I just got it on the sled and tied it down when I saw Wantalook running toward me growling. I barely had time to see the bear when he knocked me down. Still wearing the snowshoes, I didn't even have time to move my feet. I was pinned down in the snow. The bear had my left forearm in his mouth. I was trying to keep him off my head and neck. My right arm was underneath me behind my back. I could not get it loose to reach my gun. Wantalook was all over the bear with a fury I didn't think he had. I couldn't see much with the snow in my face, still fighting the bear with my arm. I was pissed to say the least, being brought up around animals since I was little. You never let an animal get the best of you. I never did then. I wasn't about to now. It felt like the bear was about to rip my arm off. If my feet and legs weren't pinned down and held by my snowshoes, I could have a better chance. Wantalook was not letting up. As hard as I tried I could not get my right arm free. Then all of a sudden my left shoulder snapped and excruciating pain went all the way down my arm. My arm was useless now. Damn it. I came too far and did so much to survive out here and now to be taken out by a fricken bear. I knew if he let go my arm I wouldn't be able to protect my hand. I was thinking this is about the end when Wantalook must have hit pay dirt; the bear howled and let go of me and went for Wantalook. He had hit Wantalook with enough force that he was flying through the air and I could hear his yelp as it happened. It had given me enough time to free my arm and grab my gun. Wantalook was back on his feet and attacking the bear. Wantalook had hit the ground and when the bear turned back on me, I had the barrel under his chin and started pulling the trigger. The bear flopped down alongside of me but was still on my feet and legs. I was ready to shoot some more but when I saw I blew open the top and back of his head I knew it was over except the nerves.

I looked over to see Wantalook laying on the ground bleeding bad. I dug my legs as free as I could with my one arm and used my knife to cut my feet free. My heart just sank when I saw Wantalook. That bear had ripped him up good before I could help him. I've got help myself. I removed my coats and I could see my shoulder was out of place. My lower arm had some teeth holes but no arteries were damaged. I had to move fast to get my shoulder back in place before my adrenaline wore off. I hope I can do this on the first try, even the slightest movement was painful. I needed to pull my arm outward and slam my shoulder into a tree. I was in tears by the time I got pressure on my arm when I slammed the tree. It went back into place. I had to sit down before I fell down. My hands were shaking from the pain and my stomach felt nauseous. I got my one jacket on and put Wantalook inside my other one. I cut my T shirt off me to use on Wantalook. He knew I was trying to help and doing my best not to hurt him anymore. At times he yelped with his teeth against my hand but not biting me. I got him wrapped up the best I could and grabbing my jacket that was around him, picked him up with my right arm and put him on the sled and secured him with rope. I had my left hand in my coat pocket and used rope around me to keep the arm still. I slipped on the showshoes and started toward the cabin as fast as I could. I didn't know if I could save Wantalook but I would try my best. I didn't stop the whole way back to the cabin. I couldn't stop. I needed every minute.

When I reached the cabin, I untied Wantalook and opened the door, carried him inside and put him on the table. I started a quick fire and got out my first aid kit. He was in bad shape and lost a lot of blood. I had to tie him down even as weak as he was; it would be safer for both of us. He was so weak. I cleaned his wounds and put muscles back in place the best I could and sewed each one closed. I didn't have any suture material for internal stitches. By the time I finished Wantalook was out. He was breathing but that's it. I made a bed for him by the stove and covered him up. My arm was killing me. I didn't take time to take any pain killers myself. I had blood all over me from the bear, from Wantalook and my own. I took some pain relievers and ampicillin and unwrapped my arm. I had bite marks from my wrist to almost my elbow with several puncture wounds that will need stitches. I cleaned each one and the alcohol brought tears to my eyes. This is going to be hard doing the stitches one-handed. I had to use my teeth to tie knots; that was the easy part. Pushing the needle through the skin was another thing. By the time I tied the last I was in a sweat and breathing hard.

I finished getting cleaned up and changed my clothes, then made a sling for my arm. Wantalook looked so bad laying there lifeless and wrapped up. His breathing was still good. I just hoped he would make it. I didn't want to lose my friend who fought so hard to save me and had been the most unlikely companion a person could have. I put my clothes in soap and water to soak till tomorrow. I took my watch out of my pants pocket to clean it up. The crystal was cracked but still running. My old Timex took a licken and it's still ticken. I couldn't believe the time—it was after 10:00 and all this happened this afternoon. I got out my bourbon, sat on the edge of the bed and had a drink. I stayed awake most of the night checking on Wantalook plus my shoulders won't let me sleep long anyhow.

Wantalook was still out when morning came. I started a pot of moose stew on the stove so it will be ready when he wakes up. I need to get fluids and nourishment into him, fluids mainly. I still need to get the last of the meat into the food shack too. I'll do that later. While the stew was cooking I washed all the clothes out and had them hanging to dry. I went outside to pull the hind leg up into the food shack. I had a hard time doing it but it's done. I went back inside to be with Wantalook. He was still out. I took my solar lights outside to get charged up. I drained them down yesterday. I went in to lay down. I was still very tired. I laid there looking at Wantalook thinking about all we have done and been through these past few months. But Wantalook was in good shape and strong. I am sure he will pull through this. I don't want to lose a friend especially now with winter starting. I had fallen asleep and I woke up dreaming about Wantalook and I playing. I looked down and he was still the same.

I got down beside him and started petting his head and talking to him trying to get him to wake up. I wasn't getting any reaction so I kept talking to him and stroking his head. A couple hours went by and I was feeling about as sad as anyone could. I wanted my friend back. I touched the hair on the edge of his ear and the ear moved. I touched it again and again it moved. I had water ready for as soon as he came around. I kept talking and tickling his ear and he started to move and opened his eyes. I was so happy. I was in tears. I dropped some water on his mouth and he licked my fingers. I got the pan of water by him and held him so he could drink and he did.

He laid his head back down. He was weak but he will make it now. Later on I got him to eat some and drink some water, that was a good sign. I stayed by his side the rest of the day and by evening he was starting to move more and holding his head up. Well, Wantalook, it looks like our wrestling days are over for a long while. Don't we look a sight, we're both crippled and bandaged up but we won the war. We had some more to eat before it was time to get some sleep. I fell asleep happy that night. I had my wolf back. He had saved my life and I saved his.

When I opened my eyes Wantalook was watching me. I got down beside him and gave him his loving. He was a lot perkier today. I liked seeing that. I got him fresh water and food; his appetite was coming back too. Well, what are we going to do today, Wantalook? How about we lay around the cabin and lick our wounds? He just looked at me as if I lost my mind. Wantalook was not too crazy about having his leg and shoulder immobilized but he's getting used to it. Wait till I go to take his stitches out at the end of ten days, that will be an event in itself. I got back up and sat on the edge of the bed—that's when I noticed the black and blue on my hand. I took off my shirt and my arm and shoulder was black and blue. Well that explains why it still hurts like hell. I will need to ice it down or stand outside half naked for a while. I can just imagine how Wantalook feels. He was not only torn up but severely bruised. It was a wonder he didn't receive broken ribs. I put my shirt half on and went outside.

I put snow on my arm and shoulder for about twenty minutes until I thought I was turning into Chilly Willy. I know it helps but it still hurts. I was glad to get back inside and warm up. Wantalook just laid there probably still thinking I lost my mind. I got my shirt back on and got my arms back into the sling and tied my arm to my body to keep from moving it. After this I needed to lay down and try to relax.

It was time for lunch when I got back up. I had been sleeping for a couple of hours. I slipped my coat on and got some food out of the food shack for the rest of the day. I chopped up Wantalook's food so it would be easier for him, some fish and meat. I had some stew and fried up a chunk of meat also. We slept off and on the rest of the afternoon. I got up to add more wood to the stove. Wantalook was moving more but he wasn't ready to get to his feet yet. I had to get him more water. I was happy to see him drinking this much. I fixed up some supper and Wantalook was eating more with each meal. I laid back down. I guess I wasn't feeling the best either. I woke up around midnight and had a big drink of water and I was running a fever. I made sure Wantalook had water and went back to bed.

I woke up the next morning wet from sweat and feeling weak. I took more medicine and drank water till I couldn't drink anymore. I managed to get Wantalook his food and water and went back to bed. I woke up with Wantalook licking my face. He was up sitting by my bed. I don't know if he had made it on his feet but he was up on his front paw. I petted him and assured him I was alright. I was feeling better but still weak. When I sat up my head was spinning for a minute or two. Wantalook laid down by my feet. He was moving slow. I could tell he was hurting too. I got dressed; I wanted to step outside for some fresh air. I think Wantalook wanted the same. He staggered to his feet and slowly made his way to the door. I helped him outside. The fresh air felt good on my face as I stepped into the sunlight. Wantalook was looking for a place to relieve himself. Step by step he was getting better walking on three legs. We were outside for about ten minutes and I helped Wantalook back inside. He was ready to lay down by now. I was feeling better too and made us some food. We were getting down on water so I started melting snow. I wasn't up to making a trip to the spring and back. Wantalook just cat-napped while I stayed busy. After I got all the snow melted for water I laid down for a nap too. Rest and food and water is all we need to worry about right now.

When I woke up, Wantalook was at the door wanting out. I got my boots and jacket on and went out with him. He found another spot to relieve himself and it dawned on me he's housebroke. I sat in the chair for a while. Wantalook walked around the camp some till he came up to me and I petted him some and we went back inside. I was going to cook moose steaks tonight. Wantalook was watching me cook and his nose was checking if things were done yet. Yup, Wantalook, we're just a couple of cripples in the wilderness, but we are eating good. The cabin was filled with the smell of meat cooking and both of us were ready to eat. After supper was over we went outside one more time then returned to the warmth of the cabin. I was feeling tired and needed to lay down. My arm and shoulder were still bothering me and I drifted off to sleep.

I remember waking up several times during the night to find a comfortable spot and fell back to sleep. I think I sat on the bed ten minutes or more before even thinking about standing up. I think Wantalook felt the same way. All he did was lift his head and laid back down. I finally got dressed, put some wood in the stove and when I got on my boots and coat is when Wantalook got up. I was surprised how nice it was out, sun shining and temperatures in the 20s my guess. I felt like setting outside so I started a fire and got some fish and meat out. I like the smell of wood smoke in the open air. We sat by the fire like we have done so many times in the past. Wantalook by my side, he had two fish and was enjoying meat scraps while I cooked mine on a stick and from time to time he would get some of mine. As long as he will eat I will keep feeding him to get his strength back. I put more wood on the fire and Wantalook laid down by my feet. A couple hours went by and I got more food out. It took Wantalook a while but he ate two more fish and I was having more moose on a stick till I was full. I was starting to doze off by the fire. I looked down and Wantalook was sleeping. I sat there a while longer till my butt was getting numb. I had to get up. One thing for sure, I wasn't used to all this sitting around and doing nothing. I got my bucket and walked to the spring. I only carried it half full, full was too much yet. So I wound up making several trips till all my containers were full. Wantalook was laying down waiting for me to finish so I could set beside him and give him his petting. It was getting dark by now. I fed him more food before we went inside for the night. I had to restart the fire in the stove before I could get into bed. Wantalook was already in his spot for the night.

The next few days were all pretty much the same. Eating, resting and getting stronger. I was getting more use of my hand and arm. The muscles were still stiff and tight. I had to keep my arm in a sling most of the time. The shoulder was far from being normal. Wantalook was recovering real good and getting stronger by the day and more like his old self. He doesn't know it but today is stitch removal for both of us. This will be a challenge. Wantalook was pretty much out of it when I put his in but he won't be now. I removed his bindings and bandages. All his areas looked real good. This was the first time his leg and paw had been free. I got out my travel bag and removed the tweezers and nail clippers. I was hoping I wouldn't have to tie him up for this. I had a lot of stitches to remove.

I could tell he was still tender so I started out slow I removed the easy ones first so he would get used to what I was doing. I could see some that wouldn't be easy at all. I had removed over thirty so far and Wantalook had been pretty good a few times to let me know it hurt when he put his teeth against my arm. I kept talking and petting him, reassuring him it will be alright. I was making progress but his patience was getting a little thin. So I started a game with him. I would be ready to pull and cut after I would give him a piece of meat just big enough to keep his mouth busy for a few seconds. It worked but after a while, he was wise to my trick and wasn't having anymore to do with it.

Well, plan B. I wrapped his back legs in a blanket and got his back against the pile of boards and knelt on his stomach and neck. I had to scream no at him several times till I got the rest out. One quick look over everything. I was done! After I let him up, it took a while before we were friends again. But with coaxing and food, he was fine. After seeing the scars and all the stitches I took out, I can see why it took me several hours of putting him back together. It will be weeks before he will even start using that leg. Now it was my turn. Wantalook was watching me take mine out. I think he liked it when I showed pain on a few of mine. When I finished Wantalook laid down and started licking and cleaning himself. I know I need a short rest. My shoulder was letting me know I had moved too much.

When I got up it was time for lunch. It was still snowing when we went outside. This is the third day. I've been trying to keep up with it every day and I'll do some more after I eat. I got meat out of the meat shack and went back inside. I was out of fish, maybe I'll try to get some later. Wantalook wasn't even trying to use that leg yet. The way those muscles were torn up I just hope he lets them heal more. When lunch was over, we went outside and I started moving snow. My push board worked good using my hip to push with. After getting the yard and pathway cleared, I sat under the overhang a while and watched the snow coming down.

Well Wantalook, break time is over. Let's go fishing. I tied on my snowshoes, grabbed the ax, my pole and headed to the lake. Wantalook followed along. I chose a spot and started chopping a hole one-handed. I finally chopped through the ice and cleared out the chunks. It took a while to get a bite but the first one was nice size. But it didn't take long till the fish were biting like old times. Wantalook was enjoying his share and after a few hours of fishing, I had to drag a bunch back to camp. When it does turn very cold, I won't be able to fish till spring so I might as well catch what I can while I can. The fish were frozen by the time I put them in the food shack. I was kind of like stacking wood.

By now I was ready to go inside and get warm. Wantalook was laying down before I got my jacket off. Today is the most he has moved since the bear attack thirteen days ago. I added more wood to the stove and laid down too. When I got up the meat was thawed out and I fried up a couple of steaks for myself while Wantalook ate fish and meat scraps. Afterwards we got our quality time in, then I let Wantalook outside for his nature call and let him back in. I laid on my bed thinking about today and all I've been through since June. I thought about my family in Michigan, how they were doing and what they were feeling, not to mention what they were thinking about me. I turned over and went to sleep.

I woke up early to the sound of the wind blowing through the trees. I looked out the window and snow flying in the air was all I could see. I got dressed, slipped on my boots and jacket and stepped outside. It was like a blizzard out. I stood under the overhang. It took a while to see where the fire pit was. It was a white out. Even Wantalook was thinking twice about going out. I pulled down my hat and buttoned my collar and made my way to the food shack. The snow and driving wind was so bad even though it was only a few minutes my face felt like it froze. We got back inside. I had to warm my face and hands. Well, Wantalook, it looks like we will be inside for a while till this blows over. We ate our breakfast on the warmth of the cabin while the wind howled outside. I was setting on the bed and Wantalook leaned against me for some petting. I took a few minutes to see how his injuries were healing and there were no signs of problems or infection. I was glad to see that. I would like to get started on the inside of the cabin but the arm and shoulder aren't ready for that yet.

When the petting was over, I laid down for a while and stared at the inside of the cabin and started thinking about my family and the holidays coming up and the family get-togethers we would have. Yes, there were times one could never forget. But it seemed as the years progressed and the family got bigger, getting everyone together at the same time was harder and harder. As some go their own way, seeing or being with the rest of the family is not important to them. I guess it's that way in a lot of families. Right now Wantalook is my family and we're together through the holidays and beyond.

I got up; I had to do something. There were some clothes that needed cleaning and some clothes to mend too. So now I've got something to keep me busy for a while. I got the washing done and the clothes were hanging to dry. I made up a pot of stew and let it cook on the stove for later on. Wantalook was waiting to go outside so I opened the door. I took a quick look and it didn't take long before Wantalook wanted back in. He shook off the snow and he wanted to play. Yup, he's feeling better. When he was satisfied he laid back down. I sat at the table to start doing some sewing. My jacket was the worst, then my shirt and the sleeve to my thermals. Afterwards, I got into my food I'd been saving and got myself some dried fruit and ate a few pieces. It's been a few months and I knew I needed some vitamin C. I've still got to go through my food to see what I have left and how to ration it out for the winter and spring. I was feeling like a short nap so I took the stew off the stove and laid down.

I woke up with Wantalook in my face, I mean nose to nose. Maybe he was checking to see if I was still breathing, talk about a rude awakening. I sat up and petted his head. I gave him his food and put the pot back on the stove. I could hear the wind still blowing outside. I was glad I had no reason to be out there. When the stew was hot, I dished myself a bowlful. Wantalook wanted some too. So I got a bowl for him and let it cool. He was taking quite a liking to cooked food. I just hoped he didn't get gas like some of my dogs did. He finished his stew in record time. Damn Wantalook, you're eating like I never fed you. I cleaned the dishes while Wantalook laid down. I got out my measuring stick and was checking my plans for the cupboards and base cabinet I was going to build. I was looking forward to this project. It will take up a lot of my time and time is what I had a lot of. Wantalook was wanting out for his nature call so I opened the door. Everything under the overhang had snow on it. Wantalook didn't stay outside long and I let him back in. We played for a little while till it was time to go to sleep. I filled the stove and climbed in bed and fell asleep listening to the wind.

Wantalook woke me up with a wet tongue across my face. That wolf and I are going to have to have a long talk about this. I got up and Wantalook wanted outside. I looked out the door and it looked like the snow had stopped but there was a good amount of wind yet. I added more wood to the stove and got dressed. I put the rest of the stew on to heat up. I sat down to eat. Wantalook was still outside. Well it must not be too bad out there. I got on my heavy clothes and went outside too. I got down my push board and started clearing snow. There were some big drifts that needed to be moved along with the paths to be cleaned also. I spotted Wantalook—he was marking his territory outside the camp area. I was taking a short break when he came up to play afterwards. I got his fish out and went back to pushing snow while Wantalook watched.

It was time for lunch and a much needed rest. We went inside, it was nice to get out of the wind. I heated up the last of the stew and sat down to eat. Wantalook was eating his fish and looked up at my food. This is mine, I told him, and he went back to eating. I put on my hat and coat and went back out to attack the snow some more. The going was slow; a couple of the drifts were over six feet and with only one good arm it was a lot harder.

It was 6:00 when I got the yard and a path to the food shack cleared. I found out how tired I was after I got inside and was getting warmed up. I got Wantalook his food and started frying up some meat for myself. It didn't take long after petting Wantalook that between the food and the heat I was getting sleepy. I let him out for the last time and we settled in for the night.

Eight

When I woke up, Wantalook was waiting at the door to go out. I looked out the door; it was clear and no wind. I was glad to see that I would be able to work outside today. I put some wood in the stove and got dressed for the great outdoors. I cleaned out the fire pit and got a fire started. Wantalook wanted some playtime. It was more petting and pushing against each other than anything, that was all we were up to. I fed Wantalook and started clearing the path to the lake and took a break. I was looking at the snow on some of the mountain areas and the area to the east looked like there could be an avalanche at any time. We were safe where we were at so I wasn't worried. I didn't feel like clearing the path to the spring. I'll use my snowshoes for that. I needed more water so I made several trips to get everything filled up. I sat by the fire after that till it was evening and I cooked some moose on a stick. The camp was about normal and I had moved enough snow. If I can keep this cleaned out the rest of the winter it will be good. It's been dark for a while and it was time to go in. I've been outside all day with the exception of keeping the fire going in the stove. It was nice stepping into a warm cabin and it didn't take long before the eyelids were getting heavy. I filled the stove and pulled the covers over me.

When I opened my eyes Wantalook was setting by the bed watching me. At least I wasn't getting my face washed. He was eager to get outside. I got up and let him out and sat down, still trying to get the sleep out of my eyes. I tossed a few pieces of wood in the stove then got dressed. I could use a cup of coffee but I've only got a small amount left. It was another nice day out. The skies were clear and the air had a sharpness to it. It had to be around zero degrees out. I could feel the hair in my nose freezing when I breathed in and the cold penetrated my globes. I got the fire going in the pit, it was a nice buffer against the cold. I got food out of the shack and started cooking some pieces over the fire. Wantalook was making short work of his food. I made sure he had plenty. He was waiting for me to get done so we could have our playtime and when the last piece was gone, it was game on. We played for ten to fifteen minutes till we both were tired. I sat down by the fire a while but still had to keep turning to warm the other side. It was too cold so I went back in the cabin. I set up a board to start shaving it smooth; it takes two hands to give my arm a rest. I don't think I'll make much progress. I just keep at it a little at a time.

It was time for lunch so I checked how the temperature was. It had warmed up to livable so we ate outside. I was glad to see Wantalook was doing better. He is starting to use that leg some and in a few weeks he'll be good as new. It's surprising how quiet it is with the snow on the ground, any sound is deadened out. I sat there with Wantalook for almost two hours before I got up to work some more. Wantalook wanted to come in this time and he laid down by the stove. I started back on the board I started earlier. My forearm was giving me more trouble than my shoulder, the muscles were still very tight. As the afternoon went by, progress was made. I had one board. I cleaned up and put the shavings in the pit. The temperature was dropping and it was going to be cold tonight. After we ate our supper I played with Wantalook before we went inside. I was looking at the board I had done and what a difference compared to the others. Those cupboards are going to look great and they will be what this place needs for a more homey look. It was time to get some sleep and that bed felt good. I laid there a while and realized that it was November 15th. Five months now, I've been here. One never knows what events will happen that can change your life overnight. If I never get rescued I will have experienced a dream and I have no regrets either way. With the exception of my family not knowing where I am and how I am doing. Well I better get to sleep so I can find out what tomorrow will bring.

Oh Wantalook I am awake. Do you serve towels with the face washing? Damn something wound him up this morning. He wanted out big time and I barely got the door opened and he was gone. I shut the door and sat down for a few minutes till the mind and body were running on the same wavelength. I filled the stove and slowly got dressed. I took a check outside and quickly came back in. It's too cold to be spending much time out there this morning. The trip to the food shack was a quick one. Wantalook wanted his outside. I was going to eat mine inside. After breakfast was over I set up to start another board. It was around 10:00 when Wantalook wanted back in. After he got his petting, he laid down in his spot and watched me work. The way I figured if I could get one or possibly two boards done a day for now would be pretty good and I should be ready to start building in December. I was working away to get the surface of the board smooth only stopping to sharpen my knife.

Wantalook was taking a nap. Well, he can't be taking too much of a nap. He's keeping his ears tuned in on me. It was almost lunch time and I needed a break. I fried up some meat while Wantalook ate his fish and stared at me while I tried to eat with those "give me some" eyes. What a rotten wolf. I was sure glad he wasn't spoiled, ya right. When I finished he was wanting some loving so I spoiled him some more with a lot of petting and scratching. He wanted back out when I finished scratching and not before. I let him out and went back to making smooth. Yep, that's what I'll call this job, making smooth.

By evening I had finished that board and got a start on another when I stopped. I got my hat and jacket on and went outside the cabin till I had enough. I got food out and we went inside. Wantalook was getting stronger by the day and I sure could feel it every time we played. After we ate, we just sat by each other and enjoyed our time like we always have. It was getting late. I filled the stove for the last time and went to bed.

I woke up with a dry face this morning. Wantalook was just getting to his feet after a yawn and a stretch. He was ready to go out. Hang on to your horses, I am coming. I couldn't get the door opened fast enough for him. He pushed past me and was out. I had to put some wood in the stove first before I did anything. After I got dressed I slipped on my jacket and went outside. Wantalook wanted to play and he wasn't going to leave me alone till I did. We chased each other back and forth in a game of tag, pushing, and he was trying to knock me down. I couldn't get too rough with him. I was getting winded so I let him take me down and he stayed right on top of me till I gave up. He's feeling better alright. I got to my feet and brushed myself off then got our food out of the food shack. Wantalook was ready to eat. I gave him four fish and some meat scraps. I went inside to cook my breakfast and started making smooth.

Wantalook didn't want to come in, he liked his outside time. As soon as I finished I started back on the board I started on last evening. I was working about an hour when I heard Wantalook growling and was making a fuss. I threw on my coat and was out the door with my gun out. Wantalook was at the food shack raising hell, hate and discontent. I took a while to see what had him in such a state. There was a Pine Marten trying to get in. They're of the weasel family. I was surprised it got by the snares. Wantalook was following him from one side to another, still showing he was pissed. I finally got the chance to shoot and blew it right off the platform. The second it hit the ground, Wantalook had it; it was already dead but he didn't care. Wantalook wanted to apply his hurt, then made a meal out of it. When he was done, I praised him and patted him on the head. I went back inside to work while Wantalook wanted to play watch wolf.

While I worked I thought of all the squirrels around; at least I do not have to put up with them yet. When I got that board done, I took a break with Wantalook. When I went outside he had a spot picked out on top of a pile of snow where he could see all over. He came down for his petting and to be alongside of me. Wantalook went back to his spot. Yep, everything here was his property including me. That was fine with me. I felt the same way. I started on the next board; it seems like every board is different. Some areas you can smooth out fairly easy and some spots are a bugger. I finished that one and was about to start another when I realized it was time for supper.

The temperature outside was livable so I cooked out there. I'll have the camp special tonight, moose on a stick. The fire was going good and I sat down to enjoy my meal. I was on my second piece when Wantalook finished his food. Then he sat there with that "I see you eating, give me some too," look, while following every move, every bite I made. I told him it wasn't nice to stare. That didn't change a thing. I gave him a bite and he made sure what I didn't eat, he was happy to help me with. I took a few minutes to clean up the wood shavings in the cabin, dumped them on the fire and sat down with my favorite wolf. The skies were clouding up and it looked like we were going to get more snow. We sat for an hour or so till it was getting time to go inside. Wantalook laid down in his spot as I prepared for bed. The stove was full and the only thing left was to pull the covers over me and fall asleep.

I woke up to a cold nose on my cheek and a warm breath in my ear. That meant only one thing—Wantalook wanted me up so he could get outside. I let him out and put a few pieces of wood in the stove and sat down, rubbed the sleep from my eyes and tried gathering up my senses into a collective cooperating form. Maybe a little coffee, about one mug worth, is all I need. I got out the coffee pot, measured water and a good pinch of coffee and set in on the stove. At this point I didn't care how it tasted, it will be the caffeine I need. The coffee was almost done by the time I got dressed. The aroma alone was waking me up. Oh, that first sip let my senses know it was a new day. I drank about half before going outside. I was ready to take on the furry critter that awaited me outside the door. There was a light snow coming down with around an inch on the ground. Wantalook almost knocked me over before I got out from under the overhang. It's got to be something about new snow that gets him fired up. That or the energizer rabbit gave him a jump start before I got out here. When I cleared the overhang it was game on. We chased and tagged each other around the yard, pushing and wrestling. Neither one of us was going to give up—so I thought till he tripped my legs. I didn't even have a chance to find my feet and I was covered in fur, blocking every attempt to get up. It was time to give in, he won again. After my walking fur ball got through licking my face, he let me up. I cleared the snow from my body and got him fish, then I sat down for a few minutes still recovering from the whooping Wantalook put on me. When he finished his fish he wanted some lovin' so I petted him a while. Wantalook wanted to stay outside.

I went in to start myself some breakfast. As soon as breakfast was over, I started on another board. I'll be making smooth. My arm was getting better day by day and less painful. I was glad of that. I scraped and smoothed on that board till mid-day when it was time for lunch break. I was surprised that the time went by so fast. I took a peek out the window and there was Wantalook on his mound of snow, covered in white, watching over his territory. I had a quick bite to eat and went back to work. It wasn't long before that board was done and I started another. This was going to be easy and cleaning up quick. I wish all of them were like this. It was late afternoon when I started another, not quite as lucky with this one. By 6:30 I was on the flip side when I called it quits for the day.

I slipped on my hat and coat and went outside. Wantalook was laying under the overhang out of the snow now. I gave him some petting and a head shake with both hands full of fur. We had about four inches of new snow on the ground. I was covered by the time I got back from the food shack. I had to brush myself off before I could go inside. Wantalook was ready to come in now. I put down his food and fried up mine. When supper was over it was our time to spend together. He had his head on my leg, leaning against me, taking all the petting I could give him. It was well over an hour before I got up to fill the stove. Wantalook went outside for his nature call and was back in a few minutes. He laid down in his spot as I got ready to get into bed, when I realized I hadn't cleaned up the shavings from today's work. I'll have to take care of it first thing in the morning. I covered up and found a sweat spot and was out for the night.

When I woke up I didn't move. I didn't know if Wantalook was awake yet. I was facing the wall when I felt a nose on the back of my hand. How did he know I was awake? I was awake. I turned over and got a face full of wolf and all. Enough, you spoiled rotten fur ball. I am getting up. He was dancing on his toes at the door wanting to get outside. He just about knocked me down as I opened the door. I closed the door behind him and went into my morning routine, filled the stove and got dressed. I looked out the window and it was just a light snow coming down. After breakfast I cleaned this mess up and then cleared the snow outside but first I've got this matter of a fur ball on legs to deal with.

With my hat, gloves and jacket in place, I opened the door. I didn't see him in the yard as I stepped out of the overhang.

He was waiting around the corner. It was game on now. I added snowballs in the game this time. Wantalook wasn't sure about flying balls of snow at first, then he loved it, catching a few, dodging a few, chasing each other around the yard. By the time it was over, there wasn't a spot left that didn't show where we have been. He won again. You just wait till you get healed up and I will win a few of these, now let me up. Other than the light snow coming down, it was a nice day. I got out our food and went inside. After breakfast I cleaned the snow out of the fire pit and got a fire started, then cleaned up the shavings from the cabin and tossed them in the fire. I got my push board out and started clearing the yard and paths, taking a break now and then.

It was late afternoon when a deafening roar hit my ears. The ground was shaking. I looked to the east; it was an avalanche. Wow, what a sight. I never in my life ever witnessed anything like that. It only lasted seconds and it was over with a dead silence. The edge of it was several yards away. I knew I was safe. All the signs I saw earlier this year showed no signs of an avalanche any closer to this area. Well, I can sit back down and start breathing normal again. That is another thing I can add to my list of been there done that. It didn't seem to faze Wantalook. He watched it and laid back down. I didn't sit long. I wanted to get started back on the boards. I was finished with the one from last night and it was time for lunch.

When it was over, I put on a pot of meat to cook the rest of the afternoon. Wantalook was still content to be outside so I started another board. Other than stirring the pot and the short breaks, I kept a steady pace on the boards of the day. I will leave the rest of it till tomorrow. I cleaned up the mess and took it outside to the fire pit. Supper was ready so I got Wantalook's fish out. I set my chair under the overhang and got a bowl of food. When I finished the last bite, it tasted like more so I had seconds for dessert. Wantalook was giving the eye, wanting some of mine. I had some left in the bowl so I let my poor wolf have the rest. After that Wantalook took his favorite position leaning against me with his head on my leg. I sat there with him for over an hour before we went in for the night. He went to his spot and laid down. I put away the rest of the food, filled the stove and laid down. While I was waiting for sleep to come, I was thinking back to the avalanche today and what a sight it was. Seeing them on TV is nothing like in person. I soon turned over and went to sleep.

Well, good morning my amber-eyed, big-toothed fur ball. That's all I could see at point blank. For my order this morning eggs over easy, bacon, coffee and hold the tongue. Wantalook no tongue, too late. He made sure I got lots of tongue. OK, I got my face washed. Let me up. He was waiting at the door before I got to my feet. I let him out and sat down. I wasn't through drying my face. I added some wood to the stove and got my clothes on. I looked out the window and it wasn't snowing so I could get a few things done outside. I guess I am as ready as I am going to be. Now to face the opponent. Wantalook was waiting for me as I came out the door and didn't waste any time when I was clear of the overhang. He wasn't expecting a snowball right from the start. I had it ready from the night before. But after that hit it was game on. I mean Wantalook was going to hand out some payback. I was tossing snow when I should be trying my best to keep on my feet. The more I pushed him away the harder he came back to get me. A few times it was a stand-off, waiting for me to make a move and we would go at it again. We finally wound up in a snowbank. I almost had him pinned but with all the snow he slipped loose and he pinned me. OK, OK, I give up, you win. Now he's going to give me another face wash before he lets me up, twice one morning. I had to go inside to dry off and remove the snow from inside my clothes before I went back out. Wantalook was ready to eat so I got out his fish and my food was heating up on the stove. I think I'll wait till later on when it warms up a little to work outside. After breakfast I started back on the board detail. I finished the first board by 10:30, got on my hat and coat to clear the snow out that had come down yesterday. It was a little warmer out when I started. There wasn't a lot so it didn't take long. When the snow was cleared, I made a few trips to the spring and filled up the water supply in the cabin.

I sat with Wantalook while I ate lunch. I'll need to catch more fish soon to keep the food supply up. There is enough for a few more days. I returned to my woodworking for the rest of the afternoon, only stopping for short rest and a knife sharpening. By evening I had four boards done for today. When I went outside to get out food, the wind had come up and it was too uncomfortable to set outside. Wantalook came inside till after the eating was over then he wanted back out. I was cleaning up the shavings from today, when I heard Wantalook howl. I never heard him do that before. I looked outside but couldn't see him. I tell ya, the sound of his voice seemed to go right through me. I got chills up and down my spine. It was a whole lot harder when I stepped outside. I couldn't hear any other wolves but he probably could. Maybe he was planning another outing soon. He was a lot better and using that leg now. I went back in to finish cleaning. Afterwards, I sat down on the bed. Wantalook wasn't howling anymore. I was waiting for him to come to the door so after a half hour I went outside and called him; he was nowhere around. Well, if he comes back, he'll let me know. I went back inside and got into bed. If I do three or four boards on one side. I can start building the cupboards. That is what I was looking forward to.

It seemed different to wake up and not have a face full of wolf. I looked out the window but didn't see him. I tossed some wood in the stove, got dressed and went outside. Wantalook was nowhere to be seen; that means I get a break this morning. I had a small amount to eat for breakfast. I wanted to get the last four boards scraped. I was through in a couple hours and now to make peg stock one-quarter inch this time. I marked out several boards to cut the edges to fit side by side. The strips from them I could make pegs. I cut as many strips just over one-quarter wide before the final cut. Then cut the one-quarter by one-inch strips in half and used my knife to trim them down and used a piece of metal with a quarter-inch hole drilled in it to get the final size of a quarter-inch. It took most of the afternoon to get all the peg stock made. I took a break and went outside for some fresh air. Wantalook was still gone so I didn't stay outside too long. I then marked out the boards for the bottom, the shelf and top of the cupboard, two boards equaling fifteen inches wide eight feet long, six boards all total. The four backboards come to twenty-eight inches long and sixteen inches total. It was after 7:00 and time to call it quits for the day.

I cooked some meat for supper. It seemed different not having Wantalook around but he'll be back when he's done doing his thing. I sat on the bed, picturing what the cupboard was going to look like on the wall and couldn't wait to get it done. Any other time I would be back up working till I was exhausted but I've got all kinds of time so there is no rush. I checked one more time for Wantalook and went to bed.

I slept good last night and felt great when I got up. My arm has been feeling better by the day. It's still a long way to go for the shoulder yet so long as I don't get crazy using it, I'll be fine. I added wood to the stove, got my clothes on and went outside. I was expecting to see Wantalook at any moment coming in for a surprise attack but nothing. Checking around the corner of the cabin and behind piles of snow, still nothing. He's got to have a girlfriend to be gone this long. I got my food out of the shack and went back inside. I fried up two steaks, one to eat at noon and the other later on today. I needed to sharpen the drill bit before I get started. I laid out the four backboards and started drilling and pegging the first end boards on, first drilling all the holes on an angle. Then I fastened half the top board, the shelf and the boards. I had to cut four corner supports, one inch by two inch by fifteen inches long. After pegging them in place, I fastened the other two end boards, then the last top, middle and bottom boards. I took a break to eat since it was afternoon already. Wantalook wasn't back yet so I ate alone. Next I needed to cut out brace boards four inch by fifteen inches by one inch to support the top, middle and bottom. I needed six of them. Then I needed to cut out four face boards, four inches by twenty-seven inches for the ends and over the shelf supports. When I got them pegged in place, it was ready to hang. I'll make the doors for it when it's on the wall.

I was finishing cleaning up when I heard the big bad wolf at my door. Well, it's about time he got his butt home. I opened the door and my bouncing ball of fur bounded inside and was all over me, licking my face and it seemed he couldn't get close enough. When things calmed down, I got on my hat and coat to get us supper out of the food shack. Wantalook was bouncing around like he was on springs. I was glad to have him back home. He wasted no time getting his fish and meat scraps down. I gave him two more for good measure. I'll be catching more tomorrow. I cooked up my supper and ate while Wantalook laid down in his spot. When I was done eating, he came over for his petting time with his head on my leg. I sat there for a long time with him and I was starting to nod off. Well Wantalook, it's time to get to bed. I filled the stove and crawled into bed.

You'll never guess what I could see; a big set of eyes looking at me. Morning, Wantalook, as I patted him on the head. He had to get his licks in before I could get out of bed. Settle down, I'll let you out. He was at the door, a moving ball of fur trying to let me know I wasn't moving fast enough. As soon as the door was wide enough open he was out. I sat down; that wolf has got too much energy. I got dressed, put on my hat and coat and got ready to face the fury of Wantalook. I didn't have to wait long when I stepped outside—the big bad wolf was ready to show me how bad he was.

I was holding my own for about five minutes. He had me down in a snowpile, blocking my every move to get free. So I played opossum and didn't move. He got off of me, nudged me with his paw and I still didn't move. He was about to lick my face when I grabbed him with my arm and legs and he couldn't get out of my grip. After a few minutes he started licking me. I won this one.

After I removed the snow from myself I climbed up the ladder and got our food out. It was cloudy and maybe in the 20s for the temperature, with a light wind. I think I'll eat outside this morning. I got the fire going in the fire pit and had moose on a stick. When we were done, I got my ax and pole and headed to the lake. Wantalook was running circles around me all the way onto the ice. I got a hole chopped through the ice and cleaned out the chunks.

It took a while to get the first bite after everything got quiet. But after the first one, the rest came easy. Wantalook ate two more while I fished. I wanted to catch enough to last a few weeks and I wanted some for smoking too. I stopped fishing long enough to drag the first bunch up to camp and get them in the food shack. I stopped long enough to warm my hands and headed back for more. When I filled the rope the second time, I figured we had plenty. I cleaned ten big ones for the smoker and got a fire going in it. Wantalook cleaned up the area. I cleaned the fish. I stood by the fire till my hands felt normal, then added more wood to the smoker.

I went inside to work on the cupboard. First I moved the table over to the wall where I was going to hang the cupboard. I set two gallon buckets on top then picked up the cupboard and set it on top of the buckets. I had to use wood to get the height I needed and used my bottle level to make it level. Then I started drilling holes on an angle and driving pegs in. I figured ten will hold nicely. I removed the wood and buckets and got back for a look. I like it. Wait till I get the doors on it. I moved the table back to my work area. I had to choose to make three big doors or six smaller ones. I'll make three big ones, less hardware to build. I picked out three boards to shave to get the width. I need just under twenty-seven inches per door. I went out to add more wood to the smoker, then came back in to start on the boards. These have to be smooth on both sides so it will take a while. When I went out Wantalook was on his pile of snow where he could see everything. He was content to stay there while I tended the smoker. I spent the rest of the afternoon scraping boards and I still wasn't done and it was time to eat and the fish were ready to take out of the smoker.

The evening was getting colder but nothing that a good fire couldn't take care of. The smoked fish tasted good. It's been a while since I had some. The fire felt good against the cold as we sat and ate our supper. Afterward it was our quality time of petting and being by each other. The fire was getting down and the cold was taking over so it was time to move inside. I could really feel the cold on the short walk from the fire pit to the cabin. I was glad when we got inside. I filled the stove and hung up my clothes. It was time to newspaper my boots again. They are too damp inside to keep your feet warm. I hung up the liners too. Wantalook was laying down while I sat on the bed looking at the cupboard on the wall. I finally laid down, covered up and went to sleep.

The morning was greeted with the face of Wantalook. I pulled the covers over my head and here comes a nose trying to find my face. He found a way in and the tongue wasn't far behind. He wasn't going to stop till I got up. I sat on the edge of the bed but he wasn't going to have that, he wanted outside now. I went to the door and let him out now. I would have a few moments of peace while I finished waking up. I had to feed the stove before I could feed myself. I got dressed and looked out the window. It was clear out and it looked cold, really cold. I put on my hat and coat and when I got outside, I could feel it biting at my skin. The hair in my nose was freezing. I did my trick of setting down when Wantalook wanted to play. I gave him about five minutes of time. I was not dressed for this. I quickly got his food out and went inside.

I was chilled to say the least. I will definitely need to put more clothes on to go out again. After I ate some fish I looked out to see what Wantalook was up to. He was on his mound of snow. So I started back on the last board scraping it smooth. When I finished it was time to cut out the boards to length and width. With three boards per door I need to cut out six hinge boards and three support boards so between the hinge and support it will look like a Z door. The six hinge boards were two inches by one inch by twenty-seven inches with one end rounded for the hinge with a slow taper to the other end being one inch. I put the three boards together and drilled and pegged the hinge boards in place. Then I cut the support board to fit and pegged as well. I had to cut out hinge blocks six all total two inches by four inches. Next I drilled the peg for the hinge. I set the door in place and drilled and pegged the hinge block. It opened and closed perfectly. I'll make the latch later.

It was lunch time and I was ready to eat. When I went outside Wantalook was ready too. This time he came inside. I don't blame him a bit but with that coat of his, it's just another day. I gave him some petting after we ate then he wanted back out.

So now since I had all the pieces cut out and the first door put together, the next two shouldn't take long at all to build. So one by one, I finished the two doors and started making the three latches. I kept it simple, a swing drop latch, two pegs to hold the block, one peg for the arm. I will wipe out the shelves and doing a little finish trim and smooth and this project is done. I stood back for a look. My gosh, someone call *Better Homes and Gardens* for a picture in their magazine. Now I have to get out the food I've been saving that I brought with me and put it away. I'll do that after I eat supper. Wantalook wanted to stay outside and eat fish. It was too cold for me to set out there.

When supper was done I opened the polyurethane container the food was in. It's been a few months since I've looked in there. Let's see, I've got one box of bisquick, a half gallon of flour, two large bags of noodles, dried fruit and dried vegetables, about a quart of beans and a bag of peas. I had more than I thought I did. I put it all in the cupboards along with the dried meat and my cooking utensils, dishes, pots, pans, and silverware. That sure changed the look of the inside of the cabin, having everything put away. I moved my calendar, that is when I realized that tomorrow was Thanksgiving Day. I guess I will have to make myself up a little something special to eat.

Wantalook was at the door so I let my big bad wolf in. I told Wantalook that all traces of piggys is gone. He just looked at me strange. I sat down with him for a while getting in our quality time before I go to bed. It was getting late and my eyes were starting to close. I filled the stove and crawled into bed.

Just like clockwork, Wantalook was there to wake me up, wet nose and all. I tried to push him away but he still managed to get few licks in before I could sit up. I was wiping my face and trying to get the sleep from my eyes while Wantalook was dancing by the door wanting out. Hey, just give me a minute, you rotten piece of wolf meat. I got to my feet, went over and opened the door. He was gone like someone lit his tail on fire. I'll feed the stove and sit down to gather my senses. I was still tired and I sure wasn't running on all eight cylinders yet. Coffee would be nice but I'll save what little I have left. I really felt like going back to sleep but needed to get dressed and feed my wild child and myself. I think when I go outside, I'll give Wantalook five or ten minutes then go down for a ten count. I'll let him win today. So I got my clothes on and stepped outside. I didn't see him, it's going to be a surprise attack. I no more stepped out from under the overhang and was jumped so hard, I didn't have time to recover. I mean I was out of the cleared yard into the deep snow. I managed to clear the snow from my face with Wantalook still on top of me. After five minutes or so he let me up. You just wait, Wantalook, one of these days I'm going to pay out back big time. My face felt like it was frozen as I cleaned the last of the snow off me.

I gave Wantalook his fish and took some meat to cook today. It took a while for my face to warm up. I left the meat out to thaw. I ate my smoked fish and started setting up to scrape boards. I put a pot of water on the stove and added some dried bear meat, vegetables and peas. Then I cut up the moose into chunks and put that in the pot. Now to let it slow cook. Later on, I'll make myself a couple of biscuits. I spent the rest of the morning shaving boards. It was getting close to lunch so I made up some flour and water to thicken up the broth and made up a couple of biscuits in a pan. I got Wantalook to come in. I was surprised, maybe it was the smell that helped. I waited till he ate his fish before giving him a bowl of food. Well Wantalook, Happy Thanksgiving, we are all the family there is out here. I couldn't help think about my family back in Michigan and all the food and fun. I can only imagine how they are feeling right now. But I am alive, don't give up because I never will. The biscuits were good. I had gravy to dip them in and I had two bowls of bear-moose stew. I was stuffed. One other Thanksgiving tradition, a nap in the afternoon. Wantalook wanted back outside. He went out and I laid down.

It didn't take long, I was sawing logs. When I woke up it was after 3:00, I had to lay there a few more minutes before getting up to start working. I scraped boards the rest of the afternoon into the evening before calling it quits for the day. While the stew was heating up, I cleaned up the work area.

I slipped on my hat and coat to get Wantalook food out of the food shack. Wantalook was waiting for me and it wasn't just food he wanted, he wanted to play too. After a few minutes of play I got him his food. I went back inside, got a bowl of stew and joined him. I didn't feel like starting a fire this late so I set in the cold a while. I was ready to go back in when I finished but Wantalook wanted to stay outside. The heat of the cabin felt good when I stepped inside and soon the chill was gone from the body. I sat on the bed a while thinking over the next project to build. I think I sat there over an hour before the bad wolf was at the door. Gee, if I let the wolf in he might eat me. If I don't let him in, he'll kick my butt tomorrow morning outside. I think I'll let him in, he's a good wolf. We sat for a while enjoying our quality time till I started to fall sleep sitting there. I got up, filled the stove and got into bed.

I must have been tired. I barely remember shutting my eyes last night. Wantalook was setting by my bed waiting for me to wake up. I patted his head and I got to my feet to get the door open for him. Wantalook was out the door like he was on a mission. I tossed a few pieces into the hungry stove and sat on the bed a while. After getting dressed, I had some fish before going out to face the animal that waits for me outside the door. I slowly opened the door and stepped out. No Wantalook in sight. He's planning another sneak attack. I'll be ready for him this time. I looked around the corner of the cabin; he wasn't there. I was looking around the snowpiles, still nothing. Then I spotted him hiding behind the fire pit, waiting for me to head for the food shack. I know what your attack plan is, wait till my back is turned. The path to the food shack was right across from the fire pit. I was at the path when I turned and charged toward the fire pit where Wantalook was hiding. You would think someone lit a firecracker off under him the way he sprang into the air. It was perfect. I had him and we both were rolling in the snow. We chased each other around. I was throwing snow trying to keep him back till I could get to the cleaned out part off the yard. This time we called it a draw. I was glad of that; another five minutes he would have won. I cleaned the snow off me and got Wantalook's food down. While he ate I sat down to rest and enjoy the view of the trees and mountains blanketed in white. There were some dark clouds coming in from the west and you could see the snow in the higher elevations. It won't be long before it gets here.

It was time to go in and get started on the boards again. I spent a few minutes to get my hands warmed up then set out the boards I wanted to work on today. I kept up a steady pace, stopping only for short breaks. At noon I put the stew on to heat up while I continued to work. It was snowing when I went inside to feed Wantalook. We ate under the overhang. I was enjoying seeing the big flakes come down and the way they seemed to float at times. If it keeps up like this we are going to have some inches to deal with in a short time. Wantalook didn't want to come inside so I went in to work.

After about three hours of scraping, I took a break. When I stepped outside, I was surprised at all the snow that fell, four inches and counting. I got out the push board to clear out the bulk of the snow so there would be less to deal with later on. I spent over an hour clearing the yard and paths. I then cleaned the snow off myself. I sat down with Wantalook while I rested, giving him more petting. I don't want him feeling deprived of any attention. When the spoiling time was over I went back inside to finish the fourth board of the day. It was evening when I finished scraping. Now it was time to clean up the mess. I took the scraps outside to the fire pit.

I got Wantalook's food down so we could eat. I had some stew left but I'll eat later. I just had some smoked fish. The snow wasn't showing any sign of letting up soon. By the time I went inside for the night, we had several more inches of snow. Wantalook wanted to stay out yet so I filled the stove and got ready for bed. My arm and shoulder were letting me know they were alive and they weren't pleased with the use of them today. Oh well, it comes with the territory. I opened the door and called Wantalook. I didn't see him around and he didn't come. I shut the door and laid down waiting for him to want back in and I fell asleep. I woke up during the night and checked outside for Wantalook. He was gone. I went back to sleep.

I woke up the next morning with a dry face and no eyes watching me. I fed the stove and checked for Wantalook. He wasn't back yet. I got dressed and ate the last of the stew before going outside. I had more snow to move, it looked like seven or eight inches worth. When I started clearing snow, I was glad I had a head start on it yesterday. I made Wantalook's lookout mound about two feet higher not to mention how much bigger the rest of the piles were getting. I took a short break after an hour; I still had a long way to go. I kept after it till almost noon. When I finished I even had the top of the piles pushed back. I was ready for a rest by the time I went inside. After hanging up my clothes, I sat down to some smoked fish and a much needed break.

When lunch was over I had to make a water run to the spring. So I got on my hat and coat, stepped inside and put on my snowshoes. It was a nice view with all the snow on the trees and sound didn't travel at all. I had to clear away ice and snow to fill my bucket. I only needed to make one more trip after this. With the trail broken it made it a lot easier going back. I emptied the bucket and went back for another. I had just filled the bucket and snapped on the lid, when I slipped on some ice and twisted my ankle. I hurt like hell but I don't think I broke anything.

When I got to my feet after about ten minutes, I could hardly stand to put any weight on it. It hurt more with the weight of the snowshoe. Great, I don't need this, not here, not now. I tried walking, going about ten feet. I wasn't going to make it back to the cabin this way. I had to empty the bucket. I can drag that back. I took off the snowshoes and turned them around where I could grab the tail end with my hands and kneel on the front end. I crawled on my hands and knees holding my foot up behind me. Thank goodness I had a trail already. My shoulder sure didn't need the strain but I had no choice. When I got to the yard, I could stand up and use the snowshoes to help steady myself as I hopped into the cabin.

I was glad to sit down; my hands were so cold I couldn't grab the zipper of my coat. After a few minutes of heat from the stove the fingers were letting me know they were still alive. Damn that smarts. I got my coat off and now to look at the ankle. I removed my boot then slowly removed my socks. It was black and blue. From what I could see nothing broken or sticking out. I got out my first aid kit and wrapped the ankle, took some pain reliever and laid down with my feet elevated. My ankle got first place for hurt, my shoulders were second.

After about forty-five minutes, I was feeling better. I had to get up and get some snow to put on the ankle. This ought to be interesting. I slipped on my boots and tightened my right one as tight as I could. I used one snowshoe to keep my balance. I could barely stand to set my foot down. I made it outside and scooped a bucket of snow and hopped and hobbled back in. I filled up two zip lock bags with snow. I removed my boots and put my foot up with the bags of snow around my ankle. I must have laid there for an hour before I moved again. The stove was needing more wood; at least I didn't have to move. I had enough wood inside for three or four days. I laid back down again and wound up falling asleep.

    I woke up to the sound of Wantalook at the door. I hopped to the door and let him in. It took a while to calm down his excitement of seeing me, protecting my ankle all the while. When he realized I was hurt, he calmed right down and tried to comfort me. I wasn't going out or up the ladder tonight so I gave him some dried bear meat and smoked fish. I had to lay back down and put my foot up. Wantalook was right by my side. At times his head was on my chest. And a occasional lick on my face. I remember dozing off a time or two. Oh, he was there watching me when I opened my eyes. It was getting late. I filled the stove and got back in bed and covered up.

    I had a rough night between my ankle and shoulder waking me up. I felt like I didn't sleep much. I sat up for a few minutes before putting my feet down. Wantalook was right there watching my every move. I added some wood to the stove and hopped to the door to let Wantalook out. By now my ankle was starting to throb so I sat down in the chair and put it up on the bed. I hate this crap not being able to move or do what I want. I had some smoked fish left so I ate that; maybe by tonight I can try to get to the food shack. I laid back down keeping my foot up. Now it's going to be weeks before things will be normal again. Water no problem. I can melt snow. I've got wood. I've got plenty of dried bear meat and when I can make it out to the food shack, I've got 1½ arms and one good leg when I do. I'll get enough for several days. For now I'll use a bucket to do my nature calls. Wantalook just won't be eating as well as he has till things get better.

    I laid back down and stared at the inside of the cabin. This just wasn't fun for me. I heard my big bad wolf at the door so I got up to let him in. I sat down to give him his petting till I couldn't sit anymore. I gave him some scraps and dried meat then laid down. Wantalook laid down by my bed instead of his spot. Every time I moved he was checking on me. I'd pat him on the head and tell him I am OK and he would lay back down. I fell asleep for a while when I woke up. Wantalook wanted outside. After I let him out, I needed to add wood to the stove and laid down again.

It was evening when I heard Wantalook at the door. I got up to let him in and I couldn't believe it. He came in carrying a rabbit he caught and dropped it at my feet. I praised him up and down and gave him a bunch of petting. He was fine with the leftovers when I cleaned it. After the cooking was done, I got the back legs. Wantalook got the rest and my leg bones. Afterward we shared our quality time. I couldn't help but smile when I looked at my Wantalook. He was quite a friend. It was getting late so I filled the stove and crawled into bed. Wantalook sat beside me a while before laying down beside my bed.

When I woke up Wantalook was watching me. I gave him a quick head rub and he moved in for the face lick. I got up and sat on the bed a minute before letting him out. So far I was feeling a lot better than yesterday. The stove was screaming feed me, feed me so I made sure it's belly was full. I took my snowshoes that were by the door. I overlapped them to make the right height and tied them together for a crutch. I tried a few steps, it worked good. I got dressed and tried how the boot would feel if the weight would be too much or not, so far so good. I haven't put any weight on it and didn't want to yet. So I put on my coat and made it out the door.

Wantalook looked at me as if I lost my mind but he walked by me to the food shack. I moved the ladder in place. I managed to climb it with one leg. When I got the door open, I dropped down enough fish and meat for a week. When I got down I filled the bucket and took it back to the cabin. I went back for more till I had it all. I put it in the urethane container and kept it outside the door. I made sure Wantalook had plenty to eat. I'll cook mine after I sit down and put my foot up a while. It didn't feel too bad, just a mild scream, but after a half hour of being elevated, I could live with it now. I cooked up some meat on the stove and gave Wantalook a few bites as I ate mine. He wanted back outside so I let him out and laid down for a little while. I was glad I could make the trip to the food shack and back and the snowshoes worked out good for me. When I got up I set up a board to start scraping, standing for ten to fifteen minutes then rest with my foot up. It worked out quite well. As long as I was getting something done I was happy. It was funny. Wantalook would come in and check on me from time to time.

After lunch I laid down a while and so did Wantalook. I was doing better but I had to keep reminding myself to not overdo it. It was mid-afternoon when I got up and let Wantalook out. I went back scraping on the board. It was evening when I finished with it. I did a quick cleanup and sat down. I was happy with what I had accomplished today. It wasn't long till my big bad wolf was at the door. I let him in and got his fish out of the container and went back inside. I could hear the wind picking up out there as I shut the door. There will be drifting again. When supper was over we settled in for our quality time we share every evening. The time went by so fast that it was almost 9:00 when I got up. I filled the stove and waited for Wantalook to come back in. I looked out the door and the snow was flying everywhere. What was on the trees is gone now. Let it snow and blow. I don't need to go outside for a while now. Wantalook didn't spend too long out there before he was back inside. I got into bed and he still laid beside my bed.

When I woke up I could hear the wind howling outside. When I let Wantalook out, I couldn't see anything outside. The air had a sharp bite to it. Everything under the overhang was covered with snow that blew in through every crack there was and the open side too. Needless to say I wasn't outside the door long. I filled the stove and started cooking breakfast. I was done eating and Wantalook hadn't asked to come in. I looked out the door and he was laying under the overhang watching, playing guard wolf or whatever. I gave him his fish and went back in. He'll let me know when he wants in.

I set up the next board and started scraping. The ankle was feeling better but I was still staying off it. The boards I am doing now only need to be scraped on one side. I'll be able to get more done now. I was still taking breaks throughout the morning to give my good leg rest too. When I stopped for lunch I had two done and started on the third. Wantalook came in for a short while to eat and get some much needed attention before going back outside.

Wantalook checked on me twice but still wanted to spend most of his time outside. It seems the colder and nastier the weather the better he likes it. I went outside for a little while and I had enough. I finished two more boards making today's total five. I was tired by the time I sat down to eat. Wantalook laid down while I cleaned up the wood shavings. As soon as I sat down, Wantalook had his head on my leg getting in his quality time with me. We sat for over an hour before I had to quit. I was falling asleep. Wantalook wanted out one last time. I got the stove filled and he was back at the door. We both laid down and I was soon asleep.

Wantalook, get that cold nose off me. When I said that I got the tongue treatment. What a way to wake up in the morning. Maybe since he can't beat me outside, he figures he can lick me in here. Enough, enough I am getting up. He was dancing at the door waiting to get out as I sat up. I hobbled to the door, he helped push it open before I could. The wind was still blowing as I looked out and the cold gave a sharp tingle to my skin. I shut the door and rubbed my bare arms. It's a good day to stay inside. The fire was down in the stove and it required some immediate attention. So after a little stir of the coals and some fresh wood, it was cooking now. I got dressed, slipped on my jacket to get some food out of the box. Wantalook wanted to eat outside. I sure wasn't. It was too cold for me. I might venture out later with all my heavy clothes on but definitely not like this. After cooking up a little breakfast, I picked out the boards I wanted to work on today.

I was getting to where I could put a little weight on my ankle now and then. I am still going to give it a few days more to heal before I start using my full weight on it. I got the first board set up and sharpened the edge on my knife and got started. Wantalook came in a couple hours later to check on me, get some petting and went back out. The weather hasn't changed yet but that didn't bother Wantalook at all. I was making better progress today on the smoothing of the boards so in a few days

I can start building the cabinets. Before I knew it, it was time for loving and a short rest. Wantalook came in and joined me; afterwards we played till he wanted back out. From what I could see the bare spot under the overhang is where he is spending his time. I went back to working on the boards till taking short breaks so I don't overdo it. Wantalook came in twice during the afternoon. He was still checking on me. It was after 6:00 when I finished the last board. That made today's count seven.

After cleaning up I started cooking supper. Wantalook came in to eat his and some of mine. I had some dishes and silverware to clean. I let things pile up the last few days. Wantalook laid down and watched me do my job, waiting for quality time when I finished. We got over an hour of Q.T. in before it was time to go to bed. Wantalook didn't stay out long. I had the stove filled and was ready to climb into bed when I let him back in. I gave him his last petting and covered up.

Wantalook was waiting for me for my first movement of the morning. After that there wasn't any going back to sleep. No matter how I covered my head he managed to find my face and get in his licks. I tried to lay there more but he wasn't going to have it. He was up and he was making sure I was too. Before I even got sitting upright, he was doing his door dance, waiting for me. I let him out before he could try the two-step. It was a calm morning, clear and cold, with not an inch of yard that was drifted full. I closed the door, shook off a shiver and moved to the stove to build up the fire. After things got warm, I got dressed, put on my heavy clothes and went outside. Wantalook was ready to eat his fish. I gave him four to eat while I checked out the yard and all the snow. Everything looked so different, not only around the cabin but the landscape as well. It wasn't long till the cold was getting too much for the face and hands and I had to go back in. Wantalook was on his mound of snow, his eyes and ears checking out the countryside. When I went in, my face was very cold.

I need to make a face mask out of something. While I was going through my clothes, in the pocket of my hunting suit, I found my leather fleece-lined mitts. Well the hands are set now. I didn't realize I had them. I picked out a pullover shirt to make a face mask out of. It was big enough to double the material. I got out my little sewing kit and started cutting and fitting till I had it all laid out ready to sew. It took a couple hours to complete it but it fit just right. I even stitched around the eye holes and it was long enough to tuck inside my collar. So this along with my stocking hat I should be good to go.

So I got my heavy clothes on and new headgear and stepped out. Wantalook thought there was a stranger in camp. I had to show him it was me. I took a while before he stopped watching my every move. I kept talking to him till he settled down on his mound of snow. I got some of the snow moved by the overhang while standing on one leg, using the other to balance myself. I only worked twenty minutes. I had spent enough time on the ankle. My face mask worked just fine. The cold didn't bother me at all.

After stripping down for my inside work, I picked out more boards to work on today. But first, before I get started, I am going to sit a while. It's going to be an hour or more till lunch so I should get one board done before then. I was just starting to scrape when I heard and felt the rumble coming from outside. It was only one thing, an avalanche somewhere. I took a quick look outside and the area east of the cabin was where it was. That's the second one so far. I rushed back inside where it was warm. I finished that board before I took time to eat. Wantalook was Johnny on the spot ready for his too. When we were through eating, Wantalook was doing his door dance to get out. With Wantalook back outside, I went back to scraping boards the rest of the afternoon. On my breaks, I looked out to see what my favorite wolf was up to. He was on his mound playing watch wolf. I called it quits after the 6th board, got on my clothes and went outside for a while. It was still cold but I wanted some fresh air. I played with Wantalook a few minutes before moving more snow. It was dark by now but the white of the snow laminated against the shadows of the dark. I had spent an hour outside before grabbing our supper and got in where it's warm.

Wantalook was watching me as I cooked my supper. He had already eaten his and a taste or two of mine was next on his plans. I've tested him many times through these past months; he never once bit my fingers, no matter how small the food was.

His gentleness showed every time. When supper was over, I cleaned up the shavings from today before we could get to our quality time. I looked forward to it as much as Wantalook; spending an hour or two every day like this tightened our bond all the more. It was time to hit the sack. My eyes were going closed quite often. I filled the stove while Wantalook did his nature call then we settled in for the night.

I slept good last night. I don't remember waking up at all, till a cold nose touched my face. I knew when I opened my eyes, the tongue was next. OK Wantalook, that's enough. I am getting up. As I got to my feet, he was already doing his door dance, waiting for me to open it. He was out the door as soon as it was wide enough to get his body through. It was another sunny day out so it looked like I'll be able to spend more time outside. I made sure the stove was well fed, then got dressed to go outside. It wasn't as cold as yesterday but the air had some bite to it. I got Wantalook his fish, then started clearing snow. It's going to take a couple days at this pace as long as it doesn't snow anymore. Wantalook doesn't know it but his mound is going to get a lot bigger and taller before I get done. It was time for a break plus Wantalook's been nudging me to play. We played for ten minutes or so before I sat down, then it was petting after that. There was so much snow to deal with I had to remove the snow in layers and also make a trench to push the snow out of the area. I was getting hungry by now. I was cooking some breakfast while making up a pot of soup for later on. When I went back outside Wantalook was perched on top of his mound. He was like a king sitting on his throne looking over all that was his. The area was already cleared between the smoke house and the cabin. I was working my way toward the fire pit. I was moving my chair along with me so I could sit down right away when I needed to. I got the path cleared to the food shack, by then my ankle was letting me know it needed a break.

It was mid afternoon so I had enough hours of being on it. I put my chair back under the overhang and went inside. I added more wood, then set the pot on to cook. It felt good to put my foot up for a little while plus not having the weight of the boot on it. I still had time to do a board or two this afternoon so I picked out two from the pile and got started. There is nothing like a little sawdust therapy to make a person feel better. Stopping only long enough to stir the pot, I had those two boards done by supper.

I cleared up the shavings then got Wantalook's fish out. He was ready to eat too. I had a bowl of soup. Wantalook got the other half. I had enough left for tomorrow's meals. After putting the soup away, I sat down on the bed to get ready for our quality time. Wantalook didn't waste any time getting into his spot with his head on my leg. Who would believe that I could have such a relationship with a wild wolf? The trust and friendship we share together. By now it was getting late. I got up and let Wantalook out, filled the stove and the big bad wolf was at the door wanting in. It was only a few minutes till we were laying down and sleep overcame us.

I opened my eyes and what did I see? A big bad wolf looking at me. Morning Wantalook as I patted his head and I got my face washed. Wantalook was doing his door dance as I got to my feet. I let him out, then sat on the bed for a few minutes, rubbed the sleep from my eyes and got ready to start my day. It looked like it was another nice day from what I could see from my window. I put wood in the stove, then set the pot of soup on to heat up while I got dressed. The sun was out so I took the solar light out to charge. I got Wantalook his fish out. By now the soup was hot and I sat with Wantalook outside to eat. Wantalook was wanting playtime so when we finished eating, I put down my bowl and let the games begin. It started out as tag with Wantalook doing the running, then some pushing, throwing in a little snow too. I let him win by sitting down; he was happy with that. When the petting was over, I started back on the snow clearing. Wantalook made his rounds to all his territory, marking spots then took his positions on his throne. I'll get the fire pit cleaned out today and maybe the path to the lake. I would like to catch more fish for smoking and get Wantalook's food supply built back up.

By noon I had the area around the fire pit plus the fire pit cleaned out. I was ready for a break and have some lunch. The path to the lake didn't look as bad so it shouldn't take too long to clear it. When lunch was over I began on the path. The deepest part was by the shore. Once that was done I was ready to go fishing. When I grabbed the ax and my pole, Wantalook came to life off his mound and even beat me to the lake. The ice was thick and it took quite a while to chop a hole through at least twenty-four inches thick. This may be the last time fishing. After things got quiet the fish started biting. Wantalook ate three right off the bat then I started putting them on the rope. When the rope was full I dragged them to camp and went back for more. Over the course of the afternoon I made this trip five more times. It was dark when I got the last of the fish in the food shack. I had twelve nice ones picked out for the smoker and two for eating. I cleaned and prepared the twelve for tomorrow and Wantalook cleaned up after me. What a wolf. I fried my fish up for supper and had some soup with it. I had put the lights back in their spots. I only needed to use one at a time so I was set for a few days. I still had my battery lantern to use if I needed with a full set of batteries I haven't touched yet. Wantalook was waiting for me to sit down but it's going to be a few minutes yet. I got a little cleaning to do first. He was ready and waiting when he saw me head for the bed to sit down. Our quality time lasted till 9:00. I couldn't hold my eyes open any more. Wantalook went out for his nature call while I filled the stove. When I laid down and covered up I was out.

I slowly opened one eye that morning to see if Wantalook was up. I knew if I moved in the slightest, I would have a face full of wolf. I was doing good till I yawned. Wantalook was on his feet and in my face. Enough, you licking fur ball. I am getting up. My feet didn't even touch the floor yet and he was doing his door dance to get out. He was gone the second the door opened and closed the door behind him. I made sure the stove was well fed before getting dressed myself. I started cooking my fish so it would be ready when I went outside to feed Wantalook. It was another nice day out, the same as yesterday. I got out Wantalook's fish, then went in to get mine. While we ate I couldn't help but look at the beauty of the winter wilderness, the green trees standing out of the glistening snow, blue skies and mountains. I have been blessed with a chance to see and enjoy this. I must have been caught up in my thoughts because the next thing I felt was Wantalook nagging my arm, letting me know it was playtime. We pushed and shoved our way around the yard till I was out of breath, then I laid on my back and gave up. Wantalook was on top of me declaring himself the winner with his triumphant face licking. I finally got my licking fur ball off me, cleaned off the snow and dried my face. He was still playful, pushing against my legs till he got on his throne.

I cleaned out the smoke house, then got a fire going in it. When the last of the snow was melted and the inside dried out, I put in the twelve trout and shut the door. It was a good day to spend outside so I started a fire in the fire pit and set up my chair. I love the smell of wood smoke in the open air like this. It was nice to sit by the fire again. It didn't take long before Wantalook was sitting beside me, getting a little extra attention. I got out a pan to melt snow. It will be a good job while I'm outside today. It was time to add more wood to the smoker. I got back to the fire; that batch of snow was melted. I added more till I had a pan of water. When I got a bucketful, I took it inside. After I got a second bucketful I had decided to catch more fish. I had room for more and I needed to fish while I still can.

When Wantalook saw me with the axe and pole, he was ready to go. It didn't take long to reopen the hole in the ice and soon the fish were biting again. Wantalook made sure he ate his fill, then he wasn't so excited now. He more or less laid on the ice and watched. When my rope was full, I took them back to camp, checked the smoker and went back for more. I repeated this through the afternoon. I filled up everything there was to put fish in and they were stacked up like firewood inside the food shack. I should have enough to last till spring now. The smoked fish were ready to eat. I put more wood on the fire and sat down to eat. Wantalook was laying down. He made a pig of himself today and it showed. I got to admit as well as he has been eating, he had a nice coat of fur. I put the rest of the smoked fish away and put more wood in the stove so the cabin will be warm when we came in later on. I built up the fire and sat down. It was a clear night and I wanted to look at the stars and maybe a light show if the Northern Lights show up.

Wantalook finally got up and put his head on my leg. We were getting our quality time in, which I had a front row seat to the stars. The sky was clear with no light or any other pollution, that the stars and Milky Way stood out with such clarity, even more than it was when I was young boy. We sat out under the stars till 10:00.

I was getting ready to go in; the fire was down and it's been a long day. I stood up and grabbed my chair where I saw the first flash of light across the sky. I sat back down; the light show began. I was getting more goose pimples from watching the Northern Lights, than I was from the cold. Every minute there was something new, such a mesmerizing sight. When I got to the point of constant shivering I had to go in. I think I stood by the stove twenty minutes till I got warm. I was shocked when I looked at my watch—1:40 in the morning. That's the latest I've stayed up yet since I've been here but it was worth it. I filled the stove and slid between the covers and fell fast asleep.

Needless to say my plans were to sleep in this morning but there was one wolf that had definitely plans. I don't think he waited for me to move. I was getting the tongue treatment before my eyes were open. I was up so fast, he didn't have a chance to do his door dance. I had it open. I shut the door and got back into bed. When I woke up again it was almost 10:00 and the big bad wolf was at the door. When I opened it, he just stood there looking at me. I grabbed some fish out of the container for him and stepped back inside. Burr, I wasn't dressed yet. I gave the stove the attention it needed then got my clothes on. I grabbed myself some smoked fish and joined Wantalook outside. I was liking this weather we were having. I'll take all the days there is like this. Wantalook was waiting for me to finish eating. I knew what he had on his mind, playtime.

He probably has plans to slam dunk me in a snowbank for sleeping in this morning. When I stood up, it was game on. We tagged and pushed each other from one end of the yard to the other. When I added snowballs to the fun, it got him going all the more. We carried on like this close to a half hour before I had to give up. I tried to get to my chair but he kept blocking my way. It wasn't till I got on the ground, when he felt he had won with him on top of me. When the licking was over he let me get to my feet.

After getting a fire going I was ready to sit a while. Wantalook got off his mound and joined me. He wasn't about to miss a chance to get his head and ears scratched. It was too nice of a day to be inside. After setting about an hour, I had to get up and do something. I cleared a path to my pole pile of wood, got out my saw and started cutting more firewood for the cabin. I'd rather make sure I have plenty so I don't get caught low on wood during a long storm in the first three months of next year. Wantalook was back on his throne watching over me and his territory. I just kept a steady pace and rested when I wanted. When I got the space filled back up under the overhang, I would be setting good for wood supply. It was time for a lunch break in the middle of the afternoon. I only ate a half fish before going back to work. When I finished splitting what I cut, I stacked it under the overhang. I still had room for more but I think I will finish tomorrow.

I built the fire up and sat down. The skies still had a little light left as I watched the shadows grow into darkness. The stars were appearing more by the minute but I wasn't going to stay up late tonight. We ate our supper under the stars and shared our time together. It was our tradition that will keep going. It was time to go in; as I got to the door Wantalook wanted to stay out. I've seen that look before—he's got plans for the night. I patted him on the head and told him to have fun. I went in for the night, filled the stove and checked outside. He was gone. It didn't take long to fall asleep once I got in bed.

When morning came, it took a minute to remember that Wantalook wasn't there. I was expecting a cold nose or a wet tongue. After a few yawns and stretches, I got to my feet, fed the stove and got ready to start the day. It was another nice day I realized as I stepped out the door. I had to check for Wantalook in case there was a surprise attack. He wasn't back. I started a fire and sat down to eat. The temperature had to be in the 20s and no wind. I can handle that. I got out my saw and went back to cutting wood. As I worked throughout the morning I kept expecting Wantalook to pop up at any time for a surprise attack.

But by the time I got the last of the wood stacked under the overhang, he wasn't back yet. All morning I had planned to have moose on a stick for lunch. I haven't had that in a while and was looking forward to it. The meat I got earlier is thawed out. All I need is my knife and roasting stick and I am ready to eat. Slicing the meat one-quarter inch thick only takes a couple of minutes on the fire to be done. Plus I like my meat with a little kick left in it so that works out fine with me. I noticed I was starting to have some squirrel problems around the cabin and after I checked, the food shack too.

I guess I will need to set up snares and maybe I will have to trap some. I knew it was only a matter of time before this was going to happen. So now I've got something to do this afternoon. When I checked the backside of the cabin, there were at least ten places they were digging into the moss. If they want to come around like this Wantalook and I will add squirrel to our list of things to eat. I didn't have as much wire as I thought but I managed to make up five snares. The other wire I had was too stiff to use. I put the three up on the most traveled spots. Now we'll see what happens. I had some scrap pieces of wood left over from the cupboard. I got them out and cut them into one-quarter inch thick strips. It was getting dark by the time the last scrap board was cut up. I took all the strips inside, to make a drop door cage later on. It was time to go in where it's warm. I've been outside all day. It wasn't long before the warmth of the cabin had me falling asleep. I took one last look for Wantalook, then got into bed.

I slept so sound that I couldn't believe it was morning already. I turned over and found a sweet spot and more sleep was soon to come, I thought. The big bad wolf was at my door. He wasn't huffen or puffen but he wanted in. When I opened that door, he was all over me with excitement, almost knocking me over. Damn, I am glad we're not in a china shop. There wouldn't be a thing left unbroken. Wantalook finally settled down enough for me to get my clothes on so I could get his food out. I put more wood in the stove then picked up my fish and joined Wantalook outside. Wantalook was finished with his when I sat down. I gave him two more fish so I could eat mine in peace. Wantalook could barely wait for me to finish to start playing. When I stood up it was game on. I tell ya, this wolf is wound up this morning. He had me all worn out after fifteen minutes. Tossing snow didn't slow him down at all. I think it made it worse. I tricked him and got to my chair; it still took a while for him to accept my loss and settle down.

After a short rest, I checked the snares I put out. I got one! Wantalook was excited when he saw what I had. He sure didn't turn down the leftovers after I cleaned it. I then put it in water and will cook it tonight. I couldn't believe the good fortune we were having with the weather so far. I set up my log horses so I could do the edge cutting on the boards I already had shaved. I needed some of the scraps to make my cage trap so I was killing two birds with one stone. I only need four strips one-half inches thick over twenty-four inches long. When I was ready to start cutting Wantalook was laying on his throne watching. It was nice to do all this cutting outside and not have the mess in the cabin. When I would finish marking and cutting a board, I would take it in and bring out another. When I finished with the last one, it was noon time. I picked up all the strips. I set them in the corner of the cabin to use later on a project or burn in the stove. When I sat down to eat, Wantalook joined me to eat too. I got a few minutes of petting in before I went back to work. I then took all the quarter-inch strips I cut yesterday and cut them to twelve inches long. I was finished within an hour. I took all the pieces inside. I need to use the table and have warm fingers to put it together. Wantalook was content to stay on his mound while I went inside.

I had seventy pieces, sixty-four for the four sides and six for the one end. Each piece was marked out to cut a quarter by half inch slot. $1\frac{1}{2}$ inches apart, with the sixty-four marked out to cut. I started to cut and trim each one so when I put them together, I had a square of rib with the inside of $9\frac{1}{2}$ inches. I will take sixteen ribs with half-inch space between them to make twenty-four inches.

Around 4:00 Wantalook was making a fuss outside so I slipped on my coat to check it out. When I saw him on the back of the cabin I knew what it was another squirrel. I thumped it with a stick and removed it from the snare, then set it back up.

Now we will have two for supper. Wantalook helped me clean the squirrel, then I put it with the other one. Wantalook stayed outside while I worked on the trap. When I quit for the evening, I had half of the ribs for the cage together. I got out my cooking rack, put the two squirrels in it along with some moose. Gee, we're going to have a cartoon supper, moose and squirrel. I dressed for the outdoors and got a fire going in the pit. I gave Wantalook a few fish to hold him over till I was done cooking. Granted there wasn't a lot of meat on the squirrels but they will taste good. I ate all the back legs and the front shoulders of one and Wantalook had the rest. When I finished the moose I was full. I added a few more pieces of wood to the fire then we settled in for an hour or two of quality time. It was nice to have Wantalook back. I've just to find a way to calm him down when he does come back home. He was too wound up and excited when he saw me this morning. It was time to go in for the night. Wantalook was soon at the door to join me. The stove was full and I spent a while setting on the bed, making plans for tomorrow before I went to sleep.

What a rude awakening. A cold nose in the ear. I turned toward Wantalook and he got me good with his tongue and I knew better than to do that too. As I sat up on the bed for a good stretch and yawn, Wantalook was doing his door dance. So I let him out before he could get to the song and dance part. I got dressed, fixed the stove, now to feed Wantalook and myself. My bouncing fur ball was waiting, when I came out. After getting out his food then I could sit down and eat mine. It looked like it would be another nice day, only a few clouds in the sky. I tried to remain setting after I finished eating but Wantalook wasn't going for that trick. You can't blame a guy for trying. We started in the second I stood up. He almost knocked me down on the first try. We chased and tagged, pulled and wrestled. At one point I thought I had him this time but he wiggled loose and knocked me over backward into the snow and jumped on top of me. I was grabbing all the snow I could, covering his face and everywhere else it landed. It didn't matter, he wasn't going to quit till I gave up. So I had no choice, he won. I had forgotten to close my collar and I had snow all over inside my coat. After another face licking, he let me up. It was snowy and wet when I got to my feet. I took a quick check of the snares and went inside.

I hung up my clothes to dry and started back, working on the trap. I had to finish cutting out and assembling the ribs next. Then I picked out the half-inch by one-inch strips. I needed and cut and trimmed them down to a half-inch square. I then trimmed down one edge to look like a quarter-inch round. These four pieces will hold the ribs in place. They will be tied on the four corners of the ribs on the outside of the cross lap that sticks out with the leather strips tied on the outside. They can't be chewed from the inside. The leather strips had been soaking for over a day. It was late afternoon when I finished tying the sixteen ribs in place. I cut out the top and bottom pieces to hold the end strips in place, then cut the six remaining rib strips to size. After tying the top and bottom pieces in place, I used some of the copper wire from the plane to secure each rib in.

It was time for supper. I didn't bother with eating lunch. I got dressed and went outside, got the fire going first. I was going to have moose on a stick again. Wantalook was ready to eat too. He wasted no time on devouring his fish. Then watched me eat, waiting for his portions. What do you do with a spoiled rotten wolf? You spoil him more. When I finished, Wantalook settled in with his head on my leg to get our quality time started. As I scratched his head, I looked at the stars and stared off into the darkness thinking how lucky I was to have Wantalook with me and all we have been through these past months. I wouldn't trade this experience for anything. The fire was dying and time to go in. Wantalook laid down, while I cleaned up the wood shavings from today, filled the stove and went to bed.

Nine

When I woke up I was facing the wall. It wasn't long before I could hear a nose getting closer. I guess there is just no way to fool this wolf. I turned over and grabbed his head with both hands as I tried to hold back the licking. It didn't work. The only way he'll stop is when I get up. I sat on the bed a while. I wanted to see his song and dance routine before I would open the door. I didn't have to wait long before he added a song with the door dance and I let him out. I had to laugh a little when I sat down, that was cute. I added more wood to the stove, then got out a bunch of bear meat to make a pot of stew. It may be hard and dry as a piece of wood now but it will be just fine when I get done with it. Afterwards I went out to feed my furry friend.

Wantalook was waiting with excitement. I opened the door. I made sure he had plenty to eat before I sat down to eat mine. I knew Wantalook would be waiting to play when I finished. I think I will flop on the ground right from the chair and see what happens. Wantalook just looked at me till I started to laugh; we both were rolling in the snow then. When I got to my feet it didn't slow down till he knocked me over and I gave up. He's always got to lick my face before he'll let me up.

I checked the snares then went inside to work. Wantalook settled down on his throne to watch over his territory. I first made the sliding door for the cage trap with slide rails all smoothed for quick closing. It was noon when I had that in place. Next I built the tilt floor on a triangle pivot with a peg on the door end, tapered on the upper end to hold the door open four inches. When I pushed the other end down, the door went shut. I tied a rock about the size of my fist to the top of the door and tried it again, it slammed shut. I tried it ten or more times. It never failed. I made a spot to hold the bait on the inner end and it was ready to use. I made up a small ball of Bisquick and put it in place. I took it outside and set it on a squirrel trail down from the cabin. Wantalook was curious about the strange object but he never bothered it.

I had to get back inside the cabin, clean up the mess and finish getting the stew ready to start cooking. The pot is on the stove so I sat outside with Wantalook a while. The skies were clouding up and the air had a different feel to it. We were in for more snow. An hour had passed and I needed to check the stew, it was almost ready. I checked the trap one last time. It was almost dark now, nothing yet. I got Wantalook his fish and dished myself up a bowl of stew and joined Wantalook outside. It was just starting to snow when I sat down. Well the nice weather was great while it lasted. I finished the bowl and got some more. I had one-quarter of a bowl left that I gave to Wantalook; he liked it too. We sat under the overhang till it was time to go in; even though it was dark I could see everything had a new covering of white already. After putting away the stew, I filled the stove and laid down. I was tired but could not fall asleep. I'd been having thoughts about my family, especially my daughter, and I still was. I laid there. I eventually turned over and went to sleep.

It snowed the next four days; other than push snow around and spend time with Wantalook, I spent most of my time in the cabin making pegs for the cabinet building coming up and resting. I've got to reteach myself to slow down. All my life I've been doing something and sitting on my ass has not been one of them. If I get everything done, the only thing left to do is count snowflakes. So I am putting off building the cabinets for a while. It's a few days now till Christmas. I'll make up something special to eat for Wantalook and myself. This will be my first Christmas without my family. I know they are going to be down too. But they will keep up the tradition that has been set many years ago. All I can do is pray they get my thoughts that I am fine and someday I will see them again. I've got washing to do today—clothes and myself.

Wantalook has been out all morning. He likes fresh snow. It's been a few weeks since he went out on his outings so I imagined in a few days he'll be gone again. So far I've caught three squirrels in the trap and one with a snare. I'll check again this evening if I got anymore. Well, my clothes and myself are as clean as they are going to be. It was more like rinse the dirt out and off. I've got soap left for dishes and that's about it. I sure would have packed different if I knew I was going to be spending a year or more instead of thirty days. It's been over six months now. All the clothes aren't dry yet so I won't be setting outside tonight. All the traps are clear and Wantalook joined me inside to eat. We got a little quality time in after supper but he was restless and wanted out. I petted him on the head and told him I'd see him when he got back. Sure enough when I checked before going to bed, he was gone. I thought to myself, I know my wolf.

I slept in the next morning long enough that the fire was almost out in the stove. I got it going again and got dressed, went out and got another squirrel, cleaned it and put it in water for tonight. It took about a half hour to finish clearing the snow from the yard. It seems strange not to have my bouncing fur ball around but he'll be back in a day or two. The air is colder today and with the wind makes it feel colder yet.

I went back inside where it was warm. I decided to start on the cabinet, just do a little on it each day. That will be hard for me. Once I start something I am on it. Hour after hour till it's done. Today I will mark and cut out the base. The base will be four inches high, twenty-two inches wide and ninety-six inches long with brace support at sixteen inches apart. Everything is made from one-inch boards. After I cut the two sixteen pieces, I cut the seven to twenty pieces for both ends and brace supports. I stopped to eat some lunch. I looked outside to check the weather and to see if I had anymore squirrels. No Wantalook and no squirrels. I spent the rest of the afternoon assembling the base, drilling and pegging three pegs per joint, forty-two in all. It was solid and looked good. I've got to stop now so I will have more to do in the days ahead. I was setting at the table eating, going over the plans in my head, when a scrap piece of wood reminded me of the wood whittling I'd done years ago, making statues and figurines, using nothing but a pocket knife. I do have my pocket knife. I sharpened the blade. Sometimes you can see what's in the wood waiting to be cut out and sometimes you don't know what, that's when you get started into it. I've got thicker pieces of scrap wood in the corner. After looking them over, I found one that had the look of an animal in it. It took over an hour to see what was inside coming out; it will be a bear. Wow, I forgot how fast time goes by when you do this. It was late already. I filled the stove for the night and went to sleep.

When I woke up I was eager to get started. After feeding the stove and myself, I went out, checked the traps, then came back in to get started. I picked out the boards for the bottom of the cabinet, trimming the edges for a tight fit and cutting the boards to ninety-six inches, with the total width of fourteen inches. Making sure everything was square. I started drilling and pegging the three boards down to the base with a total of fifty-six pegs. It was so solid you could toss this puppy around and it wouldn't come apart. It was almost dark out and I needed to check the traps. I had two, one in a snare, the other in the cage trap. After cleaning them, I let them soak in water a while before cooking them. I put the guts and head and remaining scraps away for Wantalook. I cleared the wood shavings up before starting supper. I was almost done eating when I heard the familiar sound. The big bad wolf was at my door again. Well, in comes excitement on four legs. Wantalook barely gave me a chance to shut the door. For the first five minutes, he couldn't get close enough. When the food started being served, he slowed down then. While he was finishing the squirrel scraps, I got him a few fish to get his tank filled for the night. Afterwards he moved in beside me to get his petting and log up more quality time till it was time to go to bed. When Wantalook came back in, he laid by my bed. I laid there awhile scratching his head before falling asleep.

It was a cold nose morning as I woke up. I didn't expect any less. Wantalook managed to get his licks in before I could get up. I was rubbing the sleep from my eyes, while Wantalook was doing his door dance waiting for me. I let my four-legged fur ball of excitement out, fed the stove, then sat on the bed a while before getting dressed. It was cold when I went out to feed Wantalook. We played for a while. Afterwards I gave up early to get back inside. Wantalook wanted to stay out and do his thing; for me I wanted to eat and get back to work. I fried up some moose and got a pot of stew started. When breakfast was over, I started marking out and cutting the inner framework for the corners, shelves and top. Wantalook came in once to check out what I was doing, got some petting and went back out. The stew was done so I took time for lunch. Wantalook joined me to eat. I gave him some after he ate his fish. He stayed inside for part of the afternoon, watching me work till I saw him doing his door dance and I let him out. I finished cutting out the rest of the framework and assembled some of it. I had done enough for today, cleaned up and carved on the bear figurine till supper. It feels like it's colder out now when I got Wantalook's food out. I didn't waste any time getting back inside. After supper we settled in for our quality time before going to bed.

As usual Wantalook was waiting for me to wake up; his tongue was ready and I was not. When he sensed I was awake, he was nothing but tongue till I got up. He didn't have to dance long before I opened the door. If I wasn't awake then, I am now. That cold air was an eye-opener. I had to shake the cliff off on my way to the stove. I put in a few pieces of wood and I had to step back a little. I got on my heavy clothes before going outside. It had to be around zero out. The hair was freezing in my nose. I gave Wantalook his food and went back in; if he wants to play some, he would have to come in for it. After I warmed my face and hands I put on my face mask and mitts to check the traps. We played some tag there and back before I got back inside. I heated up some stew for breakfast. Then afterwards, I marked and cut out the boards for each end of the cabinet then shaped each one for a tight fit as I drilled and pegged them in place along with part of the inner framework. Next I'll cut the shelf boards, fitted, drilled and pegged them in place. It was already into the afternoon when I realized what time it was. I looked at my pile of pegs I made. I may have to make more. I used 130-plus today and I've got the back, front and top to go yet, plus doors and hinges. Wantalook came in again to check on progress, get some petting and went back out. I made pegs for about an hour.

It was starting to get dark and I needed to check the traps. I bundled up for the great outdoors and stepped into the cold. I got one in the cage trap. Wantalook was more than ready to help clean it when I got back. I grabbed Wantalook's on my way in. I wasn't going out anymore today. I cleaned the squirrel and Wantalook enjoyed the leftovers and his fish while I ate my stew. Wantalook laid down while I carved on the bear figurine. Boy, if this isn't a Rockwell picture in the *Saturday Evening Post.* Man setting by the stove whittling, wolf at his feet inside a log cabin. I could set the camera up for a delay shot. I got the camera set up and sat down quick whittling. Flash and Wantalook was on his feet ready to kick ass. I forgot I never used a flash on him before. After a little assurance, he was fine. All the other pictures have been outside. We settled in for our quality time after that. When I started to fall asleep sitting there, it was time to go to bed. I filled the stove while Wantalook was out, then we settled in for the night.

Face to face and nose to nose is the first things I saw, when I opened my eyes. I was getting licked before I could focus on his face. Wantalook, give me a break, you big-tongued licking fur ball. He was doing his door dance before my feet hit the ground. I let him out and dried my face. What a spoiled rotten piece of wolf meat. I sat down to finish waking up before even thinking about putting wood in the stove. I think I will have a cartoon breakfast, moose and squirrel. When I went outside to get our food out of the container I could really feel the cold bearing down. It had to be well below zero. Wantalook wanted his food outside. I am eating mine inside. I saved my scraps for when Wantalook comes back inside sometime this morning. I started marking out the boards for the back of the cabinet. After cutting them out, I shaped and pegged each one in place so when I put on the top, I'll have a four-inch back on it sticking up. Wantalook came in when I was about halfway across the back. I played with him and gave him his petting before letting him out. It was late afternoon when I drove the last peg in. The back was on, 130 pegs' worth. This thing is solid as a rock. I really didn't want to go outside but I needed to check the traps and get more food out of the food shack. The traps were clear and after I got the food container filled, I was glad to get inside. Wantalook came too. I set the meat up to thaw out. It wouldn't be time to eat for a couple hours.

When I got the hands warmed up, I sat down to whittle till supper. Wantalook was in his spot catching a few Z's, while I carved on the figurine. My, time sure does fly by when you are having fun. While the meat was cooking, I cleaned up the shavings from today's work. When the meat was ready, I went out to get Wantalook's fish. After supper we settled in for our quality time. I think Wantalook would take this all night if I could hold up. It was easy to relax during this time so after an hour or so I was ready to go to sleep.

When the morning ritual of cold nose and wet tongue was over, I let my dancing wolf out. I got goose bumps when I opened the door. I soon made a move toward the stove to fight off the chill. When the stove got fed, I looked out the window. I could see crystals in the air and the skies were clear, that's cold. Well today is Christmas! I will cook up a few things special for today. I was getting dressed to step outside when I heard my big bad wolf at the door. I wasn't surprised. He wanted to come back in where it was warm. When I opened the door, I noticed the frost on the edge of the door and door casing. The last time I saw anything like that was on an ice fishing trip when it got down to twenty-seven degrees below zero. I quickly grabbed our food and got inside. After breakfast was over, I started making up a pot of bear-moose stew with veggies and noodles. Later on I'll bake up some biscuits.

As I prepared the food I couldn't help but think about some of the Christmases we had when I was a boy. The great smells coming from the kitchen of turkey or ham, pumpkin pie, mashed potatoes and gravy, cranberry sauce, stuffing and cookies. Not to mention all the times my brothers and sisters and myself would be up early waiting for mom and dad to get up. All the presents under the tree and the mess of paper, ribbons and bows that laid all over the floor afterwards. It was the same way with my children too. I remember seeing them shoulder to shoulder at the foot of the bed waking us up at six in the morning. I remember seeing the looks on those faces and the excitement in their eyes as they opened their gifts. I couldn't keep from crying some. I missed everyone so much. I hope their Christmas is a good one this year.

Wantalook got up and sat next to me, I think to cheer me up. Well, old friend, it's just you and me this year. I held him in my arms and had a good cry. He kept licking, trying to comfort me. Afterwards we played and snacked on some food. It was time to make the biscuits then we can eat. I added some flour to thicken the stew like a gravy. Wantalook had fish and a bowl of stew and a biscuit. I had stew with gravy over my biscuits and had dried fruit for dessert. I was full and there was enough left over for supper and breakfast. Afterwards Wantalook wanted outside and I was going to lay down for a nap. I woke up an hour later; Wantalook was wanting in. He laid down while I sat in my chair carving on the bear figurine till supper. When supper was over we sat side by side till bedtime. Wantalook did his nature call while I filled the stove. I soon fell asleep after laying down.

Wantalook was holding down his spot when I opened my eyes—to his cold nose in my face. Enough with the tongue. I am getting up. He was doing his door dance. I had to hit the door with my fist and foot to break the frost loose so I could get it open. Well, we had a nice warm spell, now we'll have a cold spell. I filled the stove and got dressed, put on my hat, mask, and gloves, grabbed Wantalook's fish and use my knife to scrape some of the frost off the door and casing before going back inside. Wantalook was right behind me as I entered the cabin. I finished the stew and cleaned the dishes from yesterday too, before starting back on the cabinet. I had three nice grained boards saved out for the top, after cutting and fitting to size. I drilled and pegged in place. It took sixty pegs to do the top. After lunch I'll cut and smooth each one flush with the board.

It was late afternoon when I finished. All I have left to do is build the front and the doors. I thought about making drawers maybe later on. Wantalook is wanting to go out. He was doing his dance routine. After he went out, I figured I'd better check the traps today. I made the trips as quick as possible even though it only took minutes. The cold seemed to go right through me. I was inside cleaning up when the big bad wolf was at my door. I think he wanted to get the frost off his chinney chin chin. He came through the door like his tail was on fire, got a couple pets on the head then laid down to enjoy the heat. I sat for a while carving then made supper. For some reason I really felt tired tonight. I sat with Wantalook a short while before going to bed.

In the morning, I let him out and laid back in. I woke up later when Wantalook wanted back in. I sat petting him till I needed to lay down again. Whatever it was, I wasn't feeling the best. By evening I was feeling some better. I had a small amount to eat and had to lay down. Wantalook's head was on the bed next to me watching. I would pet him now and then. I let him outside one last time then went to sleep.

It took three days of this before I started feeling like normal again. The only time outside was to get food out. The cold is not as harsh as it was a few days ago. I might venture outside for a while later on. It was midmorning. Wantalook was on his throne again watching over his territory like normal. I sat inside and carved on the figurine for an hour or so. I got dressed up in my heavy clothes and went out for some fresh air. Wantalook came to greet me; he wanted to play. We pushed and wrestled around for five or ten minutes. I had to call it quits. I got out a couple fish for him and went back inside. I marked out the rest of the boards for the front of the cabinet then cut and fitted each one to their spot then drilled and pegged them in place. That changed the looks tremendously. The last thing left is the doors and hinges. I had made soup for supper and I just put it on the stove to heat up. I was glad I was feeling a lot better. When I finished cleaning, the soup was hot and I had Wantalook's fish ready for him and I didn't even have to call him to eat. He was in the second I opened the door and did a great job of making his meal disappear. Well Wantalook, this is a new year, we have a few more months left till the start of spring. Our wood and food supply is good so we shouldn't have any problems. We settled in for our quality time before turning in for the night.

Wantalook was my alarm clock every day. It was nose and tongue. I really didn't mind. I've gotten to look forward to it, most of the time. Some mornings Wantalook goes overboard on the tongue but that's part of our daily routine. Wantalook was doing his door dance before I even made it out of bed. He couldn't wait for me to open the door. I filled the stove then got dressed to go outside. It had warmed up. It looked like our cold spell was over. While Wantalook was eating, I got a fire going in the pit. I was looking forward to sitting by the fire. Wantalook was ready for some playtime now. We started out with push-tag, chasing and challenging and ended up with a good wrestling match. I was ready to sit after that. After a short rest, I got myself a bowl of soup and sat back down by the fire. It sure was nice to sit outside again. It had to be in the 20s and with the sun shining it made for a beautiful day.

    I went to bring the case trap back. I had an idea for it. I cut a strip of aluminum and mounted on the top of the cage with a piece of cloth attached to the end. It will work like a flag on a tip-up, when the door goes closed, the flag will be waving in the air. This way I can check it from a distance. I want to set it up farther away from the cabin. After testing it several times, it was ready to be put out. I put on my snowshoes and we headed out to find a spot.

    About 100 feet from the cabin, I found a well-used trail from tree to tree and set it up there. When I got back to the cabin, I found that if I stood on the snow mound, I could see if the flag was up. I put more wood on the fire and sat down. Wantalook was next to me to get his petting. Other than the occasional sound of some birds, the sound of the fire was all I would hear. Yep, this is life in the wilderness, just take each day and make it the best it can be with what you have. I know if I had an auger or an ice spud, I would be fishing right now but the ice was too thick to chop with an ax.

    Come on, Wantalook, let's take a walk. I slipped on the snowshoes and headed west toward the stream. I wanted to see what it looked like completely frozen. On the way there I found several good squirrel trails and a few rabbit spots too. When I got to the stream it seemed so different. The eerie quiet of winter's grip. Where before the sound of water was all one could hear. I can only imagine what the spring thaw sounds like. Well, that will be an event I can look forward to. On the other side of the stream, I found more areas to trap at so fresh meat will be on the menu the rest of the winter.

When we got back to camp, I stepped up on Wantalook's mound and the flag was up on the trap. Damn I came up with a good idea. I got the squirrel and reset the trap. Wantalook always gets excited when I catch something. He gets to jumping and running around like he's half crazy and more than happy to help clean them. We spent the rest of the afternoon by the fire. I just had to turn around now and then to warm the backside. The moose meat was thawed so I could cook it with the squirrel. I filled the cooling rack and let it slow cook over the coals. Wantalook was right there to supervise, watching me turn the meat. When it was done, I got out his fish and we chowed down. When his fish was gone, he was ready for his part of the squirrel. I had cooked enough moose to save for breakfast in the morning. We sat by the fire for another hour till I had enough of being outside for one day. I filled the stove and it wasn't long before the heat had me falling asleep sitting there. When I laid down and covered up, that was the last of the day.

My four-legged friend alarm clock was right on time, tongue and all. I sat up right away. When I did, he went into his door dance routine, till I let him out. From what I could see, it was going to be another nice day. I ate the leftover moose from last night as I got dressed, tossed a few pieces of wood in the stove and headed out the door. Wantalook was staying as I stepped out. I gave him his fish then checked if the flag was up on the trap, nothing yet. By the time I got the fire started and sat down, Wantalook was ready for phase two of the morning routine playtime. He kept nudging me with his nose till I got off the chair. Now it's game on. I've got to admit he's fast on his feet. Always staying inches out of my reach. We went at it for twenty minutes, at least till the bugger tripped me. The second I went down, he was on top of me with his winning pose, pinning me down. Afterwards he gave me his victory licks then he let me up. As I walked to my chair, I swear he has his own victory dance with an "I beat you attitude" look on his face, rotten wolf. But I love him anyhow. The sun was out and not a cloud in the sky.

The air was still as if time itself had stopped long enough to take in all that nature had laid out before me. With each day there is something new, something different to see and enjoy. Winter is the holder of the promise of spring. I'm a person who wants to be with nature, they must learn to live with nature. If they fight nature, nature will win. I sat by the fire the rest of the morning watching how the light and shadows changed the looks of everything from the snow to the mountains. I was getting ready to have some moose on a stick for lunch. I looked again to see if the flag was tripped on the trap. It wasn't so Wantalook and I ate our lunch.

Afterwards I put on my snowshoes, grabbed a bucket and broke the trail to the spring. I was surprised to see how much ice built up. I had to go back and get my ax so I could make a spot to get my bucket in. I took off my snowshoes this time so I wouldn't slip again. It took several trips to fill up everything but now I am good for water for a while. After taking a break by the fire, Wantalook and I took a walk to the east, stopping short of the avalanche area and staying well out of range. I found more good spots for rabbits and squirrels too. On our way back the flag was up on the trap. I had another squirrel. Wantalook couldn't wait to get back to help me clean it. I checked the snares on the back of the cabin and found I had another one. The snares were clear at lunch time. Wantalook was cleaning up the last of the second one when I went inside to put them in water. Afterwards I built the fire up good. The sky was still light and the temperature was dropping. I could see beyond the mountains, a wall of dark clouds slowly coming in this direction. Another storm is on the way. I refilled the container from the food shack before starting supper. Wantalook ate his fish while I was cooking the two squirrels and moose. By the time we finished eating, the temperature had dropped tremendously. We can do our quality time inside. I filled the stove first before I sat down with Wantalook. Several hours had passed since I had sat down and it was late. When I let Wantalook out I could smell it was already snowing. We settled in for the night and were soon fast asleep.

I woke up during the night to the sound of wind blowing through the trees. It was far worse than what I've heard before. I took a quick look out the door; it definitely was a full-blown blizzard. I laid there in bed listening to the wind till I fell back to sleep. It still sounded bad, when Wantalook woke me up. I noticed the frost on the door when I let Wantalook out. The air had a deadly feel to it. The likes I've never felt before and zero visibility. Blowing snow was the only thing you could see. I was out in the blizzard of 1978 but it was nothing like this. Wantalook was wanting back in. I don't blame him a bit. He had snow planted all over him. I brushed off what was left, then filled the stove. After I got dressed, I had to go out to bring our food in. I wasn't outside four minutes but I got chilled in that short amount of time. There wasn't any outside adventure for a while. When breakfast was over I made a pot of bear stew for later today. It was nice to get back to wood carving. I almost had the bear done. I had more wood set aside for the next ones. The sound of the wind is all I could hear the rest of the day. By supper time, I had finished the figurine of a bear. I was very pleased how good it turned out. Things hadn't gotten any better outside when I got Wantalook's fish. After supper we did our quality time, then went to bed.

The storm raged on for the next twelve days. I only ventured out to get food and came back in. Once in a while I could get a glimpse of the yard. I was almost finished with the figurine of a wolf. I tried to make it resemble Wantalook as much as possible. I felt it was my best work yet. By the evening of the 12th day the wind was letting up. I went to bed that night with the hope of getting out tomorrow.

When Wantalook woke me, the sound of the wind was gone. I jumped to my feet and opened the door. Wantalook ran out. The snow was so hard packed that he never left a track going up the drift. From the overhang it was uphill to get on top of the drift next to the cabin. The top of the smoker and the food shack was the only thing sticking out other than the cabin. Well, it looks like I will be busy moving snow a while. Wantalook was busy checking out his territory, while I was making my plans of attack on the snow as far back from the yard area as possible.

I remembered what I used to do at home—make a snow wall to let the wind clear the driveway. I got my sled down and used it to move snow from the yard to the snow wall west of the cabin. I worked all morning and had only a small area cleared but the wall was taking shape. The snow was hard so a lot I could cut in chunks. I could handle it. I took time out for a quick lunch then back to work. I made my way to the spring but I figured it was covered over with about eight feet of snow. I'll melt snow for now.

When I got back to the cabin, I kept clearing snow till I reached the outhouse. I had snow to remove inside and out now. I can empty my bucket. I made good progress on the yard and snow wall today. I'll spend the rest of the evening melting snow. Wantalook was enjoying his time outside after all those days in the cabin. We played some off and on all day otherwise he was setting on the highest mound of snow in the yard. The sun is down past the mountaintops and the shadows are turning to darkness. It's time to call it a day and start supper. By the time I finished eating, I was ready for bed but I stayed up with Wantalook till I couldn't hold my eyes open anymore. I filled the stove and went to sleep.

Wantalook was waiting for my first movement of the morning. I could feel his breath on my cheek. I tried to pretend I was still sleeping but his tongue knew better. As I tried to push him away, he made sure the licking woke me up. The only way to get him to stop was to sit up. I am wiping my face while he's already started his door dance. You've got to move so I can get to the door, you bouncing fur ball. He was out the door like he was shot out of a cannon. I set back down, took a deep breath and rubbed the sleep from my eyes. My mind and body was now working together. I filled the stove and got dressed. I ate breakfast before going outside. By now I had a hungry wolf on my hands. I got out his food the minute I got out the door. That would give me some time to get ready for the next event, playtime. I had a plan for today's game. I was going to win this time. I had snowbanks to use now. Wantalook was ready to get started and so was I. We pushed and chased each other and wrestled, each trying to get the upper hand. When we got into the area I had stopped clearing the day before, I had him where I wanted. I grabbed tight with both arms and picked him up. I had a face full of fur from the back of his neck, with his feet off the ground, he couldn't get free no matter what he done. I swear it took five minutes before he gave up. I was laughing by the time I let him down. He shook himself then jumped up on me and licked my face. I am enjoying this moment. It's one of the few times I won. I sat down to rest a minute or two before getting back at moving snow. When I get the snow wall built, the wind we get now should keep most of the yard clean.

Today I plan to make it to the food shack then on to the fire pit. By noon I was up to the path to the food shack. After a short lunch I was back at it. Wantalook was content with watching me make trip after trip to the snow around the base so if anything tried to get to the food shack the snow wouldn't help. The snow wall was completed, across the open area between the trees in most places five to six feet tall. The closer to the fire pit the less snow there was. I made a path for the sled to dump snow over the bank toward the lake. I got the fire pit uncovered and cleared out, then uncovered the wood pile. I would get the rest cleared out tomorrow. It was getting dark by now. I was looking forward to setting by the fire tonight. After the time was started, I set out some meat to thaw so I could have moose on a stick. Wantalook was ready for his fish by now. I like the way the snowbanks kept the heat closer to one. The cold air stayed over my head when I sat down. The meat was thawed enough to slice it now so I could get it on the fork to cook. It was a nice evening out. It was cold but between the fire and the snowbanks, we were cozy for the rest of our time sitting there. My butt was telling me it was time to get up; when I looked at my watch it was 10:30. I thought it was maybe 9:00. We headed inside for the night, filled the stove and crawled into bed.

My four-legged alarm clock was there to make sure I got up, cold nose first to get me to move and tongue for the rest. What's wrong with sleeping in a little? I jumped to my feet and opened the door. I could feel it in my muscles from the two days of moving snow. Sat back down a while to give the body a chance to get used to moving again. I slowly got myself dressed. I really wasn't ready for Wantalook. When I stepped outside I gave him his fish, got the fire going and sat down. Wantalook was nudging me to play. I wrestled for a while with him, then I let him pin me down. I give up. Wantalook got his licks in before letting me up. I didn't have that much more to go and the rest of the area would be cleaned out. The body was back to normal by the time I finished. I slipped on my snowshoes and with my shovel, I dug out the cage trap, it was completely covered. I moved it to a new traveled area. Hopefully I'll have one before too long. It was time for some lunch and a rest, a few more pieces of wood on the fire and I was ready for some sit time. Wantalook joined me to get his share of the eats and petting too. I had the pot on the fire, melting snow till I had everything filled inside the cabin. I took it easy the rest of the afternoon, enjoying the nicer weather while it was here. Wantalook didn't lay around as much as normal. I've seen that mood many times already. He will be heading out for a day or two. I made sure he had all he wants to eat for supper. I only planned to set by the fire a short while. Afterwards Wantalook went on his way as I went in the cabin. I filled the stove and settled in for a long night's sleep.

I had woke up several times but went back to sleep that morning. When I did get up the stove was out and the cabin was cool. I got the fire going right away then got dressed. From what I could see out the window, it looks like it's going to be a nice day out. After cooking breakfast, I went outside.

It was cold but nothing that a good fire couldn't handle. It didn't take long before I had a big one going so I could sit down. It always seemed strange around here when Wantalook wasn't around. I would like to know what he does when he's gone like this. I keep asking him but he doesn't tell me a thing. He's probably looking for a girlfriend; if he had one he wouldn't be hanging around here. If I remember right, a wolf's mating season is December or January, it tis the season.

After being roasted and toasted, I put on my snowshoes to check the trap. Flag up. This is almost as much fun as tip-up fishing. I forgot to bring more bait so I will have to come back and reset it. I am doing good. I got a squirrel and getting a walk in. After resetting the trap and cleaning the squirrel, I took my spot by the fire. I've got work to do inside but I'll save that for bad weather. As long as it's nice enough to be outside, that's where I'll be. I've got a few spots I should take some of the snow down. I'll start that in little while. The lake ice sure is noisy today with its crackling and groans. This is the loudest I've heard so far this year. I might as well get off my butt and take down the snow to around four feet, except for Wantalook's mound. At least now I can see out around camp.

It will be a cartoon lunch today, moose and squirrel. I hung around the fire the rest of the day enjoying the scenery. I don't think I will ever get tired of looking at this place. The evening shadows were setting in. I was glad to get back inside. After building the fire up in the stove, I sat down to work on the figurine of Wantalook. I had an hour or two to go and it would be finished. I really like the way it turned out when it was done. I put it on the shelf with the bear. It only took a couple minutes to clean up and then I went to sleep.

Ten

When I first woke up, I was expecting a nose or a tongue till I remembered Wantalook wasn't here. I tried to go back to sleep but couldn't so I got up. I fed the stove, then got ready to go outside. The clouds had moved in and it would be snowing before long. I took a walk to check the trap; the flag was down. There was a light snow coming down when I got back to camp. I got out some meat and went inside. When breakfast was over, I got started on the doors of the cabinet. I should get everything cut out today and start putting them together tomorrow. Each door will be two inches wide, four doors all total. Three boards per door. After those were cut to size, I marked and cut out the eight hinges boards that will hold the three boards together. Next I cut out the cross support boards so when assembled, they will look like the Z doors of the cupboads. Shaping and smoothing the hinge boards took longer than the rest combined.

    I made a pot of bear stew for supper. I'll let it cook on the stove till the meat falls apart. I cleaned up the cabin, then checked the trap before it got too dark to see. There were a couple inches of new snow from today. It was still coming down. The stew was ready when I came back in and I was ready to sit down to a bowl or two. After supper I laid down waiting to hear from Wantalook at the door. I had fallen asleep and woke up around 10:00. I got up and looked outside to see if Wantalook was waiting. I called several times. Wantalook was not around. This is the longest he's been gone. I crawled back in bed and went to sleep.

    When I woke up the skies were just getting light. I got up and looked for any tracks in the snow but there were none. This reminds me of the saying—do you know where our kids are? NO. I filled the stove then heated up the stew. When I finished eating, I began assembling the doors, drilling and pegging each piece. Later on that morning, I heard the sound of my big bad wolf at my door. I was happy to see my bouncing fur ball again. We greeted each other at the door but he wouldn't come inside. So I got on my heavy clothes and joined him outside. Wantalook was acting strange as I petted him, then ran off. I thought, what the hell is he up to? In a short while I found out.

Wantalook had a mate. She wouldn't come any closer than maybe forty feet. Her color was darker than Wantalook's. She had two socks on her feet. Well Wantalook, you just had to get yourself a friend, didn't you? Well she is definitely not dog ugly. Now I got to come up with a name for her now. Well Wantalook, she is a good looker, there you go. I'll call her Goodlooken. I'll use food to bring her around and Wantalook will do the rest. I got some fish out for the two of them and sat down. I tossed the first one about twenty feet away. Goodlooken took it cautiously and moved away. The second one I tossed and she stayed put. It was a start. It was so neat to watch those two together. I just stayed still in my chair as they played. Every once in a while Wantalook would come to me for some petting while Goodlooken watched. We spent the rest of the afternoon outside. I had started a fire around 3:00. Goodlooken was curious for a while but Wantalook kept her reassured. I could move around more by now and she didn't run, just watched. Wantalook and Goodlooken were on the snow mound for a while, that was a Kodak moment. I'm not going to bring out the camera yet. We have come a long way for the first day.

When it was time for supper, I brought out the pot of stew to heat up and got out more fish. Goodlooken didn't run, she kept her distance. After supper, Wantalook took a few minutes of quality time then laid down by his mate about ten feet away. I kept talking to them so she would get used to my voice. It was time to go in. Wantalook came to me to get his petting before I went in. After I filled the stove, I sat on the bed a while thinking about today and the new addition to the family. They will have to do some hunting on their own. I don't have enough food for the three of us for the rest of the winter. I was tired but happy. I'll have two wolves for friends now. I covered up and went to sleep.

I woke up early, got dressed and went out to greet the happy couple. As I fed them, I petted Wantalook while he ate so Goodlooken could watch. She liked the fish but still kept her distance. I wasn't sure about me and Wantalook playing and how she would react so I kept the play light and only a few minutes. She was very interested in what we were doing. I didn't want her to get too excited and jump in for a bite. It was turning out to be another nice day. After I eat breakfast, I'll get the fire going. When I came back out Wantalook and Goodlooken were playing. She stopped to look at me and what I was doing and went back to playing. I'll have my hand on her within a week. I got the fire going and sat down to watch those two carrying on. Wantalook would still come up by me to get petted. Goodlooken still stayed back. When they finished playing, they laid down by me. Wantalook was closest. I could get up to tend the fire and Goodlooken stayed put. While I sat there I was making more plans on the food supply. First I'll take a walk to see if any of that bear is left that I killed; if not, I'll set up a trap line to check every day.

I got out more fish for lunch and fed them both. I ate the last of the stew. I changed clothes for walking, slipped on the snowshoes, grabbed the ax and sled and started out down the lake. Wantalook and Goodlooken came along. The woods looked a lot different than it did a couple months ago. When I got to the spot of the attack, I didn't see anything. I started probing with a pole where I was sure the bear was. After a few minutes I found what I was looking for. I used my snowshoe to dig three feet down. I saw fur. I kept digging and the carcass was not touched. When I got enough uncovered, I chopped off both back legs across the back. It was on its belly. I had a sledful to bring home. I had enough pieces to keep my wolves busy eating. I had enough time to get back before dark. They were down eating on the carcass when I started back. When I reached the lake, the clouds were lit up in colors from the sun's last rays of the day.

It was dark when I walked in the yard. I put their food away, then started a fire and sat down. That was the most I've walked in snowshoes since the attack. It felt good to get them off. It wasn't long before the kids showed up. Their bellies were bulging too. Wantalook sat down beside me and Goodlooken alongside of him. She is coming around real good. We had our quality time before I went in. I had to get a fire started in the stove. It was cold in the cabin but it didn't take long till it was comfortable, then I could go to bed. It's still hard to get used to Wantalook being outside but he's dressed for it—plus he's not alone.

I woke up with the anticipation of what today will bring. After filling the stove, I got ready to go outside and greet the happy couple. They were waiting for me when I stepped out the door. I was surprised to see Goodlooken was excited to see me too. I got them some fish, then got the fire going. Wantalook came up to get his petting, while Goodlooken watched closely, almost wanting to get some too. I kept talking to her as I played with Wantalook and at one point she almost joined in. When she is ready she will. I figured a few bites of food will help too so I hacked off some pieces and sat down. So with the food and Wantalook doing his part, Goodlooken was getting closer. I didn't expect her to take anything from my hand yet but picking up food at two feet away was fine with me.

With the weather being good right now, I figured I would start the trap line and move the cage trap to a different spot. I got out the last of the wire I'd been saving and pliers, I slipped on the snowshoes and headed out. Wantalook and Goodlooken played and chased each other as I made my way to the cage trip. I moved it to a spot about 100 feet away. Then I started looking for the traveled areas to set up snares, keeping clear of the avalanche area. I set out four snares within a half mile always staying two to three hundred yards away from the danger area. All the spots looked good. I'll check them this evening. I still got areas to the west yet to set up. I'll save them for later on.

I was glad to get back to camp to eat and rest a while. Wantalook and Goodlooken took their spot on the mound to lay down. I got the fire built up and got food out for lunch. I had some meat thawing out by the fire so I could slice it for moose on a stick. It was only when I got the fish out that the king and queen came down from their throne. Since they finished theirs right away, they had to sit and watch me eat and cook mine. I knew with the two sets of eyes watching, I would have to give them some too. I swear, it was like two kids looking through the windows of a candy store. Afterwards, Wantalook got next to me for some petting and Goodlooken was next to him. I thought to myself it won't be long. We sat there about an hour before I got up. I needed to chop the bear up in chunks so I can make it last longer. I wound up using my saw to cut through the meat and the ax to break the bones. The cleanup crew was on the spot when I got done and not a piece was wasted.

It was time to walk the trap line and my wolves walked with me. It turned out to be good for the first day, one squirrel and one rabbit. Needless to say the kids were excited even when we got back to camp. They both were eager to help with the cleaning and one time Goodlooken was next to my leg till she realized where she was. I let the meat soak for an hour before I put it in the rack to cook. Wantalook and Goodlooken had their spots picked out while I cooked the meat. I waited till it was done before I gave them each a fish. I cut up the meat into pieces after I ate the back legs of each. I am liking this close range attention. When the eating was over, we settled in for some quality time. When I was petting Wantalook I stopped with my hand on his shoulder and she sniffed my hand for the first time and was no in hurry to quit. It only lasted a few seconds. I kept talking to her as I petted Wantalook. It was getting late so I headed inside, filled the stove and laid there awake thinking about the days ahead till spring and I soon fell asleep.

I couldn't believe it was morning already. It seemed like I just laid down. I sat on the edge of the bed till all my senses were working together before I got up to feed the stove and the kids. I felt like having some coffee so I made up a small amount and set it on the stove to perk. The smell alone was waking me up. I filled my mug and took a sip, sweet nectar of the gods. I forgot how much I miss this stuff. I finished getting dressed and went outside. Wantalook and Goodlooken were there to greet me, excited like always. Goodlooken was joining in on the play. It looks like you two have been out eating last night, your bellies are bulging. I managed to get a stroke or two on Goodlooken while the three of us played. I was down on my knees with Wantalook as he licked my face.

Goodlooken licked my hand. Then I got a chance for the first chance for the first pet, she liking it. The three of us are bound together now. I got up and started a fire, then sat down to enjoy my coffee. Wantalook and Goodlooken were playing around the yard, jumping on each other, putting on a show for me. When they did settle down, I could really see the tenderness they showed toward each other. I guess the three of us makes a pack now. I finished my coffee.

Now it was time to walk the trap line. I slipped on my snowshoes and the three of us headed out. Wantalook and Goodlooken were having fun running circles around me as I walked. Occasionally they would brush my leg on a run by, playing tag. We got one rabbit on that trip on the way back. The two were getting crazy on me with the rabbit in my hand. They wanted to help clean it on the spot. The two settled down some by the time we got to camp.

When the cleanup was over, Wantalook and his queen laid down on their snow throne to rest. It looked more like making out with all attention they were giving each other. I was hungry by now and cooked up some moose and the two lovebirds stayed where they were while I ate. Who needs food when you got love? Afterwards, I melted more snow and brought in a wood supply into the cabin. The air outside was starting to change. I could feel it; we definitely had another cold spell coming. By late afternoon, I could feel the drop in temperature when we checked the trap line again.

We came home empty-handed this time. I built the fire up good. When we got back, I got a couple fish for each of them and cooked up the rabbit with some moose too. When everyone in the pack was fed, I had a wolf for each hand now. Being friends with one wolf is a chance of a lifetime. I've been given two chances. The only thing left they haven't done yet is howl together but I have a feeling it will be coming.

It was getting too cold for me. I didn't want to move but there will be more quality time in the days ahead. They wanted to stay outside but I had to offer. It felt good to get out of the cold. My backside is what needed some serious warming and after I filled the stove, that's when my backside was facing the stove. It's been quite the day with my wolves and Goodlooken has come a long way. I said I would be petting her in a week and I did. I had a smile on my face when I went to sleep that night.

    I couldn't wait to get outside when I woke up. After filling the stove and getting on my warm clothes, I stepped outside. What a temperature shock from warm to below zero. I mean freeze the hair in your nose, grab your breath in your hand cold. I got Wantalook and Goodlooken their fish and got back inside to add what I had left to put on. I'll do an outside test when I play with them and see how long I last. Well, I didn't last long. After ten minutes it hurt to breathe even with a frozen face mask. It is by far the coldest I've ever experienced. Until it warms up, I won't be checking the trap line either. After I warmed up some, I went back out to pet Wantalook and Goodlooken. Even after fifteen minutes the cold was penetrating right through me and I had to go back in.
    After making breakfast, I started back on the door. It was an hour or so later when I heard Wantalook at the door. When I opened it, Wantalook came right in. Goodlooken not so eager. I tried talking to her in, Wantalook helped too. I went to the cupboard and got a few pieces of dried meat. When I did coax her in, she jumped in instead of walking. Wantalook was assuring her and so was I. Now to shut the door and see how she reacts so far so good. The cabin was cold and so was I after having the door open for fifteen minutes. It didn't take long before the cabin was warming up. It looked like Goodlooken was liking it too. It was a little cramped with the three of us but we settled in fine. Wantalook laid down and Goodlooken joined him. I wanted to take a picture but it was too soon for the shock of a flash.
    I went back to work building the doors. Wantalook was used to watching me work. Goodlooken watched with curiosity, watching my every move. After a while she just laid her head on Wantalook and I caught her a couple times with her eyes shut. I couldn't help but smile when I saw that.
    It was getting close to lunch time so I put on my hat and coat and made a quick trip to the food container outside the door and back in. Needless to say my two wolves were wide awake as I put down their fish. When they finished, I got some petting

time in. I was still waiting for my food to thaw out. After twenty minutes, Wantalook wanted outside. When he went out Goodlooken jumped through the doorway like she did when she came in. I fried up my lunch after that, then went back to assembling the doors.

Around 3:00, I made a pot of stew and let it cook the rest of the afternoon. I was working on the fourth door; when it was completed, I had to trim and smooth the pegs and fit each door to its opening. The only thing left is to cut out the hinge blocks, handles and latches but that's another day. My stew was ready so I got dressed to get out the fish. Wantalook and Goodlooken were laying down under the overhang. They wanted to eat outside. I went back in. After shaking off the chill I sat down to eat. I will have to wait till later to see if I will have company tonight in the cabin. As I sat at the table, I was looking at the stack of boards I had left. I didn't figure to build anything else, well maybe a bench or stool. I could use them for a floor since the cabin was twelve by sixteen. I could cover just over half. The only board on the floor is the two by my bed. Plus I won't have to set the base cabinet on the ground.

Things must be bad, the wolves are at my door but that's good. Wantalook came in first, Goodlooken paused then jumped in. She will overcome the doorway one of these days. After the greetings were over, we settled in for our quality time of petting, love and attention. I don't believe this, I have been petting these two for almost two hours. When I stopped they were pushing their noses under my hand wanting more. I just shook my head, what have I created? I petted them a while longer and it was time for bed. I got up to fill the stove and they laid down together. As I got into bed, I wondered what my wake-up was going to be like. Well, I'll find out in the morning I told myself as I fell asleep.

I got my answer when I opened my eyes. I was being doubletongued. Wantalook was first and it was a second or two, Goodlooken joined in. I am up. I've got a couple of happy wolves on my hands. As I sat up, Wantalook was showing Goodlooken how to door dance. I quickly got to my feet and let them out, only a small jump this time. I dried my face and sat down. I had to laugh a bit at those two. I loaded the stove and got my clothes on to face the cold outside. Wantalook and Goodlooken were chasing each other around the yard when I came out. I wasn't sure if it was going to be play or eat time first. When they both came up and started rough-housing, it was play. We rolled and tumbled around the yard, pushing, shoving, tagging each other. It was a sight to see. I had to stop. I couldn't go anymore. My sides hurt from laughing and being out of breath. I got to my feet, brushed the snow off, while they pushed against my legs still wanting to play. I got them their fish and went back in to get my hands and face warmed up. The stew was hot so I dished myself up a bowl. Afterwards I slipped on a few more clothes and went back out. When they saw me slip on the snowshoes, they got excited and were ready to take off. As I walked down the trail to check the traps, the rest of the pack ran around chasing each other and rushing me to make contact play. I got to the cage first and we had a squirrel. They both had to get a sniff. They were excited but when I came up with two rabbits, there was no control in their excitement.

When we got back to camp, they were more than ready to help me clean them. The squirrel was no problem. The rabbits I had to warm up first. They were frozen solid. After a few hours inside they were thawed out enough to clean. I did it inside. My fingers were cold enough handling the frosted meat without trying to do it out in the cold. Guess who was waiting at the door for their share when I was done? When they came through the door, there was no time wasted on the cleanup. I got some petting time in before they wanted outside.

I started scraping boards for the floor and cutting them to size. The dirt was pretty level already so with a little scraping and packing, I started laying them down as I got them done. As soon as I had enough board down, I slid the cabinet in place. This place is looking more homey by the day. It was getting toward evening so I cleaned up inside. I then got my heavy clothes on and got the fire started outside. The king and queen came down from their throne to join me. After the fire was going good I went in to get the meat. All of it wouldn't fit on the rack so I only put the back legs of the rabbits and the squirrel on the rack. Wantalook and Goodlooken wolfed down their food. I know, bad pun. Before I even had a chance to start cooking, I got them out a few fish to help fill them till I was done. I planned to save two of the legs for breakfast. Wantalook and Goodlooken each got a half a squirrel and I had the rest. I had to put the last two legs away before I could sit down to do some quality time.

The clouds had moved in and it was somewhat warmer than it was earlier. We sat for over an hour before I had to go in. It may be warmer but I was getting cold. Wantalook and Goodlooken weren't ready to come in. Oh well, they know where the door is. I filled the stove and sat at the table and started whittling since the family got bigger. I've got to make another wolf now. I sat there for about an hour. The eyes were getting tired. I looked outside and those two were nowhere around. Well they are doing what's natural. I added a few more pieces of wood to the stove and went to bed.

It was snowing when I got up. As I filled the stove, I heard the wolves at my door again. I got dressed and opened the door. They were waiting and glad to see me. After the greetings were over, I got out their food and went back in. I ate the last two rabbit legs, got on my heavy clothes and went outside. I tried setting down but they weren't going for that. So I buttoned my collar and let the games begin. Those two had me worn out in no time. At one point, Goodlooken got carried away, getting too aggressive, and Wantalook pinned her. In his own way, he let her know she crossed the line. I petted them both and all was good after that.

I got on my snowshoes to walk the trap line. Wantalook and Goodlooken were ready. They were out of the yard before I was. Today I am picking up the traps and bringing them back to camp. The area to the west is a lot better. When this snow is over, I'll set up there. There wasn't anything in the cage or snares today. When we got back to camp, there were almost five inches of new snow. After a short break, I got down the push board and started clearing snow. Five inches is easier to deal with than five feet or more. It was still snowing when I finished at noon. The king and queen stayed on their throne the whole time, content to watch me work. After a short break, I started marking and cutting out the rest of the parts to finish and hang the doors. Cutting out the handles and latches took the longest.

The hinge blocks were two cuts. It was late afternoon before I was ready to finish assembling and hang them. It took four pegs per handle, twenty-four total and four pegs per hinge block, thirty-two total when done.

It was supper time already and I wasn't finished. Oh well, tomorrow's another day. I looked outside and Wantalook and Goodlooken were covered with snow still laying there. I slipped on my coat to get food out of the container. They came alive and were off that mound of snow in a blink of an eye. There were at least three more inches of snow on the ground since I cleared it. I went back in to cook my supper, then cleaned up afterwards. I sweet talked the happy couple to come in for our quality time but when it was over they wanted outside. I think I was half asleep when I let them out. I filled the stove and was sleeping shortly.

When I woke up that morning, it seemed no different than the rest. I put wood in the stove, got dressed, went outside to feed Wantalook and Goodlooken and saw nothing but white. It was hard to say how much snow came down overnight till I stepped out into it. It was past my knees. I could see Wantalook and Goodlooken were laying down under the overhang. I gave them their fish and went back inside. Damn I got some snow to move now. I fried up some meat for breakfast. I wasn't looking forward to the task ahead. I was eating my last bit of meat when I heard the wind. I quickly slipped on my hat and coat to see what direction the wind was coming from. I was happy to see it was coming out of the west. Now I'll see how my snow wall does, making the wind clear the yard. I was under the overhang petting and playing with Wantalook and Goodlooken when the wind really kicked in. The snow was falling off the trees and the air turned white with blowing snow. Soon you could hear the trees howl as they lost their blanket of snow. It was time to go in and let this storm blow over.

I got the rest of the doors hung and latches in place. It looked real nice. I got out my camera and took a couple of pictures. Wantalook and Goodlooken wanted in again. I think it was more to check on me because after some petting, they wanted back out. I took a look out the door and nothing but flying snow is all I could see. There was even a layer of snow over everything under the overhang. I had more boards left to do and get done. So that's what I did the rest of the afternoon. When I got the last board down, I couldn't believe how it changed the looks of the cabin. Not to mention not seeing a pile of boards laying there. I took more pictures before starting supper.

The pot was on the stove when I heard the wolves at the door. As I opened the door I said sorry guys, you're stuck with me. Little Red Riding Hood, Granny, and The Three Pigs are not here, they left for warmer climate. They didn't care what I said. They wanted some food from the food shack, the container was empty. After supper we got our spot to get our quality time in. The wind wasn't showing any sign of slowing up and some of the gusts were quite hard enough to hear it in the stove. We sat for a couple hours before I had to call it a night. Wantalook and Goodlooken laid down. I filled the stove and went to sleep.

When I woke up, the wind was still intense and stayed that way for the next five days. I had finished the figurine of Goodlooken, played and laid around, only went outside for a quick breath of fresh air now and then.

I woke up to silence. After my face licking wake-up, I couldn't wait to get outside. Wantalook and Goodlooken were doing the two-step at the door when I let them out. I got dressed and was out the door minutes later. Things sure looked a lot different out, other than the snow drifted in front of the open side of the overhang. The rest of the yard was clear. The snow wall did its job. The only snow to clear was in front of the smoker and fire pit, around the outhouse and overhang. The west side of the cabin was covered to the roof but that didn't matter. The area east of the cabin was deep, clear to the woods. I fed Wantalook and Goodlooken then started pushing snow. They started playing around me as I worked, trying to get me to join in. I was done with the snow in a little over an hour. I played with them after that, till I thought I'd drop. There was no way I would win against the two of them.

I was more than happy to sit down and watch them. The day was turning out nice weather-wise. The sun was out and the air was calm. I cleaned out the fire pit and got a fire going.

I'll be spending the day outside. After setting up my chair and getting out my roasting stick I settled in for some moose on a stick. I had to give Wantalook and Goodlooken a chunk of bear meat so I could have a little peace eating my food. I'll put the snares and cage trap out tomorrow, if the weather stays like this tomorrow morning. I will have good travel areas to choose from. After the petting was done, Wantalook and Goodlooken took their spot on the mound of snow and laid down. I was happy to stay where I was and feed the fire and enjoy the day. I had a little house cleaning to do, melt snow to get the water supply back up and dump the bucket into the outhouse. I melted snow the rest of the morning to get everything filled back up.

After lunch, I would go for a walk and check out the snow in some of the other areas. The king and queen were still on their throne till I got the food out. After we ate I slipped on the snowshoes and headed off to the west. The only thing that slowed those two down was soft deep snow spots. The rest of the time, it was full tilt boogie across the hard snow. After I crossed the frozen stream, I traveled along the lake shore to the west end of the lake. I thought about walking around the lake but I decided that will be another day so I headed back. When I walked back into camp I was ready to sit a while.

I hung up my shoes then tossed more wood on the fire. Wantalook and Goodlooken joined me as I sat down. They both were wanting attention. We sat there the rest of the afternoon till the daylight was fading. I got up to stretch my legs and get supper out of the food shack. When supper was over, I had to put more wood in the stove so the cabin would be warm when I came in later on after our quality time was over. The skies were clear so I got the chance to look at the stars too. I knew when it was time to go. Wantalook and Goodlooken wasn't going to spend their time indoors tonight. When I reached the door, they were heading out over the snow. The cabin was warm and I needed to warm my backside first. I couldn't do that with a wolf at each leg when I was sitting. I filled the stove for the night and was looking forward to a good night's sleep.

When I woke up I could see that the skies were clear. It would be a good morning to get the traps out. After adding wood to the stove I got on my heavy clothes then stepped outside to greet the family. Damn, they get excited when I come out the door, each trying to get closer than the other for attention. Gee, I feel loved. I got a short break after the food was handed out, long enough to get the fire going and start cooking mine. They started to play while I ate; it sure was comical to watch those two at it. It wasn't long before they wanted me to join it. I wanted to save my energy so I gave up after ten minutes. They still wanted to play but when they saw me slip on the snowshoes and grab the traps, they were ready to head out. Those two just have too much energy.

I set the cage trap up first with one snare this side of the stream and the other five beyond it. I was glad that Wantalook was keeping Goodlooken back while I set the snares out. He seemed to know what I wanted. He has watched me do it many times. We played on the way back to camp. Their favorite thing was come in running and hit my leg. I could usually block or grab but when you got a tag team going, at times I had a hard time staying on my feet. The madness slowed down when we got back to camp. Those two had me worn out. I put more wood on the fire and sat down for a much needed rest. Wantalook and Goodlooken laid down on the mound. I was glad to see I wasn't the only one tired. I sat there over an hour before I even thought about moving. I was concerned about the food supply. We had the rest of February, March and April to go yet. Rabbit and squirrel isn't going to make up all that we will need. I need to try to get a hole through the ice for fish. I got out the ax, shovel, trim saw, slipped on my snowshoes and went out on the lake. Wantalook and Goodlooken came along. I started chopping a hole three by three feet. When I couldn't use the ax anymore, I used the trim saw and hatchet trying to keep the hole as big as possible. The further down, the narrower it gets. I knew once I broke through, I had to knock the bottom out as soon as possible. When I got to around thirty inches, I kept chipping away inch by inch till water appeared. I quickly grabbed my shovel and slammed the bottom through. After clearing away the loose ice, I had an 8-inch hole in the bottom. I took my tools back to camp, warmed my hands, then went back out with my pole and rope. It wasn't long before I had fish flopping on the ice. Wantalook and Goodlooken were having a field day eating all they wanted. When I got one rope full, I took it back to camp, emptied it and went back for more. I made four more trips that afternoon and by the time I emptied the rope it was dark.

I put all but twenty in the food shack, the twenty are for the smoker. When I got the feeling back in my hands, I cleaned them, put them in water overnight. I decided to clean one more for supper. It's been a while since I had fish. There wasn't much quality after supper. It was late plus I was tired and getting cold. It felt good to get inside. I filled the stove, then stood next to it. I was warm all over, then got into bed.

Morning was here. Way too quick for me. I laid there a while before even attempting getting up. But I must get everything going. I got places to go and things to do. After feeding the stove, I got ready for the great outdoors. Wantalook and Goodlooken were waiting with much excitement, anticipating my appearance for attention and food. I had a bunch of the older fish ready in the container to give them as soon as the petting was over. When I gave them their fish, I got the chance to get the fire started in the pit, then got the smoker started. After the frost and moisture was gone, I loaded the fish in. I cooked up some moose for myself for breakfast. I added more wood to the smoker before heading out to check the traps.

Somehow I managed to make it beyond playtime. They will probably make up for it on the trail, they did. So as I am walking along, they're coming at me doing this running tag against my leg. I added some snow to the fun. I could see the flag was up on the cage traps. After I removed the squirrel, I reset it and went on to the first snare. It was empty. I then crossed over to the other side of the trout stream to check the remaining five snares. We got lucky this morning. We had two rabbits to bring home. Needless to say I had two excited wolves keeping me company on the way back to camp.

They wouldn't even let me sit down. They wanted to help clean. I did something a little different this time. I just kept the back legs and gave them the rest. The squirrel I saved for myself too. The smoker was needing more wood. While I was taking care of the smoker, Wantalook and Goodlooken made sure the area where I cleaned the game was clean too. Now I can sit down by the fire a few minutes a while. Wantalook and Goodlooken joined me for a few minutes before going to their spot on the mound. It was another sunshiny day to enjoy. I'll take them when I can get them. It sure beats being locked up in the cabin for days during a storm. The rest of the day is smoked fish and kicken back by the fire.

I got out my cooking rack. I am going to have the rabbit and squirrel for lunch. I didn't eat breakfast and smoked fish is on the menu tonight. Since the light is good, it's a good time for Goodlooken to get her picture taken. I went in and got my camera. They were both in a good pose on the mound. When that first click of the camera went off, Goodlooken almost jumped to her feet; after a few words, she settled back in alongside of Wantalook. I moved over and took another. She wasn't sure if she liked it or not. Wantalook just laid there. I got three or four good shots after that. I put the camera back inside. The fish were looking good; a couple more hours and they will be ready to eat. I was looking forward to it too. It's been weeks since I had smoked fish. It was a nice relaxing afternoon. I even caught myself dozing off a couple times.

Well, it's time to check the fish. Good, done to perfection. I slid a nice one on a plate and sat down. Yes, I had company too. Wantalook liked smoked fish. This will be Goodlooken's first. It turned out she liked it as much as he did. I was still hungry so I got out one more. Afterwards I put the rest of the fish away and put more wood in the stove. When I sat back down, I tried to get a howling session going between the three of us. It took a few minutes. Wantalook opened up first and Goodlooken joined in. Boy, if this isn't the coolest thing. It felt like their howls were going right through me. I mean I had goose bumps. Wow, I don't think it gets any better than this. It didn't last long but what there was, was great. After that we settled in for a couple hours of quality time before I had to call it a night. It was nice stepping into a warm cabin. After filling the stove, I sat on the bed a while, thinking about today and all the fun I had. As I laid down, I couldn't help but smile. It was a good day.

I woke up feeling good. I slept well and was ready to have another great day. First I'll feed the stove, get dressed then feed the rest of us. Mr. and Mrs. excitement were waiting as I stepped out. Two balls of fur, each trying to get more attention than the other. As soon as I could, I got their fish out so I could sit down and eat mine. They had four times more fish to eat than me and they still beat me. It was playtime now. We went at it for at least ten minutes. When I grabbed my snowshoes, they gave me enough time to put them on and the rest of the playtime was on the walk to check the trap. We got one rabbit on the last snare. One is better than nothing. I was Wantalook and Goodlooken's bestest friend all the way back to camp.

I saved the back legs for myself and divided the rest up for them. I put the legs in water and got the fire going. It was another nice day out. Wantalook and Goodlooken still wanted to play as I sat down. I was getting some petting in between the pushing, when all of a sudden a rabbit ran through the yard. When Wantalook and Goodlooken realized what happened, they took after it. I got on my snowshoes as fast as I could. I wanted to see this. When I stood up they were out of sight. I took off at a good pace following their tracks going east. I was close to the avalanche area when I stopped. Their tracks were still heading toward it. It was 200 yards from the devastation area. I had a very bad feeling about this situation. Then all hell broke loose. I turned and put more distance between me and the devastation of snow that was coming down that part of the mountain. The sight of that much snow, rocks and boulders coming down was heart-stopping. It was like a huge explosion when it hit the trees. There was so much debris, flying trees snapping off like twigs. My heart was pounding so hard, I could hardly breathe. It stopped as fast as it started. When the snow settled, the snapping of popping of trees and limbs was all I could hear with the creaking of snow. I took off running as fast as I could around it, looking for tracks out, hoping they were past it before it started. There only a few trees left standing in its path and the destruction was 200 yards and more beyond the old.

When I reached the other side, my heart sank, no tracks. I started across the destruction area looking for any sign of Wantalook or Goodlooken. I didn't care how out of breath I was, I had to try to find them. Taking a wild guess with the lead they had on me and the size of the area, I figured they were in the second half from where I was standing when it happened. It was looking hopeless. I was running all over like a wild man, still finding nothing and minutes were passing by. I had to stop to catch my breath, Lord, I need your help now more than ever.

As I turned to take off again, I spotted some hair in under some trees. I dove in head first and grabbed it. It was the tip of a tail. As soon as I started digging, I knew it was Wantalook. As I dug, there was no movement, he was pinned between two trees, trunk across his chest. There were ten to fifteen feet of tree top past me. I got his face uncovered but he wasn't breathing. I planted my feet on the lower tree and put my shoulder on the upper as I stood up, I pulled Wantalook free. I grabbed his mouth, cleared his nose and blew in while rubbing his chest. I think at one time I hit his chest with my fist still blowing air into his lungs. Wantalook, don't die, buddy. I was doing everything in my power to bring him around, rubbing his chest, trying to get him to breathe. I was in tears by now when I got a nose snort. I ripped off my hat and put my ear on his chest. The heart was going strong and his breathing was fast at first, then slowing down. I held him in my arms even though he was limp as a wet dish rag. I rubbed his body and kept talking to him, not even taking time to wipe the tears that constantly streamed down my face.

His breathing was close to normal now. I kept up talking to him, rubbing his body. What I did before to wake him up was touch the hair on his ears. It worked. Soon after a few times of that he opened his eyes. Welcome back, my friend. He licked my hands and face and soon got to his feet. He was wobbly at first. After a few minutes he was fine. He was looking for Goodlooken now and so was I but with this much time passed, I knew we wouldn't find her alive if we did find her.

About thirty feet away Wantalook found the spot. He started digging and I did too. We found her five feet down wrapped around a broken off tree stump. No air pocket around her and broken up inside. Wantalook sniffed and pushed her with his nose and paw. The sight broke my heart. My heart was sad with the loss of her not to mention the puppies she had inside. I must have been on my knees with Wantalook an hour.

I put on my snowshoes and picked Goodlooken up in my arms and carried her back to camp. Wantalook walked by my side lifting his head only to sniff her and his head would hang low again. It was a sad time for both of us. When we got back to camp I laid her down by the overhang. Wantalook laid alongside of her, then laid his head on her with the saddest look in his eyes. I had to turn away. I couldn't hold back my tears anymore. I went inside the cabin to get a drink of water and sit down a while. I really need to get out of my wet clothes. Between the snow and sweat, I was soaked in a few areas. I changed my clothes, took a shot of bourbon, then went back outside. Wantalook hadn't moved any. I got him to drink some water, then he laid his head back down. I knelt alongside of him, scratching his head and stroking his fur, trying to comfort him. We both shared the loss of Goodlooken. I really felt bad for Wantalook. The gleam in his eyes was gone. His whole body showed the sadness he was feeling. There was nothing I could do except be there for him and with him. They say a loss of one in a wolf pack affects them tremendously. They are right. I am a witness to that fact. I tried to get him something at different times during the afternoon.

It was time for supper and I cooked up the rabbit legs and I finally got him to eat a bite and a little more water. He still wouldn't leave her side. I didn't expect he would. Back when I was hurt, he stayed by me the same as I stayed by him after the bear attack. I stayed with him as long as I didn't want to go in but I had to. I stood by the stove the longest time trying to get the chill out of me, before going to bed. As I laid there, my mind was on Wantalook and the sad days ahead.

I woke up early. I didn't sleep well at all. Yesterday's events kept going through my mind. I got dressed and went outside to check on Wantalook; he was still laying by her. My heart was going out to him as he picked his head up to greet me. I got him to drink some water and a few bites of smoked fish but that was all. I tried to get him to play hoping to cheer him up, but getting petted was all he would do. I spent an hour with him before getting up. I put on my snowshoes so I could take up the cage trap and snares for now. There was plenty of food and I didn't need to take anymore from this land. I tried to get Wantalook to come along, he wasn't ready. The cage trap was empty and out of the six snares, there was one rabbit. When I got back to camp, I put the traps away. When I showed Wantalook the rabbit I got a little rise out of him. I needed to get the fire going before I started cleaning the rabbit. Wantalook got up and joined me, ate what he wanted, then laid back down. Well, it's a start on the long way back.

It wasn't till the third day when Wantalook left her side. He didn't have his spirit back yet that I loved but he was spending more time with me. I was still learning the ways of the wolf so I was playing it by ear, day by day. I had picked out a spot to bury her east of the cabin. A snow grave will have to do till spring. Wantalook didn't seem to mind what I was doing as I prepared her spot and laid her down then covered her up. He stayed by my side and watched every move. I went in the cabin to get the board I made to mark her grave. When I came out Wantalook was laying on the mound of snow that covered her. I put the board in place. The words read, Goodlooken you were loved and you are missed. Wantalook joined me by the fire with his head on my leg making every minute of our quality time count.

It took weeks before Wantalook was back to his old self. As I witnessed his mood changes, his good days and his bad days, there really wasn't any difference than what humans go through.

By the end of March was when the big changes came. Spring was right around the corner and I think we both could feel it. Hopefully all the big storms were behind us. We made it through four bad ones, since Goodlooken died. I needed to set the traps out so we'll have fresh meat again. Wantalook was himself again, playful as ever and his amber eyes had the look of the proud spirit that was in him. After breakfast we were ready to get this day started.

I got out the cage traps and snares, slipped on my showshoes and headed west. The snow was a lot deeper now since I was here last. The traveled spots were different. Wantalook watched as I set everything out. He knew what the traps were for. We played along the way setting things up and all the way back to camp. I sure liked having my wolf back. I was ready to sit by now.We covered a lot of ground today and with the playing as we went along, I was beat. Wantalook laid beside me till I got up. I've got chores to do today, like melt the snow to get the water supply up. Get some clothes cleaned, more like rinse out, no soap left. Clean the ashes out of the stove again, then bring some wood inside. I'll make it last till this afternoon, then I will check the traps again. Wantalook went to his spot on his throne of snow so he could watch over his territory. Today was the warmest it's been, mid up to high 20s, my guess. I'll be glad to see the snow melting away. It's been a long winter and when the stream starts flowing, that part of the lake will open enough to catch fish again. I got the clothes as clean as they are going to be and got 'em hanging outside. The containers are full of water, the wood is in and the ashes are hauled out.

Time to check the traps. I didn't need to say anything to Wantalook, he knew where we were going. Mr. excitement was ready before I got my snowshoes on. We played tag on the way out as we got closer to the cage trap, the flag was up. I got the squirrel and reset it. Wantalook was right there, sniffing with excitement. I wasn't sure if we were going to get a rabbit, their travels are mostly at night. Our luck was good, we got one on the 5th snare and it was still warm. Wantalook was bouncing after this find. I had to laugh, the way he was acting. So when we got back to camp Wantalook was right there for the cleaning. If he was any closer, he would have to be in my clothes. I let the meat soak in water till supper. Wantalook was doing the final cleanup when I sat down then he joined me by the fire. After an hour, I took the clothes in to finish drying then started cooking supper. It wasn't long before the smell from the cooking was in the air. Wantalook was eating his fish when the cooking was being done. The taste of fresh meat was a welcome change. It's been a long time. After the last scrap was eaten, we settled in for our quality time, till it was time to go to bed. Wantalook was still staying by my side, when I went, he went. That will change when the snow melts. I filled the stove, while Wantalook laid down by my bed. I patted his head one last time, then I laid down and went to sleep.

I was greeted with a wet nose when I opened my eyes. I don't have to wash my face in the morning. Wantalook does that for me. The longer I laid there, the more tongue I get till I get up. Wantalook was doing his door dance as soon as I sat up. I stood up and stretched then opened the door. I put a few pieces of wood in the stove, then I got ready to go outside. When I stepped out the door, my bouncing fur ball was waiting. I gave him his fish and meat scraps, then went to get the fire started. It was turning out to be another nice day. If April stays like this, it won't be bad at all. Wantalook was ready for playtime. So I got to my feet and we started in. Keep away was one of his favorite games, when I'd try to grab or touch him. Needless to say after the pushing, tagging and wrestling, I laid on my back with a face full of wolf, yelling I give up, you win. After a few licks on the face, he let me up. I got to my chair and sat down. Every time he wins, he gets this special walk. He doesn't just to show he's the winner. Gloating would be a good word to describe it, gloating!

It was time to check the snares, there should be something waiting for us. As I walked down the trail, Wantalook liked to play brush or bump tag. It's fun till he steps on the snowshoes and I wind up face first in the snow. If I keep swinging my arms, he stays back some. I could see ahead that the flag was up on the cage. Wantalook always gets excited when he sees I've caught something. I reset the trap then moved on to the snares. We had rabbit in the second and fourth. Wantalook was my very bestest friend now, sticking to me like glue and on his best behavior, ready to help me clean them. When we got back to camp, he was ready to start.

I put more wood on the fire and sat down. It was another nice day, very close to thirty-two degrees. It was still calm at 10:00. I like it now, the days are getting longer and the sun is getting higher in the sky. When things start melting, I won't be crossing the stream for a while. When it does, I'll pull up the snares and set them up to the east, till a spot opens up on the lake. I haven't been there once, since the accident in February. There are safe areas to trap but I just didn't want to venture that way.

Wantalook was laying on his mound now, dozing off in the sun. Granted the sun does feel good sitting here. About the only thing left to do around here for a while is wait for the snow to melt. As long as the trapping is good, we'll do fine, till a spot opens up on the lake. The meat that's left in the food shack is not that great. I think Wantalook will have most of that. The dried meat is still alright, that should last till the end of the month. The only food left from what I brought is some beans, peas and potato eyes wedges I saved for seed. I saved some seed from dried veggies. I'll see if I can get anything started from that. I'll make planter boxes to get things started. The area where I removed the moss will be a good spot for a garden.

If time flies by when you're having fun, daydreaming works good too. It was past lunch time and the stomach was starting to scream feed me. I got out one rabbit and started cooking it. Wantalook chowed down on fish and moose meat, then waited for his share of the rabbit and all the bones. I wound up eating most of the rabbit but Wantalook didn't mind. Afterwards I noticed some puddles were appearing in the yard. My gosh, it is warming up. I slipped on the snowshoes and headed toward the stream. Sure enough we were starting to get runoff. I crossed it and picked up the snares to take back. When I got back to the stream I could hear water under the ice, making its way back to the lake. This thing could open up in a day or two, if the weather stays like this. I'll keep checking it. The sooner it flows, the sooner I can fish.

I'll get back to camp. I sat down a while before setting up the snares again. I think this winter has took its toll on both of us, me more than Wantalook. I know we could have a nasty spell or two of cold but winter's grip has been broken. When this snow gets down, I will have to set up my bell alarms again. I hope I don't have another bear encounter.

It was already late afternoon so Wantalook and I left camp to set the snares out to the east. I found good travel areas for all of them covering quite the distance away from camp. By the time we got back, evening was setting in and the temperature had dropped to below freezing. I got the fire going again, got out Wantalook's food, then started cooking up the rabbit and squirrel. It was calm out this evening. The best it's been in a very long time. I just hope it keeps up like this. The meat was done and I was ready to eat. I'll save some of this for breakfast. Wantalook was there by my side getting what scraps he could. Afterwards we enjoyed our quality time till nothing but embers were left in the fire pit. I got up to go in for the night. Wantalook wanted to stay out. After starting the fire in the stove to take the chill out of the cabin I was more than ready to get some sleep.

When I stepped outside, I could feel the sunlight doing its work. Wantalook was ready to get playtime started too but I'll feed him first before we get playtime started. When I finished the leftovers from last night, Wantalook had already finished his food and was ready to start. As our morning tradition goes, we kept it up for about twenty minutes or more. I was close to winning once if that counts. After my face licking, he let me up. I slipped on my snowshoes and we left camp to check the traps. Wantalook was having fun, running circles around me and dove in for an occasional big bump as I got closer to the cage trap. I could see the flag was up. After removing the squirrel, I planned to move it to another spot. As I got closer to the stream, I could hear water a lot more than yesterday. As I got closer, I could see it had opened up a lot and the ice at the mouth are starting to open up too. I told myself, if this keeps up, I'll be fishing in a few days. I took the trap back with me. I've got some spots east of camp where I want to set it up.

After a short break at camp, we headed out to check the snares and set the cage trap up in its new spot. I was sure we would do good in the new territory. When we finally got to the last one, we had three rabbits to bring home. We will be eating good the next couple days. Wantalook couldn't wait to help when we got back, after the cleaning was done. Wantalook looked quite heavy around the middle and soon laid down on his mound to recuperate. That should keep him satisfied till tonight. The weather was turning out great today. The temperature was above freezing already.

I got out some of my scrap wood. I started building some planter boxes. They will be ready when we start getting some warmer days. I can get a head start on the growing season. I spent the rest of the day marking and cutting all the pieces, enough for five trays twenty-four inches long with slide in dividers. I'll start putting them together tomorrow.

It was time to get a fire going and start supper. Wantalook finally decided to get up and come down from his throne and joined me. The fish were gone so he will be eating from the remaining meat from the food shack. I cooked up two rabbits for supper so I could have leftovers in the morning. As I was eating, I noticed how much the snow had melted today especially where I had spread the ashes around. That's a good idea. Tomorrow I will clean the stove and fire pit and spread the ashes on the snow, where the garden's going to be. It's been a good day so when our quality time was over, I was ready to head in for the night. It didn't take long for sleep either.

It was another nice day from what I could see from the window. When I stepped outside, I could smell spring in the air. After we ate and played a while, we left to check the traps. Walking along, you couldn't help but notice the change from yesterday. We were lucky again, one squirrel and one rabbit. This afternoon I'll check the lake at the stream and try to figure when I'll be able to fish again. After the cleaning was done and the meat put away, I started hauling ashes to the garden site. The snow there was only a foot or so deep. When I finished I had a large area covered, now to let the sun do its job. After a short break, I got out my tools and wood pieces then started to assemble the planter boxes. I had made two different sizes for small seeds and larger seed, like potatoes. With a little luck, I should grow enough to get me through the coming winter and have plenty of seeds for the next year. Because it doesn't look like I'll be leaving here. It was already late afternoon when I put the boxes away. I still needed to go to the stream yet. I could hear the water long before I got there. Wow, what a torrent of water moving past me and into the lake. There must be thirty feet of lake opened up at the mouth. I should be able to try some fishing tomorrow. Then I won't have to trap anymore. I was happy with that prospect. I walked back to camp.

Well it's time to get supper started. All the while cooking, I was thinking about fresh fish and smoked fish, it's been awhile. Then after a month of eating fish, I'll be ready for some fresh meat again. The skies were starting to cloud up by the time supper was over. I will know by morning if it's rain or snow. The fire was dying and Wantalook and I have been setting here for hours already. My butt was numb when I stood up to go inside.

Wantalook joined me. I think he knew we had a change of weather coming. I got the fire going in the stove, then we settled in for the night.

It snowed and rained for the next three days. On the second day, I caught two fish. It was too cold and wet to stay out for any length of time. The stream was totally out of control by now and it made it very hard to fish. When I woke up the morning of the fourth day, the storm had passed and I could see the sun shining again. I got dressed and joined Wantalook outside. There was an area of water pooled up all over. I petted Wantalook a little, then grabbed my shovel and tried to drain what I could. We had a lot of snow the past three days and more bare spots were showing. I took a walk to the garden area and it was bare. Now the sun can start warming the ground. I slipped on my boots, grabbed my fishing equipment and Wantalook followed me to the lake. A large spot was open now from the stream. The water was fast and furious. I had to add more weight on my line to keep the lure down where I wanted, then I started catching fish. I was glad it didn't take long to get the fish I needed for cooking and smoking. I got a couple for Wantalook too. We then headed back to camp.

I cleaned and washed the fish, put ten in the smoker and got the fire started in it and soon the smoke was coming out all over. Next I got my cooking fire started to cook the two remaining trout. At least now I don't have to worry about food anymore. I made it through the winter. After I ate my fill, I removed the last of the meat from the food shack and put it in the container with ice and put snow around it. It will last about a week or so till Wantalook has eaten it all. With that project done, we went out to pull up the snares. I was glad there was nothing caught in any of them. It's been days since I checked them. I guess with all the brush and food exposed, they were eating elsewhere. I spent the rest of the day tending the smoker. I couldn't wait till they were ready. As the time got closer, I couldn't help but sneak a pinch now and then. While I was waiting, I chopped away at the ice so the water could drain from the yard.

Supper was most enjoyable. If I had salted it, it would better yet, but I am not complaining, I put the remaining fish away and spent the rest of the evening with Wantalook till it was time to go in. Wantalook wanted to stay outside tonight so I'll see him in the morning. I started the fire in the stove then laid there till I fell asleep.

When I opened my eyes I could see the sun was up. I had to lay there a while longer. I had found a sweet spot and did not want to move from it. Then I could hear the wolf was at my door. Well, so much for my sweet spot. I got up to let him in. He just wanted me up, bad wolf. I had no choice but to get dressed and join him. I got out his food then set down with my fish. It was going to be above freezing today. That will work with my plans. After eating, I played with Wantalook but not to the point of getting muddy or wet.

First I wanted to start getting the hole made for Goodlooken's grave. The snow was gone so I can just keep chipping away at the soil till I get it deep enough. The warmer temperatures and the sun will help too. I went to the garden area next to scrape up all the thawed ground I could so the sun could make more. If I keep this up and start working chopped up fish and parts into the soil, it should be ready when I plant in the end of May. I'll need to build a fence around it too. One moose could wipe out everything. I've got time to get that done. I went back to camp to eat some fish for lunch. I only ate one. I'll have a lot more for supper.

The rest of the afternoon, I worked around camp. I gathered some poles and made a rack to set the planter boxes on the south wall of the overhang. It's a warm spot with plenty of sunlight. I had Goodlooken's grave almost done. I will get it a little deeper tomorrow. I've got some time left till supper so I got the sled out and gathered the rocks I need to put on top of the grave. I was ready for some fire and sit time by now. I sure am liking this weather and getting the chance to do things again. I could only imagine what Wantalook was thinking as he watched me all day. Probably what the hell is that crazy man doing now? After supper we sat by the fire doing our quality time till it was time to go in. I tried to get Wantalook to come in but that was not in his plans. That bed is going to feel good tonight. As I laid there

I thought about today and what I'll do tomorrow till I drifted off to sleep.

In the morning, I was awakened by Wantalook at my door, wanting me to get up. I was sleeping good too. I got to my feet and opened the door. The bouncing fur ball was ready to get the days started and sure didn't want me to miss out either. So after the morning greeting and I know you're awake now, he went out in the yard. After a yawn and a stretch, I got my clothes on and joined him. The weather was a repeat of yesterday. I was glad to see that. Wantalook wanted to play. I found out if I feed him first, it slows him down. That works for me. So after a peaceful breakfast, Wantalook was waiting to start. We carried on with our morning game for twenty minutes. No matter how hard I tried, I just couldn't get a hold of him long enough to win.

Afterwards I got the fire started and sat there a while recovering and taking in the beautiful morning. I was thinking since we are into the last half of April, I better get started with planting the seeds. I got the potting boxes out, then drilled drain holes in each chamber. Then get some soil and filled each spot. A few hours in the sun with the heat reflecting off the side of the overhang I will be able to have the seeds in by noon. Then all I'll have to do is take the boxes in at night. Every day that it's warm enough, I'll set them out.

Next I finished digging the grave and laid Goodlooken in it. Wantalook was with me the whole time while I put the marker up and covered the spot with stones. After lunch I checked how the soil in the boxes were doing, warmed up nicely. I planted all the potato seeds I had first, twenty-six in all. Then the beans and peas, then whatever else I picked out from the dried veggies. I wasn't sure about them; if I get anything it will be a plus. I liked the way the heat was reflecting off the wall. I think I will make a wall for the garden; plants need sunlight and warmth. It should work. I went to the garden area to scrape more thawed soil plus all I could from the entire area I had removed the moss from. I picked out the spot for the wall and the fence. I'll get good sunlight all day. I plan to have twenty-four inches of good soil to work with so I'll be well above the permafrost. I started gathering logs and poles that afternoon. I was really getting excited about having a garden. It was starting to cool off so I took the boxes for tomorrow. In ten to fourteen days, I know what I've got.

As I sat by the fire with Wantalook that night, my mind was on the garden and the weeks ahead, getting ready. One thing for sure, I was going to put up all the berries I could this summer. The fire was down and I was ready for some sleep. After adding wood to the stove, I went to sleep.

The next two weeks, I was busy every day between catching fish, running the smoker, and building the garden wall and fence six feet high, railing about one foot apart and the wall five feet high and twenty feet long, total garden size twelve by twenty feet. I even had a gate. The soil was coming along and I am still working chopped fish into it. The plants are up, twenty-one potato plants, three didn't start, and all the beans and peas came up. I figure in three weeks around May 24th, I'll transplant everything. I've still a lot to do before then. There's still ice on the lake yet. We have had nice days but nothing in the 40s yet. Cold night and a few days of cold and snow mixed. Today I want to cut out aluminum squares from the left over sheet metal to make noisemakers and light flashes for the garden. I think Wantalook thinks I lost my mind by now but I keep telling him, there is a method to my madness. I've got all the bells set up around camp and left two on the food shack. I spent the rest of the day cutting out metal squares using a hammer and chisel.

It was time for supper. We were on a fish diet now. All the meat's been gone for a while now. I'll get that started after I take the plants inside. I'll go fishing again in the morning. I want to start another batch in the smoker too. I cooked up two trout for myself. Wantalook ate three for his supper. As our quality time started, my thoughts went back to all we've been through since he first showed up at camp last year, what a change. From the weeks of getting to trust each other, to a bonding friendship, where we each risked our lives to save the life of each other. No matter what came along, we faced it together. Well, it's getting late. I've got another big day tomorrow. I told Wantalook good night and went inside. He only comes in now once and awhile. I don't mind. Maybe it's to protect me. I am his property. I sat on the bed looking at my plants for a few minutes. It's neat to see how much they grow from day to day.

I think I woke up two minutes before Wantalook was at the door. After I let him know I was awake, I got dressed, then stepped out the door. There was frost on everything so it will be a while before I can set the plants out. I needed to catch breakfast for both of us so I cut short our playtime. When Wantalook saw me grab my pole, he was ready to go fishing. The area at the mouth of the stream was the only place open yet. It didn't take long to get the fish I needed after Wantalook ate his four.

When we got back to camp, I got the smoker going and loaded ten fish into it, then got the fire started so I could cook the remaining two. I still have a lot to do on the garden area yet. I'll get back on that project after I eat.

By 10:00 the frost was gone, I set the plants out. I think I will try something. I got out the survival blankets and put two of them on the wall of the overhang. What a difference. You could feel the heat and sunlight reflecting off it. Every little bit helps. I went back to drilling the metal squares. I used sand then steel wool to shine them up and my knife to remove the sharp edges and smooth the holes. The smoked fish were on the final stages of heat when I finished the last square. So I sat by the heat till they were ready to come out. Wantalook helped me eat one before going back to work. I got out my fish line to use to hang the squares from the railing of the fence. It took me till into the evening to get them all up between each rail and on the two ends. I put some close together so they would touch in the wind. It all looked like a deterrent place to me.

When I got back to camp, I took the plants in for the night. Then I cooked some fish for Wantalook and for me in the morning. When I got the fire going again, then I could sit down and enjoy my supper. Wantalook was by my side to make sure what I didn't want wasn't wasted. During our quality time, I was making plans for the rest of the garden area. I was starting to doze off so I better get my butt to bed. I started a fire in the stove then went to sleep.

My wolf clock woke me up, hell who needs an alarm clock. I opened the door to let him know I am awake, then shut it. Coffee sure would be nice right now but that is not a reality right now. I gave Wantalook his fish while I got the fire going so I could cook mine. It was another nice day and as soon as I finished breakfast, I can set the plants out. Wantalook will have to wait till after breakfast and plants before our playtime. I had to tell him NO several times. When I set the last planter box down, I grabbed Wantalook up in an arm lock, holding him off the ground. What an armful. He twisted and tossed, trying to get free. I had him. I won! When he gave up, I let him go. I was laughing by then. He shook himself with a look I should have recognized. As I turned away he knocked me down. He wasn't going to let me up. After he gave me his victory lick, he let me up. We chased each there around for a while after that, then I had to get busy.

I got out my trim saw and started cutting dead limbs thirty inches long, for around the bottom of the fence on end to keep out rabbits. I'll need a lot to go across the front and both ends. I had cut and hauled a big pile that morning, then after lunch I started burying the sticks six inches in the ground and used the pegs I had left over from the cabinet making, to peg the upper end to the bottom rail. Each stick was one to 1½ inches apart. I had enough pegs made to do about half so I'll need to make more now. I spent what was left of the afternoon into the evening making pegs.

I had to take time out to catch fish for both of us for supper. After I ate I didn't feel like working on pegs anymore today. I took the plants inside for the night and couldn't believe how much they are growing. I sat with Wantalook for over an hour before turning in for the night. After starting a fire to get the chill out of the cabin I soon fell asleep.

When I was awakened by the big bad wolf, I could hear the rain outside. When I opened the door, Wantalook came in. You decided to come in where it's dry and warm. After a short greeting, he laid down in his spot. I added more wood to the stove then got dressed. When I stepped outside to get the last two fish out I could see just how much it was raining. At least it wasn't snow. I started making more pegs after breakfast. It was like old times having Wantalook in the cabin with me. Doing what he does best, watch me work. I spent the rest of the morning making pegs till I figured I had more than I needed. After I cleaned up, I sat petting Wantalook. The rain wasn't letting up so I might as well take a nap plus extra rest won't hurt a bit. I woke up a few hours later. The rain was spotty now. I slipped on my raingear and we headed to the lake to catch fish.

I caught enough for tonight and tomorrow morning. I got the fire started in the fire pit. The rain was still spotty so when the fish were done, I sat under the overhang to eat. The cold wasn't too bad to put up with but the dampness with it, made it feel a lot worse. I got up and finished eating inside. It felt good to get out of the dampness. Wantalook was waiting for me to get done. I wonder what he wants as if I didn't know. As soon as I finished, he put his head on my leg, quality time had started. We sat up till around 10:00. Wantalook wanted out so I opened the door. I waited a while for him to want back in but after twenty minutes, I went to sleep.

When I opened my eyes, I looked out the window. The rain had stopped. As I was getting dressed, there was a knock on my door, more like two paws making noise. I yelled out I am awake. I'm coming out. Sure enough there was my bouncing fur ball waiting to greet me. After a good head rub and a couple of pets on his side I gave him his food. While he was eating, I set the plants out. If they keep growing like this, they will be a nice size when I plant them in a couple of weeks. I played with Wantalook for a while but not to the point of getting on the ground. I grabbed the pegs and my tools. I was anxious to get back on the fence. I couldn't help but notice the flashing as I walked toward the garden and the tingling of the squares bumping each other in the light breeze. I spent the rest of the morning putting the sticks in place. All I had left to do was the one end. After I finished the last of the smoked fish, I started back on the fence. As I completed the last couple of feet, I couldn't think of anymore I could do to keep the animals out, with what I had to work with already. Chance of frost will be the only thing to fight off now and I think I've got that covered. I took my tools back to the cabin, then got down my sled. I planned to build four fire spots, one on each end and two on the front side. I needed to gather rocks now. Most of the snow was gone except all the areas that were shadowed or the areas that were real deep. I hauled rocks for a couple of hours, then it was time to catch some fish.

Wantalook was ready for that when he saw me grab my pole. Wantalook was waiting for that first fish to be brought in, pacing with anticipation. He didn't have to wait long before the first was in my hand. Wantalook didn't waste time, that one disappeared. When Wantalook had his fill then I could start filling the rope with the ones I needed for cooking. When we got back to camp the temperature was dropping so I took the plants inside before cleaning the fish. I saved out two for my supper then put the rest away. The heat felt good on the hands. They were still cold from handling the fish. After supper, I added more wood to the fire and settled in for a couple hours of quality time. The air tonight had a chill to it, like we were going to have a cold spell. It was time to go in. I was getting cold and tired. It didn't take long for the cabin to warm and the bed was looking better by the minute.

When I stepped out of the cabin that morning, it was cold. All the puddles were frozen and the wind was blowing too. We got a cold spell like I figured. I had to go back inside to add more clothes, that wind had a bite to it. After feeding Wantalook, I got the fire going in the smoker and the fire pit. I loaded the smoker before I started cooking my fish. I think winter wasn't ready to let spring have its fun yet. Wantalook and I got our playing time in after breakfast, he won again.

Afterwards I went to the garden area and arranged the rocks for the four fire spots. If someone saw all of what I had done just to grow a garden they would think I was nuts. But if this garden fails, next winter is not going to be good. The beans and peas are a plus. It's the potatoes I am counting on. I went back to camp to start cutting wood. I had to drag more wood up to cut before I could get started. I spend the rest of the day cutting wood and tending the smoker. I had a large pile built up and hauled. A good part of it to take to the garden, the rest I put under the overhang.

The fish were ready to come out of the smoker. I got out Wantalook's fish and was looking forward to sitting down and enjoy my smoked fish. I got a lot done today, I thought to myself as I ate. I'll be glad when it warms back up. It didn't get above freezing at all today. I put the rest of the smoked fish away and spent the rest of the evening with Wantalook till I couldn't hold my eyes open any more. I added wood to the stove then went to sleep.

It stayed cold for the next five days. Even with the sun being out, it never warmed up above freezing. I wound up using what plastic I had left along with the space blankets to create a hot box so I could get some sunlight on the plants, two boxes at a time. By the end of the fifth day, the wind had changed and by the time I was ready to go to bed things were warming up.

When I woke up the next morning, I was surprised to see a big change in the temperature, things were starting to melt again. I played with Wantalook a while but I cut it short. I needed to catch us some food. When we got back with our fast food I put the plants out, then started cooking. Boy I tell ya, it really feels like spring today. Even the air smells of spring. I think winter cold has showed its face for the last time. If it stays like this I should be able to put the plants in the garden. I will need to keep working the soil so it warms up till then. After breakfast, I took down the survival blankets and got out the third then put them on the wall of the garden so the reflected sunlight could do its job.

That afternoon, I started turning the soil over. If I do this once or twice a day, we'll be good to go. With the countdown started toward planting day, there wasn't much to do now. I was setting by the plants, enjoying the sunlight and the heat radiating off the end of the overhang wall, when I thought about my next job. I still had the floor of the cabin to finish. It would be nice not to see or step on dirt anymore. I got up to find myself about four logs. Wantalook didn't know what I was looking for but he was ready to go. I picked out the ones I wanted, north of the cabin within a hundred yards. I thought to myself at least I won't have the long drag this time. It took me till evening to get the four logs cut out. I'll drags them out tomorrow. The plants perked up today. I was glad to see them doing so good. I got the fire going then sat down to enjoy my meal. I could tell my arm wasn't used to pushing that saw like that. In the morning, I'll sharpen it before I use it to cut out boards. After supper it sure wasn't hard to enjoy the evening; even the smell of the woods and soil was very detectable. Wantalook and I got a lot of quality time in that night. It didn't feel like it was going to freeze but I still took the plants inside. I only made a small fire in the stove before going to bed.

Wantalook was right on time with my wake-up call at the door. There was no sleeping in when he's around. I got dressed and joined him outside. When our greeting was over, I got out our food and sat down. I think this is going to be our nicest day yet. I can't wait to get started. I brought the plants outside then had a big wrestling time with Wantalook. I came close to winning today but close doesn't claim the prize. Afterwards, it took me a half hour to sharpen the saw, then I took my shovel and turned over the garden. By then my muscles were warmed up so it was log dragging time.

I got out my backpack framework. It was still set up for dragging logs from last fall. I got the rope on the first log and moved it about twenty feet. Damn, I forgot what this was like or I am not in as good shape as I was then. I think I'll need to use wood to roll it on till I get an open area where I can roll the log. It was noon when I got the first lot in camp. After a long break and a bite to eat, number two log was up next. When I get this next log back here, that's all I am doing today. At least I had all the wood in place, now to roll it on. As I am working this log toward camp, I kept thinking, how did I do this last year? When I reached camp with the second log, I thought about going after another, not really. It was rest time now.

Eleven

It would have been nice if Wantalook helped me. All he would do was lay down and watch me move and watch me some more. I sat for about an hour then set the first log up on the log horses then started removing the bark. There was too much sand in the bark to use the saw. My hatchet worked well for the first job since the tree was already dead over a year. It was supper time now. Smoked fish was on the menu after I catch a few fish for Wantalook. When we got back I got the fire going before I sat down to eat. It was maybe forty degrees out and it felt warm compared to what I was used to. It made the rest of the evening enjoyable with Wantalook. I took the plants inside and went to sleep.

When I opened my eyes the wolf was at the door, waiting for another chance to kick my butt again. I got up and let him know I was awake then got dressed. Wantalook wasn't waiting for food first this morning. It went from greeting right into play. After the pushing, tagging and the chasing around the yard, we ended up on the ground with him on top. He gave me his victory lick first before letting me up. It was time to head to the lake for our fast food breakfast. It took longer to walk to open water and back then it did to catch fish. When breakfast was over, I turned over the garden again, then I got ready for the log pulling contest.

There is no time limit so I've got all day to get two logs back here. Before I get started I need to strip down to my shirt sleeves. The third and fourth log were a little lighter so it was easier today. I had the first one back before noon. After a short break, I went for the last one. I was back in camp by 2:30, then I took the sled to pick up all the rolling pieces of wood and put them back into the pile. I was done with the work for today, other than catching fish for supper. I was enjoying my assets by the fire. I figure on taking four days to cut the logs into one-inch boards, one log per day. With that much arm work ahead, I don't want to overdo it. With the evening over, I was more than ready to get into bed. So with the plants inside, it was stove and bed.

I was hoping to sleep in, when I found another sweet spot that morning but that didn't happen. Wantalook was right on time with my wake-up call. I am awake, you rotten piece of wolf meat. As I sat on my bed I slowly got dressed. My bouncing fur ball was waiting for his morning greeting as I stepped out the door. As soon as I gave him his fish, I sat down with mine. Our playtime this morning will be a short one. I'll try to keep it to five or ten minutes. I think Wantalook sensed how I was feeling. He was taking it easy on me. After the fun was over, I set the plants out, then went to the garden to turn the soil over again. Well, that got all the stiffness out.

Now on to the board cutting. I marked out the log for one-inch boards, then started making the ten foot cuts. With each cut, I just took my time, letting the saw do its job. You won't cut a straight line by forcing it. I stopped each cut at around nine feet so it would hold all the pieces in place till I could cut the remaining foot. When I had finished that afternoon, my arm was tired. I stacked the wood inside, then set up the next log on the horses. After a short rest, I removed the bark so I would be ready for tomorrow. It was time to catch supper. Wantalook was well rested after watching me all day. I only needed to catch what I needed for tonight. Tomorrow I'll do another batch in the smoker. When I got to the fishing spot, the ice was changing and it looked like the lake will open up in a few days. Wantalook ate his four before we left the lake. I saved one more for him for a snack for later. It wasn't long before the fire was going and the smell of fish cooking was in the air. It was nice not having to wear heavy clothes to enjoy the outdoors. When my fish were done, I gave Wantalook his fish so he wouldn't bother me so much. It sure was going to be a nice evening to get our quality time in. As we sat there, the sound of the fire was the only noise to be heard. It was getting time to go in. I thought about leaving the plants out but not yet. I got a small fire going in the stove, then crawled into bed. It sure felt good to lay down.

When Wantalook woke me up in the morning, I didn't feel too bad. When I stepped outside, it felt like comfortable. Maybe it will get to the 50s today. When our playtime was over, I set the plants out. They were getting a nice size to them and they should do quite well when I plant them. It's time to head to the lake for fast food. Wantalook was packing down the ground waiting for that first one. He ate his fill before I could get the twelve I needed for today. I was looking forward to smoked fish tonight. When the cleaning was done, I got the ten going in the smoker before cooking up my two. Afterwards I went to the garden to stir up the ground. It was looking good and it will be ready soon.

It was board cutting time but first I've got to feed the smoker first. When I got it all marked out, it was time to start some sawdust therapy. Between the rest breaks and tending the smoker, I was making the last short cuts by the time the fish were done. The arm and shoulder were tired but nothing like yesterday. I opened the smoke house door to let them start cooling, while I put the boards inside. I don't know where my head's at, didn't have anything for Wantalook. I closed the door, picked up my pole and caught four trout for Wantalook. I got a fire started then sat down to eat. Two more days of cutting left if this weather stays like this. I will put the plants in on the 21st of May, three days from now. The rest of the evening went by fast and before I knew it, it was time for bed as soon as I put the plants away.

The next two days, I completed all the board cutting. I have enough to finish the floor of the cabin with wood left over. The weather's been great and the garden is ready for tomorrow. The ice on the lake is breaking up now. It shifts around when the wind comes up. I am looking forward to fishing again in front of the cabin. I think I wore Wantalook out watching me. He's still laying there. The rest of the evening, I am doing nothing, just setting back and take in the scenery around me. It's surprising how fast the new growth is coming out on the trees and new plants seem to pop up overnight. It was getting to be supper time so Wantalook decided to join me when I got the food out. After supper, I made a water run to the spring and back. I'll get more tomorrow. I need to get some washing done. Now for some afternoon, I've been thinking about my daughter, wondering how she is doing and what's going on in her life now? I swear at times I can feel her thoughts and I can only hope she has been feeling mine. The time was late and I need to get some sleep. I patted Wantalook on the head and went inside. I was tired but I felt happy tonight and at peace. I haven't felt this way in a long time.

    I slept good last night and couldn't wait to get this day started. Wantalook was letting me know it was time to get started too. Our morning greeting turned into play. We chased and challenged each other around the yard so much for the clean clothes as we rolled in the dirt. He got me pinned down so the only thing to do is to give up and take my licks. After I brushed myself off, it was time to catch breakfast. Wantalook must have been hungry this morning, he ate five. Tomorrow I'll make another batch of smoked fish. When breakfast was over, I checked the garden. What a change from yesterday. I am happy about the way the garden was turning out.
    I was anxious to get back on the floor. I only had a few boards to go and I should be done by noon. Wantalook had his spot picked out where he could watch as I worked. When I got the last board in place and fastened down, it was time for lunch. I ate the last of the smoked fish, then did the cleanup inside and out. There was a board that I had an eye on for the outside of the cabin. I've wanted to do this for a long time. I'll carve out the lettering this afternoon.
    It was late afternoon when I finished it with the letters darkened and put it up on the overhang. I stood back and read it out loud, Dunbarker cabin, Wantalook Valley 2003. Even though it's 2004, I built it in 2003 and as far as I know this place didn't have a name. It's got one now. I put my tools away, cleaned up the chips and started the fire for tonight.
    It's time to catch supper. I think in a few days, I will try to catch a rabbit or a squirrel. Fried meat would taste good right now. After supper, we got to our spots to start our quality time. I've still been thinking about my daughter off and on all day and felt nothing was wrong or something bad has happened. Whatever it is, she sure must be thinking about me. I sure do

miss her. Before I knew it, several hours had passed and the eyelids were hard to keep open by now so I petted Wantalook good night and went to bed.

Wantalook was at the door, making sure I was awake. Settle down, I am awake. I sat down on the bed a while, wiped the sleep from my eyes and got dressed. I was still thinking about the dreams I had last night. They were about my daughter, my family, Jim and Wantalook. I was almost non stop craziness that you couldn't stop. Well I got reality waiting for me outside the door. Our greeting almost turned into play but when I grabbed my fish pole, Wantalook's thoughts turned to food. The fishing was good as usual and it wasn't long before I had all the fish I needed for breakfast and the smoker. After the fish were cleaned and washed, I put them in the smoker and got the fire going then started cooking up my two fish.

Today is going to be a lazy day, tend the smoker, lay back and enjoy the calm sunny day. I checked the garden after breakfast and I swear the plants were changing by the hour. They are nothing like they were when I planted them. It was time to feed the smoker when I got back then I sat by the fire. Wantalook was beside me to get more petting since we didn't do our playtime this morning. I still had a little washing to do so I got the water I needed and started in. I hung my sleeping bag outside to air out some too.

I wasn't hungry come lunch time. I'll eat when the fish is done. The clothes were dry so I put them away and made the bed. It was a nice afternoon sitting by the fire, when I heard a plane dropping into the valley. I quickly snapped off some pine bows and tossed them on the fire and ran to the opening by the lake. The plane was coming closer in my direction. I could see two people in the plane as they flew by and waved his wings; he saw me. He traveled down the valley and around, coming back for a landing. As the plane touched down on the water, I could not believe what I was seeing. After all this time, someone has come to get me. As the plane motored in to the shore in front of me I got ready to tie him off. He killed the engine and floated in.

The pilot and passenger got out. He tossed me the rope, then I saw my daughter Angie. I didn't have my boots on but I didn't care. I was in the water and to the plane in a heartbeat. I took her in my arms and carried her to shore. I know I cried more than her. I held her in my arms for the longest time, telling her over and over, I love her and missed her so much. After our tearful reunion, I was introduced to the pilot, Sam Davis. After we talked for a few minutes he wanted to get me packed up and head out. I told him, he could not leave now. "What do you mean, we can't leave?" "No wind, you can't get off this lake without wind. Do you know Jim?" I asked. "Sure, for many years." "Well, this is his spot and he not only told me, he showed me that it takes a wind to get off of this lake." "Well, it's a little short," he admitted. "We are due in a few hours." "Do you have a satellite phone?" "Yes." "Then make a call and tell them that you will be out of here in a day or two." It was different to hear a person's voice again.

My daughter Angie and I held each other as we walked up the path. There was so much to say and ask. It was hard to know where to start. "Dad, when we came through that last pass, my hopes were high. We knew where but did not know you were still there or if you tried walking out. I was hopeful we would find you. People said, you would not make it. I told them, you don't know my Dad. As we got closer, my mind and heart was hopeful but I wasn't sure if you would still be alive or dead or we might never find you. When I saw the smoke all that I felt in my heart came true. Then when I saw you waving your arms, I couldn't wait to land, to hold and touch my Dad again." "What happened to Jim?" How did you find me?" About then she saw Wantalook. She grabbed my arm. "Dad, there's a wolf." "I want you to meet my friend Wantalook." I called him over, he wasn't sure what to make of the situation. I told Sam to stand still behind me. I am the only person that Wantalook knows. With a little talking he came up. I told my daughter not to be scared. I showed Wantalook affection between me and my daughter and introduced her and he came up and smelled her hand and we petted him together. He was fine with that. Sam took a little longer but Wantalook came around.

I showed them the food shack, smoke house and the smoked fish that was almost ready and my cabin. "Wow, Dad, this place is nice. You built all this? The cupboards and base cabinets are beautiful and the table, bed and shelves and even wood floors. How did you do all this, the cabin and everything without power equipment and only a few tools you brought with you?" "That is a long story too. I've got more to show you." We went outside. "Dad, whose grave is that? Who is Goodlooken?" "That was Wantalook's mate. He showed up with her in January and in the middle of February she got killed in an avalanche. Wantalook was almost killed too but I managed to dig him out and saved his life. When we found her there was nothing I could do."

"I need to show you my garden too." "A garden, how did you manage to do a garden?" "Very carefully." "Wow Dad, a fence and everything." I showed them the path to the spring. "Let's sit by the fire and talk." I am still holding my daughter's hand. I guess it was the touch of a loved one I missed the most. We sat down and Wantalook sat by my side. "You know how I could feel when something was wrong?" "Yes Dad." "I had times out here when I felt something bad happened to someone. One time in July of last year and another time in December and I've been thinking about you for the last two days." "In December, I was in a rear end collision and wore a neck brace for a couple of weeks. The rest I will tell you later."

I told my daughter I needed to know first and then I will tell you about me. "What happened to Jim?" "Jim was in a plane crash during a bad storm back on July 7th and has been in a coma. He is still in a facility in Anchorage." "How come no one came to get me?" "No one knew where you were." "How could that happen? I e-mailed you." "I did not get it." "I sent you a letter." "I just got it." "I left directions in my Explorer." "It was stolen."

I got her to tell me the whole story. "Well after Jim's crash, a few days later some people broke into his house, stole his computer and equipment and safe and they used your Explorer to take everything away and torched the house.

"I started calling Jim's place on the 19th, five days after your due time back and couldn't get an answer. I called every day and e-mailed and still got nobody. On the 24th, I called the police department, that's when I found out about Jim and the fire. They didn't know about you Dad, or your Explorer, and all traces of you and where you were at were gone. The Civil Air

Patrol looked for several weeks and a few other pilots spent time looking too." "I saw one plane way off in the distance last year. I had a big smoke fire but it was too far away beyond that mountain range over there." "We never gave up, Dad, even when everyone else did. I knew if there was a way to make it and stay alive you would find it. The police found your Explorer stripped and burnt around the end of August, in the woods outside of Fairbanks." "How did you just get my letter? I mailed it on June 14th. Well, I left it to be mailed with Bob Miller, the owner of the cabin I stayed in. I left it on the counter when I went to call you but I couldn't get through." "Your letter was found in a file box under the counter. Someone that was helping them, found it and put it in the mail. Bob and his wife were on a trip, matter of fact they still are. When I received the letter two days ago I called Sam here and told him I am coming and needed him to help again. Everyone had given you up for dead but not me." "I can't thank you enough, Sam. When we get back, I'll see that you are well paid for your time."

    I got out smoked fish for all of us while we talked. I wanted to know about the family and everything that's been happening in the world and any other information I could get. I asked about Jim's Beaver. What happened to it? Sam said it was picked up and brought back to the airport where his plane is at.

    I told my daughter there was something I needed to show her in the cabin. When she noticed the door clawed and chewed on, "You've got to tell me about this, Dad." When we got inside, I told her about Jim and me and the gold I found at the miner's cabin and the gold we found in the stream. "Jim had taken the gold back with him to cash in and get a claim filed in both our names so there should be around $120,000.00 in a bank deposit box when I get back to Anchorage."

    She could hardly believe it and when I opened up the cooler, her eyes got big. "Is that all gold?" "Yes, it is over a half a million in there." "Oh my gosh, Dad." "So right now this is between us till I see the claim papers."

    When we came back out Wantalook was right in front of Sam looking at him. "Could you do something with your wolf please?" I told Wantalook to leave Sam alone and he came over by us. We talked for hours till my dear sweet girl was falling asleep. She had put a lot of air time in these past two days. I told Sam that he could sleep in the cabin with us but he declined and said he would sleep in his plane. I let her sleep on my bed and I slept on the floor. Wantalook spent most of his time outside. "What are you going to do with him, Dad?" "I have to leave him here till I get back. I don't want to but he's wild, dear. He's been my friend and companion for a long time. He will not be caged. You know as well as I do, if I brought him out of the wild with me, I would be arrested, fined and put in jail and Wantalook would be caged up, possibly for the rest of his life. I will not do that to him or take a chance." "You are right, Dad." "He's a survivor like me and he will be here when I return. How long did you take off work?" "Two weeks, Dad." "Well I think you will be able to call them and tell them you are retiring. We'll talk tomorrow." And I watched her fall asleep.

I got up early, my body had enough of the floor. I quietly slipped outside not to awaken her. Wantalook was waiting for me to start our morning ritual greeting. We were wrestling and playing maybe fifteen minutes when I noticed my daughter watching us go at it. I have to admit it we do get a little rough at times. When I did spot my daughter standing there, I lost my concentration with Wantalook and he knocked me down. I tried to recover but he had me pinned down. I had to give up then he licked my face and let me up.

"Dad, you had me scared there for a minute. How often do you do this?" "Every morning." "Does Wantalook always win?" "Most of the time." Wantalook wanted his petting from her too. I started a fire and we sat down. "Dad, this place is so beautiful, the lake and mountains. It's so peaceful!" There was so much we had to catch up on. I told her to wait right there. I went and got my camera and took several pictures of her and Wantalook by the fire with the lake and mountains in the background. Then I set the camera up to take pictures of the three of us.

It was a perfect morning out, a little cool but calm and blue skies. I put the camera away and got out my two poles. "Are you ready to catch breakfast?" "Sure Dad." We walked down the path to the lake. We went down to the mouth of the stream, where we could stand on the bank to cast out. We had a great time catching trout and Wantalook was enjoying himself too. We brought back six for breakfast. Sam was setting by the fire when we walked into camp. "How long have you been up, Sam?" "Maybe ten minutes. I didn't see anyone around but the fire was going so I knew you wasn't far." "I hope you don't mind fresh trout for breakfast." "Not at all, anyone who doesn't like fish wouldn't make it out here." We ate and talked. They were telling me about the events of the last year and the search. Sam got his map out and showed me all the areas the search planes covered. The closest they came to this valley was twenty-five miles. "Actually this place is not on the map. See, here's the north and south mountains ridges, it doesn't show this lake or this valley. So other than us, Jim is the only one that's been here."

"Are we going to get some wind today?" "I don't think so, a possible breeze this afternoon. I would say a better chance tomorrow. Jim told me once he had spent five days or more here waiting for the wind. There are plenty of days that we have wind. Some would like to blow you away." It got to be noon and we took a lunch break of smoked fish. I told them it would be better if I had salt but I've been out of salt since last fall. My daughter wanted to know more about my time out here and how I came up with the stuff I had. I told them about the stove I bought back from the miner's cabin and the trip to the plane crash site and back, the building of the cabin, smoke house twice, the first bear attack, Wantalook showing up, the wolverine, getting a moose and that Wantalook saved me when the bear attacked us and the injuries we received and how I saved his life. There wasn't enough time in the day to tell them everything.

I told them it was time for supper, that we needed to go fishing. Sam said, "Stay and talk. I'll catch the fish. Where do I go?" "With boots, pick a spot anywhere, without boots, go west to the mouth of the stream. We will need ten fish unless you want more, four is for Wantalook. Sam, you got a gun?" "Yes, in the plane." "Well, take it with you, the bears are out. I haven't seen any in a few days but so far they have been staying away from camp." I had to laugh a little, he got on his boots and fished down from camp next to his plane. My daughter asked what was so funny and I told her. "I like it here, Dad. I don't know how you did it out here. I don't think anyone could have done what you've done. Even the article in the paper and in the news figured you wouldn't make it." We walked down to the lake where Sam was fishing. "Hey, do they always bite like this?" "Every day," I told him. I cleaned and washed the fish. Wantalook helped too. We went back to camp. I gave Wantalook his as I started cooking the rest. "I wish I had some moose or bear meat for you but that was gone come spring."

After supper we sat and talked. I told Sam that I was sure we could leave tomorrow, possibility in the late morning. "How can you tell?" I just smiled and looked at him. "Well, if anyone would know it would be you." As the evening went on I was feeling sad as I petted Wantalook. This will be our last night together for a while and I was going to miss him so much. My daughter could sense my feelings and squeezed my arm. She had tears in her eyes as well. Sam told us good night and went to his plane. We sat and talked and cried. Wantalook was right beside us the whole time. It was late when we turned in for the night. Wantalook came inside for a few minutes then wanted back out. We laid down and I was talking to my daughter when I realized she was already sleeping. It's got to be the fresh air, she's not used to it.

I got up early and was putting a new roll of film in the camera when my daughter woke up. "What are you doing, Dad?" "I got a job for you to do. I want you to take pictures of me and Wantalook this morning. The camera is full with thirty-six exposures so as we play just keep taking pictures." "Sure Dad, I'll be glad to." I handed her the camera and we left the cabin. Wantalook was waiting for our morning ritual to start. We must have chased and pushed each other for over a half hour till we were on the ground and I had to give up again. He let me up and I brushed myself off. "Dad, I wished I had a camcorder for that." "I do too, dear." I got the fire going and we sat there talking about my plans to come back. We went to the lake to catch some breakfast and food for Wantalook.

I woke up Sam and told him breakfast would be ready in a little while. After breakfast we got the few things I wanted to take back in the plane, the rest will stay. It was after 9:00 and we had the wind I predicted. I had a hard time saying good-bye to Wantalook. I wanted so much to take him with us but a cage or a chain was not for him and holding back my emotions was not possible. I couldn't speak as I carried my daughter to the plane as my tears streamed down my face. As I got into the plane I could see Wantalook waiting on the shore. I handed my daughter the camera and motioned for her to take a picture. At that point I lost it and broke down. Sam waited for me to collect myself before he asked if I was ready. I climbed out and pushed us away from the shore and climbed in. I told Sam what to do to get off the lake, the same way I saw Jim do it. With a half circle to pick up speed then full throttle into the wind. We cleared the tree at the end of the lake by inches and did a big left hand circle to pick up speed and altitude. I took a few more pictures of camp and my Wantalook watching me leave. My daughter put her hand on my shoulder and whispered in my ear, "He'll be waiting for you when you come back, Dad."

We cleared the pass that I climbed and showed them the plane crash site I went to. I didn't say much after that, just looked out the window and watched the mountains and valleys go by. I had lost track of time because we were dropping down and Anchorage was in sight. It looked different to me. I was glad to see civilization again but I wasn't either.

We landed on the lake and motored to Sam's place, I couldn't believe the people and all the media and TV crews upon the grass. What's all this? I am not ready for this. I look like hell, my hair and beard, my clothes. "You'll be alright, Dad. You're going to be alongside of me." We pulled up and there were people taking pictures of the plane and when I stepped out, the roar of the crowd, of clapping, wishes and cheers were deafening to my ears. There were hundreds of people and every news agency. There was a local, ABC, NBC, CBS, FOX, CNN and more. I really wanted to run. After all this time of quiet and alone and now this. My daughter held my arm as I was greeted by so many people and they had a spot ready with microphone. TV camera flash bulbs going off, it was overwhelming to say the least. The mayor of Anchorage was there to greet me and gave me the key to the city and arrangements were already made for a place to stay, transportation, food and anything else I needed. I had to spend some time answering questions and making statements.

I concluded with "I'll conduct a formal interview this evening at my hotel." We got our things into the limo and left.

My God, you would think I was the president or something. Every place we went in, they knew about me. When we got to the hotel, there were people taking pictures. I asked the driver, "How long will he be around for?" He replied, "Till I no longer needed him." I told him I would be back down in an hour. I had few places to go. After a shower, shave and a haircut plus new clothes, I felt almost normal.

We started checking banks trying to find a safety deposit box in my name and the second bank we tried, there was a manager who knew Jim and knew about me. He got the box for us and we sat down in privacy and opened it. There was the money and the claim deed in our names. He did it! I looked at the date and he did it the day after he left me. I put a thousand in my pocket and told the manager, I would be back tomorrow.

Next I wanted to see Jim. Our driver took us to the care facility he was at and we went in, the staff were real nice and they figured I would show up. I walked into Jim's room. I hardly recognized him. To see him lying there was heartbreaking, for a person that loved life and doing things the way he did and now just a body laying there. I held his hand and told him about camp, Wantalook and all I went through. I don't know if he could hear me but I do know Jim enough that he would want to hear the story. I had to leave. I was getting overwhelmed with emotions. Now I've got two friends I can't be with or share with.

It was time to get back to the hotel for interviews. When we got there, the media and everyone else was too. They had a banquet room set up and what a circus. I answered questions for a half hour, everything from being alone to being rescued. I was glad to get it over with. I did what I had to do to and use my knowledge, experience and common sense. Would you do it again? "Yes, and I will be going back."

When it was over, our driver was waiting. We got in. I told him, "I want to go to a quiet place for a steak and a cold drink." He took us to this restaurant way out of the way. We made it halfway through the meal then someone recognized me. Then the word spread and people started coming up to talk, including the owners. I said, what the hell. I started telling a few experiences I had out there. We stayed a couple hours before leaving.

When we got back to the hotel, there were a stack of messages and telegrams waiting for me. We went to our room. I wanted to spend time in the hot tub and a glass of bourbon. My daughter read me the messages and telegrams. It was a full page of congratulations to well wishes to interviews. Offers from Jay Leno, David Letterman, and more. "Wow Dad, can you believe this?" "Yes, it's unreal. The only thing missing is the book offer." "I'll bet you will get that too, Dad, before too long. What are we going to do tomorrow, Dad? First I need to know if you want to drive or fly back?" "I want to drive. I can't make the trip I already planned." "What was that?" "Drive to Fairbanks then to Prodou Bay and back down to Toh and into the Yukon and Northwest territory, British Columbia into Alberta and work my way back to Michigan. But I don't have that kind of time now. You would like to see what I did on my way here. Let's drive." "OK." "First thing tomorrow, I need to cash in most of the gold and buy a new Ford Explorer, do some banking and pay Sam and talk some business and find someone to repair Jim's Beaver." "But he's in a coma, Dad." "He'll come out of it, I know he will and we'll go shopping." "We can do that, Dad."

I was up early setting by the window, enjoying a cup of coffee. My mind was back at the cabin, watching a sunrise, enjoying the view of the mountains and the lake. But most of all, my times with Wantalook and all we shared together for so many months, when he saved my life and I saved his and helped him back to the wolf he was. The way he put his head on my leg to get his head and ears scratched. I miss all the times we played in the yard, chasing, wrestling until one of us was a winner. It's only been one day and I miss him so much. Saying good-bye, like to rip my heart out and I'll never forget seeing him on shore watching me leave. That picture was in my mind as I stared out over Anchorage. I didn't hear my daughter walk up as she touched my shoulder. "You're thinking about Wantalook, aren't you, Dad?" "Yep, I miss him and our morning playtime. Well dear, are you ready to get this show started?" "Give me ten minutes, Dad. I'll call the driver." Our limo was waiting for us when we came down and breakfast was our first stop. I wanted eggs, bacon, fried potatoes and coffee and lots of bacon. I was stuffed when we left the restaurant. Our next stop was the bank to withdraw the money, deposit part into my American Express check card and the rest cash. Then we went to the Ford dealership and bought a new full dressed Expedition and surprised the sales person when I paid in cash. I got the insurance and Alaskan plates. I gave our limo driver a couple hundred for a tip and thanked him for everything. I liked my new vehicle and it seemed nice to drive again.

We drove to Sam's place and he was home. I paid him $10,000 for all his efforts in trying to find me last year and for bringing me out this year. I talked with him about air service to and from the lake coming up and not to let anyone know about where I was for security reasons. He agreed and I told him he would be paid very well for his help. I asked him about who does plane repair because I want to get Jim's Beaver repaired back to like to new again. He said he would make the calls and get back to me later on today.

Let's do some shopping. I need to get tools and a portable air compressor, tire repair kit, and other things I lost, that I like to take with me when I travel. We both got more clothes and I talked my daughter into some diamond earrings and necklace. Then we went out for lunch. Wherever my we went people recognized me from TV and newspapers. Afterwards we went to a gold dealer and cashed in all the gold with the exception of a number of the larger nuggets and the lunker. We walked out with a check of over $500,000.00. My daughter was speechless. When we got back into the truck, I told her that this is nothing to what that is still out there. "Do you still want to work for someone else or would you want to work with me? After a year or two you can do whatever your heart desires for the rest of your life and never have to work again." "I am with you, Dad." "Of course this means as soon as we get home, we will be preparing to come back in a month." "Why so soon, Dad?" To go set up on the claim with equipment and use it for three or four months before winter sets in." "It sounds like a lot to do in such a short time." "It is, dear, but we can do it. The way I figure I will order everything we will need as soon as we get back. That should take two weeks to receive it. In the meantime I will buy a trailer and have the Expedition and trailer set up while I'm taking care of the TV show interview. So while I am doing that, you can be getting the supplies and work with Sam on arranging planes or one possible helicopter to get everything in, with trailer, equipment and supplies will be around $75,000 to $100,000 plus transportation." We went back to the hotel, picked up the messages and went to our room. I called Sam back and he found the guy that has helped Jim with his plane and would be glad to do it. I got his address and we will go to see him before we go out for supper. I'll also make arrangements with Sam for transportation and as soon as I know the size of the equipment and the weight, I will get it to him. I told him we are leaving for Michigan in a day or two and figure we would be back in about a month.

"Well guess what, Dad, here are your book offers along with congratulations and well wishes." We got changed up to go out and went downstairs. I informed the desk clerk that we would be leaving in a day or two. We left and went to see the repair guy about the plane. When we got to his place, he was waiting, had an estimate count and time down to do the job. I told him to incorporate any equipment that Jim might like inside but not take away from the original equipment. His price was $25,000 plus $5,000 for any extras. I gave him $20,000 and would check back with in a month.

We need to find out who is handling Jim's mail. We stopped at the Post Office and his mail was being delivered to the Millers." Well now, I'll get a chance to show you where I stayed before I left." When we walked in Bob and his wife were surprised to see me and apologized about the letter. We sat down and talked a while. I told them about Jim and me and our claim and I needed to find out if he got the permits and land lease and whatever else we needed. We started going through the stack of mail and all the papers were there. My signature was needed on most everything and had to be sent back. I put my information on how I could be reached, where and when and dropped them at the Post Office on our way back. It was nice seeing Bob and his wife. We had visited over an hour. On the way out the door, my daughter pointed to the Northern Pike on the wall. "How would you like to catch something like that?" "I did." Look closer, you and Bob caught that?" "The guy did a nice job on it." Bob said, "Yes, he is one of the best around." When we left I told my daughter that I had accomplished everything that I needed. Tonight we will have a nice dinner and get some rest and hit the road early in the morning.

I took my daughter to the restaurant down from Jim's place that I enjoyed when I was here last year. The owners were glad to see me again and were hoping I would stop by. We had a great time eating and talking with everyone and the evening went by so fast. It was hours later when we left. "Dad, the people up here are so friendly and nice, nothing like back home." "I know, dear, that's one of the things I like about this country. Actually I wouldn't mind moving here for good." We talked on our way back to the hotel about the day and the trip home. When we got to our room, we got everything ready to leave early in the morning. It was 10:00 now and I planned to get started by 5:00 a.m.

The alarm went off at 4:00 a.m. All we needed to do was to take our showers and get dressed. When I started the truck it was almost 5:00. I stopped in Palmer to top off the tank and get coffee and road munchies. The camcorder was set up with plenty of tapes handy and my trusty camera. My daughter had a picture of Wantalook and me on the dash that she had made up. I don't know when she did it. She was with me all the time. We drove from daylight till dark, stopping only when we needed to all the way back to Washington state. Then we did the constant push, trading off driving all the way back to Michigan.

It was nice seeing everything again. I dropped off my daughter and headed to my house. When I pulled up my driveway, it seemed like everything shrunk: my yard looked smaller, my house looked smaller, my backyard looked a lot shorter. It didn't take long before the phone started ringing. I tell ya, I am not used to sounds and noises. I know I've been out of the woods a while but I'm used to being able to hear my heart beat. Needless to say it took a while to get my things out of the Explorer with the phone calls coming in.

I finally got a chance to check my e-mails, starting with the most recent. My heart skipped a beat on the first one. It was from the facility that Jim is awake and asking about me. Please call. I grabbed up the phone and then punched in the numbers.

I was so excited, I couldn't wait to talk to Jim. They put me through to his room and a hello. "Jim, it's that crazy guy from Michigan." "I read all about you from the papers, Alan. I am so sorry about all you had to go through. I still don't know how you did it." I started to tell him the story but people were starting to show up. "Jim, it's getting crazy around here. Call me back tomorrow morning. Here is my phone card number. It's a lot cheaper than collect. Oh yes, I am having your Beaver repaired. The work has already has been started on it." When I hung up, the crowd was getting bigger with family and friends, then the local news people showed up. I was glad when that part was over and they left. Everyone wanted to hear about my experience. I figured that the best way is set them all down and tell the story once, then answer questions after. I ordered pizza and had someone go for pop and beer. I got a fire going in the backyard. I am damn good at that, then got chairs and tables set up. So with the food, drinks, chairs and everyone sitting down, my story began. You could hear a pin drop as I spoke about how the days turned into months. The friendship with Wantalook, the bear attacks, Wantalook saving my life, me saving his, the encounter with the moose, wolverine, our loss of Goodlooken right up to leaving Wantalook behind.

Then I surprised most everyone there when I announced that I was going back within a month. I didn't tell them the full reason why I was going back. I just left it that Wantalook was the biggest reason. There were a lot of questions that were asked and it was great to see everyone again. Slowly people started leaving and I asked my daughter to come over in the morning. We had a lot to get ready for. When the last person left, I poured myself a drink and sat by the fire. It wasn't like camp but I had some time to think. The only distraction was a dog barking down the road and the sound of cars going by. As I watched the fire, I was thinking about Wantalook and our quality time we spent by the fire all those many evenings. I miss that bouncing ball of fur. Then I remembered how down he got when he lost Goodlooken and now I am gone from his life. I can only imagine what he is feeling right now. It's not good. Tomorrow, my daughter and I will put into motion all that we need to do and get going so we can return.